Role Play

Role Play

KAY COVE

PAGE & VINE

Page & Vine
An Imprint of Meredith Wild LLC

This is a work of fiction. Names, characters, places, and incidents either are the product of the author's imagination or are used fictitiously, and any resemblance to actual persons, living or dead, business establishments, events, or locales is entirely coincidental. The publisher does not assume any responsibility for third-party websites or their content.

The author acknowledges the trademarked status and trademark owners of various products referenced in this work, which have been used without permission. The publication/use of these trademarks is not authorized, associated with, or sponsored by the trademark owners.

Copyright © 2025 Kay Cove
Editing by Michelle at Fiction Edit
Proofreading by Judy Zweifel at Judy's Proofreading
Cover Design by K.B. Barrett Designs
Art by Aga Olario

All Rights Reserved.
No part of this book may be reproduced, scanned, or distributed in any printed or electronic format without permission. Please do not participate in or encourage piracy of copyrighted materials in violation of the author's rights. Purchase only authorized editions.

Paperback ISBN: 978-1-964264-26-4

DEDICATION:

This one is for all the storytellers who've forgotten their own story— who measure themselves in word counts and rankings, who've traded sleep for deadlines, and joy for metrics.

Of all the things you strive for, never forget that in the end, the greatest measurement of success is your own happiness.

The world will fall in love with the voice that comes from your heart, not the one that stems from your fears.

EPIGRAPH

Either write something worth reading or do something worth writing.

- Benjamin Franklin

CHAPTER ONE

Forrest

Absolutely no one wants to date an escort.

I glance at my watch as I'm jogging down the sidewalk to my daughter's school. *Forty-two minutes.* Could've been worse.

It's been exactly forty-two minutes from the time Wesley Prep Academy called me to inform me my four-year-old daughter had an accident. Her mother, who is the primary contact, was not answering her phone. Dakota was pulled out of her pre-K class and is currently hiding in the nurse's office until I can bring her a fresh change of clothes.

In moments like these, I'm pissed I only have my little girl on Wednesday afternoons and one weekend a month. She doesn't keep a full wardrobe at my place. Not that there'd be much room for her clothes in my small apartment. In fact, the overpriced prep academy she attends is one of the reasons I live in a shoebox all the way in the South Bronx.

Unable to flag an available cab, I had to splurge for an Uber Lux, the only option immediately available. I had the driver drop me off at the drugstore around the corner, praying they had toddler underwear in Koda's size.

Plastic bag rustling in my hand, I hustle up the concrete steps to the front doors of Wesley. It's a little anticlimactic that I broke a small sweat racing here just to stand and wait at the locked front doors until Tillie, the elderly front office secretary, can buzz me in.

"Hello. How may I help you?" Her voice sounds through the intercom above me.

"Good morning, Tillie." I slap on a smile. The security cameras aren't overtly visible, but I know she can see me. "I'm dropping off a change of clothes for Dakota."

"Your full name, your child's full name, teacher's name, and the family password, please."

I refrain from rolling my eyes. "Tillie," I groan. "You know me. I pick up Koda every single Wednesday."

There's a small pause. "It's safety protocol, Mr. Hawkins. I'd like to keep my job, thank you."

After letting out a short exhale, I acquiesce. "I'm Forrest Hawkins. My daughter is Dakota Hawkins. She's in Ms. Mazer's pre-K class. And the family password is 'Go Giants.'"

Football is the only thing Hannah and I agree upon. I thought I was going to marry and grow old with her. I thought we'd give Dakota several siblings. But now, we tolerate each other. Our only thing in common reduced to our devout loyalty to the New York Giants.

"Thank you," Tillie replies. "They're really looking rough this year, huh? Cowboys gobbled them up last week. Take me back to twenty twelve, you know? I don't even think those boys know what a Lombardi Trophy is anymore."

I smirk. "Oh, come on now. The new quarterback is just getting his sea legs. This season's a wash. They'll look better next year when we pick up a few more linemen. Plus, commiserating over losses is half the fun of being a Giants fan. If they start winning, what're we going to talk about?"

"Ha." Tillie lets out a bitter laugh as the buzzer sounds, indicating the front door of the school is now unlocked. "Ms. Dakota is in the nurse's office. Have a nice day, Mr. Hawkins."

"Forrest is fine, Tillie," I remind her as I grab the door handle.

"Protocol," she answers back.

I walk through the double doors of Wesley and bank a sharp left. I made a point to memorize the school layout during orientation a couple months ago. I didn't want to look like the clueless dad who only gets to see his daughter ten percent of the time. Although, unfortunately, that's the truth.

I knock on the nurse's door expecting to see Ms. Jillian, a sweet-as-pie, retired RN who traded surgical assistance for Band-Aids, thermometers, and ice packs. Instead, a very *not* elderly, voluptuous blond woman pulls open the door.

"Are you here for Dakota?" she asks, her whisper borderline melodic.

Holding up the plastic bag, I nod. "How is she?"

She glances over her shoulder. "I assure you, the tears are just from a little embarrassment. She's not hurt. Come on in."

The nurse closes the door behind us as I make a beeline for my little girl, clothed in an adult-sized T-shirt, sitting on a small wooden chair in the corner of the office. Her cheeks are bright red and there are thick tearstains starting from the corner of her eyes and trailing down to her chin.

"Hey, baby girl."

Dakota pouts her bottom lip and crosses her small arms. "I'm not a baby." I try not to chuckle at her little scowl. She's mad and she wants me to take her seriously.

"Okay, fine. Big girl, then. Are you okay?" I squat down to meet her at eye level, but she turns her head.

"You took so long." Judging by her sniffle, the tears are about to start again.

"I'm sorry, Koda. I was all the way across town. I got here as soon as I possibly could." I bolted out of the tailor's when I got the call, right in the middle of measurements.

She lets out a huffy breath. "Too long. That was mean."

My daughter is four. She doesn't understand that I paid triple my normal rideshare fare and sprinted six blocks from the drugstore to her school in very uncomfortable dress shoes, so she wouldn't have to sit in her soiled clothes a minute longer than necessary. I don't care about being reasonable at the moment. She's hurting. "Daddy is very sorry. I didn't mean to be so late. I'm here now, though. Do you want to change?"

Dakota turns in her chair and looks me dead in the eyes. Her puckered frown breaks my heart. "I don't want you. I want Mommy," she mumbles. "Where's Mommy?"

Forget the broken heart. That was a knife straight to the gut.

I clear my throat. "Mommy is..." *Hell if I know.* Hannah doesn't work. She's a trophy girlfriend to a Wall Street guy who put her and *my* child up in his mega-penthouse in Midtown. I'm not jealous he's with Hannah. I'm jealous that he's giving my daughter everything I can't. "I bet you Mommy just lost her phone and couldn't answer. But I'm here. Is that okay?"

Maybe Dakota sees the sadness in my eyes. She's an intuitive one. Suddenly her arms are around me and she's burying her face in my neck. I feel her warm tears against my skin. "Brody M. saw and then he told everybody I was a pants-wetter. Nobody knew until he told. *Everybody*, Daddy. They all laughed at me." She wails against me. "But I'm not even wearing pants. I like dresses."

"Well, Brody M. sounds like a giant butthole."

Dakota pulls away and looks at me with bright, wide eyes. "He *is* a butthole."

The nurse chuckles behind us, then quickly clears her throat, pretending like she can't hear every word of our conversation.

"You know, baby, sometimes little boys are mean to the little girls they like. Does he pull your pigtails, too?"

She scrunches up her face in disgust. "*I'm not a baby.* I don't wear pigtails."

I stroke her thick, blond hair, curling one tendril around my finger. "You used to."

There are a lot of competing thoughts going through my mind...

I miss her pigtails. She's growing up way too fast. Why isn't Hannah here? She lives just a few blocks away. Shouldn't she have her phone close anytime she's away from our daughter? Also, I want to find out who Brody M.'s dad is and kick his ass for raising such a little punk.

"Do you want to get changed and go back to your class?" She's swimming in the oversized white T-shirt.

A mischievous smile spreads across her face. "I think my tummy hurts, Daddy." She's using her squeaky, overly cute voice because she wants something. "That means I have to go home." She even grabs her stomach and tenses her face like she's in pain, fully committing to the charade. She's faking, but you know what? Some miniature jackass just humiliated her in front of her entire class. She's allowed to play hooky for a day.

Pulling out the pack of size-4T underwear with Belle, Ariel, and Cinderella on the front, I nod. "Good idea. Put on a pair of these and I'll take you home." I look over my shoulder at the nurse, who is beaming ear to ear. "Our little secret, right?"

"As far as I'm concerned, Dakota's belly has been aching all day," the nurse answers with a big smile.

I wink in her direction. "What would you prescribe?"

"Definitely a big cookie and an afternoon of cartoons and fuzzy pajamas. Oh, and absolutely no homework." The way the nurse is smiling at me, she might've misinterpreted my wink.

"How's that sound, Koda?"

"Yes, please." She snatches up the pack of new underwear and proceeds to the bathroom.

"Do you need help?" I call after her, but she slams the door shut.

"Her other clothes are in there." The nurse points to a tied plastic bag in the corner of the room. "I hope you don't mind, we put her in an extra T-shirt from the bake sale. It's brand new."

"Does she have a change of clothes? When Ms. Mazer called, she said she just needed—"

"All pre-K and kindergarten students have to have a change of clothes for their cubby. Dakota had everything except underwear. I'm sorry to interrupt your day, but school policy, we're not allowed to give undergarments—"

I hold up both hands. "Understood. It's no problem, really. What's your name?"

"Kirsten." She holds out her hand and takes two steps toward me. "I'm subbing in for Ms. Jillian this week while she's on vacation."

Before I can shake her hand, something loud crashes from behind the bathroom door. Instinctively, I fly across the office. Jiggling the locked handle, I call through the door, "Koda, are you okay?"

"I'm okay," she chirps.

"What was that noise? Do you want me to come in and help?"

"No!" she barks.

More evidence of the fact Dakota's growing up too fast. I've changed her diaper since the day she was born. I helped pottytrain her. Now, very suddenly, she's embarrassed around me during bathtime. The universe took my baby, and gave me a clever, sassy little princess instead.

Grumbling underneath my breath, I meet the nurse on the other side of the office, this time my hand outreached to properly introduce myself. "Nice to meet you, Kirsten. I'm Forrest. Thank you for helping my daughter...who clearly wants nothing to do with me."

She shakes my hand firmly, her eye contact steady. "I'm sure it's just a phase." Cocking her head to the side, she smiles.

"What?" I ask, studying the dazed expression she's wearing.

"It's really nice to see such an involved father. Most of the time it's nannies or au pairs dropping off forgotten lunches, science projects, and changes of clothes."

"Ah..." I trail off, finally understanding the dreamy look on her face. "Well, we are indeed nanny-free." Hannah has suggested it, but I don't see my daughter enough as it is. I don't need to share her with a nanny, too.

"*We* as in...?"

"Dakota's mother and I."

Kirsten blushes, her pale cheeks turning pink at record speed. "Oh, I'm sorry, I didn't realize by 'we' you meant you and Mrs. Hawkins—"

"I didn't," I quickly add and she perks right back up.

I'm not dense. The very attractive, blond nurse is interested in me. She's sweet, probably smart if she's an RN, and clearly, she's great with my daughter. This woman is the whole package. I'm sure I'd more than enjoy her company.

There's just one problem...

The problem I always encounter when it comes to dating. Flings I can do, but a woman who is basically smiling at me with her ovaries is dangerous territory. How would I even begin to explain my job?

"Hannah's mother and I were never married. We just share custody," I clarify.

Actually, *share* is a bit of an overstatement. One of us is getting the lion's share of time with Dakota. The other is feeling supremely cheated, but also wary of poking the bear. If Hannah ever took me to court, the judge would ask about child support and what I do for a living. I could lie, which wouldn't bode well. I could also tell the truth and implicate my boss. The last thing Rina wants is the feds sniffing around her operation.

"Okay, I see. Well, in that case..." Kirsten tucks a lock of her hair behind her ear, then meets my eyes. Her smile is tepid, seemingly filled with nerves. "I don't usually do this, and it *might* be against school rules—I'm not sure, I'm just a sub—but could I take you out for a drink sometime?" She blinks at my frozen expression. "Or coffee perhaps if you don't drink?"

"Oh, I..."

Her face transforms into a look of horror when I don't answer right away. Luckily, Dakota emerges from the bathroom with both arms in the air, interrupting our awkward moment. "Ta-da." She twirls around, showing off a white dress with colorful flowers. "See? I like dresses."

"You look beautiful, Koda. Here—" I beckon her forward, then swivel my finger so she spins around. I fasten the back button on her dress. At least that she'll let me do.

"I picked Cinderella," she announces. "That's what took so

long. I almost picked Belle."

"Why Cinderella?" I fix Dakota's hair, smoothing it over her shoulders. I like moments like this, when she has problems I can actually solve.

"Ms. Mazer says Cinderella is the only princess with a job and work epic."

"You mean work *ethic*?"

She nods eagerly. I peer over my shoulder at Kirsten who has her eyes clamped shut as she stifles a laugh. Turning my attention back to Dakota, I ask, "Do you know what a work ethic is?"

"No. But I want one. How do I get a job like Cinderella, Daddy?"

"We're playing fast and loose with the word *job*, baby. Her evil stepmom made Cinderella do all that work. She didn't like it, and she didn't get paid."

The little cogs in Dakota's brain are spinning out of control. I can almost see the steam coming out of her ears as she tries to make sense of my explanation. "So, *you're* like Cinderella?"

I smooth the front skirt of her dress, feeling the expensive fabric. I have no doubt Hannah picked this up from a pricey boutique. It looks like Sunday's best for an Easter service. *And these are the backup clothes she keeps at school?* "Why am I like Cinderella?"

"You don't like your job. *You told me.*"

My daughter's stark honesty catches me off guard sometimes. At this age, the world is very black and white. She either likes something, or she doesn't. She's far too young to understand that while I don't love my job, it's the only way I've been able to stay afloat. I'm making more now than I would ever have as a lawyer. "But Daddy gets paid. That's the difference."

Surprisingly, she's satisfied with that answer. Normally, Dakota's a dog with a bone, following up everything I say with a "how come?"

"Go get your backpack from your cubby. I'll be right there to tell Ms. Mazer I'm taking you home for the day."

I linger in the doorway, watching Dakota skip down the hallway—clean, dry, and happy. I wait until I see her disappear into the pre-K class on the left. Kirsten approaches behind me, holding out the plastic bag of Dakota's wet clothes.

"So, Ms. Mazer, huh?" I ask.

Kirsten raises her brows. "I guess in her books, princesses should work."

I laugh. "I mean, Cinderella as the only princess with a job.... That can't be right, can it?" We both squint our eyes as we rack our brains.

"Snow White took care of all those dwarves, I suppose?" Kirsten twists her lips, also stumped.

"I think they more so took care of her. And the animals did most of her chores."

She nods slowly. "Right. Well, this is rather disturbing, Forrest. I need to go home to do some Disney research, because I can't have Belle disrespected like that."

I smile. "Ah, *Beauty and the Beast* fan, hm?"

"All of the Disney princess movies, really. Only the originals though. These remakes are giving me severe anxiety." We share in an awkward chuckle, and then it's time to address the elephant in the room. In my experience, head-on is the best way to approach it.

"Kirsten, about earlier, you seem really nice and I know 'it's not you, it's me' is a lame excuse, but I know I'd be a disappointment. My job has me working all hours of the night. Outside of that, my daughter is really all I have time for. My circumstances are too messed up right now. You deserve a guy who can focus on you."

She rolls her eyes but pairs it with a soft smile. "Honest, hot, and clearly communicates. Now you're just not playing fair."

My gaze drops to the pattern of rainbow squares on the floor as I suck in my lips. After letting out a deep exhale, I add, "I hope you're not upset."

"Of course not. Probably stupid and uncomfortable of me to ask you out—"

"It wasn't." I show her an earnest smile to put her at ease. "I'm flattered. And in any other circumstance, I probably would've beat you to it and asked you out first."

"Out of plain curiosity, what circumstances? I mean, are you in the medical field, by chance?"

"No." I shoot her a puzzled look. "Why do you ask?"

"You said your job has you working all hours of the night. And you're dressed like a doctor off duty." She gestures to my ensemble which is for an upscale Manhattan wedding next week with one of my regulars, Celeste. I was getting alterations completed when I got the call from Wesley. I flew out of the shop, not bothering to change. "Maybe you're too modest to refer to yourself as 'Doctor Forrest.'"

"Are you kidding? If I graduated from med school and passed my licensing exams, I'd even make Koda call me 'Doctor.' Rite of passage. But no, I'm not that intellectually inclined." That's somewhat of a lie. I did graduate from Columbia Law, I just never sat for the bar.

She relaxes her shoulders as she laughs. "So, what do you do?"

"Consulting," I say absentmindedly as Dakota reemerges from her classroom with her bright pink backpack secured around her shoulders. Ms. Mazer appears behind Koda and spots me from down the hall.

"Mr. Hawkins," she calls out while curling her pointer finger.

"I'm being summoned. I should go," I say in a hurry.

"Nice to meet you, Forrest."

"You too."

I'm about halfway down the hallway when I stop in my tracks and hustle back to the nurse's office. The door is still open, so I peek my head through. Kirsten, who was headed back to her desk, stops and turns around at my unexpected intrusion.

"Mulan," I say, a little out of breath. "She survived basic training in the midst of war. Soldier is a job, right?"

She chuckles. "Take that, Ms. Mazer."

I return a hearty grin. "Okay, take care, Kirsten."

She gives me a little wave goodbye as the corner of her lips curl down into a slight frown. *Ah, shit.* I feel bad if I hurt her feelings, but I'm trying to spare her. If she only knew the real reason my dating life is nonexistent...

No one, and I mean *no one*, wants to date a professional escort.

CHAPTER TWO

Sora

Kitchen sink cookies and assholes wrapped in pretty packages.

Holy shit. There's one left.

Papa Beans is always sold out of their legendary kitchen sink cookies, especially after the early lunch crowd. At 1:00 p.m. on a Friday, there's zero chance of snagging a jumbo, kitchen sink cookie at one of New York City's most treasured mom-and-pop coffeehouses, *but I'll be damned.* There it is, looking so alluring with its perfect golden-brown edges, defying all odds. It has to be a sign.

I stare longingly into the bakery case, reading far too much into a cookie. Most of the time, I do my best to keep my hopes in check, but this means something. A message from above that my meeting today is going to be life-altering, groundbreaking, and dammit—the wreckage of my career ends *today*. This is going to become my celebration cookie.

Let's be honest, kitchen sink cookies are a child's treat. Papa Beans throws miniature M&M's in theirs to add some color. With pretzel pieces, toffee, three different types of chocolate chips and chunks, a drizzle of chocolate, and a sprinkling of crushed nuts—yes, they absolutely look like three different desserts got together and collectively vomited into one mega cookie. But there's something about the busyness that I like. It reminds me of my brain lately. There are too many competing elements firing off at once. For my life, it's detrimental, but for a cookie, the chaos is magic.

I flinch when my phone buzzes so powerfully, I'm worried it's going to burn a hole right through my back pants pocket. *Yeesh.* "If only my vibrator performed with this kind of gusto," I mumble to myself.

I whip my head around to ensure I don't have an audience that could've heard that. All the café patrons are entranced in their conversations, seated around tiny, round wooden tables lining the back wall, and I'm presently the only person in line at the counter. I've been standing here patiently for a few minutes, just waiting for the barista texting by the espresso machines to stop smacking her bubblegum and acknowledge my existence.

With my phone now in hand, I see I missed my mother's call. Instead of putting it away, I stare at the blank screen. *Just give it a minute...she always calls twice.*

This time, I answer the moment the screen lights up. "Hey, Mama."

"Hi, love. What are you doing?"

"Oh, just embracing my last few moments of agonizing obscurity."

Used to my quippy, and oftentimes cryptic wit, Mom pauses and clears her throat. I can picture the scowl on her face as she tries to piece together the puzzle.

"Obscurity? I'm confused. Do you have a date?"

I chuckle at the notion. Me, with a date? That would be newsworthy to my mother. She has my wedding details planned all the way down to the crystal napkin holders. Unfortunately for her, the only love I'm chasing is between the pages. First, get my career sorted. Then, there's time for love, marriage, and children later.

"No. *So much better than a date.* Guess who I have a meeting with today?" After pulling my phone from my ear, I check the time. It's 1:08. Not exactly polite, but still not quite ten past. It's only rude to be late to a business meeting without a heads-up text or email at ten past. He still has some time.

"I'm lost." She hems and haws into the phone, unable to match my enthusiasm. "Who are you meeting?"

"Take a guess."

"No, thank you, Sora. You tell me so little about your life these days, guesses could range from a brand-new, free-range chicken farmer to another ghost hunter."

Tucking my wallet under my arm, I press two fingers firmly against my temple. "I'm allergic to store-bought chicken—"

"No, you're not. You've been eating Tyson chicken nuggets just fine since you were in diapers."

"—and Hepzibah is *not* a ghost hunter. She is a spiritual energy guide. Very professional."

"She's a con artist who showed up to your apartment with a bushel of sage, a shop vac, and an empty backpack. Not to mention she was wearing a Ghostbusters uniform."

I cringe. *Crap.* I forgot Mom was over at my place that day when Hepzibah came over. "It wasn't a uniform. It was overalls with a matching jacket. And it wasn't Ghostbusters, per se. She's just really into khaki." My cheeks puff out before I let out a deep, exasperated breath.

"Mhmm." I can *see* her eyes rolling. "Real professional to charge you actual money for crystals made from Play-Doh."

"For the millionth time, she was clearing the cluttered aura of my home to help me get through my writer's block. And by the way, after she was done, I wrote four chapters that night and even—"

Stop.

Why waste my breath? I've tried for the better part of a decade to explain my life choices, but they will never make sense to her. Finance managers speak numbers and statistics. Mom will never understand my plight as an author. And by plight I do mean a desperate, relentless desire to stay remotely relevant in an oversaturated, no-bars-to-entry industry, which all but guarantees financial failure.

"Are you being so defensive because you hired Hepzibah to get you through another writer's block?" Her voice is honey smooth. She's speaking to me the way she would to soothe me through a tantrum as a little girl. It's almost tender and maternal until I hear her cover her chuckle with a lazy cough.

I scowl into the phone. "I hope you have an appetite because you're about to eat your words. I'm meeting Dane Spellman." I pause for dramatic effect, but when Mom doesn't gasp, squeal, or spontaneously combust on the spot, I'm forced to reiterate. "*Dane Spellman*. Of Spellman Literary."

"You can say his name until your voice goes hoarse, that still doesn't tell me anything."

"He's an agent who represents every top dog in the industry. R.M. Mercer, Paige Gold, Jinny Michaels—and they are considered his midlist authors. *Mom*. They literally call him 'The Dream Maker.'" Dane Spellman has a contact with every Big 5 publisher and it's rumored he refuses to sign deals under seven figures. He is exactly what my dawdling author career needs.

Phone still pressed to my ear, I smile when the barista and I finally make eye contact. I give her a small wave, indicating I'm ready to order, but she quickly looks away and pretends to fiddle with the buttons on the espresso machine. *Are you freaking kidding me right now?*

"Oh, Sora." I hate the way Mom says it. Like she's disappointed that I just traded our only family cow for a handful of magic beans. "How many times have you been through this?"

"Please don't start—"

"I don't want to see you get your heart broken again. You don't need a hotshot agent to validate you. Get a normal job. Write books as a hobby. If it were just for fun, wouldn't that take the pressure off? We have some service positions open at the bank. Good benefits, great pay, and we could have lunch together every day."

The heat prickles in my cheeks as we circle back to our normal exchange. Me, telling Mom I'm at the doorstep of my big break. Mom, begging me to give up and return to earth, because you can't get anything done in life with your head in the clouds.

"Mama, I want to do something I love."

"I love *my* job—"

I cut her off with a groan. "Will you please just give me this one? Be happy and congratulate me for landing the meeting that is going to change my entire career."

I check my phone again. 1:09. We are getting dangerously close to Dane being rude. Another ten minutes and we're stepping foot in the something-came-up-and-I-have-to-reschedule danger zone. It shouldn't come to that—I confirmed our meeting this morning with his assistant.

It's taken a shameless amount of pleading, cajoling, and ass-kissing to even get this meeting. Dane's office made it quite clear he's not taking on new clients. Translation: He's not interested in small, broke, indie authors. It hurt, but at this point in my life, my engine basically runs off the fuel of rejection and humiliation, so I'm learning to take "no" as an invitation to try harder. Persistence and resilience are the keys to a happily-ever-after in the publishing world.

When Dane's assistant, Morgan, called a few weeks ago, I was on my way to snag a bagel from my favorite bagel cart in the West Village. It's a solid thirty-minute walk, but they have the best cream cheese and they don't charge extra for their generous shmears. I literally stopped in my tracks in the middle of Broadway when her contact information popped up on my phone. My heart locked up. How could I continue to walk?

Sure, I got savagely bumped and flipped off a few times for causing a pedestrian traffic jam, but it was worth it. After Morgan informed me that Dane had an opening to meet with me, I fell straight to my knees on the dirty sidewalk, right in the middle of Broadway, and cried out in glee.

I took every single precaution for this meeting. I ensured the location was at my lucky coffee shop, which was conveniently located nearby his office. Superstitious thoughts aside, with only a two-minute walking commute, there's less of a chance Dane could cancel on me.

A week out from the meeting, I re-sent sample chapters and a synopsis of my newest manuscript. Two days out, I sent Morgan a small muffin basket and a thank-you note for accommodating me. Finally, this morning, I made an excuse to reconfirm that the meeting was at the coffee shop in Tribeca, and not the location near Hell's Kitchen. It was a little white lie. Had Morgan done a simple Google search, she would've easily discovered that Papa Beans has no second location. But it slipped right by her as she confirmed the meeting for 1:00 p.m. at the location right by their office.

"Congratulations. I'm happy for you." There's not an ounce of zest in Mom's obligatory reply. She can't even fake it. But it's all I'm going to get.

"Thank you," I respond in a matching monotone.

"Call me after? I know we have plans tomorrow, but would you like to do dinner tonight, as well?"

"Two dinners in a row? Isn't that a lot of mother-daughter time?"

This time her laugh is melodic and warm. "Like I could ever get enough of my favorite child."

"Your only child," I clarify. "And I can't. I have dinner with Dad. Remember? He's on a flight to New York right now."

"Right. I forgot he still visits for your birthday," she grumbles. Mom's tone has deflated, the way it does anytime Dad is mentioned. They've been divorced for twelve years, but I don't think the wound completely healed over. They were so passionately volatile. They loved each other so much, but they hated each other more.

I was fourteen when they called it quits. They promised me after the divorce we'd still do family things...

They tried. It was short-lived.

The first year after their breakup, they made the effort to get together for my birthday. That night ended with confetti cake in my dad's hair and Mom subtly threatening him with a butcher knife. And for the record, he had it coming.

My father is a legendary writer, but he has a chronic mouth-filter issue. Barely a year after their divorce, he made a few not-so-sensitive comments about my mother's reemergence into the dating world, and the new risqué dress hanging in her closet. The very closet my dad most definitely shouldn't have been snooping in. After that night, they decided birthday celebrations and holidays should be independent of one another moving forward.

For a while, it was Christmas Eve spent with Mom. Christmas morning with Dad. Christmas dinner with Mom. My family really doesn't give a rat's ass about Thanksgiving, so that swapped back and forth. To this day, even though I'm twenty-seven, I'm still my mom's Valentine's Day date. The years she was in a relationship, she'd ditch her boyfriend, and we'd paint mugs. The day before my birthday, I was Dad's. Day of my birthday, I was Mom's.

My wonderful, attentive, handsome boyfriend graciously attends all these events with a big smile on his face. He endlessly compliments my dad's impressive author career. He also maintains eye contact during my mother's endless boring stories about her clients' tricky portfolios and enthusiastically nods along as she humble-brags about her most recent promotion. He's tall, better looking than me, but not totally out of my league. He pulls out chairs for me, has never once bought me lingerie for a gift, and even though he's totally ripped, rugged, rides bulls, and could build me a barn with his bare hands, he's also very sweet. Occasionally, he reads poetry when no one is looking, and helps me paint my right fingernails because my left hand is too shaky with a polish brush.

To clarify, by boyfriend, I do mean my fictitious book boyfriend.

The closest thing I've had to a real boyfriend in years is my very lazy, weak-willed vibrator. It's mediocre company.

"Do you want to go to the Galbi Grill or Pajeon Palace? I'm going to make a reservation."

"Whatever you prefer, Mama. You know Korean food better than me." Of course she does. I have her eyes, her hair, her smile, and her fair skin—but Mom is *from* South Korea. I've lived in Manhattan since the day I was born. She's the final authority on the best, most authentic Korean food in the city.

"No, it's your birthday dinner. You choose. Galbi Grill has better LA Galbi, but Pajeon has better Jjamppong."

"Hey," I say softly into the phone.

"Yes?"

I sigh. "You know, when you were my age, you were married, had a master's degree, and you had me. Is it lame that I'm about to be twenty-seven and I'm still spending my birthday dinner with my mom?"

She's silent for too long, I'm sure concocting a response that won't hurt my fragile feelings. "There's no shame in the fact that I'm your favorite person in the world. Do you want to know why?"

I roll my eyes. "Why?"

"Because you're my favorite person, too."

She's so cheesy. Exactly the way a mom should be. I can't help but smile big into the phone. "*The end.*"

She lets out a sweet hum. "All these years... You're still doing that?"

It's been a habit of mine since I was a little girl. Whenever I hear the perfect closing line, the one worthy of a happily-ever-after, I just have to add, "the end."

The barista suddenly lights up with a wide, toothy grin on her face. She's staring right at me, a brand-new woman, seemingly enthused to take my order. She makes a beeline to me at the register. "I have to go, Mama. Let's do Galbi Grill at eight o'clock?"

"Sounds great."

"See you tomorrow." I end the call before checking the time once more.

1:13 p.m.

Dangit. Not good. Not good at all.

No, it's fine, I assure myself. Maybe a prior meeting went late, or Dane stepped in gum just up the block and is currently cleaning off his shoe. There are a million and one excuses for him running a few minutes behind. He's Dane-freaking-Spellman. There's no choice—he's forgiven.

"Hi, what can I get you?" According to the crooked name tag on her brown apron, the barista's name is April. She *is* smiling, but not at me. Following her gaze, I glance over my shoulder. Too focused on my phone call, I didn't realize I now have company in line.

I quickly give the man behind me a once-over. My stomach flutters uncomfortably as I register why the barista's mood suddenly improved. He's tan, tall, and has neatly combed dark hair. Gun to my head, I couldn't conjure up a sexier guy. His strong jaw is cleanly shaved, and his haircut is fresh. He's definitely attractive, but admittedly the most noticeable thing about him is the magenta backpack slung around one shoulder, and his hand, which is securely attached to a little girl's. *She's three? Four, maybe?* Her eyes are glued to the glass bakery case. She's practically drooling as she bounces in place with excitement, making her honey-blond hair dance.

I check his left hand. *Ringless.*

I snap my attention back to the barista before the man catches me gawking. I wasn't really looking at him anyway...more so his daughter. I struggle to write the mannerisms of kids in my stories. Whenever I see a child, especially a little blond-haired, blue-eyed cutie patootie, I try to pay attention—how they point, smile, or wiggle in place when they are excited about something. I don't want it to be so painfully obvious in my writing that motherhood might as well be a different language for me.

"Anything to eat?" the barista asks.

"Oh, yes. One kitchen sink cookie, but can you pack it to go? And then two flat whites for here."

The barista scoots a table tent number across the counter. "Any flavors?"

"No, thank you." A flat white seems sophisticated. I want Dane to see a mature, levelheaded author who also has a decent mind for business. I'll double back after the meeting and get my caramel crème latte with extra whipped cream and a chocolate drizzle.

After swiping my debit card in a hurry, she hands it back, failing to offer me the receipt. "We'll bring the coffee out." The barista is already turning her attention to hot dad behind me. "Hi there. How are you guys today?"

I stifle an eye roll. That greeting was far warmer than the one I received. "Thanks, April," I offer, glancing at her name tag just to make sure. It always makes my day when someone takes the time to notice my name.

She responds with a curt nod. "Oh, wait. Your cookie." Swiveling around, she fetches a pair of silver tongs and opens her side of the bakery case. The very second the tongs clamp around the last kitchen sink cookie, there's a loud wail from behind me. A painful, guttural, howl of agony that pierces through the entire coffee shop. Looks pour in from every direction. It takes me a moment to realize the sound came from the little girl behind me. I pictured her voice to be bright and squeaky, but what just came out of her was more akin to a Spartan war cry.

"M&M cookie," she musters out through her hysterics. There's a light thud as she stamps her teensy foot hard against the tile floor. "That was *my* cookie."

Oh, no. Oh fuck.

Heat races up my cheeks. *I'm the asshole that just stole the cookie this little girl had her eye on.*

Hot dad squats down, sinking to eye level with her. He strokes her back soothingly and whispers into her ear. Her bottom lip puckers, then quivers as she tries to protest against what he's saying. But he stays calm and continues to talk into her ear until she stops blubbering.

For a split second he glances up and we meet eyes for the first time. His light brown eyes don't match his daughter's beguiling baby blues. I show him an apologetic smile as I shrug one shoulder. My knees nearly buckle when he shoots me a quick wink. Translation: *Don't worry about it.*

After gently wiping the tears from the girl's cheeks, he kisses each of them. "You're going to be just fine, my baby," he murmurs. Then he rises, collecting his daughter's hand once more, fastening it firmly into his. She's calm now, only quietly sniffling.

My better sense tells me to get lost and let this man and his devastated daughter be, but my urge to "fix it" kicks into hyperdrive.

As soon as the barista hands over my cookie in the brown paper packaging, I turn to face the little girl. "Hi there. Was this the cookie you wanted?"

Her cheeks are blotched with red, evidence of her meltdown. With big, sad eyes, she nods.

Hot dad squeezes her hand gently. "Koda, what did we just talk about? There are other cookies to choose from. This one isn't yours. Tantrums won't get you your way."

Actually, in this situation, it kind of will. Tearstained, chubby cheeks are my kryptonite. And she is particularly precious. I give her a quick once-over. She's wearing a fancy sundress, paired with Golden Goose tennis shoes. I'm also convinced the prim pink Chanel backpack her dad is carrying for her is real. *Mmmk, so Daddy's rich.* We have that in common.

He's certainly dressed like he's well-off. Hot dad is wearing black slacks with a white, long-sleeved, button-down shirt. I'm willing to bet he's a finance guy. His business attire looks subtle, but throw in his dress shoes, and I bet that ensemble cost over a grand. Money in New York City is weird. People want to pay a small fortune to blend in. You only notice their net worth by the tiny logos peeking from their shirt pockets or belt buckle. The designer labels that scream, *"yes, correct, passerby. I'm glad you noticed. I am indeed out of your league."*

I yank my attention back to the little girl before he notices me studying him. Just like her dad did moments ago, I squat down to meet her at eye level. "Here, sweetie." I hold out the cookie. "My gift to you. I'm not that hungry anyway."

"No, thank you. Please keep it," hot dad says.

"I insist," I say, shrugging him off.

The little girl wrestles out of her dad's grip and grabs the package with both hands. This time, she lets out a shriek of glee. She has the deepest dimples when she smiles. It's infectious.

I'm feeling like a damn hero for putting that smile on her face, but then I notice hot dad's scowl.

"Oh, there's nuts in there. Is she allergic?" I rise, grasping for some sort of explanation as to why my hero-move was poorly received.

He shakes his head. "Not at all. But you did just undermine me in front of my daughter. I'm trying not to raise a spoiled brat who stamps her feet and cries to get her way."

A warm flood of shame washes over me. My palm meets my forehead as I shake my head. "Shoot. I didn't think of it like that. I'm so sorry." I glance down at his daughter who is clutching on to the cookie, eyes wide, like a feral animal, daring anybody to steal her treasure. "What can I do to fix it?"

A small smirk creeps over hot dad's face. "Well, I'm going to need you to be the bad guy and take the cookie back. There will probably be more tears. But at least we won't be reinforcing bratty behavior, right?"

My jaw sweeps the floor. "You actually want me to take the cookie away from her?"

Hot dad shrugs. "That about sums it up."

I hold up my palms in surrender. "I can't do that. That's one small, adjacent step away from taking candy from a baby."

He grins mischievously and nods. "Agreed. Total villain move. You are not going to come off good in this scenario. But you said you wanted to make it right."

"Please don't make me do this," I plead, gaze fixed on the little girl's twinkling eyes that are filling with horror. She understands where this is going.

"It's my cookie," she mutters weakly.

Her dad quirks his eyebrows at me. That's hot-dad speak for, "*Get on with it.*" Reluctantly, I squat back down, like I'm obeying my executioner's command. *Oh, she's going to be so upset.* Once me and the little girl are eye level, I begin, "So, listen, sweetie, I'm sorry, I, um... I should've asked your dad first—"

"I'm just messing with you. Please get up." His eyes are in big, wide circles, and his smile is in full force. I have never wanted to slap a stranger so much in my life. "I didn't think you'd actually do it." His breathy chuckles aren't helping my disposition.

"You're an asshole," I bite out as I rise to my feet. Immediately, I cringe, remembering his daughter can hear us. "Shit. I didn't mean to curse. *I mean shoot.*" I clasp both hands over my mouth. My entire neck is hot as lava.

"It's fine," he says, still smirking, observing me intensely with his stupid smoldering gaze. "She's with her mom most of the time, who cusses like a sailor." He smooths his hand affectionately over the top of his daughter's hair. "She knows what she's not allowed to say."

A glint of sunlight from the café door opening catches my eye, nearly blinding me. I look up to see Dane Spellman in a sophisticated, light gray suit, then instinctively check my phone. There are no emails, missed calls, or text messages, and the time reads 1:20 p.m.

Twenty minutes late for a meeting with no heads-up. *So fucking rude.* But at least he showed.

Dane spots me, holds up his palm and gestures to a few sofa chairs in the back of the café. It's my signal to join him. "As much as I'd like to continue this uncomfortable exchange, that's my meeting." I give the innocent little girl a scrunchy-face smile, then narrow my eyes at hot dad. "Has anyone ever told you you're funny?"

His expression turns quizzical. "Not particularly."

"Good," I snap. "Then you know no one's lying to you."

I didn't mean to make him laugh again, but the soft rumble of his chuckle is all I hear as I collect my table number from the counter and turn toward Dane.

"Wait," hot dad calls out as he nudges his daughter forward.

"Dakota, say thank you to the nice lady for sharing with you."

"Thank you," she parrots absentmindedly, still staring at the cookie like it's the new love of her life.

"You're welcome. That's the best cookie in the whole world. Enjoy." I step around hot dad, but catch his stare one more time. His honey-brown eyes cause my heart to jolt, jumping two whole beats. I can't help but glance at his ringless finger again. If Mom were here, she'd probably want to grab his hand and tattoo my phone number on it permanently.

He really is the perfect specimen.

But it's the wrong place, wrong time. There's only one man on my mind at the moment, and he's in a gray suit, holding my entire future in his hands. Nothing, and I mean *nothing* is going to distract me from what I'm sure is going to be the best day of my life. Whatever offer of representation Dane Spellman is about to make, the answer is a resounding *hell yes*.

CHAPTER THREE

Sora

It's simple. The readers want dragons.

Dane Spellman is not an ideal book boyfriend. In fact, if I'm being honest, he has antagonist energy. I've never seen a man with resting bitch face, but lo and behold—it's possible. I'm staring right at it.

"So"—I take a pretend sip from my empty coffee mug, out of sheer discomfort—"did you have a chance to check out the chapters I sent you? And please know, I'm not one of those authors who is too proud to take feedback. I personally feel like the pacing could use direction, but I'm particularly fond of—"

Dane interrupts me by holding up his hand. "Just take a deep breath, honey. I can tell you're nervous."

Honey? Lovely. Terms of endearment, laced with condescension. "More excited than nervous. I really appreciate you taking time out of your schedule to meet with me. I can't imagine the number of queries you receive."

He levels a stare at me, a cruel smirk curling at the corner of his thin lips. "Thousands."

"Wow."

His smile turns a little sinister. "Most of them don't make it past my assistant's spam folder, though."

I press my lips together, trying to contain my zealousness, but I can't help it—the need for validation wins out against my better judgment. "May I ask, what made you finally open my email?"

Dane runs his hands through his flowy blond hair and grimaces. "Honestly? I didn't. One of my assistants did and passed it along to a junior agent on the team."

It's a sucker punch right to my heart, but I force myself to breathe in steady inhales and exhales. Don't be a child, Sora. This is the number one agent in the game. So, Dane didn't read your work, his junior agent did. Deal with it. You're here, aren't you? Thousands of authors want to be here. Be grateful.

I tuck my hair back behind my ears. "Dare I ask what your junior editor thought?"

He shrugs. "She said it was fine."

I stare at his expression, trying to gauge if I should smile at that. "Fine as in 'fine wine' or 'fine dining'? Or fine like lukewarm fries at McDonald's when you're starving?"

He hangs his head and peeks up at me through his sparse lashes. "Like I said, *breathe*. Fine is just a word. Don't read too far into it. Why don't you tell me a little bit about you?"

"Sure." I nod so eagerly, my hair clumsily untucks itself from the anchor of my ears and falls right back into my face. "I've been self-published for three years now and have twelve books in my backlist and one more releasing in a couple months," I explain as I smooth the loose strands away from my forehead and cheeks. "Now, I know that's a long time and a lot of books without representation, but the first few years I was really finding my footing. I dabbled in women's fiction, but ultimately fell in love with romance. I like angst and emotional depth in stories, but personally, I just can't read a book without a happily-ever-after, so I knew romance was the lane for me."

Dane nods along, but when I register his disinterested expression, my eye starts to twitch. My hand flies to my eyelid and I rub gently like I'm trying to dislodge a rogue eyelash from my eyeball. I hate having this tell. It's been this way for years. Every time I have to bite back a "fuck you" and smile politely instead, my eye twitches.

"I'm sorry. Is that not what you were asking...?" I trail off, silently begging Dane to fill in the blanks.

"You've been in this industry long enough to know all stories are recycled in some way, shape, or form, right? There's no such thing as originality. Same dish, different plating."

I twist my lips. "Okay," is all I offer because I don't necessarily believe him. To an extent there are linchpins that all stories mirror in some way, but that has more to do with the human condition. Heroes triumphing over adversity, healing from trauma, love against the odds—those are universal recipes for a great story, but originality isn't dead. *Is it?*

"When I sign new authors, what I'm looking for is personality. I need versatile authors, who are ready to deliver whatever the market is calling for. Every story has been told, and retold, and retold again. The only valuable thing a writer brings to the table is their personal style. So, tell me, author business aside—who are *you*? What do you like to do?"

Public speaking is my superpower. Years ago, when I briefly endured corporate work, I was the weirdo who loved interviews. *This is my freaking jam.* Never once have I choked when it comes to talking...until right now.

"Um...well, I'm Sora, obviously." I flush and giggle like a fool. My brain has split into two. Half is trying to buy myself time with nervous chuckling, the other is desperately racking through the last few years of my life since I became a full-time—struggling—author. *What do I like to do?* I like writing schedules, word count sprints, and taking writing craft classes. But outside of that, it's blank.

Dane's eyebrows climb his forehead like twin caterpillars. "Why don't we start with what you read for fun?"

Indie marketing guides on Facebook and Amazon Ads... But I can't freaking say that out loud. It's starting to dawn on me why my mom is worried about my mental health. What was the last book I read for fun? Hell, when was the last time I *had fun*?

"How's your social media presence?"

"Wildly unimpressive." I show him a half-smile and half-cringe as I playfully point at his chest. "But hey, at least you know I'm honest."

He lets out a weak chuckle, then drags his hand over his face. He doesn't need to say anything. I can read his mind. This is a casting call, and he's thinking there's absolutely nothing unique about me that stands out.

I hold up both hands as if I'm trying to stop him from leaving. It's a bit of an overreaction because he hasn't budged. "I need this, Dane. I *really* need your help. I'm old-school. I care about storytelling, but all the other stuff? I can't do indie publishing anymore. It's a giant popularity contest and I can't seem to fit in. But somehow, I do still believe this is meant for me."

Dane's gaze snaps to mine as the thin veins stretched across his temples bulge. That apparently catches his attention. "What do you mean?"

I clench my fists under the table, preparing to unleash my bleeding heart. "If there's anything remotely interesting on my social media accounts, it's the brainchild of my unpaid personal assistant, who I'm certain has only stuck with me out of steadfast loyalty. I'm not polarizing. I don't do hot takes. I'm not good at getting views and asking for attention. I just really love to write. I don't miss deadlines. I don't cause drama. I'm never going to be TikTok famous, but I swear, I will work harder than any author you have on your roster. I want this *that* badly. You want your authors versatile? I can do that. Just tell me what the market wants right now and I'll write it."

His smile is small. It doesn't touch his eyes. Actually, it looks a lot like pity. "It's simple. The readers want dragons. Can you do that?"

I quirk a brow. "Dragons in contemporary romance? Please tell me how that can work."

Dane purses his lips. "It can't."

"So, you want me to switch lanes and start writing fantasy?"

He cinches his thick brows together seemingly in anguish. Exactly the way people do when they are about to deliver bad news.

"The truth is, Sora, the market is so oversaturated. Everybody is an author these days. And I'm sorry to say, but the genre you write is a dime a dozen. We're not taking any new authors right now unless they are bringing their own lucrative opportunities to the table. Then, we'll happily manage them."

"For a cut of the deal," I deadpan.

"Well, of course."

What a scheme. Their authors bring in the deals with the publishers, then the agency swoops in and takes a percentage to forward a few administrative emails. How is that fair?

"If you want my opinion, you can make more money staying on the indie publishing path. Keep writing. Wait for your big break, and then when the publishers are swarming with offers"—he points to his chest—"I can make sure you get every single penny you're worth."

My cheeks are stiff and my mouth goes dry. I hate this feeling so much. It's the same feeling from when I auditioned for Ariel in the elementary school play but got cast as singing seaweed instead. It's when my very first crush in junior high asked me to pass a love note on to my best friend. It's the moment my high school boyfriend dumped me because I wouldn't put out. The next day the entire school was gossiping about how I was still a virgin during senior year. There was even a rumor that I wouldn't take my pants off because I had "weird" equipment down there.

It's the same feeling I had when I took the subway by myself for the first time and experienced racism. I'd never really heard derogatory names for a Korean woman before, but I learned every single one on one bus ride from a cracked-out hobo on the subway.

This same feeling brings me back to my first awful book review. The first time I spent a month's worth of rent on an influencer to help me promote my book, but instead of helping me, she made it her full-time job to humiliate me on socials by picking apart my backlist one by one. I lost way more than money in that bad deal.

Rejection hurts everyone. But I wonder if humiliation makes

other people want to shut their eyes and never open them again, like it does to me. When is adulthood going to stop feeling like the torturous hell of grade school?

Trad publishing is my out. An agent like Dane was supposed to be step one of my master plan of survival. I need support. I need someone in this industry to have faith in me because after three long years, I'm starting to lose faith in myself.

"Can I ask you a question?" I say finally.

Dane cocks his head to the side, meeting my gaze. "Sure."

"Why take this meeting if you had no intention of representing me? Was it just to get me off your guys' back?"

"I hear you did email a shocking number of times...*long emails*." He pumps his brows playfully. "I'm teasing you, Sora. I really wanted to meet you."

"Why?"

He leans back into the green, tufted sofa chair and rubs his hands together. I glance over his shoulder to see the hot single dad from earlier across the café seated directly in my sight line. As if my quick glance is summoning, he suddenly looks up from his takeout cup and matches my stare. He lifts his dark, angular brows as if to say, "*Caught looking, missy.*"

Dammit. He probably thinks I'm into him. He's sorely mistaken.

"There's a rumor going around the office I was hoping you could clear up," Dane says, reclaiming my attention.

My stomach lurches. The word "rumor" is triggering for me. It usually ends in some kind of cat fight that I most definitely don't want to participate in. "That rumor being?"

"Is Sora Cho your pen name or your legal name?"

"Both," I reply, hesitantly, careful not to offer any further details. My stomach continues to churn as I slowly piece together exactly where this is going. The real reason why Dane Spellman wanted to meet with me. "Why?"

"How can it be both?" he asks. I think he's smirking because he's catching me in a trap. This is going to be much easier if we get this over with quickly.

"My legal name is hyphenated. Sora Cho-Cooper. Cho is my mother's maiden name. I dropped Cooper from my author name... for obvious reasons."

"You're shitting me. So, it's true... You're J.P. Cooper's daughter? *The J.P. Cooper?*" Dane scoots forward in his chair, showing genuine intrigue now. "Are you guys in touch? Are you estranged? Pardon me for asking, but with your father's name, how the hell are you struggling with your author career?"

Dad, aka J.P. Cooper, writes literary epics as commentary on societal structure. His books sit on shelves next to George R. R. Martin and Tolkien. His first series sold at auction for well into seven figures. Studios are fighting over the development options, wondering whether they'll make more money on HBO or the big screen. Emmys are all but guaranteed for anyone attached to the project.

But to answer Dane's question, I'm struggling because Dad does not give out free lunches, not even to his own daughter. When I told him I wanted to become an author, he tried to deter me. When that didn't work, he made it clear I was to keep my career far away from his.

"My dad prefers I keep his name off of my projects."

"It's your name too, though, isn't it?"

Is it? My eyes drop to my lap. I rotate my thumbs in slow circles, contemplating Dane's response. "I guess—"

"I read in an article that his agreement with Meek Publishing is about to expire, and he's considering going back to auction with the *Hell & Heroes* series. Is that true?"

"If you read it in a public article, then you know as much as I do." I wish he'd stop interrogating me about this. My dad's wild publishing success is not a sore subject for me, it's a throbbing, infected, open wound. *Stop poking at it.*

"He doesn't have an agent listed anywhere."

"Because he doesn't use one. He finds a lawyer for paperwork, but otherwise, the publishers go directly to him." I bite the inside of my cheek until it hurts.

Dane clears his throat as his stare grows more intense. And now I'm the one losing interest in this conversation. "But I also heard he's working on a new series. That has to be a lot to manage. Surely, he could focus more on writing if he had a team to represent him, right?"

Trying to avoid Dane's eager stare, I pick up my empty mug once more. Bone dry. I can't even fake a sip without looking ridiculous, so I set it back down. "I suppose."

When I finally look up, Dane is holding out his business card, wiggling it between his fingers. It's a bland professional's card but I notice there's a handwritten number scribbled on the front.

"I think I've sent your dad about as many emails as you've sent my agency." He chuckles as if his joke is funny. "It's been years. He never responds. I heard he hates agents, but Spellman Literary could do some great things for J.P. Cooper. I wrote my personal cell phone number on this card. I never give that out, but if your dad calls, I will drop whatever I'm doing and answer. Do you think you could pass this along?"

I want to lug my empty mug at his head. This was never my meeting after all. I was simply bait.

"Sure," I mutter, plucking the card from between his fingers.

Dane clutches his chest, and ducks his head in what seems like gratitude. "You're a sweetheart, Sora. Thank you. If I could snatch up J.P. Cooper"—he blows out a sharp breath—"I mean, that's it. My dream list would be complete."

Keep dreaming. Dad is going to file this business card with all the others—in the trash.

Dane's palms collide against the top of his thighs with a loud smack. "Whew, okay. Well, I should get going, but I have to say meeting you was the highlight of my week."

"Thank you. Likewise," I add. *Bleh! What?* Damn my word vomit. I can't even control it. I'm hardwired to spew out niceties. It's why I'm getting my ass kicked in this industry. I'm too soft. Meeting Dane was not the highlight of my week. Not even close.

In fact, scalding the roof of my mouth on hot soup this past Monday was preferable to learning that my dream agent thinks I'm unremarkable, "dime a dozen," bait.

When Dane rises, I do as well, extending my hand. I glance at the mugs on the table in front of us. Mine empty, Dane's untouched. Maybe he doesn't like flat whites. Perhaps that's why he didn't even thank me for ordering him something.

"By the way, I know a guy who could probably help with your situation," he adds, shaking my hand.

A little flutter of hope tickles my chest cavity. "Oh?" I fail at sounding nonchalant. "An associate of yours?"

"In a way. He's a marketing guru a lot of my well-established authors use. Indie publishing is built on luck and ads. Sounds like your luck hasn't been fantastic, but my guy could get your ad game going strong. The only problem is, he only takes on serious investors. Can you rummage up about sixty thousand to start?"

What the fuck? He better mean sixty thousand pennies. "Um...what?"

"Too steep?" He scrunches his nose.

That's more than I make in a year from all my books combined. But I want to save face and not sound as low on the totem pole as I feel. "Is he worth it?"

Dane nods slowly. "Worth every dime. I'll have my assistant email over his information. Sound good?"

I nod, wordlessly.

Dane pats my shoulder, pairing it with a quick wink. "Take care, Sora. Keep writing. I can't wait to see you on a bestseller's list one day."

When Dane is through the café door, I release the low growl of agitation I've been holding in for twenty minutes. I don't have words for whatever that was that just happened. Today was supposed to change *everything*.

I clench my fists together, feeling my skin stretch over my knuckles. With a deep breath I try to tell myself it's just business. Of course Dane would seize an opportunity for access to J.P. Cooper.

The commissions from selling my dad's series could probably carry Spellman Literary single-handedly. It isn't personal, except it *is*, because there's a big part of me that is so sick of being jealous of my own dad.

I've never read his books. Not because I'm bitter. I'm too scared to be humbled...or maybe more accurately, humiliated. I come from greatness, yet I'm not great. I'm not even a little bit great. My dad's readers think he's the next Messiah. What I did not just need is a wakeup call to everything I'm lacking.

I slump back into my chair and slide Dane's untouched coffee to my side of the table. Running my fingers over the rim, I debate drinking it. Instead, I stare at the coffee that's cooled, ruminating over how rude it was for him to not take a sip, not thank me, not even acknowledge the gesture. I would've done all those things to be polite. It's moments like these that I feel like my brain is just on a different wavelength than most people—shackled by conscientiousness.

"She didn't eat it. It's still sealed."

My eyes fly to the tall man standing in front of me. Hot dad holds out the still-wrapped cookie, but I don't take it. Issuing a thick sigh, he places it on the table next to me. "Truce? Sorry. It was a crappy way to break the ice earlier."

I force myself to match his gaze. "Thanks. But I'm not hungry."

"Well, chances are you'll get hungry later." His lips twitch into a small smile as he taps the cookie. "All yours," he answers as he glances past me.

I look over my shoulder to follow his stare. He's angled himself so he can speak to me and also watch his daughter who's sitting at a nearby table, mindlessly eating a bag of pretzels. She's fully immersed in the phone she's holding. Once hot dad is satisfied that his daughter is fine, he continues, "How was your meeting?"

I'm not about to pour my bleeding heart out to a stranger. So, I change the subject. "If she didn't want the cookie, then why was she crying over it?"

A glint of amusement flashes in his face. "Because she's four."

It triggers me. Maybe it's the simplicity in his explanation. Like I'm the only childless spinster in the world who doesn't understand crocodile tears.

"You know what? I'm having a really bad day, and I just can't take one more conversation with a snarky asshole wearing a charming smile. So, if you'll excuse me."

He sucks in his lips and raises both eyebrows. "Wow. Unexpected."

My eyes, on the other hand, narrow. "What? The charming part or the asshole part?"

He chuckles. "I suppose the combination of the two. Bittersweet I guess."

I rise from my seat. He moves backward, making room for me to step past him. "Don't read into it. And for your information, your daughter is wearing Golden Goose sneakers. And based on the solid-gold C on her little pink Chanel, that backpack costs more than my rent. If you're worried about spoiling your child, you have bigger fish to fry than a freaking cookie."

His smile disappears and I swear I see him blush. For a moment, we say nothing as we study each other. My heart is racing, adrenaline flooding my veins, but I hold the moment as long as I can because I want to remember this forever. Regardless of the fact this is a stranger I'll never see again, this is a powerful moment for me. I finally said exactly what was on my mind instead of playing nice. It's dangerously exhilarating.

Recovering from his stunned silence, he asks, "What are Golden Goose shoes?"

I shake my head, deciding I don't have the patience to explain how people are spending hundreds of dollars to buy custom shoes that look like they are already beat to shit. I point to the cookie on the table. "That was supposed to be a celebration treat. I don't need it now. There's nothing to celebrate."

I take a few steps toward the door, then feel an emotional anchor holding me back. I walk right back up to hot dad. I have to angle my head all the way back to meet his gaze. "I realize that was rude of me," I admit, pairing it with a sigh. "I'm sorry. It's just I'm—"

"Having a bad day."

My nod is small as my eyes drop to my shoes. When I look up, he's smiling. This time, with the tilt of his chin, and soft eyes, the smile seems more genuine. "I won't hold it against you."

I show him my palm in a half-hearted wave goodbye before retreating for the door. Once my back is turned, I let one tear of frustration loose.

CHAPTER FOUR

Forrest

My punishment? A date with Ursula.

Watching the dark-haired woman storm out of Papa Beans, I can count at least three things I should've done differently in that conversation. I only approached her again because Dakota begged me to. The woman looked near tears after that guy she was with left. Maybe I caught her in the midst of a breakup?

I was a fool in line earlier. I'm pretty sure I did the adult equivalent of pulling her pigtails to get her attention. I still don't know what threw me off my game. I know how to be whatever a woman wants. But they usually tell me as part of my employment contract. I might've forgotten how to talk to women when I'm not hired to.

Not to mention, I probably should've kept my mouth shut about the parenting stuff, but it's a sore spot for me. If Hannah says no, everybody respects that. When I try to set rules, it's laughable. I'm Dakota's parent too. It'd be nice to be treated as such sometimes.

When my parents got divorced, my mom was the "fun" one. She bought me everything I wanted, then would disappear for months. As a kid, it was great. Mom would bust in like Santa Claus with a sack full of bribes in the form of toys and electronics. She never made me do anything I didn't want to. My rancher dad, on the other hand, made me do chores to earn an allowance. He taught me to take pride in a day filled with hard work. Dad made sure I got a good education and even set me up with a savings account that he faithfully contributed to for over a decade. I'm twenty-eight now... Guess which parent I respect.

And guess which parent I still talk to.

"She didn't want to play?" Dakota asks, looking up from my phone as I sit down across from her.

"What's that?"

"Where did your friend go?"

I shrug. "She left. I think I upset her."

Dakota frowns as she eyes the bakery treat still in my hand. "You didn't give her the cookie."

I nod, then relax into my seat. "I tried. She didn't want it."

"Daddy, do you have friends?" Dakota crosses her arms and grabs her elbows. Her smile is weak...almost pitying.

"Of course I do. You've met Taio and Saylor."

She presses her fingers against her temples and groans. "No, *girlfriends*."

I laugh at the annoyed expression on her face. "What, you're exasperated with me now?"

She screws up her face in confusion.

"Yeah, that's right, smarty pants. Bet you don't know what that word means."

Dakota scowls at me. "I do, too."

"Mhm, sure." I give her a teasing wink. "Why are you suddenly worried about if I have friends? Or girlfriends?"

"Because...who do you play with when I'm at school or when I'm with Mommy and Henry?"

I pout at her, puckering my bottom lip. "I don't play. I sit and sulk until I get to see you again."

"*Daddy.*"

"*Koda,*" I mimic in her whiny tone. "Is that why you wanted me to go give the lady her cookie back?" For fuck's sake. Apparently my dating life is so sad that my four-year-old daughter is trying to be my wingman.

She hangs her head. "She's pretty."

She definitely is...

"What's her name?" Dakota asks.

It suddenly dawns on me that I never even asked for her name. Nor did I introduce myself. Okay, make that *four* things I should've done differently.

Before I can save face and make up a name for the woman to appease my kid's curiosity, my phone rings. Dutifully, Dakota hands over my phone. That's the one rule she respects. I let her play Kiddopia as much as she wants, but she is never, *ever* to answer my phone. My burner number still connects to my device and one of my worst fears is my clients knowing about my daughter. These are two worlds I work desperately to keep apart.

I mouth "thank you" to my daughter, then glance at the caller ID. *Finally.*

"Hannah, where are you?" I ask, slightly panicked. "Are you okay?"

"I'm fine. I just finished a hot yoga class at the club. Why?"

"Koda's school called you like four times. They said you didn't answer." I press my lips together hard, bracing myself. "I took her home early. She's with me. I know it's not my day, but some punk in her class was bullying her and—"

"Forrest. It's fine."

"You're not mad?" Now, I'm puzzled. Taking our daughter without her permission is a prime opportunity for her to yell at me. Hannah loves any excuse to bite my head off. She's still mad at me for being the cause of our breakup, and I think she's determined to punish me until the end of time.

"No. She's been asking for you, anyway. It's good you're spending some quality time together."

"Were they handing out edibles at this yoga class or something?"

Hannah chuckles, and now I'm very suspicious. "No. I um... Well, hey, can you keep Koda tonight?"

I tap my fingers against the table. "Why?"

"What do you mean why? Don't you want to keep her?"

"Of course, but it's not my weekend. And I have to work tonight."

Hannah grumbles into the phone. "What kind of financial consultant has to be on call on Friday evenings?"

"It's for a big acquisition overseas. They requested a video chat. It looks better if my client's advisor is there as a show of support." I stare at the wall as I lie. I hate to say it, but it's becoming easier and easier to fool everyone into believing my pseudo-career in financial consulting. No one wants to hear about finance portfolios, so my fake profession tends to shut down probing questions quickly.

"Well, fine. Can you bring Koda to my parents' house, then?"

"Will they be there?" My eyes snap to my daughter who is lost in her bag of pretzels. She's sticking her finger deep into the bag, trying to catch the loose grains of salt.

"I don't know... The housekeeper should be, though."

"The housekeeper? Do you even know the housekeeper?"

"Forrest, don't tell me how to be a mom. My parents have security cameras all across their estate. It's fine. She'll be safe."

I can't believe the words that are about to come out of my mouth. "Can she just stay with Henry if you're going out? At least that's her home and her toys are there."

"No... Henry and I have to sort some stuff out tonight. In private."

There's something tension-ridden in her response, but I can't understand what's going on. "Hannah, I'm about to text you."

I pull the phone from my ear and quickly send her a message so Dakota doesn't hear.

Are you pregnant?

As soon as the swoop of a sent message sounds, Hannah responds into the phone, "*God, no.* Why would you ask that?"

"Because last time you sounded this cryptic and stressed out, you were. Then, Koda came along."

"Well, I'm not," she snaps.

"Okay, okay. I just wanted you to know, if that's what you and Henry want, it's fine. I wouldn't give you a hard time about it."

Hannah scoffs. "It's most definitely *not* what Henry wants. So, drop it, detective."

"Sorry."

There's a silent lull between us. I watch Dakota tip the pretzel bag into her mouth, then lick her lips as she savors the last remnants of salt and crumbs.

"I'll keep her tonight," I finally say, running my fingers down the buttons of the client-gifted, expensive shirt I'm wearing.

"What about your meeting?"

"I'll figure it out."

"But—" She stops short. "Okay, never mind. Thank you. Kiss Koda goodnight for me."

"Do you want to talk to her?"

It takes a few seconds of silence for me to realize that Hannah already hung up. Sighing, I quickly make another call.

"Yes?" Rina, my boss, never answers "hello." Always "yes" or "what do you need?" In her defense, I suppose none of us ever call her to chitchat, only when we need something.

"Hey, what are the chances you can get coverage for me tonight?"

"None. Impossible."

"*Rina*. You didn't even check."

By the extremely loud clicking of her acrylics against the keyboard, I know she's holding the phone on speaker right next to her laptop. "Look at that," she says immediately, "just checked. *No chance*."

"Hilarious," I grumble. "But I can't make it tonight."

"It's a five-thousand-dollar night, Hawkins. She *specifically* asked for you. No one has deeper pockets than Mrs. Connor. I'm not going to risk pissing her off."

"Saylor told me Mrs. Connor is aggressively handsy. And that's before additional payment."

Rina laughs into the speaker, causing a crackle in my ear. "What you guys do off the books is your business, but you better keep it clean when you're on the clock. Her limo is picking you up at seven. Before I forget, she also requested that when you shower, you can use scented soap, but absolutely no cologne. It triggers her migraines."

"Are you even listening to me?" My eyes hit the ceiling. "I said I can't make it."

She grumbles in agitation. "What's your excuse? And, Hawkins, it better be *damn good*."

"My daughter." I smile at Dakota across the table. She pokes out her tongue and crosses her eyes, making a silly face. "I unexpectedly have my daughter tonight."

Based on Rina's long, exaggerated exhale, I know I've won the argument. "Playing the kid card? You're a real pain in my ass, know that?"

"Cam's free tonight." I picture Rina scowling at my very helpful suggestion.

"Cameron is a buffoon."

"A buffoon who doesn't mind being shamelessly groped."

"Fine," she huffs. "I'll figure it out. But you owe me, and I'm going to make it hell. You think Mrs. Connor is handsy? Your next job is going to be with the woman Levi calls the human octopus."

"Wait, what—"

But like Hannah, Rina also ends our call without saying "bye."

Human octopus? That can't be good.

I unzip Dakota's pink backpack that was resting by my feet. "Any chance you have pajamas in here, baby?" Dakota only has two pairs of PJs at my shoebox of an apartment, and not expecting her until next weekend, I haven't done laundry quite yet.

She shakes her head aggressively, her hair whipping her in the face.

"I guess we're going shopping."

"Why?"

"Because I just talked to Mommy, and you and I get to have a sleepover tonight."

Her big blue eyes widen to startling proportions as she clenches her little fists tightly. "*Yes!*" she squeals, attracting the attention of our fellow patrons.

The look of glee on her face almost makes up for the fact that my next job is going to be with a woman that I'm mentally picturing as the sea witch from *The Little Mermaid*.

I stare at Dakota's smile that's so big, her eyes cinch closed.

Ah, who am I kidding? That smile definitely makes up for a date with Ursula.

CHAPTER FIVE

Sora

A svelte Santa Claus...just not as cheery.

Dad's at least two shades darker than I remember. The last time I saw him was six months ago during the holidays. He's been bouncing back and forth from California to New York, ever since he signed on as a writer and executive producer for his series film adaptation.

I thought for sure we were ready to retire our birthday tradition. I'm not a kid anymore, but the older I get, the harder he seems to hold on to the past. He hopped on a six-hour flight just to take me to dinner, the night before my actual birthday, at this hoity-toity restaurant. I mentioned to him last year that I always wanted to eat at The Gilded Perch but couldn't afford to. He's been planning this...*for an entire year.*

"You look good, Dad. *Tan.* The Hollywood sun suits you."

He huffs with disdain. "The only time I'm in the sun is the walk from the writers' room to my car. California is too damn sunny."

I meet his grouchy reply with a doe-eyed smile. "*Writers' room,*" I muse softly. "Please tell me all about it. And I mean every single detail. What's it like?"

"It's like work," he answers dryly.

"No, I mean being in an actual studio's writers' room. You're working with some of the best screenwriters in the industry. I know screenwriters and novelists have different crafts, but that's still a hell of a lot of writing talent in one room. What are the conversations like?" Exhaling a slow breath, I try to calm down. I am about ten seconds away from drooling at the notion of writing a book so revered, Hollywood is fighting over the film adaptation. My dad is living my wildest dreams.

"It's a lot of chattering monkeys mincing my words is what it is." He waves off the conversation. "But I don't want to talk shop on your birthday."

"My birthday is tomorrow," I mumble in a weak excuse, but it's no use. This is how Dad always is. He's so tight-lipped about his job, you'd think he was involved in wet work for the CIA.

Accepting defeat, I show him a begrudging smile before poking my fork into a small piece of my garlic-herb-crusted barramundi. Quick mental math tells me this fish is about six dollars a bite. I chew slowly, savoring the luxury that only my dad's wallet can afford.

The servers are all wearing black from head to toe, except for their white gloves. It's like mimes are walking around replacing every sip of water I take the second my glass leaves my lips and hits the table. There's great service, then there's table stalking, and I fear The Gilded Perch is toeing the line.

"Why are you chewing like that? Is the fish bad?" He already has two fingers in the air, flagging down a mime.

"*No.* Put your hand down. It's phenomenal. I never eat this well. I'm *experiencing* my food." I glance at his clean plate which looks like a Labrador licked it clean. There's not even a drop of Béarnaise sauce left. Dad took down his bacon-wrapped filet mignon in two bites, right before grouching about the tiny portions here.

He lifts one bushy, salt-and-pepper brow. "What do you mean you never eat this well?"

"I mean my idea of fancy is topping ramen with a little chili crunch. Add some day-old rotisserie chicken, and voilà." I sprinkle my fingers over my plate. "Culinary masterpiece."

"You're still eating ramen noodles for dinner, Sora?"

"Yes. My life is regal," I deadpan.

Issuing a raspy sigh, Dad leans back into the tufted-fabric dining chair. With his head lowered and eyes lifted, he matches my gaze, but doesn't return my smile. "You need money."

Obviously. But I shake my head like it's preposterous. "I was being glib. I'm fine."

"Ramen is for broke college kids trying to figure out their lives."

"Take out the college part..." I shrug innocently. "Pretty accurate."

"How much?" he asks so seriously.

I reach across the table for him, but Dad's too far away. Instead, I trill my fingers against the surface, the thick table linen turning my taps into muted thuds. "I don't want your money." I blink at him a few times. "Well, except to pay for dinner, because I absolutely can't afford this meal. Did you know the cocktail I ordered cost thirty dollars?"

His lips twitch into an almost-smile, but it's clear he's distracted. "It's your birthday dinner. Order everything you like."

"Then I'm ordering more fish to go."

His grin quickly widens, then disappears just as fast. "You still have the same bank account? I'll set up a wire."

Forcing sincerity into my expression, I shake my head slowly. "Jokes aside, *no.* Thank you, but no. I don't want to be *that* kid with my hand out. I'm still in my ramen-eating phase but it won't be forever. One day, I'm going to take you to a restaurant like this and cover the bill with the money I earned, not the money Daddy gave me."

There's a flash of pride on his face. It's almost a sweet daddy-daughter moment until he opens his mouth again. "Why wait? It's all yours when I die anyway. Start the celebration early."

My eyes roll so hard I swear they nudge my frontal lobe. "Perhaps shocking, but I'm not really looking forward to your death just to collect on an inheritance check."

"You'll never cut it in Hollywood with that attitude, kid."

"Well, if my writing career continues to tank, I will ditch my independent attitude and seriously consider nepo baby as my next profession."

His guffaw cuts through the low murmur of voices in the restaurant, attracting the attention of nearby diners. I bite the inside of my cheek, wondering if someone will recognize him. There's been a time or two when shameless, diehard J.P. Cooper fans have crashed our private meals. But not tonight. The diners turn their attention back to their own plates.

Weaving my hands together in my lap, I pray my dad asks me about my writing. I just gave him the bait. *My career is tanking.* He's quick to offer cash, but money isn't the most valuable thing he can offer me. When it comes to advice, he's so damn stingy. It's like if Michael Jordan refused to show his kid how to shoot hoops. Senseless.

Leaning down, I reach into my purse to produce Dane Spellman's information. "Before I forget, I have something for you." With one finger, I slide the business card to Dad's side of the table.

"What's this?"

"Have you heard of Spellman Literary? I met the owner today. He asked me to pass this along to you." I tap the card where Dane scribbled in his personal number. "That's his cell. He said to call him day or night."

Dad picks up the business card and rips it in two. "Well, he can hold his breath waiting, then suffocate."

"With all that charm, you must have to beat the ladies away with a stick."

"Why do you have this?" he asks, ignoring my clever jab. "What the hell are you doing meeting with sleazy agents?"

Oh, geez. Here we go. "Why does he have to be sleazy?"

"Is he an agent?"

"Yes."

Dad holds out his open palm. "Case in point."

"For your information, he's the best in the business. I was lucky to even get a meeting. He was friendly enough. He introduced me to a book marketing expert who can help me grow my readership. I just have to get a little investment money first."

"Ah, and by marketing expert do you mean a lost Nigerian prince who is caught in the midst of a corrupt regime and needs your bank account number to restore peace to his rightful kingdom? After which, he'll reward you richly with a magical bestselling author career, of course."

I narrow my eyes to slits. "You know, people ask me where I get my sarcasm from. I just don't know what to tell them."

"Oh, Sora." He throws his hands in the air, pairing the gesture with a sharp exhale. "You're a smart girl. Use your common sense."

"Common sense? What is that supposed to—"

"I heard we're celebrating a birthday," our waiter-mime interrupts in a singsong as he approaches the table. He beams at me, all of his teeth on display. "How old are you turning?"

I shoot a dark look at Dad. "I'm turning pretty upset at the moment."

The waiter opens his mouth, then clamps it back shut when he realizes he doesn't have a viable response.

"Sorry. Twenty-seven. Tomorrow," I continue. "This is my dad. He's working on a long-term project in LA, but flew all the way across the country for one night, just to treat me to dinner."

The waiter didn't need my explicit explanation. That was more for me. I needed a reminder of what this night is—Dad, making an effort. A big one. He wasn't around much for the majority of my adolescence. When he was around, he was constantly distracted. It's obvious now he's trying to make up for lost time.

"For your birthday, the chef would like to comp your dessert, whatever you like." The waiter hands over a skinny, long dessert menu. The font is so swirly, I can barely make out the options.

"Um..." My eyes sweep up and down the menu. "I'm debating between the berry Chantilly cake and the mocha chocolate cheesecake. What would you recommend?"

"They're both so decadent. You won't be disappointed with either," the waiter says, waving his mime-hands around like spirit fingers.

"Then bring her both," Dad interjects. "Me, the praline pie. And two espressos." He glances at me. "You still drink coffee, right?"

"Only on the days I'm breathing," I answer with a wide grin that signals, *truce*.

The waiter scuttles away after topping off my water glass. He's slipping. I've already had two sips since he last addressed my cup.

"You look beautiful." Dad shows me a shy smile, very uncharacteristic of his normally more surly demeanor. I'm wearing minimal makeup and a simple black dress that barely satisfies the restaurant's dress code.

"Thank you."

"You look so much like your mother."

That blindsides me. *He's bringing up Mom?*

"I've been on this planet for fifty-four years, and I'm still convinced she's the most gorgeous woman I've ever laid eyes on."

Now my jaw falls open in shock. "That's so sweet. See? How come you can't say stuff like that directly to Mom? Then we could have one birthday dinner with all of us."

He's quiet for a while, pensiveness seeping into the lines between his brows. "Is she seeing anyone these days?"

I cock my head to the side, having a hard time reading the obvious writing on the wall. Dad wants to know if Mom is single? That can't be right. Mortal enemies aren't usually concerned with their nemesis's relationship status. Then again, enemies to lovers is all I tend to hear about on bookish social media. Maybe there's something to it.

"No. She hasn't dated anyone since Richard. They ended a year ago."

He perks up in his chair. "Why?"

"He was nice, but boring. Too much of a couch potato. They had an amicable breakup."

Sucking in his lips, Dad bobs his head. He waits a moment longer, maybe not wanting to seem too eager, then he asks, "Do you think I'm a couch potato?"

"Yes." My answer slips out before I can collect it. "But like a *refined* potato. You're a rosemary, parmesan Duchess couch potato if that helps."

"Jenni—*your mom* always wanted us to take a family trip to South Korea. She wanted to show us where she grew up and where your grandparents are buried. Eat street food, shop at the local markets, sightsee, hike...a lot of non-couch-potato activities."

I nod. "I know. She still talks about going sometimes."

"We should've done it back then." His mouth tenses into a grimace, like he's fighting off an unwelcome emotion that's reared its ugly head. "Maybe for your birthday next year, you, me, and your mom can take a trip. What do you think?"

I think even if hell froze over, Mom wouldn't entertain the idea of spending time with Dad. "When's the last time you talked to her?"

"I texted her about a month ago, letting her know I'd be in town today."

I quirk one brow. That's news. Mom tells me everything, but she didn't tell me that. "And what did she say?"

"Nothing, just a 'read' receipt." Dad averts his gaze.

If she won't return a text, a fun-filled international family vacation is certainly out of the question. "What are you saying right now? You miss Mom all of a sudden?"

He releases a deep exhale. "I tried dating. I joined a site."

I want to ask him which site but I don't know if I can really stomach the visual of Dad on Tinder, so I sidestep further inquiry. "Cool...cool. Are you ordering another whiskey sour?"

"The women are... I don't know. Dating is different when you're in your fifties."

Apparently we are having this conversation. Fantastic. I grab my own cocktail and guzzle down the remnants of the berry Cosmo with lavender syrup. "How is it different?"

"I put in my age and interests, assuming my matches would be women in their fifties as well. But oddly, most of the women who message me are in their twenties and thirties. We have nothing in common. I'm not sure what to talk about. It's unclear what they're after."

Wrong. It's crystal clear: his wallet. But I don't want to cheapen his efforts or hurt his feelings. "Oh, come on, Dad. You're a catch."

"I'm old. I don't know what these young women want from me."

"Age-gap romance is in right now. You're like a svelte Santa Claus...just not as cheery."

Dad flattens his expression, thoroughly unamused at my joke. "Age gap?"

"Yeah. You're in your zaddy era."

"Zaddy?" Dad parrots. "Are you still speaking English?"

I chuckle under my breath. Dad's always the most confident—sometimes arrogant—man in the room. It's endearing to see him a little insecure about this. "It means women of all ages are attracted to confidence and sophistication."

"Hmph," he grunts. "Well, it's bizarre. I find myself wanting to talk to someone about it. Maybe even laugh with someone or get advice about how to navigate this. But at the end of the day..."

"Mom was the only person you ever really talked to, huh?"

"Your mother was the only person in this world I ever felt connected to. I always lived with my head in the clouds, my mind in a different dimension. But your mom had a way of keeping me tethered to this earth. I didn't realize what a gift that was until recently."

He seems to shrink right in front of me. The great J.P. Cooper, humbled by the love he let get away. My dad never cheated on my mom, to my knowledge. He was never abusive. Dad was simply absent, and my mom got tired of begging for his attention. Writing was his true love and commitment, his wife—simply a mistress.

"Do you want me to talk to her?"

I was not anticipating his eager nod of agreement. "Would you?"

I thread my fingers together, rotating my thumbs like a proud mafia boss. My dad is my latest victim, and I have him right where I want him. "I will...under one condition."

"Being?" He raises both brows, before he throws back the rest of his drink.

"Give me one *real*, honest piece of advice, author to author."

"My pockets are deep, Sora. All you want is career advice?"

I let out a low growl of frustration. "No, Dad, what I want is for you to take me under your wing. I want to sit down and do writing sprints with you. I want to drink whatever brand of coffee you do so I can also piss excellence. But every single time I bring up this topic, you shut me out. Do you realize how cruel that is? You're *the J.P. Cooper*. Your only daughter can't get her author career off the ground, and you could help me if you wanted to, but instead you've left me in the dust. *Why*?"

Dad plants both elbows on the table. He wraps one hand around his fist and rests his chin on his knuckles. He takes a few steadying breaths. "You want my advice?"

"Desperately," I reiterate.

"Quit."

One word clobbers my heart and it shatters into a million pieces. "Quit?" I echo in a weak whisper. What are the chances that Dad actually picked up a romance book I wrote, read it, and then decided the only solution to my problem was throwing in the towel? "Because I'm that bad?"

He shakes his head. "I don't know what kind of writer you are, Sora."

"If only there were a simple solution to that," I snark.

He ignores me and continues, "But what I can tell you is that you're too much like me. You're looking for validation in all the wrong places, and this career you want is going to ruin your life. The odds are against you, and failure is all but imminent. If there is anything else in this world you can do that will bring you a sliver of joy and satisfaction...*do that instead*. Don't torture yourself."

I don't even bother fighting my tears. I let my eyes water so Dad can see what he caused. "Thanks, Dad. Great advice."

"I didn't mean to upset you—"

"It's fine. I asked for honesty...I got it."

The silence between us becomes deafening. I finally addressed the elephant in the room, but it didn't go away, it only got bigger. I'm no longer in the mood for dessert. I really just want this evening to be over.

"May I give you your birthday present now?"

I could be a petulant adult child. My dad hurt my feelings and I think I'm well within my right to make a scene. But I can't ignore the fact that he's here. I'm well past childhood. My father owes me nothing. Yet, he's trying to connect. How many daughters would kill for their father to make an effort?

"This dinner is more than present enough. It means a lot to me that you flew all the way here to spend time with me."

His lips twitch into a smile as he reaches into his pocket. "Dinner is dinner. This is your present." He dangles a set of keys before setting them on the table and sliding them toward me.

"Please tell me these unlock a treasure chest," I joke as I scoop up the two silver keys, identical in shape.

"The brownstone. It's yours."

My soul floats right out of my body. For a few moments I swear I'm staring at my own jaw, mopping the floor of the restaurant. When my speechless, catatonic state simmers, I croak out, "Are you serious?"

"I am."

Dad's brownstone was worth millions when he bought it after the divorce. In the twelve years since, it's doubled in value. "Where are you going to live?" I ask.

"LA, for the time being. The studio wants me to stay close as a consultant on set when filming starts."

"It's a lot of house for one person," I mention.

"So fill it. But with people, not stories."

"What?" I ask, rotating the keys in my hands, watching the dim glow of the overhead chandelier reflecting in the silver.

"I spent so much time lost in the fantastical worlds I built on page, I forgot to live my real life. While I have brief moments of happiness, like tonight, I'm not a happy man. Don't be like me, Sora. Be better."

I don't understand the sadness in his eyes. He sacrificed a lot for his career, but it paid off in spades. Dad has fame, fortune, and a legacy that every author alive envies.

What the hell could he possibly be regretting?

CHAPTER SIX

Sora

Tropey reader stuff.

Movement at the foot of my bed jostles me awake. My eyelids reluctantly peel apart and I'm greeted by my best, and only friend, Daphne, sitting cross-legged at the edge of the bed, squishing my toes.

"I am thoroughly convinced you would not survive a home invasion," she deadpans.

A wide yawn escapes my lips as I un-wedge my toes from under her ass. I sit up, leaning against my rickety, wooden headboard. "If you're the intruder, all I stand to lose is Toaster Strudels and maybe some box wine."

"I'm serious, Sora. I've been here for thirty minutes. I purposely dropped a mixing bowl in the kitchen to startle you awake."

I blink at her. "How'd that work for you?"

She rumples her nose. "To be honest, I'm surprised you own mixing bowls. What do you use those for? Popcorn?"

Her glib smile is because she's right. I can't cook anything without a microwave. "Perhaps," I mumble, stretching my arms overhead.

Daphne's smile softens. Her thick, blond hair cascades over her right shoulder when she cocks her head to the side. "Happy birthday, to my best friend, and the world's best romance author.

This is going to be your year, babe. I can *feel* it."

I believed her last year. And the year before. Also, the year before that. Daphne's enthusiasm is now losing momentum. "Thank you."

"I also have some great news for you." She claps her hands together in glee. "Guess what your amazing personal assistant extraordinaire did for you?"

I show her a froggy, close-lipped smile. "Break into my apartment at the crack of dawn?"

Daphne pretends to check her nails. "First off, I'm popping all the balloons I got for you on my way out. Second, you're going to regret your sourpuss mood when I tell you what I pulled off. But wait! First, how did yesterday go?"

"Fine. Dad was...*Dad*. He gave me the brownstone."

Her jaw falls apart. "*The brownstone*? As in the West Village brownstone?"

I nod. "He's staying in LA because he insisted on babysitting the showrunner for *Hell & Heroes*."

"That does not surprise me remotely," Daphne says, lying down and curling up on top of my goose down comforter, like a loyal labradoodle. "Coop is a control freak."

"He hates that you call him that, by the way."

She laughs. "And here I am just flattered he knows I exist."

Of course my dad knows Daphne. She's my only friend, and my PA out of the goodness of her heart. Without her, I am borderline pathetic. I like to remind Mom and Dad every now and then I have at least one real-life friend. Otherwise, they might circle back to the antidepressants they so desperately think I need.

"But that wasn't what I was talking about," Daphne continues. "I thought I'd pop by this morning while you still speak to us lowly folks. How did it go with Dane? I thought you'd text me at least. Did he bring a contract, or do you have a follow-up meeting?"

Her big green eyes sparkle with hope and it instantly brings tears to my eyes. I wake up every day and have my heart ripped to shreds by this industry. Whether it's a mean-spirited review, being ignored by influencers, my sales dashboard telling me I can't afford to chase this career anymore, or my dream agent telling me I'm just not good enough, I know how to function with a broken heart. But crushing Daphne? For some reason that hurts the most. She believes in me.

And maybe she shouldn't.

"Babe...tears?" she asks, crawling up the bed to sit beside me.

"He didn't want me. He was looking for an in with my dad." That's all I manage before I'm wrapped in her slender arms. I mean to clarify and present the rejection in some kind of sugarcoating of "it's not the right time," or "it's still early in my career and I might have a chance down the road," but I can't muster the strength to ignore the simple truth: Dane saw no value in me.

"What do we need to do?" Daphne asks. "Because I have to leave for work in fifteen minutes, and I won't abandon you crying here on your birthday." She kisses the top of my head, then scoots backward to examine me. "You're going to be okay, Sora. You're unbreakable."

She's wrong, though. I'm broken. But she needs a smile so she can get on with her day, so I don't say that. Instead, I do what I'm best at—placating.

"Thank you. I just need a day to shake it off." Clasping my hands together, I rub them furiously like I'm trying to start a fire. "Oh, I forgot. I know you were asking last week. I found one more foiled special edition of *Lovely* for that big influencer, RoxyReadz. I got a bunch of cute stuff for her package and got it sent last week, so keep an eye out on socials for an unboxing. Her following is huge, so hopefully that'll help with visibility before book two comes out."

Daphne's eyes descend to her lap. "Shit."

"What's wrong?" I ask. But I already know.

Her eyes come up to meet my gaze. "She's one reader with one opinion. Don't give it a second thought."

The familiar ball of lava settles in my gut as shame washes over me, head to toe. I am brokenhearted every time my imagination doesn't appease a stranger's preference. But there's no room for apologies in publishing. The authors who can't learn to swallow the bitter pill of rejection and humiliation quickly find their cancel button. Those who learn to smile through the pain, weather the storm.

I duck my head, nodding in understanding. So Roxy already read it...or maybe not. But either way, she certainly formed an opinion on my story. "How bad did she roast me?"

"It doesn't matter. Hot takes are the industry standard right now. It's just for attention," Daphne assures me. She shrugs her shoulders, brushing it off like it's nothing. "How much did that package cost?"

"A hundred and fifty dollars with shipping."

Daphne bunches up her fists. "I'll reimburse you. I'm so sorry. I didn't realize what kind of person she was when I initiated a collaboration. I just wanted to help you get some views. I've already unfollowed and muted her on socials so she can't tag you in anything else so aggressive. Don't look at it, Sora. In fact, I'm changing your Instagram password."

Curiosity tickles my intrigue in a dangerous way. Nothing good can come of me knowing what she said. And there's no way Daphne would allow it. She does a better job of protecting my mental health than I do these days.

"Reimburse me?" I ask, lifting one eyebrow. "You want me to take money from my best friend because you tried to help me? Don't be silly. I don't know. Maybe I just need to write something better."

"*Lovely* is a fantastic book. It's my favorite of yours." She grabs my knee over the covers and squeezes. "I love everything you write, but that one"—she taps against her heart—"spoke to my *soul*."

"Then why do you think it doesn't sell? What am I doing wrong?" I ask her point-blank.

"I don't know, babe. I'm trying. I really am—"

"Hey," I interrupt, meeting her sad gaze. "I am nothing but

grateful for you. You are not the weak link here...I am."

Social media is the bane of my existence, but it's an arena in which Daphne thrives. Her personal account, just for shits and giggles according to her, has ten times the following of my author account. She's full of personality, and knows how to attract an audience.

When I found out authoring meant building a social media presence, I almost didn't publish. Luckily my best friend jumped in to save the day. Daphne graduated from NYU with me, but didn't get into Columbia Law like she'd always planned. Since then, she made helping my career her life's mission between bartending and waiting tables. Of course, my plan was always to reward her richly. Except, after years of sleepless nights, hustling like we're invincible, we don't have much to show for it.

My phone rings from the nightstand barely once before I scoop it up. "My mom," I tell Daphne.

"Take it," she says as she rolls backward off the bed, landing on her feet, showing off her cat-like agility. "I'll cut us some cake."

"Hey, Mama," I answer, bracing myself for a painful serenade of "Happy Birthday." My mother is not a talented singer.

"Happy birthday, my sweet girl. Twenty-seven beautiful years of bliss." Something seems a little off in her tone.

"Twenty-seven years and nine months of bliss," I correct.

"No. Pregnancy with you was not pleasant, love. Prepare yourself. Chos have terrible pregnancies. Get comfortable with vomiting."

"Wonderful," I gripe. "Are we still on for eight tonight?"

"That's why I'm calling. I'm very sorry, sweetheart, but I've come down with a stomach bug. I've been lying on the bathroom floor all night. Can we take a rain check for later this week?"

"Oh, Mom." I pull back the covers, a light breeze chilling my bare legs. "Can I bring you something? Tea? Soup?"

"No, no," she insists. "I don't want you catching whatever this is. Very contagious. My whole office is dropping like flies. Plus, it's your birthday. Go have fun."

"I'm not leaving you alone to rot over there. I'll get dressed and come by first thing."

"*Sora*," Mom emphasizes before she goes off in Korean. I was always supposed to learn the language, but never made time. Mom often speaks to me in her native tongue as if it will magically seep into my brain.

"You'll call me tonight and let me know you're okay?" I ask once she's done.

"Don't worry about me. I just hate to miss your birthday. It's the first time in—"

"Ever," I finish for her. There's a pang of embarrassment in my chest when I realize how much I let my mom coddle me. Somewhere along the line, I stopped seeing the importance of a social life. I'm loved fiercely by my mother, by Daphne, and even by Dad in his own way. I've been so focused on getting my career off the ground, I never asked if that was enough.

"Maybe it's good though. I'm sure your friends would like to take you out." Oh, she's mighty generous for adding the plural.

"I hope you feel better, Mama. I'm only a call away if you need anything."

She ends the call after a quick, "Gotta go." I shudder knowing she probably needs to put her head in the toilet again. Poor thing.

"How's Mama Cho?" Daphne asks as she reemerges in my bedroom. "Did you tell her I've mastered the bunny chopsticks and am ready for my next lesson at Pajeon Palace?"

My stare is glued to the plate of chocolate cake in Daphne's hand. My stomach rumbles. In her other hand is a small gift basket of assorted candies and other goodies. "Believe it or not, you don't come up in conversation every single time I talk to my mom."

Daphne scoffs, whipping her hair around in a diva-like fashion. "That's just offensive. We've been going steady for ten years now. Kind of feels like the sun should rise and set on my ass. But you know, that's your call." She winks. "Since you're up, you want to eat in the kitchen?"

"I'm kind of feeling cake in bed," I say, nestling deeper into my mattress.

"I've seen you maul chocolate cake like a starving bear. It's messy, and your comforter is *very* white." My lips part, but before I can protest, Daphne adds, "Deny it all you want, but I have video evidence of it."

I roll my eyes as I follow her into the kitchen. "One time in the past three years I got completely shit-faced, and I hadn't eaten all day. Of course you were there with your phone, recording."

She smirks over her shoulder. "It's in the best-friend job description. I'm collecting content for your wedding video montage."

I'm not sure what's more hilarious, the idea of me getting married, or that Daphne thinks I'd allow a video montage at said imaginary wedding.

I sit down at my kitchen counter in front of the plate of cake. I don't have a dining table. My apartment is just shy of six hundred square feet, which is a blessing in New York City. Thanks to a rent-controlled sublet, I can afford to sleep with a roof over my head.

"You're not having any? I can't eat my birthday cake alone."

Daphne sucks in her lips as she shakes her head with firm resolve. "I have setup in half an hour. It's a lot of manual labor and you know sugar makes me sleepy."

"Where are you working tonight?" I swipe a small dollop of frosting with my pinky and pop my finger into my mouth. The frosting is sinfully delectable. Who needs orgasms when you have triple chocolate cake with a cookie-crumble crust?

"A wedding at The Plaza. Servers are getting paid one hundred bucks an hour. I couldn't turn it down."

"One hundred?" I gawk at her. "Damn. It's a good time to get into serving."

"This is basically the U.S. version of a royal wedding. A billionaire's event. They had custom-made couture uniforms for the women servers. We had to verify we didn't have any visible tattoos in a strapless dress. I went through a background check. The only thing they didn't do is a cavity search, but who knows what'll happen when I get there."

"Hopefully not a cavity search."

"*Anyway*," she says, pointing to my gift basket. "I got all your favorites. Chocolate with almonds. The little Scandinavian sour candies you special order like a weirdo. And there are some gummy bears to help you relax. Okay?"

"Are you trying to help me relax by putting me into a sugar-induced coma?"

She flashes me a toothy grin. "You're not a big drinker. I had to take liberties."

I glance at my basket of goodies and my favorite kind of chocolate cake in front of me. "You arranged this basket and shrink-wrapped it yourself?"

She nods. "I know it's no Chanel clutch or anything, but I've had to start saving—"

I grab Daphne's hand. "*It's better*. This is so thoughtful and wonderful. Thank you for always making me feel special. Not just on my birthdays. Even on my shittiest days, I'm okay because I have you, Daph. I don't know what I'd do without you."

"I'm always here for you." She says the words with a soft smile but there's a touch of sadness wrinkling the corner of her eyes.

"What're you saving for?" I ask, squeezing her hand before I let it drop.

"Life," she answers rather cryptically.

"Move into the brownstone with me. That would help you save on rent, right? The house is paid off. All we'd need to come up with is utilities."

"That's generous, friend. Really sweet of you." She tilts her head. "Can I think about it and let you know?"

I was expecting an automatic "hell yes." Daphne has two other roommates that she despises. We should've moved in together from the get-go but I opted for this place thinking I'd need the solitude to write masterpieces. So far it's just been a fortress of writer's block.

While I don't understand her hesitance, I dare not tell her

it kind of hurts my feelings. "Of course you can. No pressure." I bite back all the questions on the tip of my tongue, sensing her reluctance to share any more.

"But hey, can I tell you what I pulled off for you? I'm so excited, I'm going to burst."

"Go for it," I say.

"You know that signing event in Brooklyn, City Nights and Novels?"

"Vaguely," I answer. But of course I remember. I've applied to the major signing in my own backyard, but they turn me down every single year. The event is hosted by a big PR company called Cupids, which has also rejected me for services three years in a row. That one stings. I've been rejected by agents, readers, publishers, you name it. But it hurts a little more when someone you're *offering to pay* still deems you unworthy of their attention.

"An author dropped out last minute, and after a few incessant DMs, I got you a table." Her grin is so wide I see all of her teeth on display.

"You're kidding."

"I am not. That gives us one week to put everything together, but I know we can do it. You just have to see what inventory you have on hand, but even if we don't have a ton of books to sell, we can still network and rub some elbows."

My initial shock morphs into excitement. *There it is.* The little glimmer of hope after the gut punch that was my meeting with Dane yesterday. I slide out of my chair and wrap Daphne up in a rib-crushing hug. "You're my favorite human on this planet."

She can't move her arms because I'm wrapped around her like a python. "Of course I am," she wheezes out. Her tone returns to normal once I release her. "I know you have dinner with your mom tonight, but how about after we meet up for a drink?"

"She's sick. She canceled."

"Oh, babe—"

"It's fine," I insist. "I actually need to go through Ellie's edits. I do not mind a quiet birthday at home."

"Working," Daphne adds.

"But when you love it, it doesn't feel like work." Neither of us believes my excuse. Lately, writing feels more exhausting than a ten-hour shift in a coal mine.

"It's your birthday, Sora. You can't stay holed up in here doing nothing. I have an idea. How about you come with me? I have a plus-one for the event."

I squint in her direction. "I thought you basically needed a security clearance to work this wedding. How did a server get a plus-one?"

"Strict on staff, a little loose on the guest list apparently." She shrugs. "Don't ask me why, but I'm allowed to bring a guest to the reception. It's a black-tie affair with a dress code though. Do you still have that Marc Jacobs ball gown?"

"The one that gives me uniboob?"

"Only when you try to wear it with a bandeau. I've told you a dozen times, you have to let your girls swim free in that dress."

I puff a little air into my cheeks and swish it back and forth as I debate. "I don't know."

"I do." Daphne grabs my shoulders and waits until I look up at her. She's at least five inches taller than me. "You need a life outside these four walls."

"I think I need to focus. I have to write another book. I'm torpedoing toward the ditch of failure, and I'm not going to be able to climb back out."

"You *just* finished *The Way We Were*. How about you take a little breather and do something fun? Maybe a weekend trip?"

The truth is, I'm debating scrapping my next release. Ellie, my editor, who I've dubbed "the robot," has always been tight-lipped with feedback. Her focus is on structure and syntax. But normally I get a few comments sprinkled throughout my manuscript about relatable moments or things that made her giggle. My latest book, all she said was: *Here you go.*

I emailed her back and asked what she thought of the book. Her reply was even more painful: *It's fine. Also, my rates are going up.*

Over one hundred and twenty thousand words where I poured my heart out on the page, and the best she could come up with was, *fine*. And it's possible she hated my story so much that she decided she deserves more compensation moving forward. If that's not an ego check, I don't know what is.

"I don't want to have fun, Daph. I want to write a bestseller. I want an agent. I want to stop waking up every day and feeling like I'm sprinting in place."

"All right, how about this?" Daphne releases me with a long exhale. "Come to the wedding, eat a fancy meal, drink the free booze, then after cleanup, you and I will sit down with pen and paper and I will map out all the tropey reader stuff that makes a bestseller and we'll stuff your next book chock-full of all the viral crap social media wants."

"Tropey reader stuff?" I quirk an eyebrow.

"Yeah, we're talking about two different things, Sora. Being a bestseller and being a talented writer are not the same. Bad books make a ton of money, and some of the best literature of our day and age will die, unread, in obscurity. If you want to go viral, you have to pander to the trends."

"You mean sell out."

"No, I mean have a strategy. You don't need to work so hard at being a great writer. You already are. But if you want to be seen, then yeah, we're going to need your characters to get trapped in a snowstorm overnight and the only inn in walking distance has one room with only one bed. Or, you need a man in a mask chasing a woman through a forest with a machete. Make your hero someone's older brother. If all else fails, you could just write anything romantasy, because that genre apparently can't miss."

"Readers and their freaking dragons," I grumble. "But okay, yeah. I'm open to anything at this point. It's a date."

"Good. I have to get going, but I'll text you the details. And for the love of God, Sora, do *not* wear flip-flops. I don't care if they have rhinestones on them. You need at least a kitten heel, mk? You have my apartment key if you need to raid my closet." Daphne leans down to press her cheek against mine. "Happy birthday, my friend. I love you. Don't worry too much. It'll all work out."

"Love you," I answer back as she heads for the front door.

I smile at my best friend in the world who knows me to my core. Because, yes, I was most definitely debating wearing my bedazzled flip-flops tonight.

CHAPTER SEVEN

Forrest

I'm bored of you now, cabana boy.

My date's eyes dart over my shoulder to the precarious situation behind us for the millionth time. It's odd to see Celeste so unnerved. She owns a billion-dollar, celebrity-endorsed fashion empire. She's an icon amongst the Manhattan elite. The world is at her fingertips, yet every time she sees her ex-husband, she visibly shrivels.

I'm really starting to hate that fucker.

The wedding band playing in the corner shifts to a slower song, something romantic. I take the opportunity to unbutton my tux jacket and grab the bottom of her chair, yanking her closer to me. With my lips grazing her earlobe, I drop my voice low. "Celeste, honey, I'm going to need you to take a deep breath, and *stop* glancing over at your ex. He's going to notice you staring. You are blowing our cover."

Ignoring me, she looks over to his table and the voluptuous brunette he brought as his arm candy. The woman laughs loudly from across the room. Even from here, I can tell that was fake, simply a girl trying to appease her new sugar daddy. She looks like she graduated from high school yesterday—barely legal. That shit never used to bother me until I became a father.

"I'll hand it to him, she's pretty."

"Are you jealous?" I ask her as I eye my glass, the champagne still bitter on my tongue from my last sip.

She pulls her head back, then fixes her gaze on me. "Not for the reasons you think."

I run my thumb over her lip gently, so her deviously red lipstick doesn't smudge. "He's delirious with jealousy. It's taking everything in him not to come over here and snatch you away."

She scoffs, the corner of her mouth twitching. "He hasn't looked at me even once—"

"Because he's been watching me. He's busy sizing up his competition. Hate to say it, but he's better at this game than you are."

She slides me a disingenuous grin. "I take it as a compliment that Greg can easily out-petty me."

"He accosted me at the bar while you were catching up with your friends," I admit before taking another sip from my glass flute. Honestly, I hate the smell and taste of champagne. But I obediently drink whatever Celeste does without a complaint. Getting paid four thousand dollars per night means I don't grimace at expensive alcohol I don't enjoy. "Would you like another?" I ask, nodding to her empty flute.

"And have you risk another verbal lashing at the bar? No. What did Greg say to you?" She looks genuinely concerned, her forehead creasing with guilt perhaps, like she sent a puppy to a lion's den.

"He just asked me how serious we were, and what my intentions were with his ex."

It was actually more intense than I let on. Twenty minutes ago, while I was dutifully fetching Celeste another glass of bubbly from the open bar, Greg cornered me. He reeked of expensive cologne as he threatened me, whispering profanities with a clipped smile on his face, so no one would suspect his adult temper tantrum. He called me a broke, small-dicked cabana boy—wrong on all three counts, by the way—and referred to Celeste as his spoiled leftovers. But she doesn't need to know all that.

She lifts a well-manicured brow, surveying the wicked grin I'm wearing. "And what did you say?"

"I told him we preferred to keep our relationship status private. And as far as my intentions"—I playfully pump my brows—"I told him all I knew for certain is that I was going to tear your pretty dress to shreds before burying my face between your thighs all night."

She roars in laughter. It's the first authentic smile I've earned all night. "You did not, Forrest."

"I most certainly did."

"He probably doesn't even care." She shrugs it off, reaching for her empty glass, then sets it back down when she remembers she finished her drink.

"Let me grab you another," I insist, scooting my chair back, but she wraps her hand around my forearm, keeping me in place. Her touch is cool against my hot skin, the tux jacket making me swelter. I can't wait to take this thing off.

"I'm sure the server will come around shortly. Just stay with me." She keeps her head held high, but I see the anxiousness behind her eyes, the slight tremor in her lower lip. Not only is Greg being here at their friends' wedding an added stress, but over our past few dates, I've learned Celeste has social anxiety. She loves being a fashion designer, but she hates being the face of her brand. If she could do things her way, she'd stow away on a remote island. Just her, a sketchbook, and a tropical breeze.

I weave my fingers between hers and squeeze twice, feeling the delicate bones of her hand. "I'm here. It's okay. You're doing great, by the way. My apologies to the bride, but you are the most captivating woman in the room tonight."

"Except for my ex-husband's latest conquest. She's gorgeous."

I'm biased. All I see in Greg's date is fake breasts, bleached teeth, and hair big enough to shelter a small family of birds. From earlier, I caught a whiff of her perfume—way too much of it. *Is she attractive? Physically...I guess*? I'm not sure. His date is a young woman, dressed up like a Barbie doll, begging to be noticed. But Celeste? She's class, grace, and humility, far too busy with all her innovation to beg so desperately for attention. Not to mention she's still a knockout nearing forty, making Greg the dumbest fuck on this planet.

I hate the effect he still has on her. But from what she told me, they were high school sweethearts. She loved that man for almost twenty years. Their divorce was barely six months ago. She's more than allowed to be vulnerable at the moment.

"Her dress is nice I suppose." I offer a shallow compliment, while dodging any further confirmation of her appearance. I don't praise the young woman, but I don't insult her either. I don't know her story. Maybe she's a victim of the circumstances. Who knows? Maybe Greg hired his date the same way Celeste hired me. Wouldn't that be ironic?

A server walks by with a tray of chocolate-dipped strawberries. I silently sulk when Celeste waves them away. This woman eats like a bird, meaning, when I'm with her, I tend to also go hungry.

"It's one of my upcoming pieces from my new fall line."

"Pardon?" I ask, momentarily distracted as I fantasize about a thick peanut butter and jelly sandwich.

"The dress she's wearing. I designed it. Greg only has access to the samples because he's still a chairman on the board of my company. The lengths he went through to pour salt into the wound. That lace is so delicate..." She lowers her voice. "They massacred it. They added fabric to the sides that doesn't match the original design to accommodate her—" Celeste cups her hands in front of her breasts, acknowledging the woman's plentiful chest. "The back is bunching because the bodice is too small. I bet she can't breathe in there. Poor thing."

"Now you pity her after she stole your dress?"

Celeste smirks, a hint of mischief dancing in her eyes. "Absolutely, I do. She has to go home with Greg. That's punishment enough." Celeste holds up her pointer finger and curls it, a conspiratorial gleam lighting her face. "Four and a half inches at best, and it's crooked. How's that for petty?"

I smother my laugh behind closed lips, feeling my chest tighten with the effort. "Very petty. Well done." And the asshole had the nerve to insult my manhood? Projection at its finest.

Her eyes drop to the ivory-colored linen at our small table. We were supposed to be seated with another couple tonight, but they never showed. We've had all the privacy we could ask for.

"Who cares who he's with and what she's wearing? It's not you, so he's already lost. Why are you looking at her?"

"She's hard not to notice," Celeste quips back, adjusting her earring.

"You want her number? I'm happy to be your wingman. That could be a fun twist in your breakup saga. What if Greg's mistress left him for you?"

She narrows her eyes, the corners crinkling with suppressed amusement. "On our first date you were so docile. What happened?"

I break out in a grumbly laugh, the sound rumbling from deep in my chest. "I'm sorry. I'm getting too comfortable around you."

I normally never do repeat clients. It's a dangerous game to play. It's easy to cut ties after one salacious evening. Once you start spending too much time together, lines get blurred. I'm paid to be a woman's fantasy, and I've become excellent at playing the part. But it's an act. It's not real. And it's not forever.

But Celeste is an exception because we don't have sex. She made that clear from our first date. All she's paying me for is my company.

She swipes at my nose like she's half-heartedly disciplining a kitten, the tip of her acrylic nail barely grazing my skin. "Anyway, sorry to disappoint you, but I'm not having lesbian thoughts about Greg's date. What bothers me is the hypocrisy."

"What do you mean?"

She exhales, pushing away her empty glass, making room to fold her hands together on top of the table. "Before I started working on the fall line, I told the board, Greg included, I wanted to start designing based off a different body prototype. I wanted to launch dresses that were made to honor a curvy woman's body. Women should be proud of their breasts and hips. They shouldn't have to hold their breath and suck in their stomachs all night like they're ashamed they carried children. High fashion can be for everyone. They shouldn't have had to frankenstein my work with cheap polyester for her to wear that dress tonight."

Judging by the anguish wrinkled between her brows, Celeste didn't get her way. "They turned down your idea?"

"Vehemently. They want runway fashion. All samples in sizes double zero to two. They want to call a size six, plus size. *It's vile*. And now I'm sitting here wondering how Greg can sleep with a woman like *that*, but won't advocate for her."

"My ex, Hannah, nearly gave herself an eating disorder trying to fit into Versace. She wanted this unbelievably expensive dress, but they never had it in stock in her size. She decided she had to shrink her body."

"They probably never even made it in her size," Celeste confirms, shame clouding her expression, her shoulders slumping slightly. "She fell victim to an old trade trick. They add the bigger sizes to the website, but it's always marked out of stock. We make everything limited edition to create a sense of urgency. They get desperate enough and they change their bodies to fit the dress instead of vice versa."

"Seriously?" I quirk a brow, the string quartet transitioning to an up-tempo waltz that fills the momentary silence between us. "That's a thing?"

Celeste's eyes fall to her lap, fingers mindlessly twisting the napkin. "It's a thing."

"It's *your* company, Celeste. If you want to make a change, make one."

She laughs at my naivety, the sound tinged with resignation. "I'm the designer, not the decision maker. I couldn't have built what I have without Greg's early investment. So, I do the work, and he and his fat-cat board of advisors call the shots."

"On behalf of men, I'm sorry…if that helps."

Running her fingertips through my hair, her lips relax. "We're friends, right? Odd friends, but still—"

"Definitely friends," I assure her. "I would've joined you tonight whether you paid me or not." I place my hand on hers, turning over her palm to trace small circles with my thumb. It's a gesture that always calms her.

"Then friend to friend, why do men cheat?" Celeste asks, disarming me. I wasn't expecting that question of all things. Her hazel eyes—usually guarded—now hold mine with unsettling directness.

I clear my throat, the sudden dryness making me wish I had another drink, buying time for an enlightening response, but I can't come up with anything helpful. "I don't know. I never have," I admit.

"Greg made all of this so messy. There was no prenup. If he didn't want to be with me, why didn't he just break up with me? Then, he'd be free to screw all the dimwitted, busty, gold-diggers he pleased, guilt-free. Why did he have to cheat and make a mockery of me? I don't want him back, Forrest, it's just..."

The bitterness in her voice contrasts with the painful vulnerability in her eyes. They're glossy under the dim mood lighting, but she keeps her unshed tears at bay.

"Your pride is hurt?" I offer gently, my voice barely audible over the clinking glasses and murmured conversations surrounding us.

She nods solemnly, a strand of dark hair falling across her face. "I'm about to be forty. I thought I was past all this. Greg's the only man I've ever been with. Now, I have to date again? I can't do it. I can't even wrap my head around that."

"You're on a date right now," I counter, gesturing between us with a slight smile, hoping to ease the heaviness that's settled over our table.

"It's not the same." The corner of her mouth twitches upward, almost a smile but not quite. "We both know this night isn't headed anywhere further than this."

"It could if you want."

That gets her full attention. Her eyebrows shoot up into high arches. "What do you mean?"

I pop my shoulder, showing her an earnest smile. My heart rate quickens against my better judgment. "If you need to break the ice with someone you trust, I'm here. You pay me for my time. What you choose to do with that time is up to you."

She leans in close. "I'm more than ten years your senior. Is sex with an old lady really what you want?" She lowers her tone but fiery boldness flickers in her irises.

"I want you to never call yourself an old lady again, Celeste. Stop talking like your life is over. Start a new company you control. *Date*. Fall in love again. It's not over for you." I bring the back of her hand to my lips. "Not even close."

For a moment, she melts into my gaze. I instantly regret my offer. If Celeste wants things to go any further, it'll change our dynamic. I've opened up to her about a lot. She's the only client who I've ever told about my daughter.

"What do you think? Do you want to get out of here?" The bride and groom have already left the reception. The guests are slow to clear out, probably reluctant to leave such a fanfare. It's without question the most luxurious wedding I've ever been to. With butter carved into little roses, a miniature ice sculpture at each table, I'm pretty sure the theme of this wedding is *We have a shit-ton of cash*.

"I do." Her brows lift marginally. "But not with you."

I clutch my chest like it's wounded. "Ouch."

She chuckles, relaxed and sweet, her playfulness washing away the uncomfortableness. "As odd as this sounds, you're the most comfortable relationship I have with a man right now. I don't want one night of good sex to jeopardize that... Or, at least I'm assuming it'd be good."

I wink flirtatiously. "It'd be great." But I also breathe out in relief, my shoulders dropping as the tension flows out, learning we're on the same page. "How about one more slow dance and then I call your chauffeur and get you home?"

"Sounds like bliss."

I push back my chair, the legs dragging softly on the plush

carpet, intent on helping Celeste up in the most gentlemanly way possible...except I just collided with a body behind me. The soft fabric of a dress brushes against my arm. "I'm sorry. Excuse me—"

Turning my head to address my poor victim, I lose my words when I see who I've rammed into. She's wearing a pink ball gown-style dress that's covered with black tulle. Her hair is in a neat twist, resting at the nape of her neck. And her eyes are red and swollen, tears streaking down her cheeks.

Cookie girl. From the coffeehouse.

"Are you okay? Did I hurt you?" I slide out of my seat, my sudden concern well out of the realm of a stranger's politeness.

"Oh that's not what this is." She paws at her face, wiping her tears so aggressively that she's practically smacking her face, the sound surprisingly sharp. "But you're on my dress."

I glance down to the chair leg which I slid right over the base of her gown. With unnecessary Hulk-like enthusiasm, I rip the chair off her hem, releasing her. I notice the damage in the tulle I most definitely caused. I squat down to assess it, and see what I can fix, but cookie girl leans down at the same time and somehow my forehead lands right between her breasts.

She leaps away but trips over the extra fabric of her gown. Instinctually I reach out to prevent her from toppling backward into the table behind her. All I manage to grab, though, is the front of her dress. This time, I hear the fabric tear.

"Shit!" I exclaim. *What the fuck?* Is this dress constructed of toilet paper?

Once she's steady on her feet, I release her. She has to clench the V-neck of her dress together so she doesn't risk exposing her tits. I unwittingly catch a hint of perfume—something sweet, like peaches and cream. "That was not on purpose. I'm sorry, I didn't mean to touch you. It was a reflex."

Her head is down, fresh tears replacing the ones she wiped away. "I'm not accusing you of anything. You were trying to keep me from falling." She holds her palms up for a millisecond before clutching her dress again. "We're good."

Does she recognize me? Maybe I'm forgettable... She sure as hell is not.

"I'll pay to replace it," I awkwardly offer, my neck roasting from embarrassment.

"Don't worry. It's fine." She sniffles, forcing a smile as she nods at me, then Celeste. "Have a nice evening." Then, she whisks away, presumably toward the ladies' room, the damaged tulle trailing behind her.

Celeste smirks at me as I hold out my hand to help her out of her chair, finally. The satin of her dress gracefully cloaks her slim frame as she stands. "Wow, Forrest, that was...not smooth."

"Thanks," I mutter bitterly, my eyes still on cookie girl as she weaves through the ballroom, her hands still firmly clasped around her chest, disappearing among the crowd of gowns and tuxes.

"You looked shocked to see her. Someone you know?"

When cookie girl is finally out of sight, I tilt my head to the ceiling, noticing the dozens of crystal chandeliers overhead. "Sort of."

"She's very pretty. Her Marc Jacobs is a little out of date, but she wears it so well."

"Until I ripped it," I bellyache.

"It's salvageable. Tulle can easily be replaced."

Good grief, Celeste knows her industry. She's like a bloodhound when it comes to designer brands. She could tell you what everyone in the room is wearing without looking at the tags.

"What's her name?" Celeste asks, not bothering to hide her curiosity.

"I don't even know. A couple days ago, I bumped into her at a coffee shop. I was trying to make a joke, but I came off like an ass. I apologized. That didn't go great either."

Celeste nods in agreement. "Based on the interaction I just witnessed, I fully believe you."

"Ha-ha," I deadpan. Holding out my hand to her, I ask, "Ready for that dance?"

She assesses me head to toe, giving an obvious once-over. "You know what? My feet hurt." She pulls out a miniature sewing kit from her gold clutch and wiggles it between her fingers. "I always bring this for emergencies. I'm going to call my driver, how about you go do some damage control?"

I shake my head, ignoring the knot of uncertainty in my chest. "Don't be silly. I came here with you. And Greg is supposed to see us leave together."

"I'm tired of worrying about Greg for tonight. And plus"—she shoos me with a flick of her hand—"I'm bored of you now, cabana boy. Get out of here." Celeste nods toward the corner of the room where cookie girl disappeared, her eyes dancing with encouragement.

"You sure? It's not what you think… I just humiliated her and I want to make sure she's okay."

Celeste gives me a close-lipped smile, showing off her amusement. "You're answering questions I didn't ask, Forrest." Her eyes gleam knowingly as she nods to the right again. "Go."

Before I can second-guess myself, I peck her on the cheek, and then I'm off to find the woman who I should probably stop pursuing, because quite frankly…

She keeps throwing me off my game.

CHAPTER EIGHT

Sora

For the right price.

I'm no stranger to shitty birthdays, but this one takes the cake—and then smashes it into my face for good measure.

After ensuring the coast is clear, I scrutinize myself in the large bathroom mirror—smeared eyeliner creating shadowy wings beneath my lower lashes, torn dress exposing far more cleavage than I'd intended, and while this isn't super consequential at the moment, I'm now realizing the lipstick shade I'm wearing clashes horribly with this ensemble. Magenta lips with a pale pink dress under black tulle? Who let me leave my apartment like this?

Me. I'm the problem. Always the architect of my own fashion disasters.

Daphne aggressively underestimated how much downtime she'd have, working this wedding. Over the past three hours, I've glimpsed her in passing maybe four times. Every single time she was scurrying past the bar with a tray in her hand, mouthing an apology to me, her eyes wide with the stress of serving Manhattan's elite.

Since I'm not an actual guest at this wedding, just a suckerfish that latched on to my best friend looking for a free fancy meal on my birthday, there was no seat assignment for me. I had to eat my chicken standing up, balancing my weight from one aching foot to the other. When I got my food, I waited for a spot to clear at the bar. I threw my plate down on the flat surface and used my knife like a katana, rapidly chopping my beautiful herb-crusted chicken into bite-sized pieces. Then, to make room for inebriated wedding guests who wanted to get more drunk in a hurry, I abandoned my small square of bartop and melted back into the wallpaper. With my fork in one hand and my plate in the other, I resigned to people-watching for the evening.

Had I worn my flip-flops, my feet probably wouldn't be throbbing at the moment, each pulse of pain a reminder of how out of place I am here. Had I not come at all, I might not have been so bored and uncomfortable that I decided to log into my secret Instagram account and watch RoxyReadz's video about my book—a decision that ranks somewhere between "cutting my own bangs" and "sending a text to my ex" on the scale of self-sabotage.

I always believe some criticism can be helpful. But there was nothing remotely constructive about Roxy's review. It was the most vague roast I've ever endured, each casual dismissal landing like a dart in my writer's heart. She didn't connect to the characters, she thought the spicy scenes were weird, and she even hated the nickname my hero called my heroine. And this is a content creator I *asked* to read my book, after sending a very expensive PR package. So, essentially, I bent over and begged this reader to wedge her foot so far up my ass I can taste it in my throat. It wasn't even my first time doing that. Hadn't I learned my lesson before?

But Roxy's entitled to her opinion. I try my best not to take it personally, even though it feels very, very personal, like she's critiquing not just my writing but the very essence of my creative soul. I try to find gratitude for the fact she even gave me the time of day. There has to be some sort of silver lining to this whole debacle I'm just not yet privy to. After watching her review, I gave myself a little pep talk and forced myself to shake it off, mentally dusting the negativity from my shoulders.

Now, had I stopped there, I might not have fallen victim to hysteric tears. Except here's the real kicker—the cat called curiosity is a real bitch, one with sharp claws and a taste for writer's blood.

I know Roxy thought my book sucked, but I got to wondering...

Who else agreed?

The descent into madness was swift and merciless, like sliding down a waterslide greased with butter. I'm convinced that as an author, reading your bad reviews is just as addictive and destructive as a meth habit.

One by one, I read the mockery and ridicule, paired with endless thumbs-down and vomit emojis, each one a tiny knife slicing away at my confidence. One girl even one-starred me because she thought my pen name was stupid. Sora Cho isn't a pen name, it's my real name, so she can take that concern up with my parents.

A better author...no...a stronger woman, would laugh at the ridiculousness. She would choose to give her haters the amount of attention they deserve—none. She would stand tall, shoulders back, and march forward toward her next masterpiece.

I guess I'm not a strong woman or a good author, because it hurts. *Miserably.* The pain is an actual, physical sensation in my chest. I find nothing amusing about the teasing reviews, or the page-long dissertations picking my story apart piece by piece. They had so much to complain about, they could've pieced together their own novel. Working title: *Sora's Career Ends Here*, subtitle: *How One Romance Writer's Dreams Died in the Bathroom of The Plaza.*

The cruel comments swim laps around my brain as I reach into my clutch and pull out the contents one by one—travel-sized eyeliner with a cap that's seen better days; the lipstick in the wrong shade, clashing even worse under the bathroom's harsh lighting; blotting sheets for my oily skin that have begun to stick together from the humidity; and cream blush that's beginning to cake. *This'll have to do.*

My dress, thanks to hot dad, went from elegant to slutty with one tug from his mammoth paw. *The jerk.* Although, I don't think I'm agitated that he clumsily tried to save me from landing backward on an ice sculpture in the shape of a lotus flower. That was quite chivalrous because there's a ten percent chance that thing could've impaled me with its petals, turning this disaster of a birthday into a freak-accident headline: "Local Author Meets Frosty End at Stranger's Wedding (That She Wasn't Invited To)."

No, what's annoying is that he's here at this wedding with a woman who, based on the gossip I overheard from wedding guests, is a fashion designer who has enough money to make Bruce Wayne look like a penniless pauper. His eyes were glued to her eyes all night. *Her eyes.* Not her body. That's a man in love, not in lust. And I can't blame him. She's a bit older, stunning, and all-around regal.

What's further annoying is that the excited flutter in my chest when I first spotted hot dad at the wedding, paired with the guttural churn in my stomach when I realized he wasn't alone, can only mean one thing...

"*Fine*. I thought he was kind of cute," I mutter at myself in the mirror, knowing full well by "cute" I mean inferno-level, panty-dropping sexy, the kind of man who could play the lead in any romance novel and have readers burning through pages with feverish intensity.

To make matters worse, he's so good with his daughter. I might have let myself fantasize for a nanosecond, making plans to casually pop by Papa Beans a few more times in the next week for another chance encounter. But that's over now.

I got it so wrong, but in my defense, he wasn't wearing a ring. He mentioned a woman in his life as his daughter's mom, not his wife. The way he was smiling at me seemed flirty, the corner of his mouth lifting in that telltale way that makes your insides melt like chocolate left in a hot car. I thought...

Well, it doesn't matter what I thought. There's nothing less attractive to me than a taken man. I don't know what the opposite of a homewrecker is, but that's my lane. Call me paranoid, but I'll fetch a broomstick in a grocery store to reach something off a high shelf before asking a married man for help. There's too much girl-on-girl crime in this day and age. I can't stop the trolls from ripping me a new asshole online; that's out of my control. But I can continue to be a woman who respects a relationship.

So sorry, "hot dad." You just got demoted to "someone's dad."

There's a chime from my clutch, the sound cutting through my internal pity party. Welcoming a distraction, I lunge for my phone, causing my small tin of breath mints and Daphne's gifted gummy bears to topple from my bag and spill onto the floor.

"Dammit," I grumble, as I squat down to retrieve them, momentarily ignoring the succession of chimes coming from my phone, the alerts playing like an impatient, digital symphony.

The mints are a goner. The tin broke open, little white discs rolling underneath the stalls. This place is clean, but not *that* clean. I'm not eating Altoids off the bathroom tile, not even for fresh breath. My gummy bears are safe in their sealed package. I tell people I might be borderline hypoglycemic which is why I'm always armed with candy. The truth is I might be severely addicted to sugar. But once you acknowledge a problem, there's all this pressure to "fix it," and I'd rather glue corn kernels on my naked body and run right through a chicken coop than commit to a diet.

> Daphne
> **Babes, I'm so sorry.**
>
> Daphne
> **We're about to start cleaning up.**
>
> Daphne
> **They aren't going to let me go for another two hours at least.**
>
> Daphne
> **I ruined your birthday.**
>
> Daphne
> **I'm fired from my job as your best friend.**

> **Save your pity party 🙄. The chicken was the best I've ever had. And all you have to do to keep your job is feed me.**

Daphne
I'll pop by tomorrow to take you to breakfast.

Daphne
We'll go to our favorite brunch place.

Daphne
And we're not leaving until we plot out your next bestseller.

Daphne
Prologue to epilogue. Get some good rest.

Daphne
We'll need your brain firing on all cylinders in the morning.

It used to drive me crazy how Daphne would text. Every line of thought is a new message, like her thumbs are too eager to let her mind finish a full sentence. Now, it's one of my favorite things about her. The rapid *ping, ping, ping, ping* is her signature ringtone, as distinctive as a fingerprint.

> **Sounds great. Can't wait!**

Fuck. My response is so phony it makes me cringe, the words dripping with artificial enthusiasm like syrup on a stale pancake. I debate whether or not to tell Daphne what I did. The problem is she's going to want to know why I would choose to punish myself by reading every hateful, mean thing written about me and my work on the internet. Truth is, I don't have an answer. For some sick reason, when I'm feeling low, I seek to get lower. Maybe in a way I think that if I can survive all the abuse, then I can make it. I can endure anything.

Except I couldn't take it.

I melted into a puddle of heaving tears in the middle of Manhattan's most sophisticated wedding. I've never felt more like a loser, especially here, surrounded by all these rich people who found their success, their laughter and clinks of champagne glasses a constant reminder of what I haven't achieved. And maybe never will.

What if...

What if I just let the haters win? I'm so tired of trying to fit a square peg into a round hole. What if I take Mom up on that entry-level bank job?

Life would be simpler.

More than anything, I just want a break from feeling this hopeless.

I sink onto the bathroom floor in my ruined dress, not caring that I'm one sneeze away from my nipples popping free. I rip open the top of my gummy bear package, trying to focus on the good parts of today. I pop a gummy treat for every blessing I have in my life. *A red bear.* I have an incredible best friend who is always on my side. *A green bear.* My parents love me. *An orange and a blue bear.* I have my health and a roof over my head. I pop a handful more of the colorful assortment, convinced there are more things to be grateful for that simply don't come to mind at the moment.

Running my tongue over the roof of my mouth, I feel an odd film, slick and slightly bitter. These bears have a weird twang to them. Daphne is knee-deep in her homeopathic-organic-grass-fed phase. I bet these bears are made of dead sea algae or something harvested by moon-dancing shamans. I should've swiped the sweet-and-sour Scandinavian gummy skulls from my birthday basket, but the gummy bear package was small and nestled perfectly in my clutch, like it was meant to tag along tonight.

Knock, knock.

There's a firm thud on the bathroom door, the sound reverberating through the tiled space. I flick my eyes along the stalls, one by one, as if the person on the other side of the door can see my bewilderment. "Uh, it's open." *Who knocks on a public bathroom door?*

"Cookie girl? Are you in there?" he bellows through the heavy wooden door, his voice deep and unmistakable.

Huh? I clamber to my feet, then clickety-clack in my black kitten heels over to the door, each step sending a fresh jolt of pain through my arches. I pull open the door to see his stupid, handsome face. He's cleanly shaven, showing off his masculine, cut jaw, the kind that could slice through bread and break through hearts with equal efficiency. *"Cookie girl*? Are you looking for a stripper?" I retort, my voice dripping with sarcasm.

He smiles when he sees me, a grin that unfurls slowly across his face. Then, his eyes slip for a fraction of a second to my chest, the torn fabric leaving little to the imagination. He recovers quickly, finding my gaze and flashing me that million-dollar smile. Actually, considering who he's dating, maybe it's a billion-dollar grin. "I'm looking for you. I'm sorry, I don't know your name," he confesses, his voice softer now.

"And I don't know yours... So why are you looking for me?" I hold out my arms, letting him assess the wreckage he made of my dress. "Are you back to finish the job?"

"No, of course not. I'm Forrest." He holds up a small, clear container that's encapsulating a needle and a colorful array of threads. "I thought maybe I could help."

I blink at him, slow and deliberate. "Do you think just because I'm a woman, I know how to sew?"

His eyes pop into startled circles, widening like a cartoon character who's just stepped on a rake. "I wasn't implying—"

"Because unless you're packing super glue or duct tape, I don't think you can help me. Also, this is the ladies' room, so..." I wouldn't say I slam the door on him, I simply let go of the handle.

Gravity is out of my control, folks. The laws of physics are not my responsibility.

But it's no use anyway. His cat-like "reflexes" kick in again, and he stretches out his arm, catching the door with his flattened palm. He's able to hold it wide open with his large wingspan, like a magnificent tux-wearing eagle. "Is there anyone else in here?" Forrest asks, his gaze scanning the space beyond me.

"Obviously," I sass, stretching each syllable like taffy. "A whole crew of us. We're prepping for the grand finale flash mob. So, if you wouldn't mind, we need a little privacy."

"Mk, so you're alone," he says, shrugging one shoulder, the fabric of his tuxedo shifting smoothly across his frame.

"Yes."

His smile widens, creases forming at the corners of his eyes. "I knew you were sassy, but I didn't realize you were feral."

I curtsy with a shit-eating grin plastered on my face. I realize after, due to my torn dress, the gesture is both ridiculous and slightly obscene. "I'm Sora. Jokes aside, it's nice to officially meet you, Forrest." I raise my eyebrows so high, they've surely disappeared into my hairline, perhaps never to return. "Where's your girlfriend?" I ask accusingly.

"I don't have a girlfriend," he replies, his expression remaining neutral save for a slight wrinkling of his forehead.

I roll my eyes with finesse that would impress even the most insolent of preteens. "Don't be a pig."

"Excuse me?" His jaw slackens and his eyes narrow, like shutters closing on windows. I can't tell if we're still bantering or if I've truly offended him. *Whatever.* It's owed after his little prank at the coffeehouse. And it's my birthday. I'm allowed to be a brat... and cry...and unapologetically eat too much sugar.

"I clearly saw you with your girl—woman, I mean. And even if I didn't, you guys were the talk of the wedding. Everyone knows you're an item, so you're not slick, you're just sleazy. I don't think she'd appreciate you flirting with me in the ladies' room," I declare, my chin jutting out defiantly.

He wiggles the little sewing kit between his fingers, ignoring my accusations. "Believe it or not, I'm a whiz with a needle and thread. I grew up humble, working on a ranch. I had to learn to patch my Levi's."

"A ranch?" I balk, my interest piqued despite my best efforts to remain aloof. Damn my curiosity, always getting the better of my righteous indignation. "But you seem so...*Manhattan*."

"And you seem like someone who jumps to conclusions," he counters, with a smirk. He gestures behind me, his movement smooth and controlled. "I'll explain, but I need the door closed first."

I eye him suspiciously, ignoring the butterflies bouncing off the walls of my stomach like they're in a freaking pinball machine. "Your girlfriend won't be upset?"

"She's not my girlfriend. She's my client." His voice drops to a whisper, the words barely audible over the hum of the ventilation system. "I was working tonight."

Working? It's the way he says it, like it's a dirty little secret wrapped in expensive paper. *Oh. My. Fuck. It can't be...can it?* But I saw his young daughter. There's no way. Maybe his date has a medical situation and he's a caretaker?

"Are you a nurse?" I inquire, my brow furrowing with confusion.

He squints his eyes, befuddled, his forehead deeply creasing. "Why does everyone assume I'm in the medical field? Am I giving off a vibe?"

We're getting closer and closer to the prior conclusion I jumped to, my mind racing around like the last lap of a relay. "So what do you mean you were working tonight?"

"Not another word until you let me in, Sora," he answers, dead serious. He locks his eyes on mine and I hold my breath, a haze of his allure holding me in place and slowing down my movements, like I'm suddenly swimming through honey.

I step backward, giving him room to enter the women's bathroom. He advances, then softly shuts the door behind him, the click of the latch oddly unsettling. "I need you to make me two promises before I explain further."

"Okay." I audibly gulp when he turns the lock, the sound of metal sliding into place making my heart race.

I ignore the wild thoughts galloping through my mind. Let's be honest, this situation is the preamble to a steamy scene right out of one of my books. But even if my fantasy were to leap right off the page, I'd never be as bold as any of my heroines. Not to mention I look like a wet raccoon with my eye makeup in total anarchy.

Forrest holds up one long finger. "First, you can't tell a soul what I'm about to tell you. I'm going out on a limb here by trusting you." He holds up another. "Second, you have to try not to judge me. Are we clear on the terms?"

I wordlessly nod. My eyes are so wide, they've gone a bit dry in my state of shocked anticipation. Now, I'm getting worried he's not a prostitute. I'm getting hitman energy from the laser-focused stare he's giving me.

"Good." He makes his way past me to the vanity. His movements precise, he neatly scoots my items to the side and sets down the sewing kit. After unwedging the needle, and collecting the small spool of black thread, he licks the tip of his finger. "I'm an escort. I was hired to attend this wedding with Celeste." He casually threads the needle, twisting the thread and securing a knot.

I breathe out in relief, the tension leaving my body in a rush. "Okay, so you're just paid arm candy. You don't actually sleep with women for money."

"No, I do." He finds my stunned expression in the mirror and dishes out a cocky smile paired with a wink. "For the right price."

CHAPTER NINE

Forrest

Ma'am, you keep touching me, and I'm going to bill you.

"If you don't stop moving, I'm going to accidentally stitch your breasts together." I focus on the cinched fabric of her neckline between my fingers, trying to find the right spot to spear the fabric.

The harsh fluorescent light of the bathroom bounces off the white tiles and I hesitate. Denim I can work with; this material is a pain in the ass. Her fidgeting isn't helping because every time she shifts, her chest jiggles around, begging for attention. The bathroom smells like expensive hand soap and the faint trace of someone's perfume—probably from one of the wedding guests who was in here earlier.

"Sorry. My feet hurt," Sora says, holding out one leg and shaking her foot. "These shoes are unforgiving." The thin straps of her heels have left angry red marks across her feet.

After tucking the needle flat against my palm for safety, I grab her slim waist and plant her on the bathroom counter. The cool marble surface makes a solid thud as she lands. She loudly sucks in a short heave of surprise. I thought she was going to scold me for manhandling her, but she's silent as I remove her short heels one by one, my fingers brushing against the warm skin of her ankles. "Better?" I ask, before returning my focus to her neckline.

Music from the reception thumps through the wall—some overplayed dance track with too much bass. A couple of drunk voices laugh as they pass by the bathroom door. I freeze. The door is still locked, but for the love of God, *please don't knock... please don't interrupt whatever this is.* I breathe out in relief when a different door opens and slams shut, making the voices disappear.

Now, back to my mission. This would've been much easier if she took the dress off, but I didn't suggest it because it seemed predatory. In hindsight, this circumstance is worse. Stitching up her V-neck with her perfect tits an inch from the tip of my nose is sending very aggressive thoughts to my crotch. I shift my stance, hoping she doesn't notice.

"Thank you."

"Welcome," I mutter distractedly, trying to reposition the needle. It's easier now that she's sitting on the vanity and more level with my height. The thread catches on my callused fingers as I try to line up the torn edges of the fabric. The aftermath of last weekend's overly competitive game of paintball is showing on my hands.

Sora shuffles again, causing the needle to slip.

"*Hold still.* I was serious about stitching your breasts together."

"There it is again. You're really calling them my *breasts*?" she asks.

"Yes. Why?" My eyes shoot up to read her expression, then back down to my task at hand. I steady the needle against the satin fabric. I'm going to butcher this, but my main goal is to ensure she can walk out of here without flashing anyone. She'll need to take this to a professional seamstress to salvage the gown.

"It's so anatomical. Sounds a little funny coming from a guy like you."

"*A guy like me*? What was our second term, Sora? Because you're starting to sound judgy." I jab the needle through the fabric with more force than necessary, my jaw tightening.

She chuckles nervously, the sound echoing slightly in the tiled bathroom. "I didn't mean an escort. I meant an attractive guy...who probably has a lot of sex."

Pushing the needle through, I bark out a sharp laugh. "It's

not as much as you're thinking. And anyway, what's a guy who has a lot of sex supposed to say when he's referring to your chest area?" The tip of the needle catches the light as I pull it through the satin.

"Tits, I'd assume," she answers matter-of-factly.

I swear I'm ninety percent gentleman, but ten percent of me likes to test the waters every now and then. I'd be a blatant liar if I said I wasn't intrigued with Sora. I still have no clue what kind of girl she is, though. She's giving off preacher's-daughter vibes. But then again, she's awfully investigative about tits, so I decide to figure this out *my way*.

"I use 'tits' during dirty talk when I have a woman completely naked, face in the pillow, ass in the air. 'Breasts' is for when I'm trying to do a favor for a friend, like stitching up the dress I massacred… Again, I'm sorry about that." I keep my voice low, watching her reaction from the corner of my eye. Her perfume—something sweet and floral—pleasantly drifts between us.

"You're already forgiven," she answers, her voice cracking slightly. "You can stop apologizing."

I poke the fabric a few more times, securing the thin thread around the two-inch tear. The needle pricks my finger and I swallow a curse, tasting copper as I quickly suck away the blood. After I assure Sora I'm fine, I tell her to sit up straight. The bathroom lights cast a shadow across her collarbone, highlighting the triangle of skin still visible above repaired fabric.

"All right, then. Take a deep breath. Let's make sure the stitches don't pop free when your rib cage expands."

She draws in a long breath, her hand pressed flat against her stomach. The material stays firmly woven together. She chuckles to herself, the sound warming the small space.

"What?" I ask, matching her smile.

"I thought you were bluffing, but you are indeed handy with a needle."

"Told ya." After tucking the needle back into the plastic case, I toss the sewing kit onto the vanity alongside Sora's other belongings. The clatter reverberates off the marble. "Keep that just in case."

We lock eyes as I take a moment to appreciate the color of her deep brown eyes, but I must linger too long because she bashfully glances away, faint red coloring her cheeks. The overhead light catches the slight sheen of sweat on her forehead. I resist the urge to wipe it away. Way too intimate too fast, especially after what I've already confessed to her. *But I want to.*

Instead, I pull my phone from my pants pocket and hold it up. "Do you have Zelle?"

"Yeah. Why?"

"Could you pull it up?"

"Sure?" She cocks her head to the side like she's confused, but obeys without hesitation. The blue light from her screen illuminates her face as she navigates to the app. Once she has her bank app open, she hands her phone over. My lips part in surprise at her transparency with a stranger. I can see all her account totals. I was with Hannah for four years and never once did she hand her phone over nonchalantly like she had nothing to hide. Sora's earnestness is jarring...but in the best way.

"I'm going to program myself in here. Celeste told me your dress is designer. When you get it repaired, I want you to bill me." I type my information into her phone, my thumbs moving quickly across the screen. The phone chimes as my contact info is saved. "There we go. Just start a money request from your contacts. I'll pay whatever."

I hand her phone back and she peers at the screen. "Is Forrest Hawkins your real name or code name?"

A dismissive grunt escapes my lips. "Real. I said I was an escort, not a secret agent." I would hide my name if I had an open call for services on the web. But all my clients are discreetly obtained through Rina. There's an unspoken code. Escorts and the clients who hire them keep their business to themselves. None of us want law enforcement poking around. Rina and her ex-husband, Sean, who financially benefits greatly from her side-endeavor, are both revered lawyers, and could talk a judge in circles, defending their legitimate business. However, what me and the guys do *off the books*—that Rina most definitely turns a blind eye to—is harder to justify.

"But what you do is illegal, isn't it? Shouldn't you be a little more discreet?" Her question hangs in the air between us, heavy with implication. Stepping backward, I hold out my hands for Sora's. She secures her fingers around mine and leverages my support to hop off the counter. The slight pressure of her hands sends an unexpected shot of nerves through my arms. She hisses when her feet hit the floor. "Oh, gross. Forgot my shoes were off."

"Shit. Sorry." I snatch up her shoes and drop to one knee, adorning her feet one by one, like a scene out of *Cinderella*. She plants her hand on my shoulder to steady herself, while I fasten the straps around her ankles. When I'm finished, she doesn't let me free. Her hand remains clamped around my shoulder as I rise.

I show her a crooked grin. "Ma'am, you keep touching me, and I'm going to bill you."

I meant it as a joke to lighten the mood, but her face goes from mesmerized to mortified as she rips her hand from my body with such gusto she falters back. "I wasn't—"

"I'm kidding. Geez, you're really freaked out, aren't you?" My humorous tone doesn't match my internal trepidation. I hope she can't hear my heart pounding against my ribs. *See?* This shit is my worst fear every time I consider a genuine, non-client interaction with a woman. Once good girls learn my profession, they're disgusted with me.

"I'm not freaked out," Sora assures me, even though she's taken two more paces backward. Her heels click against the tile floor with each step. "I do have questions."

I hold up my pointer and middle finger in a peace sign before leaning back against the counter. The edge digs hard into my lower back. "You get two questions."

"Three," she blurts out. She grins sheepishly when she sees the look I'm giving her. "I'm sorry. I think I'm programmed to argue."

"Are you studying law?" I ask. Although, I doubt it. I tend to not be attracted to lawyers. The thought of Sora in a courtroom, firing off objections, doesn't fit the woman standing in front of me.

"No. Although as of tonight, I'm very seriously considering a major career shift. Any suggestions?"

A half-smile hooks my mouth. "Is that one of your questions?"

"Depends. Do I get three?"

I chuckle, the sound ping-ponging off the bathroom walls. "Sure."

She twists her lips. "Meh, forget the career advice. I have three specific questions in mind."

"Shoot." I cross my arms, my dress shirt stretching tight across my shoulders.

"How long have you been a...?" She tugs on her bottom lip with her top teeth. "I mean, been in business?"

I lift my brows at her, amused at her awkward politeness. "You can say escort. I'm not offended."

Her chest lifts as she draws in a deep breath, then forces it out in a sharp exhale, like she's hyping herself up to take a plunge in the dark, deep end of a pool. "Okay, then. Official first question: How long have you been an escort, Forrest?"

"Four years. It started a few months after my daughter was born." Sora's jaw drops and I roll my eyes in tandem. "I'm going to give you a bonus question for free, so I can clear up the nonsense I *know* is circling your mind. I did not cheat on Dakota's mom, nor was I an escort at any point in time when we were together. Hannah broke up with me shortly before she gave birth."

"Really? Why?"

I point at her chest, right at her repaired neckline. "Now, that question will cost you."

She squints one eye. "Nope. Don't answer it, then. I have other questions in mind. My next one is kind of embarrassing."

More embarrassing than being accosted like this about my job? I straighten up, my back cracking slightly, still tension-ridden from hunching over for so long. "I'm not shy. Go ahead."

"Making the assumption that you're sleeping with multiple women in a short time frame...how do you stay, um...clean?"

First, the interrogation about "tits." And now she wants to know about my sexual health? Hm, maybe not a preacher's daughter after all. I study her face, trying to figure her out.

"To be candid, condoms and routine testing. If a client requests an encounter without protection, it's extra, and they have to provide me with clean test results from the clinic." I keep my voice matter-of-fact, like I'm discussing the weather instead of my sex life.

"Holy shit. You're not messing with me. You really do this as your job, don't you?" Her eyes widen, pupils dilating.

"Why on earth would I lie to you about this?" I kind of want to. What I wouldn't give to honestly tell Sora I'm a firefighter or something.

We both turn our attention to the door when the music from the reception shifts to something slower, the bass no longer vibrating through the walls.

"Why not lie? I'm a stranger. You don't owe me anything."

I glance at her chest again, my desired view now obstructed by her patched-together neckline. "We're a little more than strangers now, right?"

She turns toward the mirror, watching me through the reflection, like she's trying to check me from a different angle. "I guess."

Sora proceeds to the counter and fumbles with her makeup. The contents of her small purse scatter across the marble surface. She reaches for her eyeliner, but misses, like her depth perception is off. Reeling, she rotates her hand slowly in front of her face, looking mystified, and sluggish, like she's moving through water.

"Are you okay?" The question comes out sharper than I intended, worry edging my voice.

"I feel a little funny...lightheaded." Her words slur at the edges.

"Funny like how?" I inquire, growing concerned with her

suddenly offbeat mannerisms. I move closer, ready to catch her if she falls.

"I'm not a big drinker, and I had a couple glasses of champagne. I think it's going to my head. Probably just need to eat something." She pins her gaze to the counter, like she's hyperfocusing. There's a loud crinkle from the packaging when she successfully snatches up her small bag of candy. "Want some?" she offers.

I shake my head when I eye the leaf on the top-right corner of the bag. I recognize the label. "No, thank you. My roommate, Taio, always uses that brand. I tried them once and they knocked me on my ass. Too strong for my taste. But I have to say I'm impressed you can handle all that."

"You're blurry," she answers abstractly, her gaze unfocused. The candy bag dangles loosely from her fingers.

I let out a breathy chuckle. "Oh yeah? Are they kicking in?"

"What the hell are you talking about?" Her voice rises, echoing. Her eyes burst wide at her own loudness.

Realization washes over me. *Oh, fuck.* She must think this is regular candy. "Sora, those are really strong edibles. Two pieces will keep a grown man, twice your size, high as a kite all night. You didn't know that?" She shakes her head silently. Her pupils have fully dilated now, nearly swallowing the brown of her irises. "How many did you eat?"

The shocked fear slowly soaks into her expression. "Six," she murmurs. "*At least* six."

"Well...*fuck*." I run a hand through my hair, mentally calculating how bad this is going to get. "You should probably get home to sleep it off."

Nodding in agreement, she makes her way to my side. With the elegance of a clumsy sloth, she hoists her ass back onto the counter, the side of her thigh pressing against my hip. "Good idea."

"Want me to escort you?"

She shows me a sleepy smirk. "I doubt I can afford you."

I bite back my chuckle, trying not to tease her too viciously. "No, I mean *escort you out*, Sora. Maybe help you call a rideshare home?"

"Oh, yes. Okay, thank you." Except she still doesn't move. She tilts her head backward, her eyes resting on the ceiling.

"Should we get going, then?" I suggest, trying not to burst out in laughter. She's goofily adorable at the moment.

"You go ahead. I want a moment with all these pretty stars," she monotones, staring at the speckled overhead tile that she's mistaking for a celestial view.

"All right, that does it." I wrap my hands around her wrists, gently coaxing her off the countertop. "No way I can let you go on your own now. I'll take you home."

"Don't be silly," she insists. But in contradiction to her protests, she melts into my chest, using my body for support. "No need to fuss. Let me go, Forrest."

"Can't," I murmur, leaning down to secure my arm around her slim waist, steadying her.

Don't want to.

CHAPTER TEN

Forrest

Panty-dropping delicious…

I'm at least eight inches taller than Sora, so naturally my stride outraces her. But at the present moment, she's also moving so slowly I have to practically walk backward to pace with her as we make our way to the Upper West Side on foot.

The night air has cooled considerably since we left the wedding, and the streetlights cast long shadows across the sidewalk. My dress shoes click in a steady rhythm against the pavement, a stark contrast to her wayward shuffling.

I wanted to hail a cab, but Sora insisted on walking to try and sober up. *Good luck.* She's pipsqueak-sized and consumed enough edibles to sedate a rhino. She's going to be high until spring. Her eyes are glassy, reflecting the neon signs we pass, and every few steps she stumbles slightly, like she's walking on a moving ship instead of solid ground.

"So, did we learn our lesson about taking candy from a stranger?" I ask, weaving my fingers between her dainty digits.

Her hand is cold against mine, and I can feel her pulse thumping in her wrist. I'm holding her hand half out of protection, as we approach a burly homeless man planted on the sidewalk ahead, but also partly to drag her along. If she doesn't pick up the pace, we might as well sleep on the streets tonight. The homeless guy eyes us as we pass, the stench of cheap liquor and unwashed clothes hitting my nostrils.

"Wasn't a stranger. It was my best friend," she defends, her voice slightly slurred.

"Your best friend drugged you?"

She exaggerates a long sigh, her breath visible in the cool night air. "I think she wanted me to lighten up. *Oh!*" she suddenly exclaims, pointing across the street. "Bingo. Pretzel cart." She halts, pulls her hand from mine, and looks up at me with big, doe eyes. The streetlight catches the remnants of glitter from her makeup, making her skin shimmer.

"You want a pretzel?" I ask, amused by the sudden desperation in her eyes.

"No, Forrest, I *need* a pretzel." She puts both hands against her stomach like she's dying of hunger.

I take a few steps into the street like I'm testing the structural integrity of the road. My eyes scan for cars, spotting only a parked cab several blocks away. Safe from oncoming traffic, I gesture Sora across. "All right, cookie girl. Let's go handle your munchies."

"Oh, a cookie sounds good too," she mutters as she shuffles past me in a hurry, the fabric of her dress brushing against my leg. Sure, to get home she's moving like molasses, but she'll sprint to carbohydrates.

"Well, don't you two look nice," the cart owner says as we approach, his thick mustache bouncing as he speaks. The steam from his cart warms the air around us, a welcome relief from the chill. I was expecting stale, grayish, day-old soft pretzels but all his inventory looks freshly baked. The smell of warm butter and soft bread swells all around the sidewalk, making my own stomach rumble. He even has elevator music playing from his cart's speakers that are hooked up to his phone. It's quite the sophisticated pretzel cart. "Heading home after a nice night out? Yous look dressed for a ball."

"A wedding at The Plaza," I confirm before holding up two fingers. "Two, please. One cinnamon sugar, and one plain." I glance at Sora, who is frozen in place, nearly salivating over the illustrated image of the giant salt-crusted pretzel on the side of the cart. Her eyes are so wide she looks like she's in a trance.

"I gotta sit," Sora abruptly announces, then makes a beeline to a nearby bus bench. The metal bench creaks as she drops onto it, her dress bunching up around her. After paying for our food, I make my way to her side, holding out both pretzel options. The warmth bleeding through the thin paper wrapping heats my palms.

"Salted or cinnamon sugar?"

Her grabby hands gravitate to the salted one, her fingers brushing against mine. A huge chunk is in her mouth before I have the chance to offer her the toxic cheese sauce crap that goes perfectly with a warm, soft pretzel. The sound of her enthusiastic chewing fills the quiet night. "Oh my god, *I love you.*"

"That good, huh?" I unwrap the plastic seal on the cheese sauce and set it by her leg before taking a seat next to her. The bench is cold through my pants. The night air is beyond crisp. I've offered Sora my coat several times, but she refused to take it. I'm not sure if she was worried about me getting chilly, or the cannabis is keeping her toasty.

I take a big bite out of the cinnamon sugar pretzel, remembering how hungry I actually am. Sweet crystals stick to my lips as I chew. Rotating my wrist, I point my food toward Sora. "Want a bite of this one?"

She answers by leaning over and taking a chomp out of the side, cinnamon sugar dusting her lips. "Panty-dropping delicious," she mumbles between her slow chewing, crumbs falling to her lap.

I let free a rumbly laugh that echoes in the empty street. "You're easy to satisfy."

She quirks her brow, showing me a suggestive grin. "When it comes to food, sure."

Her response, teeming with innuendo, makes my stomach twist in intrigue. "I see your current state of inebriation hasn't muted your wit."

She shrugs cutely, then feasts on her pretzel, taking the entire thing down in about five more colossal bites. When she comes up for air, she looks a little chagrined, wiping crumbs from the corners of her mouth. "That wasn't ladylike, huh?"

Isn't she way too high to be self-conscious? "I like to see a woman with a healthy appetite. I could never be with a girl who orders side salads on a first date." I stretch my legs out in front of me, my muscles tight from standing all evening.

Sora shows me a frog-lipped smile. "I actually do that to be nice. The last date I went on, the guy took me to a fancy restaurant he couldn't afford. My side salad still cost twenty-eight dollars. It was bananas. I felt so bad for him."

"Maybe don't date boys. Date *men* who can afford to buy you a real meal." *Ah, shit.* That sounded pompous, but agitation awoke in me the moment Sora mentioned dating. I flex my jaw, feeling the muscle tighten. I'm annoyed at the competition in a game I'm not even playing.

She scowls at my unforgiving reply, her eyes narrowing. "For the record, it was a great date. He was nice and funny and an absolute gentleman in the ways that matter. Money doesn't make you a man, Forrest."

Funny. That's not what Hannah told me for our entire relationship. Maybe I'm now conditioned to think the worst about women's intentions. "Fair enough," I answer. "Sorry, that was bullheaded of me to say." I run my hand over the back of my neck, trying to wipe away the discomfort.

"I'll forgive you if you give me another question." She flutters her lashes, the light from the streetlamp overhead gleaming in her brown eyes.

"Don't waste your feminine wiles on me, cookie girl. I've already told you too much." Not to mention, she's already seen me with my daughter which makes me more than uncomfortable. My stomach clenches at the thought of Dakota confronting me about my job. "You haven't even asked your last question yet."

After crumpling her pretzel wrapper, she sets it aside on the bench, then presses against her temples like she has a headache.

The paper rustles in the night breeze, threatening to blow away. "It's too much pressure."

"You probably need to lie down. I don't think we need to go to the hospital, but you most definitely overdosed." I scan her face, noting the dilated pupils and slight sheen of sweat on her forehead despite the cool air.

"No," she snaps, looking at me like I'm clueless. "*The question*. I only have one more, and I don't want to waste it. I'm curious about so many things." She looks up, and at least this time she's admiring the real night sky, and not psychedelic-induced stars in a public bathroom. I follow her lead, curious about what has her so entranced. The stars are barely visible through the city's light pollution, just a few pinpricks of light against the dark canvas.

"How's this?" I ask. "Keep your final question, but I'll offer you a one-for-one trade. Answer one of mine honestly, then I'll answer one of yours free of charge." I shift on the bench, the cold metal seeping through my pants.

"Deal," she eagerly responds. "How much—"

"Whoa, whoa," I interrupt, holding up my hand. "I go first. If I deem your answer worthy, then you get your question."

"*Inebriation...deem...* Why do you talk like you have a doctorate?" she sassily asks, swaying slightly even while seated.

"Because I do," I quip back. A juris doctorate is indeed a doctorate.

Her eyes expand. She opens her mouth, but clamps it back shut, not willing to waste one of her final questions by pulling on that thread. My shoulder brushes against hers as I adjust my position. This time she doesn't flinch, growing more and more comfortable with our bodies colliding.

"Your turn, then," she croaks out in a whisper, touching her throat like it's dry.

"One sec. Stay right here," I command before hustling a few yards to the right to fetch a bottled water from the pretzel cart.

The cart owner waves me off when I fish out a bill, offering me the drink for free. "Thanks, my guy," I sing out before returning to Sora, prize extended. The bottle is cold and slick with condensation.

"Oh, you sweet angel," she murmurs before grabbing the water, twisting off the cap, and guzzling it down like a fish. The sound of her desperate swallows fills the quiet night. I wait until she releases a sigh of relief and replaces the cap, a smear of water wetting her lower lip.

"Why were you crying earlier? I mean, before I ripped your dress. You seemed really upset." The memory of her tear-streaked face in the bathroom makes my chest tighten.

Now she grows quiet, head hung in something that resembles despair. The wind picks up, blowing a strand of her hair across her face. "It's hard to explain."

"Try me."

Reaching around her back, where she safely stowed her purse, Sora pulls out her phone. She types slowly, her eyes growing to wide saucers as she tries to focus on the keys. The blue light from her screen illuminates her face in the darkness. I catch a glimpse of her wallpaper—a picture of her and a blonde with their faces smashed together for a selfie, smiling like loons. I don't know why, but their smiles make me grin in return, like I can feel the joy the image captured.

"Here," Sora says, handing me her phone, her fingers brushing against mine.

I scour the screen, a little confused as to what she's showing me. It's a review site of some sort, filled with posts and reciprocal comments. The text is tiny, and I have to squint to make it out. I read a few before I understand what they're all criticizing. While brutal, it's nothing surprising, simply internet trolls being trolls, this time about a romance book. I glance through about ten of the varied criticisms that don't have a common theme. Some complain about the characters and lack of chemistry. Some wanted more sex in the story, others less. One commenter brutalized the book over a single typo.

"Do you see why I was crying, now?" Her tone has dropped a

decibel, sadness deepening her voice. She hugs herself like a wall of protection, her shoulders hunched forward.

"Not really. It's just real people working out their aggression by complaining about fake people. Have you read it?" I hand the phone back, our fingers brushing again as she takes it.

"About a hundred times...when I drafted it, edited it, and then prepped it for publishing. They aren't complaining about fake people, they're complaining about *me*. I'm the author," she adds sullenly, her voice cracking on the last word.

"Oh." I wish I had a better reply, but my mind is spinning out as the cruel comments come back to life. I was apathetic before, but now I'm pissed knowing these were the source of her pain.

"Do you get reviews from your clients?" Sora asks. She then points right between my eyes, her finger stopping just short of my face. "That's just conversation, not a chargeable question."

I let out a rumbly chuckle, the sound vibrating in my chest. "Fine. But, no. My clients operate with the utmost discretion. If they have an issue with me, they take it up privately with my boss."

It rarely happens, but there've been a few instances where a client has blindsided me into a situation I didn't agree to and I had to walk away. Rina has a strict pay-upfront, no-refunds policy, so when I wouldn't participate in the cuckold situation I unexpectedly got roped into, Tabitha Rossten was furious.

Some dudes are into watching their wives get nailed by stud-like strangers, but Mr. Rossten was almost in tears about the circumstance. It certainly didn't seem emotionally consensual, and I wasn't going be the one to tear his soul apart. There are other escorts who wouldn't give a shit about who they hurt, so I told the couple to keep fishing. *And damn*, did Rina get an earful afterward.

"Well, my criticisms are very public...and embarrassing." My heart twists uncomfortably when I see a fresh tear slip down her cheek, glistening in the streetlight. She doesn't hide the evidence of her emotions. There's a good chance her face is too numb to feel the tear. Maybe she doesn't realize I can see her pain, clear as daylight.

"If I did get reviews, I probably wouldn't read them," I offer, still resisting the urge to mop up her tear with my fingertips. "It's the negative people who tend to be the loudest."

She nods, her eyes wide and unblinking, staring ahead. "That's the advice I keep getting. But I don't know, I was looking for a reason."

I slide a little closer, the bench groaning under our shifting weight. "Reason for what?"

"A reason for why I'm failing at this. All the pieces are there, but the puzzle just isn't"—she clasps her hands together, charading her point across—"coming together."

I nudge her shoulder with mine. "How long have you been an author?"

"Going on four years," she mutters, her breath fogging in the night air. *How is she not freezing?*

"I read an interview not too long ago featuring a really famous author. He doesn't write romance books, but have you heard of *Hell & Heroes* by J.P. Cooper?"

I cower under her cold-as-ice, side glare. "Sounds vaguely familiar," Sora bitterly chides. I'm not sure what that reaction was about, but I continue anyway.

"He said it took him a decade of failing before he found success. Cooper was about to give up before his big break came through. I think the advice he gave to writers is to spend more time worrying about what *they* think about their stories than what the critics think. So maybe focus on that? How do you feel about your stories?"

I can't tell if I'm being helpful or doing that man-thing where I try to fix the problem instead of listening. Sora's mood drastically shifted. I must've said something wrong. *What's wrong?* is on the tip of my tongue, but before I can get it out, she finally cracks the silence between us.

"I think...maybe I want this way too much to see the truth."

"What truth?" The streetlight flickers above us, casting

strange shadows across her face.

She pivots, her gaze capturing mine as her dress drapes over my knee. The slight weight of it, warm through my pants. "Have you ever wanted something so badly that you convinced yourself it was your destiny? Except you wake up each day thinking, if it was meant to be, should it be this hard?"

"I don't necessarily think writing is easy—"

"No, I don't mean the writing part." She balls up her fists on either side of her head like she's trying to fight the compounding pressure. "*Belonging.*"

That renders me speechless. Because what am I supposed to say? I agree with her conclusion. It's why I'm an escort to begin with.

I could've taken the bar and sold my soul to the corrupt, corporate law firm I already agreed to work for with a fifteen-year binding contract. But something was off that I couldn't shake. My classmates and future colleagues told me that being a lawyer doesn't make you some sort of hero-vigilante. It's just a job. Hannah told me to grow up, pull my head out of my ass, and focus on the mass amount of money I'd be making. But I didn't want to commit my life to making the world a worse place.

As I was trying to make a decision about my future, and my family's future, all these bullshit opinions were swarming around my head like violent bees, clouding my better judgment. I felt like the odd man out and didn't belong because my classmates would've killed for the opportunity I received.

The only person on my side, willing to help me, was my prior professor, Rina Colt.

Now, I owe her everything. She didn't just save me from a sordid fate. She found a loophole, saved me from her ex-husband's villainous corporate law firm, and gave me a way to provide for my daughter.

"I think I'm done," Sora says. "It's time to give up and grow up, you know? I turned twenty-seven today."

"It's your birthday?" It makes her crying so much worse.

She's an after-school special in a torn dress, tears tracking down her cheek, spending the last few minutes of her birthday with an escort on a public bench. My gut twists with a weird mix of sympathy and something else I can't name.

"My best friend Daphne was working at the wedding as a server. She invited me to come along so I wouldn't be alone tonight. We were supposed to spend the evening figuring out what was wrong with my backlist, and mapping out a future bestseller. But she got stuck on the cleanup crew. So, here I am with you." Sora reaches out to pat my leg. Her movements seem more intentional and coordinated. Perhaps the painful introspection about her writing career is sobering her. Her warm touch lingers.

"Happy birthday," I offer. "If it wasn't so late, I'd offer to take you to dinner."

She points to the cinnamon sugar pretzel I'm still holding, the paper wrapper crinkling when she pokes it. "You already did."

"This isn't a real dinner. Just cheap street-cart food."

She shrugs, then pats her belly. "It filled me up just fine."

"Classy gal." I shoot her a wink before setting my pretzel down, then clapping my hands together to brush off the sugar dusting. "Now, before you go quitting on your dream, how do you feel about your books? Screw the haters. How do *you* feel about your writing?"

"I feel like... I don't even know what romance is anymore," she answers miserably. A distant siren wails, growing closer, then fading away down another city street.

"Care to elaborate?"

"Readers want fairy tales that suspend reality. It's hard for me to write that way. I tell stories based on what I know and have experienced. The stuff that's popular is so far left from what I want from love. That's why I'm never going to go viral or fit in with all the bookish girlies. I don't understand all the tropes they hold so dear. I've never once fantasized about getting a hand necklace, with my hands cuffed behind my back, while a masked stalker shoves the thin side of his Louisville slugger between my thighs until I come messily all over it."

When I hear romance, my mind goes to that Nicholas Sparks book women lose their minds over. Although, that might have more to do with the movie adaptation and Ryan Gosling with his shirt off. Whatever Sora just spewed out sounds like a nightmare that would happen on Elm Street.

"What the hell are you talking about?"

She closes her eyes, her head lolling to the left like it's loose from her neck. "It's not important. All I'm saying is I've been rejected, ridiculed, and beaten down so much, I've lost my mojo. I don't even enjoy big romantic moments when I write them anymore. They're all so contrived." She pumps her brows. "That's right, mister. I know big words too."

I chuckle. "Clearly."

"My point is," she continues, "I just don't know what romance readers want. I don't know how to make them fall in love with me and my stories. It's useless."

"I'm at a loss. Seems like it'd be easy to fall in love with you," I admit. Her eyes grow to startled owl proportions, so I add, *"As a reader."*

What the fuck is wrong with me around this girl? It's all clumsy interactions, and enough word vomit to fill a toilet bowl. I clear my throat, trying to recover. "Your market is mostly women, right?"

"Yeah, so?" she asks defensively, her shoulders tensing.

"I didn't mean anything by it. I'm simply saying that I may not know what readers like, but I know what women like. That's why I still have a job."

Her eyes land very obviously on my crotch. "I think there are more significant reasons you still have a job."

My mouth twists into a mocking half-smile. "Eyes up here, ma'am."

She blushes furiously and I've found my new favorite game. I'm like a schoolboy with a crush. Every time I catch Sora checking me out, all I have to do is call her out to see her cute cheeks turn red. The cool night air can't chill the heat that keeps rising in her face.

"All right, I have an idea. But first, do your feet still hurt?"

She shakes her head. "Not remotely. Can't even feel them. Those gummy bears are magic for achy feet."

"Good."

I dart over to the pretzel cart once again, this time with my phone in hand. The metal clinks as I set it on the counter. After pulling up Spotify and selecting a song, I bribe the cart owner with a twenty-dollar bill to plug in my music and turn his speakers up loud. "Press play when she's on her feet, okay?"

He nods in understanding, tucking the money into his pocket, and I head back to the bench to sweep Sora right off her feet.

"Come on, Your *High*ness. Up we go." Cupping my hands under her elbows, I peel Sora off the bench.

"My legs feel like jelly."

"You had three servings of edibles. It's a miracle you can feel your legs at all." I yank her tight against my body and guide us a few strides away from the bench. "It'd probably be best for you to let me lead."

"Lead what?" she asks, right as the music starts to swell over the cart speakers. Leaning away, her mouth parts in surprise. "We're dancing? You cheeseball, you're so lame. And I love this song."

"That's a lot of mixed signals, Sora. Do you want to dance or not?" The music fills the empty street, bouncing off the buildings around us.

"Kind of. But I don't really know how."

I draw her in close with my hand planked firmly against her lower back. Her dress is silky under my palm. "Just lean into me. I'll do all the work."

She rests her cheek against my chest, and hums along a few bars before she murmurs, "This is such a sad song."

"Why do you think that?" Dido's "White Flag" rings through

the speakers, the melody clear in the night air.

"Because it's about unrequited love. Listen to the lyrics...she loves someone she's never going to have."

"Can you twirl?" I hold her hand tightly.

"I guess we're about to find out," she mutters, as I spin her around. It would've been incredibly romantic if Sora's reflexes weren't slightly delayed and she wasn't tripping over her own feet. She collapses back into me, her body solid against my chest.

"Whoops, okay, no more spinning. Just stay close." I guide her head back to my chest and sway us back and forth. The concrete is rough under my shoes, but I tighten my core to keep us moving in smooth, fluid motion. "And by the way, I think you misinterpreted the song."

"I didn't, but go ahead and show your work."

I rest my chin against the top of her head, not an inch of space between our bodies. I breathe in the faint smell of her perfume that's faded. "It's about a woman who hurt someone she loves. But instead of walking away and calling a loss a loss, she wants to go down with the ship. I think the song means it's still better to have love, even if it's messy and painful. Real love is worth surrendering to, regardless of the outcome."

"Fuck's sake," she grumbles against my chest, her breath warm through my thin shirt. "Maybe you should write romance books, then."

"Maybe you shouldn't give up just yet. It sounds like you're in a slump. Take a quick break from it all. Back in law school, whenever I was in a studying rut, I'd leave campus for a few days. Go home. Reset. I always came back refreshed, and performed so much better."

Her feet glue to the concrete when the music stops. With the most peculiar look on her face, she studies me quizzically. "Hold on." Sora darts back to the bench and snags her phone. After typing ferociously, she returns to my side, heels clicking against the pavement. Two notifications from my phone chime through the pretzel cart's speakers.

"Go check," she instructs, her eyes wide and expectant.

After thanking the cart owner for his time, I yank out the auxiliary cable and scour my alerts. Sora's made two payments to me. One for ten dollars. The second is for ten thousand. Shocked, I turn around to face her, my heart pounding in my chest. "What is this about?"

"The first is paying you back for the pretzel and water," she says innocently, cupping her hands around her elbows.

"Unnecessary... And the second payment?" I lift my brow, guessing where this is headed. My pulse quickens, blood rushing in my ears.

"Here's my third question, Forrest..." Sora looks nervous and shaky, like she's about to commit a crime. Her teeth catch her bottom lip for a second before she continues. "What's your going rate? Is that enough for you to take me home and...um...stay with me tonight?"

This isn't how my jobs are booked. It has to go through Rina for legal purposes. But right now I'm not concerned with any of that. I'm more interested in what the woman in front of me is suggesting.

"If I take you home and stay..." I take a step closer to her. "...what do you want to do?"

Nearly trembling, she asks, "What does ten thousand dollars get me?"

I take another step, closing the gap between us. Her chest is pressed tightly against my abdomen as I speak in a growly whisper against her ear. "It gets you anything you want."

CHAPTER ELEVEN

Sora

A confusing cocktail of lust and fury and a blatant web of bullshit.

I've made worse decisions in my life. Probably...*possibly*.

I pace the bedroom floor like a caged tiger, my steps muffled by the plush rug that probably cost more than my entire apartment's security deposit. Every few seconds, I steal a glance at the man sprawled across the California king, his muscular arm flung over his face, his breathing deep and rhythmic.

An escort. I brought a freaking escort to my dad's—*my*—brownstone.

In my cannabis-clouded judgment last night, this made perfect sense. The brownstone was closer to The Plaza than my apartment, and I was in no state to give coherent directions to a cab driver. "Take me to the multimillion-dollar house my famous, rich author dad just gifted me out of guilt" was a mouthful, so I alluded to Forrest that this was *my place*. He didn't question why the home is so staged—immaculately decorated and devoid of even a speck of dust. To me it's obvious no one lives here. Forrest didn't seem to notice.

The memories from last night swim through my brain—scattered, hazy snapshots. Stars overhead. Stars in my eyes. Nerves prickling my body. Me, finally out of my own head, saying whatever came to mind. The pretzel-cart man—our unlikely cupid—transforming his humble food stand into a moonlit ballroom with tinny speakers and a Spotify playlist.

Forrest's arms were around me, steady and sure. The way his voice dropped, all smoke and honey, as he explained "White Flag" wasn't about hopeless longing but about glorious surrender. About diving headfirst into love's messy waters, knowing you might drown but jumping anyway. About refusing to raise the white flag even when the battle's already lost.

God, the way he looked at me when he said that—like I was the battle he'd gladly lose. Like I was worth the surrender. I know he was merely proving a point by creating a moment...

But it worked. It lingered. The next morning, it's all I can think about.

This man is *excellent* at his job.

And that performance he put on is the reason I momentarily *lost my damn mind* by impulsively sending him ten thousand dollars and propositioning him like I was Julia Roberts in a gender-swapped *Pretty Woman*.

Except unlike the movies, we never sealed the deal. Somewhere between arriving at the brownstone and me showing him to the master bedroom, I apparently dozed off into an edible-induced slumber. Forrest, being the gentleman he is, just tucked me in and climbed in beside me.

The sun peeks through the blinds, casting stripes of gold across his ridiculously perfect torso. It's already late morning. Daphne will be here any minute for our book planning session, and I need this gorgeous problem out of my house immediately.

I approach the bed, debating whether to gently nudge him or just yank the covers off entirely. Gentle wins. I'm not a monster.

"Forrest," I whisper, lightly touching his shoulder. His skin is warm and smooth beneath my fingertips. "Forrest, you need to wake up."

He stirs, his arm sliding away from his face to reveal those devastating honey-brown eyes, now blinking sleepily up at me. For a moment, he looks confused, then a slow smile spreads across his face.

"Good morning, cookie girl," he murmurs, his voice rough with sleep.

"Hi," I respond lamely, immediately stepping back from the bed. "So, um, you need to go."

The smile falters. "That's...direct."

"I'm sorry," I rush to explain, twisting my fingers together nervously. "My friend is coming over. She'll be here any minute. And she can't know that I, um..."

"Hired an escort?" he finishes for me, sitting up now, the sheet pooling at his waist. I try—and fail—not to stare at his muscular chest. Of course he's topless, I'm still wearing his shirt from last night.

"Right. That."

Something flickers across his face—hurt, maybe?—but it's gone so quickly I might have imagined it. He swings his legs over the side of the bed, revealing red boxer briefs that fit him like they were painted on.

"Wouldn't want to tarnish your reputation," he says lightly, but there's an edge to it.

"It's not that," I protest weakly, though it absolutely is that. "It's just complicated."

He stretches his arms overhead, muscles flexing in a way that should be illegal before noon. "Don't worry about it. But before I go..." He stands and takes a step toward me, close enough that I can smell the faint trace of his cologne from the night before. "I want to make sure you get what you paid for."

My throat goes dry. "What?"

His eyes dance with mischief. "Did you really pay me to cuddle for one night? Or, were you expecting something else?"

"I wasn't expecting anything." This is no time for honesty. So I won't tell him that when I made that cash transfer, all I could think about was being owned by Forrest for one dirty, salacious evening. I also won't tell him that even though all we ended up doing was cuddling, it was the best night's sleep I've had in months, wrapped in his strong arms, my head tucked against his chest.

"That's it? A ten-thousand-dollar cuddle session?" he teases, his voice dropping an octave. "Well, that's your call." He surveys the room and shrugs. "I guess judging by your place, you must have money to blow."

The doorbell rings, the sound echoing through the brownstone's high ceilings. Panic seizes me.

"That's her. Daphne's here." I grab his arm, my fingers barely spanning his bicep. "Please, please don't say anything about... your job. Or the money. Or any of it. Actually, if you could just disappear in a hurry, that'd be preferable."

He raises an eyebrow. "How? We're on the fourth floor, Sora. Should I go ahead and jump out the window onto the concrete sidewalk?" he snarks.

"Depends. Could you land it?" I deadpan.

He tries to control his smile. "I'd like to live to see my daughter again, so I'm going to pass on that idea. But don't worry, I won't embarrass you in front of Daphne. I'll just quietly wave, lips sealed, and slip out."

"Wait," I protest feebly. "Daphne is not going to let you sneak out quietly. I'm not a one-night-stand kind of girl. She's going to have questions. Could you pretend, just for a bit, that we're a thing?"

For a moment, I think he's going to refuse, but then he shrugs, his expression unreadable. "Sure, why not? I can play boyfriend for a bit."

"Thank you," I breathe, releasing his arm. "Just stay up here until I call you down, okay?"

"Yes, ma'am," he says with a mock salute.

I dash down the three flights of stairs, my bare feet slapping against the Tasmanian oak flooring, and fling open the front door to find Daphne on the doorstep, one hand raised to ring the bell again, the other clutching a pink pastry box.

"Finally!" she exclaims, brushing past me into the foyer. "I texted you three times last night. What happened to you? I was starting to really worry. And *holy shit*, I forgot how nice this place is."

"Sorry. I, uh, got distracted."

"Distracted how?" She sets the pastry box on the marble island and turns to face me, her eyes narrowing suspiciously. Then they widen as she takes in my appearance—sleep-tousled hair, oversized men's dress shirt, bare legs. "Sora Cho-Cooper, do you have a man here?"

"Maybe," I answer.

Her mouth gapes dramatically. "As in, there's a man in your bed right now? An actual human male? Not your vibrator with a face drawn on it?"

Before I can answer, a deep voice from the doorway says, "Guilty as charged."

We both turn to see Forrest leaning casually against the doorframe, wearing only his tuxedo pants from the night before, riding low on his hips. His hair is artfully mussed, his chest still gloriously bare.

His amused smile widens when he meets my gaze. "You drew a face on your vibrator?"

I cross my arms. "I'm not dignifying that with a response."

"All right, then. I'll use my imagination."

While I grumble in annoyance, Daphne's jaw continues to stretch as she surveys Forrest. "Good grief," she whispers, not even trying to be subtle.

"Forrest Hawkins," he introduces himself, crossing the kitchen to extend a hand to my stunned friend. "You must be the best friend I've heard so much about."

"Daphne Jones," she manages, shaking his hand in a daze. "And I've heard absolutely nothing about you."

Forrest chuckles, the sound warm and rich. "That's my Sora. Always keeping the best parts of her life private." He winks at me, and heat rushes into my cheeks.

"*Your* Sora?" Daphne repeats, looking between us with growing delight. "So this is...a thing?"

"It's new," I interject hastily. "Very new. Which is why I hadn't told you about it quite yet."

"Babes, if you're seeing someone, why didn't you tell me you had birthday plans? After your mom canceled, I only dragged you to that lame wedding so you wouldn't be alone. You could've been with your guy, instead."

"He's not *my* guy..." I start, my lies already unraveling. Damn Daphne and her intelligence. She's blond, but most certainly not clueless which isn't working in my favor at the moment.

"I was working late," Forrest adds, draping an arm around my shoulders and pulling me against his side. "Damn meetings I couldn't get out of. But my last client canceled, so I dug up a tux and met Sora at the wedding."

Daphne narrows her eyes. "That's right...didn't I see you there with a woman—"

"My aunt? Celeste? Crazy coincidence. Actually, not really. She's the epitome of Manhattan's elite. Of course she was at the socialite wedding of the year. But yeah, her ex-husband was bothering her, so I sat with her for a while to comfort her. She gets a little handsy when she's drunk."

"Ah," Daphne says, gobbling up his story.

It shocks me how elegantly Forrest lies. He didn't even flinch. I'm over here sweating so much I'll be standing in a puddle soon.

"Well, based on the state of you two, I'm guessing your birthday didn't end up too shitty, then?"

"It was unforgettable," Forrest answers for me, squeezing my shoulder in a way that seems innocent to Daphne but feels like a private joke between us. "She's a vixen. You would've thought it was *my* birthday last night the way she—"

"Forrest!" I shriek, then proceed to choke on air. He softly pats my back.

"Easy there, tiger. Save your energy for round three," he says to me before turning his attention back to Daphne. "She's insatiable."

I'm going to murder him. Slowly and painfully. Except Daphne is absolutely devouring this, her eyes sparkling with more joy than I've seen in months.

"Look at you, finally living a little," she muses. "And here I thought I'd have to stage an intervention to get you to take a break from all that work stress."

"Speaking of," I say, trying to change the subject, "weren't we supposed to be planning my next book today?"

Daphne waves her hand dismissively. "That can wait. I want to hear more about this," she says, pointing between me and my fake new boyfriend. "So, what do you do, Forrest?"

"Financial consulting," he answers smoothly, not missing a beat. "Mostly private clients."

"How fascinating." Daphne's tone indicates it's anything but. "And *hey*, did Sora tell you about her big book signing next week? Not to brag, but I pulled some strings and got her in. Nothing says supportive boyfriend like showing up to cheer on your author girlfriend."

I freeze. *No, no, no.* He doesn't need any more details about my life. Lines blurred and crossed. The messy pile of this situation is growing to Mount Everest proportions.

Forrest, of course, doesn't join in on my mental panic. "I wouldn't miss it for the world. Where is it again?"

"It's nothing—" I start, but am swiftly cut off by my way-too-eager best friend.

"City Nights and Novels in Brooklyn," Daphne answers, looking pleased. "It's going to be her breakout moment. All the big romance authors will be there. We're a last-minute addition, so any support we can wrangle..."

"I'll be front row, center," Forrest promises, giving me another squeeze. "With bells on."

"Perfect!" Daphne claps her hands together. "Now, let's have some breakfast and talk tropes. Forrest, I got plenty for all of us. Do you like pastries?"

"Forrest has a meeting," I blurt out. "Right...um...babe?" I could not sound more awkward if I tried. "You have to get going?"

Ignoring me, Forrest flashes Daphne a toothy smile. "I

happen to love pastries."

Daphne begins unpacking the box, and Forrest finally releases me to grab plates from the cabinet. How he knows where they are is beyond me—I've barely opened a drawer in this kitchen.

"So, what are tropes?" Forrest asks, setting the plates down.

"Romance novel conventions," Daphne explains, slicing a chocolate croissant in half. "The reader catnip that makes a book sell. Enemies to lovers, forced proximity, only one bed—that kind of thing. We're trying to beef up Sora's next book to give her sales a fighting chance."

"Your books aren't selling?" Forrest asks me. His tone changes, lined more with concern than his playfulness over the past few minutes.

"Not well," I admit.

"You know what I think we need for virality? *Shock factor*," Daphne says. "So, we take what's tried and true and up the ante. For example, dark romance authors, we'll see your masked tattooed stalker chasing a woman through the woods with a knife, and *raise you* a masked stalker with tattoos *and* a Prince Albert chasing a woman through *haunted* woods with a katana." Daphne nods at me with eyes wide like she's possessed. "You see where I'm going with this?"

"I do. But I'm not following you down the unhinged path you're on." I turn to Forrest who has busied himself with a cherry tart. "I don't write dark stuff."

"What do you write?" Forrest asks.

"Don't you already know?" Suspicion lines Daphne's face.

"We're *new*, Daph. I haven't really gone into all that yet," I add.

"She's way too humble about her career. She thinks it's going nowhere but she's an incredible writer. This girl is going to be on billboards one day," Daphne proudly declares.

I catch Forrest's eye and subtly shake my head.

"So, Daphne, what kind of men does Sora put in her love stories?" Judging by the smirk on his face, his question is layered.

"Billionaires who are allergic to shirts," Daphne says, raising her eyebrows at Forrest's bare chest. "Art imitating life, perhaps?"

Forrest laughs, after helping himself to another bite of pastry. "I'm afraid I fall short of the billionaire mark. And I'm usually wearing a shirt," he adds, briefly glancing at me like after the cherry tart, I'm his next meal. "But even if sales are sluggish now, Sora seems to do pretty well for herself. This place is incredible." He rotates his finger, gesturing to the luxurious kitchen.

"The brownstone is my dad's."

Forrest blinks at me. His jaw twitches ever so slightly. "Great. If I'm also meeting your dad this morning, I'm going to need my shirt back, sweetheart."

"He's not here. He lives in LA right now. He doesn't need this house anymore, so he gave it to me for my birthday. I'm not even sure if I'm going to move in yet."

"Her father is J.P. Cooper," Daphne supplies helpfully.

Recognition flashes in Forrest's eyes. "*Hell & Heroes*? That J.P. Cooper?"

I nod reluctantly. "That's Dad."

"Wow. I feel like there was a prime opportunity for you to mention that last night, Sora." Forrest looks a little peeved, like I got caught in a lie. But this entire morning is a blatant web of bullshit, so what's he annoyed about? "So, you're a romance author who comes from literary royalty. Quite the charmed career."

I narrow my eyes, not appreciating what he's insinuating. *Poor little rich girl with laughable problems.*

"My career is far from charmed."

"When it comes to author stuff, Sora's dad is about as useful as a snail in the Kentucky Derby. He doesn't support her career at all. Just calls her a couple times a year to make sure she's alive, and flies in every now and then to buy her love with multimillion-dollar spare houses."

I hang my head, accepting defeat in trying to control this conversation. "Forrest, if there are any other wildly personal and painful details you'd like to learn about my life, Daphne is at your service."

"Good," he says, ignoring my sarcasm. "Because I have questions, Daphne."

"Fire away." If Daphne grins any wider, her face is going to rip in half. I don't like how much these two are already getting along.

I turn to Forrest, returning to my mission at hand. *Getting him out.* "Didn't you say you had to get going soon? To pick up your daughter?"

Something flickers in his eyes—surprise, maybe, that I had the gall to bring up his daughter.

"Right." He nods, setting down his half-eaten pastry. "I should probably grab my coat. Daphne, thank you for sharing your breakfast. Very kind of you."

He disappears upstairs, and Daphne immediately rounds on me.

"Daughter?" she hisses. "He has a kid?"

"Yes, a little girl," I confirm. "She's adorable." I don't offer Daphne a name or age, because I don't actually know it. But I clarify what I can. "He's a really good dad. Not just the dote-on-her-to-shut-her-up kind of dad. He's trying to raise his daughter right. It's impressive." Of all the lies I told this morning, that sentiment was genuine.

Daphne fans herself theatrically. "Hot, great in bed, and good with kids? Marry him. Immediately."

"Don't get too comfortable with him," I urge, my voice low. "We're probably not going to work out long term."

"Why?" she counters, like she's taking personal offense. "Unless he's a serial killer feeding dismembered body parts to wild hogs, there is no excusable reason for you not to snatch that man up in a hurry."

"We're just not compatible, Daphne. His job is—"

"My job is what?" Forrest asks, returning and once again unexpectedly interjecting himself into our conversation. How come I don't hear him coming down the stairs? The man moves like a ninja when he chooses to.

Forrest stands a few paces away, dressed in his rumpled tux coat from the night before, his bow tie hanging loose around his neck. "My job is *what*, Sora?" he repeats.

"Complicated."

The look he's giving me is layered with emotions. He's studying me like I'm a book written in a language he doesn't understand. "That it is," he answers shortly.

"The walk-of-shame look suits you," Daphne remarks, raising her brows at me, forcing light humor into the tension between Forrest and me.

He relaxes, grinning, returning to his easy confidence and charm. "I prefer to think of it as the stride of pride. I'm not remotely ashamed about last night." He shoots a playful wink my way, but compared to all the Forrest winks I've received so far, this one feels forced.

"Well, I should get going," he adds, buttoning his jacket, covering as much of his chest as he can.

"Shoot." I tug on his dress shirt that's blanketing my body. "Do you want this back?"

"As much as I'd like to see you strip down…keep it. It's just a plain white button-down. Easily replaceable." He holds out his hand to my friend. "It was nice meeting you, Daphne. Sora, I'll call you later?"

"I'll walk you out," I say, ignoring Daphne's suggestive eyebrow-waggling.

Outside on the brownstone's steps, the morning air crisp against my bare legs, I finally let my smile drop.

"Thank you for that," I say quietly. "For not saying anything."

"No problem." He shrugs, adjusting his jacket. "My services come with discretion included."

The mention of payment brings me back to reality with a thud. "About that. The money…"

"What about it?"

"I need it back," I say, forcing myself to meet his gaze. "I was high on gummies, and I wasn't thinking straight. That money was everything I have in savings. I was going to use it for a new marketing guy to run ads for me." I omit the part where I'm fifty thousand dollars shy of his fee, but I was going to beg for his help with a hefty down payment in cash.

His expression softens slightly, but then he shakes his head. "I'm sorry, but I don't do refunds." He glances back at the brownstone. "I'm going to assume I need the money more than you."

I narrow my eyes. "You know what they say about assuming."

"So Daddy gives you a house, but won't give you the money to help with book marketing?"

Now I'm irritated at his casual pokes to my open wounds. "That's really not your business. And I'm sorry, Forrest, but ten thousand dollars for a night of cuddling is ridiculous. You know that, I know that. You have to give me my money back. *Please*?"

"No." He steps closer, his voice low. "But you're right. You were too messed up last night to fully appreciate what you paid for. So how about we make a deal? Ten grand is enough for two nights. I'll make them more than worth your while. You already have my number from the money transfer. Whenever you're ready, just let me know. And I'll even throw in the book signing for free. I'll show up and be the world's most supportive, doting boyfriend in front of all your colleagues and readers."

My heart sinks. "Please, I just need the money back. We can forget any of this happened. I don't need you to pretend to be my boyfriend."

"Too late," he says with a grin. "Plus, Daphne's already expecting me there."

"Forrest—"

"Stop. The answer is no. Deals aren't reneged just because you're having morning-after regret. If I ran my business that way, I'd be broke, living on the street." He leans down and presses a soft kiss to the top of my head, the gesture so unexpected and tender that I forget what I was going to say next.

"No refund. I'll see you soon, cookie girl," he murmurs

against my hair before pulling away.

Unable to form a coherent response, I watch him walk down the steps. Only when he's halfway down the block do I realize I'm standing outside in nothing but his dress shirt, giving the entire neighborhood a morning show.

Rushing back inside, I catch Daphne looking out the bay window, watching Forrest disappear down the street.

"Don't say it," I warn, when she joins me back in the kitchen.

"I didn't say anything," she replies innocently. "But if I were going to say something, it would be that I've never seen you look at a man the way you just looked at him."

I gawk at her, thinking, *looked at him with what? Panic? Agitation? A confusing cocktail of lust and fury?*

"It doesn't matter," I mutter, grabbing another pastry to stress-eat my feelings. "It's not what you think."

"What I think," Daphne says, pouring us both cups of coffee from the pot she apparently made while I was outside, "is that maybe this is exactly what your career needs right now."

"A man? Really? Because that's the opposite of focusing." I sink onto a barstool, suddenly exhausted as I ruminate on my dwindling career hope. The marketing guy I can't afford was my last resort. *What now?*

"Exactly. You need a distraction. Someone to take your mind off of obsessing about ratings, reviews, and sales numbers." She sits beside me, her expression unexpectedly gentle. "I know you don't see it, babe, but every day I watch you lose a little more of your spark. You are consumed by your perceived failure. But maybe having a life outside of your job will help you put things into perspective. You know it's odd..."

"What is?" I ask, staring into my coffee cup, watching the swirls of cream dissipate.

"You write about love, *really well*, I might add. But I've known you for a long time and I don't think you've ever been *in love*. It's funny that you can write about something that you've never experienced before."

"I've been in love... I think."

I've dated a little here and there through college. I've had a few short-term boyfriends. The love didn't last, but it was there.

"Honey, if you *think* you've been in love, you never have. You'll know when it happens." She pokes my shoulder. "Or, is happening," she whispers maniacally, tapping the tips of her fingers together like a witch over a cauldron who's particularly proud of the potion she brewed.

"Let's just get to talking shop, yeah?" I don't even want to entertain the idea of something legitimate between me and Forrest. It's a ridiculous notion. He had me swooning last night. He'll have a different woman weak in the knees tonight. That's not real romance, nor is it a game I'm interested in playing.

"Nah, I want to talk some more about your new piece of man candy."

I set my coffee cup down and exhale. "Or, we could talk about how you tricked me into eating weed gummies?"

"Tricked you?" she balks. "I specifically told you they were to help you relax. The package clearly had a marijuana leaf symbol on it. Anyone with eyes could've seen that."

"I didn't recognize the symbol," I argue. "I thought the leaf meant it was *vegan*. I ate a whole handful at the wedding last night."

"*Oh...my...god...*" Daphne says through her riotous laughter. "You must've been so baked. You and Forrest must've had the time of your lives last night."

I close my eyes for a second, drifting back into the memory of Forrest and me dancing on the sidewalk under the stars.

"It was all right," I mutter. "Just a one-time thing."

CHAPTER TWELVE

Forrest

"World's Okayest Roommate"

The apartment is quiet when I walk in, which is unusual for a Saturday morning. Normally Taio has music blaring while he makes his protein smoothie, getting ready for his weekend workout routine. I drop my tux jacket on the back of our secondhand couch and head straight for the coffee maker.

Our place isn't much—a two-bedroom walk-up in the Bronx with temperamental plumbing and neighbors who think three in the morning is an appropriate time to practice their off-key rendition of "Bohemian Rhapsody." But it's relatively clean and affordable which is how I can cover my portion of Dakota's tuition. That last part makes it worth the occasional cockroach sighting.

I've just pressed the start button on the coffee maker when Taio's bedroom door swings open. He emerges in basketball shorts and nothing else, his six-foot-four frame filling the doorway.

"Well, well, well," he drawls, eyes dancing with amusement. "Someone didn't make it home last night."

"I'm home now," I reply, reaching for a mug from the cabinet.

"In last night's pants and no shirt." He leans against the counter, crossing his arms over his chest. "Did Celeste finally cave and decide to wear your dick out?"

"I wasn't with Celeste." The coffee maker sputters and hisses, filling the kitchen with the rich aroma of dark roast.

Taio's eyebrows shoot up. "New client? Do tell." He reaches across me to grab his own mug, the one with "World's Okayest Roommate" printed on it. Dakota and I got it for him last Christmas, and he treats it like it's made of solid gold.

"Not exactly." I pour coffee for both of us, stalling. Usually I don't mind Taio's interrogations after a night out. We've been best friends and roommates for the last four years. We also have the same job, so there's nothing to hide. He knows nearly everything about me. But something about last night with Sora feels private. Like sharing it would diminish it somehow.

"Dude." Taio snaps his fingers in front of my face. "You're being weird. Spill."

I take a long sip of black coffee before answering. "I met someone at the wedding. A woman. She was high as a kite on edibles and propositioned me."

Taio's face splits into a grin. "My man, coming in with the double play. Booking jobs while on a job." He pretends to bow to me. "How was she?"

"She paid me ten grand, and we didn't even have sex." I shake my head, remembering Sora's sleepy smile as I tucked her in. "She passed out, and I just...stayed."

"You cuddled?" Taio's voice climbs an octave in disbelief. "For free?"

"The ten grand wasn't exactly free."

"Still." He studies me, his expression shifting from teasing to concerned. "You like this girl?"

I shrug, not trusting myself to answer honestly. Because the truth is, I do like her. I like the way her mind works, how she can be both vulnerable and sharp-tongued in the same breath. I like that she writes romance novels but couldn't recognize an obvious advance if it wore a name tag. I even like her ridiculous stubbornness.

What I don't like is how quickly she tried to hustle me out of her place this morning, like I was dirty laundry she didn't want her best friend to see. Like what I do for a living makes me unworthy of being acknowledged.

"She's interesting," I say finally. "But it doesn't matter. She's embarrassed by what I do."

"Ah." Taio nods sagely. "The escort shame spiral. Classic. She must've been a first-timer."

"Definitely. She practically shoved me out the door this morning," I grumble. "Didn't want her friend to know she'd slept with—or rather, not slept with—someone like me."

"Someone like you?" Taio repeats, his tone hardening slightly. "What's that supposed to mean?"

I run a hand through my hair, frustrated. "You know what I mean."

"I know you've got a serious complex about this job."

"It's not a complex. It's reality. People judge."

"People like your fancy ex?" Taio raises an eyebrow.

"Hannah doesn't know what I do," I remind him. "And she never will, if I can help it."

"Well, maybe this new girl just needs time to adjust to the idea. Not everyone's as sex-positive as your boy Taio." He strikes a pose, flexing his biceps, and despite myself, I laugh.

"Yeah, well, I've got bigger problems than Sora's hang-ups." I take another sip of coffee. "I promised to show up at her book signing next week, pretending to be her boyfriend."

Taio snorts. "Sucker."

"She doesn't want me there." I run my thumb over the rim of my mug, remembering the soft press of my lips against the top of Sora's head this morning.

"Then why go?"

"To annoy her." That's not entirely true. Based on the way Sora was talking about her industry last night, it kind of sounds like she's heading right into the lion's den dressed like a ribeye. I have an unrelenting urge to protect her.

"Just be careful," Taio warns, suddenly serious. "Our line of work doesn't mesh well with relationships. Trust me. I've tried it." He makes a mock explosion with his hands with added sound effects. "That shit blew up in my face, *hard*."

Before I can respond, my phone rings. I pull it from my pocket, surprised to see Wesley Prep Academy on the caller ID. Fear spikes through me—calls from school are never good news. Plus, it's a Saturday. Am I late on tuition? I thought it wasn't due until next week.

"Hello?" I answer, bracing myself.

"Mr. Hawkins? This is Principal Vaughn from Wesley. I hope you and Dakota are having a wonderful morning."

"She's with her mom this weekend."

"Oh, right," Vaughn answers awkwardly, like the fact that Hannah and I aren't together makes her uncomfortable.

I clear my throat, then coax the conversation along. "Is everything okay?"

"Oh, it's wonderful! I'm calling with good news." The principal's voice turns bright with enthusiasm. "We've received word from Dorimer Academy in California. They've accepted Dakota into their gifted and talented program. I know it's mid-semester, but they have an immediate opening, which rarely happens. They've offered the spot to Dakota. Isn't that exciting?"

I blink, trying to process her words. Did she say California? "I'm sorry, what program?"

"The gifted and talented program at Dorimer Academy, the boarding school you inquired about?" Her enthusiasm dims slightly. "Dakota's test scores were exceptional, as we expected."

"Test scores?" My voice comes out sharper than intended. "What test did my daughter take?"

There's a pause on the other end. "The comprehensive aptitude evaluation we discussed last month. The paperwork was all in order, signed by both parents."

"I never signed anything." The coffee in my stomach turns sour. "I never agreed to have my daughter tested for a special school. We have no plans to move to California."

"It's a boarding school, Mr. Hawkins. Only students on campus. You and Ms. Novak wouldn't need to reside in California for Dakota to attend Dorimer."

"You're saying she'd be alone?"

"No, of course not alone. At her age she'd have a full-time nanny whenever she isn't under the care of her teachers. And of course, you'd be allowed to visit campus for holidays and student exhibits."

"Ms. Vaughn, all due respect, are you high on paint fumes? On what planet would I be interested in sending my child away to be raised by a stranger?"

Another, longer pause. "Oh dear. Well, we have your signature on the consent forms. Perhaps you forgot? Ms. Novak assured us you were both in agreement."

Hannah. Of course.

"She forged my signature," I say flatly. It's not the first time she's done it. I just thought we were past that childish bullshit when it comes to Dakota.

"Mr. Hawkins, that's a serious accusation—"

"My daughter is four years old," I cut her off. "She's not going to any boarding school, especially not one three thousand miles away."

"Perhaps you should discuss this with Dakota's mother," Principal Vaughn suggests, her tone now carefully neutral. "They'll only hold the spot for the weekend. We'll need an answer by Monday morning."

"Here's your answer: *no*. She's not going," I emphasize, my response full of undeserved anger directed at Principal Vaughn. I hate to shoot the messenger, but Dakota's still a baby. Who the fuck willingly separates a four-year-old from their parents?

I hang up and stare at the phone for a long moment, rage building inside me like a pressure cooker. Hannah forged my signature. She's trying to ship our daughter off to California without my knowledge or consent.

"What's wrong?" Taio asks, watching me warily. "Koda okay?"

"Hannah's trying to enroll her in boarding school." My voice sounds strange even to my own ears. "In California."

"What the fuck?" Taio pulls his mug from his lips. "She can't do that. I've read *A Little Princess*. Boarding school is gnarly."

My stare is blank. "What?"

"Sue me," Taio snarks. "I read."

"*Playboy*, maybe."

"No, my guy. Classics." Taio taps his temple. "Sometimes you have to rest the dick, and exercise your mind."

I don't have time to unpack that at the moment. I'm already heading for my bedroom, pulling a clean shirt from my dresser.

"Where are you going?" Taio asks as I return to the kitchen, pulling my white T-shirt over my head. "I need to talk to Hannah. Now. Before my brain explodes."

"Want me to come with? Play bad cop and help put Hannah in her place? Put me in, Coach." The offer is sincere. Taio might act like the perpetual bachelor, but he loves Dakota as if she were his own niece.

"Thanks, but no," I say, clenching my fist so my fingers stop shaking from anger. I take a deep breath to calm myself. "I'm sure it's some kind of misunderstanding. We don't need to ambush her."

Forty minutes and an expensive-as-hell cab ride later, I'm standing outside Hannah's building in Midtown, a gleaming sixty-story glass monstrosity that screams "if you have to ask the price, you can't afford it." The revolving doors give way to a marble-clad lobby straight out of an *Architectural Digest* spread—all soaring ceilings, abstract sculptures, and a massive wall of cascading water behind the concierge desk.

Maurice, the weekday doorman who usually gives me a friendly nod when I pick up Dakota, isn't at his post. Instead, there's a younger guy in the same crisp charcoal uniform, who eyes me with the practiced suspicion reserved for anyone who doesn't look like they belong in this temple to wealth.

"Can I help you, sir?" His tone is polite but cool, his hand hovering near the security phone.

"I'm here to see Hannah Novak." I run a hand through my disheveled hair, suddenly aware of my appearance—unshaven, wrinkled shirt, radiating the kind of barely contained fury that probably has him calculating the response time of building security. "Hannah is my daughter's mother. I'm Dakota's father, Forrest Hawkins."

Recognition flickers across his face, though not the kind I'm hoping for. "Mr. Hawkins. You're not on the weekend schedule."

Of course I'm not. *The weekend schedule.* Like I need an appointment to see my own daughter. The familiar indignity burns in my gut.

"It's an emergency," I say, forcing my voice to sound even. "Family matter."

He consults his tablet, scrolling through what I assume is a list of approved visitors. "Let me call up."

Every time. Every single time it's the same dance. Asking permission to enter a building where my child lives. Waiting for approval like I'm a goddamn salesman rather than her father.

While he murmurs into the phone, I stare at the bank of elevators—four of them, each with custom artwork etched into their brass doors. The lobby is bustling with residents coming and going: a woman in tennis whites, balancing a small dog and a green smoothie; an older gentleman with a driver patiently holding the door; a couple in matching Lululemon, heading out for what I assume is a five-hundred-dollar-an-hour personal training session.

The residents of the building move through the space with the easy confidence of people who never have to consider what things cost. It's a world I never belonged in, even when Hannah and I were together. Especially not now, with my current living situation and vocation.

"Ms. Novak says you can go up." The doorman's voice pulls me back. "Shall I announce you?"

"No need." I head for the elevator bank, escorted by a

concierge who materializes at my side. She swipes a key card and presses the PH button.

"Have a pleasant day, Mr. Hawkins," she says with professional courtesy, stepping back as the doors slide closed.

The private elevator to the penthouse rises swiftly and silently, its walls lined with something that looks like leather. A small screen shows the weather, stock tickers, and building announcements about the rooftop garden renovation and the new sommelier joining the residents-only restaurant on the mezzanine.

It's a far cry from my walk-up in Brooklyn, where the elevator breaks down so often, my calves are toned from the daily trek up six flights. No wonder Hannah looks at me with thinly veiled pity on the rare occasion she drops Dakota off at my place.

The elevator opens directly into their foyer—because of course the penthouse has its own private entrance. No hallways shared with neighbors here. Just twelve-foot ceilings, walls of glass overlooking Central Park, and the kind of pristine white furniture that makes me wonder if anyone actually lives here or if it's just a showroom for the criminally affluent.

Hannah and Henry occupy the kind of New York City home that appears in glossy magazines. Floor-to-ceiling windows with views that lesser mortals pay to see from observation decks, and furniture that looks like it's never felt the weight of a human body. It's beautiful, but sterile. Like a hotel suite rather than a home. Every time I'm here, I find myself scanning for signs of my daughter—a stray toy, a crayon mark on the wall, anything to indicate a child lives here. I rarely find any.

I pound on the door to the main living area, my initial attempt at civility evaporating as I replay the phone call with Principal Vaughn in my mind, imagining Dakota being shipped off to strangers.

I knock again, more forcefully.

The door swings open to reveal Henry, dressed in pressed chinos and a blue button-down like he's a banker on his way to brunch. His salt-and-pepper hair is perfectly styled, his smile polite but reserved.

"Forrest," he greets me, stepping back to let me in. "This is unexpected."

"Where's Koda?" I ask right away. The silver lining to this impromptu visit is I get to see my kiddo's cute little smile. That ought to cheer me up and relieve my anger so I can have a cool-tempered conversation with Hannah.

"Dakota is upstate with Mr. and Mrs. Novak this weekend. They heated the pool so she could swim."

My agitation rises again. "Henry, do you think it's odd that even though I'm Dakota's dad, I seem to never know where my daughter is or what she's up to?"

"I, uh..." Henry diverts his gaze, taking another small step backward. I'm pleased I've made him visibly uncomfortable.

"Anyway, I'm here to speak with Hannah," I say, not bothering with forced pleasantries. "Is she here?"

"She's in the study." Henry gestures down the hallway.

"Studying what?" I snark. *Gold-digging one oh one?* I think to myself. *Or has she moved on to an advanced degree when it comes to taking advantage of men's money?*

"It's just an expression," Henry adds. "It's where we keep the desk and computer. I believe she's editing some photos. I was just heading out, actually."

I nod, trying to dial back my ire. It's not Henry's fault his girlfriend is trying to abandon our daughter. "Sorry to interrupt your weekend."

He waves off my apology. "Not at all. Family matters are important." He gives me a strange look, something like pity mixed with relief. "I'll give you two some privacy."

Henry grabs his jacket and slips out the door, leaving me alone in the expansive living room. I take a deep breath and head toward the study.

I find Hannah at her desk, typing on her keyboard. She looks up when I enter, her expression guarded. "Forrest. What are you doing here?"

"Wesley called me." I leave the door open and halt two strides away from the desk. "Care to explain why our daughter is being enrolled in a boarding school without my knowledge or consent?"

Hannah's face does something complicated—surprise, guilt, then defiance, all in rapid succession. "She was accepted into their gifted program. It's a tremendous opportunity."

"She's four years old." My voice rises despite my effort to stay calm. "And you forged my signature, Hannah. That's illegal."

"Don't be dramatic." She stands, smoothing down her silk blouse. "I knew you'd react like this without considering the benefits. Dakota is *gifted*, Forrest. We'd be irresponsible not to give her the best opportunities."

Obviously, Dakota is precocious. She's been carrying on conversations like an adult since she was three. But while she's intellectually advanced, emotionally, she's still a baby. *My baby.*

"What's irresponsible is robbing her of her childhood. Take it from a guy who spent more than twenty years in school. Let her be a kid while she can."

"For fuck's sake, get over it. You didn't slay a dragon. You're not the only person to graduate from law school. I mean, maybe the only person to graduate and then piss away a multimillion-dollar employment opportunity—"

"Here we go again," I grumble.

"Anyway, Dorimer is the best educational institute in the country. The connections she'll make there, the opportunities she'll have—"

"She's a child, not a networking opportunity." I take a step closer, forcing myself to lower my voice. "What's really going on? This isn't like you. Hannah, you're a lot of things—a bad mom isn't one of them. Can't you see this for what it is?"

Hannah sighs, the fight seeming to drain out of her. She sinks back into her chair. "Henry got offered a position in Tokyo. Six months, maybe longer."

"So?"

"So I'm going with him." She meets my eyes, and I see the

determination there. "It's an incredible opportunity for his career. For both of us, really."

"And Dakota?" I ask, though I already know the answer.

"Henry feels that she...complicates things." Hannah at least has the decency to look ashamed. "He's not ready for full-time parenting. Especially abroad."

"Well, good thing he's not Dakota's parent, right?"

"Forrest—"

"Look, you want to know my honest opinion about Henry?"

"No," she snaps.

"Tough shit. He's not a bad guy, but he's too old for you and he's rigid—stuck in his ways. Just like your parents who you spent the majority of your life trying to escape. But if you really love him, I'll help you."

"Help me?" Her expression changes, as if that were the last thing she expected me to say.

"Breaking up doesn't mean we have to be enemies. Don't you know I still want you to be happy? You and Henry can survive six months of long distance. Go visit him whenever you like. I'll keep Koda while you travel. You know I want more time with her anyway."

Hannah smooths her long hair, then tucks it behind her ears—her nervous tick. So, I know bad news is coming. "Henry wants to propose. And I want to say yes. But..."

"But what?"

"He doesn't want kids. He doesn't particularly like it when Dakota's around. He made some calls to get Koda into Dorimer. And he's willing to pay for tuition, room and board, visits, *everything*. If she doesn't go, Henry's not going to ask me to marry him."

The words hit me like a physical blow. My throat tightens with fury—not just at Hannah, but at Henry too. What kind of man asks a woman to choose between him and her child?

The kind of man my mother chose, whispers a voice in the back of my mind.

Memories surface...

Mom dropping me off at Dad's ranch for what was supposed to be a weekend visit, then calling three days later to say she'd met someone new, someone who "wasn't into kids." Dad became my everything after that—steady, reliable, always there. He taught me that being a parent isn't something you do when it's convenient. It's who you are, always.

"So instead of telling this guy to fuck off, you're planning to ship Dakota away?" I ask, incredulous.

"It's not that simple, Forrest."

"It *is* that simple. She's our daughter. We're supposed to put her needs first."

Hannah stands again, insolence replacing her shame. "And what about what I need? What about my happiness? I've been a full-time mother for four years. Don't I deserve a life too?"

"Not at the expense of your child." I rake a hand through my hair, wishing she could try being reasonable for once. "Hannah, really listen to yourself. You're talking about abandoning our daughter."

"I'm not abandoning her!" Hannah's voice rises, my words triggering her. "I'm providing her with the best education money can buy."

"Henry's money, you mean."

Her eyes flash. "Yes, Henry's money. The same money that pays for her pony, her swim lessons, her dance lessons, her designer clothes. The same money that gives her a bedroom with a view of Central Park instead of some cramped hole-in-the-wall in Brooklyn."

The words sting. There's truth in them. I can't give Dakota the material comforts that Henry can. But I can give her something far more valuable—my time, my attention, my unwavering presence.

"You know what?" I say, suddenly calm. "If you want to go to Tokyo, go. But Dakota's not going to boarding school. She's staying with me."

Hannah laughs, the sound shrill and dismissive. "Where

would she even sleep? Your apartment barely has room for you and Taio."

"I'll figure it out."

"And what about your work? Those late-night client meetings? Who's going to watch her then?"

I tense, wondering how much Hannah knows or suspects about what I really do for a living. If she ever found out, she could use it against me in court. A sex worker isn't exactly the preferred custodial parent in most judges' eyes. If I lost custody in a messy court battle, I couldn't prevent Hannah from sending Dakota away.

"I said I'll figure it out," I repeat firmly. "I'm her father. I have rights. You may not want our kid, but *I do*."

Suddenly a lightbulb powers on and I see a possible solution. Sora's brownstone. Four bedrooms, a laundry room, expansive kitchen, even a backyard. Not to mention it's a stone's throw from Koda's school. She's not even sure if she'll use it. Maybe we could make some kind of arrangement—my ten grand back in exchange for letting Dakota and me stay there until I find something more permanent.

It's a long shot, but it's something.

Hannah's face grows ruddy as tears fill her eyes. "I do love her. This isn't easy for me," she says, her voice cracking at the end of her sentence.

"Then tell Henry to kick rocks." I cross the room and take her hand, appealing to whatever maternal instinct still exists beneath her ambition. "She needs you. She needs us. If you do this, Hannah—she'll remember. I still remember my mom leaving. I've never forgiven her."

For a split second, I think I've gotten through to her. Then she pulls her hand away. "I want to be with Henry. I think when Dakota is a little older, he'll come around."

"And until then?"

She blinks her tears free, staring at me wordlessly. Then, her voice hardens again. "Dorimer would give her opportunities neither of us could provide. And it's not like we'd never see her. There are holidays, summer breaks—"

"No," I cut her off, my decision made. "She's not going. Not to California, not anywhere."

Hannah's eyes narrow. "You don't get to make that decision."

"Watch me." I turn to leave, then pause at the door. "Call the school. Tell them Dakota won't be attending Dorimer. And if you ever forge my signature again, I'll take your ass to court and I won't stop until I see you strutting around in an orange jumpsuit. Understood?"

It's a bluff, and she probably knows it. I can't afford a protracted legal battle, and my job would become public record. But something in my tone must convince her, because she doesn't argue further.

"This conversation isn't over," she says instead.

"No. It's just beginning," I say before I storm out.

On the elevator ride down, I lean against the wall and close my eyes, exhaustion washing over me. The anger I felt walking in has been replaced by cold determination. I don't tell Hannah how to live her life. Never pushed back against her decisions regarding Dakota. I could never risk losing what little time I have with my daughter.

But this? I will die on this hill fighting for her. Nothing—not money, not comfort, not convenience—is more important than my little girl.

As I step out onto the street, waiting to hail another overpriced cab, my phone buzzes with a text.

It's from the last person I expected.

212-555-2929

Hey, it's Sora. I forgot to thank you.

For the cuddle?

> **212-555-2929**
> **For turning my night around. I would've gone home alone, crying on my birthday if it wasn't for you. So...thank you.**

> You're welcome, cookie girl. It was my pleasure.

> **212-555-2929**
> **For the record, I still need my money back. PLEASE.**

I type out a response, then delete it. I want to tell Sora that maybe there's a different deal we can work out, but there's too much to figure out prior. First off, this might be a momentary lapse of judgment amidst a psychotic break for Hannah. It's quite possible she'll think things through and come back to her senses, see the light, and dump Henry.

But even in that scenario, I doubt her jilted ex will be willing to pay for Dakota's education any further, meaning I'll have to double my contribution or enroll Koda in public school. But if I do that, I'll have to move anyway because the local elementary school that Taio and I live close to has full-time security guards, drug dogs, and metal detectors at every entrance. So, hard pass.

Fuck. I pinch the bridge of my nose, endless scenarios, all with dead ends, crashing together to form a tension headache. There's too much to figure out. I'm not sure about anything right now.

Well, one thing.

Brownstone or not, I still can't shake the urge to see Sora again. I ignore her prior request as I text her back.

> **Looking forward to your book signing, Sora. I can't wait to be the world's best boyfriend.**

Sora
> **You ass.**

I smile to myself, picturing her cute scowl.

CHAPTER THIRTEEN

Sora

All hail the queen of mean.

"It's got to be around here somewhere," I mutter, squinting at the printed map in my hands. The ballroom of the Grayson Event Center stretches before us like an endless sea of rectangular tables draped in black linens, each numbered with a small placard. I tug my rolling suitcase behind me, the wheels catching on the plush carpet.

"Table fifty-six," Daphne reminds me, effortlessly pulling her own dolly stacked with three boxes of my books. "The email said it would be in section C."

"Which is...where exactly?" I scan the room, overwhelmed by the labyrinth of tables and the buzz of activity as authors unpack boxes, arrange bookmarks, and set up elaborate displays.

My stomach twists with a familiar anxiety. Everyone else seems to know what they're doing, confidently arranging Instagram-worthy tablescapes. Meanwhile, I'm wondering if my hastily printed bookmarks and the single banner I ordered last minute will make me look like the amateur I am.

Daphne must sense my spiraling thoughts because she bumps her hip against mine. "Stop that."

"Stop what?"

"That thing where your eyes get all squinty and you start mentally comparing yourself to everyone else." She flips her long blond hair over her shoulder and gives me a stern look. "Your books are great. Your table will be great. You belong here."

I wish I had half her confidence. Daphne moves through life like it's a runway designed specifically for her—all five foot nine of her, with curves in places I'll never have them and a smile that could probably end wars. And yet she chooses to spend her Saturday helping her neurotic best friend set up for a book signing that will likely be a complete disaster.

"What if we didn't bring enough books?" I fret, peering into the box on my dolly. "Or too many? What if no one comes to my table and I'm just sitting there like a loser while everyone else has lines?"

"Then we'll go get drunk afterward and burn the leftovers in a cleansing ritual." Daphne grins. "But that's not going to happen. Now come on, it's probably around this corner."

We navigate around a partition, and suddenly it's easy to spot my table.

Because Forrest is already sitting at it.

My heart does a complicated gymnastics routine in my chest. I haven't seen him since that morning at the brownstone when he kissed the top of my head and walked away with my ten thousand dollars. I've been cycling through anger, embarrassment, and a reluctant admiration for his audacity ever since.

He's leaning back in the folding chair, one ankle crossed over his knee, looking unfairly gorgeous in dark jeans and an earthy-green henley that makes his eyes look almost golden. When he spots us, a slow smile spreads across his face that could only be described as smug.

"There she is," he calls, rising to his feet. "The author of the hour."

"How did you even get in here?" I ask, trying to sound annoyed instead of flustered. "This area is supposed to be for authors, PAs, and staff only during setup."

He shrugs, that smile still playing on his lips. "I told them I was with Sora Cho. I think they assumed I was one of those book-boyfriend models. The woman at the door got very flustered when I asked where your table was."

Daphne snorts. "You flirted your way in, didn't you?"

"I did no such thing," he counters, winking at her before turning his attention back to me. "You look beautiful, by the way."

The compliment sends heat rising to my cheeks. I'm wearing my "author outfit"—black jeans, a silky pink blouse that Daphne insisted brings out the warmth in my dark eyes, and my special-occasion ankle boots. My long hair is pulled back in a sleek ponytail, and I've made a rare effort with makeup.

"Thanks," I mumble, busying myself with unzipping my suitcase to hide my reaction. I refuse to let him affect me like this. The man is literally a professional at making women feel special.

Still, when his fingers brush against mine as he helps me lift a stack of books, a jolt of electricity skates up my arm. I jerk away, nearly dropping the hardcovers.

"Careful," he murmurs, steadying my hands. "These are precious cargo."

"You have no idea what you're doing, do you?" I shoot him a raised eyebrow.

The corner of his mouth lifts. "None whatsoever. But I'm excellent at following directions."

Something about the way he says it makes me think of things far removed from book signings. I clear my throat. "Daphne, put him to work."

"Gladly." She thrusts a box of bookmarks into his arms. "These need to be fanned out artfully. Think you can handle that, pretty boy?"

"For you? Anything." He winks, and Daphne giggles.

I roll my eyes, but can't help the small smile tugging at my lips. As annoying as it is to admit, having him here takes some of the pressure off. While Daphne arranges my books in aesthetically pleasing stacks, Forrest unpacks my swag items—bookmarks, stickers, and a handful of tote bags I splurged on—with surprising care.

"So, what are these about?" he asks, picking up one of my latest releases. "*The Way We Were*, huh? Like the movie?"

"Sort of," I say. "It's a second-chance romance about high school sweethearts who reconnect at their ten-year reunion."

"And do they get their happily-ever-after?"

"It's romance. That's kind of the whole point."

He turns the book over to read the back cover, his expression thoughtful. "You believe in that? Happily-ever-afters?"

"In books? Absolutely. In real life?" I shrug, arranging my banner on the front of the table. The light pink of my logo looks almost gray. The printers warned me the shade wouldn't be vibrant against white, but I foolishly didn't listen. Primrose is my entire brand—soft, subtle brushstrokes of pale flowers and wispy *I love yous* blending into the background. "The jury's still out."

"Aren't your books supposed to reflect real life, though? Isn't that what makes a story resonate—the truth in it?"

I pause, surprised by the depth of the question. "Yes and no. Romance novels offer what real life often doesn't—certainty, closure, the guarantee that love is worth the risk. That's why people read them. For the hope."

His eyes scan the other titles displayed on my table, pausing on a stack with a soft-pink cover featuring two silhouettes against a sunset. "What about this one? *Lovely*?"

My hand instinctively reaches for the book, my fingers tracing the embossed title. "That's the first in a duet. The second book, *Lonely*, is coming out in about two months." I hesitate, then add quietly, "At least, it's supposed to."

"Supposed to?" He picks up *Lovely*, examining the cover more closely.

"Sales weren't great," I confess, the admission burning my throat. "Actually, they were pretty abysmal. My editor barely had any feedback on the sequel. Just 'it's fine, here you go.' Not exactly a ringing endorsement."

"What's it about? The duet."

I take a deep breath, trying to find the enthusiasm I once

had for this story. "It's about a woman who thinks she's unlovable because of a childhood trauma. She meets this guy who sees through all her defenses, who's patient and kind and determined to show her she's worthy of love."

"And the sequel?"

"It's from his perspective. His struggles, his demons. The first book ends with their beginning, but the second shows how hard it is to maintain love when you both have scars." I bite my lip, suddenly self-conscious. "It's about how loving someone broken doesn't fix you. How two damaged people have to actively choose each other every day."

Forrest is quiet for a moment, his eyes uncharacteristically serious. "That sounds...real."

"Too real, maybe. Romance readers want escape, not uncomfortable truths about how much work relationships are." I shake my head, trying to dispel the cloud of doubt that's been hanging over me since I finished writing *Lonely*. "I don't think people want what I'm peddling. I'm too much fact, not enough fantasy."

"I'd prefer the substance," Forrest says softly. "I like to see the messy things people have to overcome to get from the start to the end. Real love isn't a destination. It's a journey."

I blink at him, startled by the insight. "Exactly."

He sets the book down, his fingertips lingering on the cover. "So why are you thinking of pulling it?"

"I don't know if I want to put my heart out there again just to have it stomped on," I admit. "Reviews for *Lovely* were...mixed at best. And it's exhausting to keep pouring everything into something that feels like shouting into the void."

"Can I ask you something?" His voice is gentle, but there's an intensity in his gaze that makes my pulse quicken. "Do you write because you love it, or do you write to be loved?"

The question lands like a punch to the solar plexus, stealing my breath. No one has ever cut so cleanly to the heart of my insecurity before. Not even Daphne, who knows me better than anyone.

"I..." My voice falters. How do I answer that when I'm not sure I know the difference anymore? When the line between creating art and seeking validation has become so blurred, I can't see where one ends and the other begins?

Sensing my discomfort, Forrest reaches across the table and briefly squeezes my hand. "You don't have to answer that. But maybe it's something to think about."

I nod, grateful for the reprieve but unsettled by how easily he peeled back my defenses. There's something unnerving about the way he sees me—not the carefully constructed version I present to the world, but the messy reality underneath.

"These are really good," he says, mercifully changing the subject as he picks up one of my flower-filled bookmarks, the roses in tight bouquets, lining the corners. "Did you design them yourself?"

"Daphne did," I reply, delivering her a grateful smile. "She's the creative one."

"Not true," Daphne chimes in, materializing at my side with a stack of promotional postcards. "I just know how to use basic designer software. Sora's the one who creates entire worlds out of nothing but her imagination."

Something shifts in his expression, a softening around the eyes that makes my stomach flip.

"Who's taking the table next to you? It's still empty," Forrest asks, nodding toward the vacant space to my right, distinguished by a star on its placard.

"No idea. The email just said it was reserved for a special guest author," Daphne informs us.

Forrest glances around the now-bustling ballroom. "Must be someone important. Everyone else is already set up."

I shrug, trying to appear nonchalant. "Probably some bestseller who can waltz in whenever they want."

"Speaking of bestsellers," Forrest says casually, leaning against the table. "Your dad's work is pretty different from yours, isn't it? Fantasy versus romance?"

I tense involuntarily. "My dad writes literary epics with fantasy elements, yes."

"That's got to be...interesting. Growing up with a famous author."

"Interesting is one word for it." I arrange and rearrange the same stack of bookmarks, avoiding his gaze.

"Was he thrilled when you decided to follow in his footsteps?"

I bark out a laugh before I can stop myself. "Not exactly. He recently told me to quit, actually."

His eyebrows go skyward. "Seriously? Why?"

I hesitate, unsure why I'm even sharing this with him. Maybe because he's looking at me with genuine curiosity rather than the usual pity or judgment I get when people learn who my father is.

"He thinks I'm torturing myself for nothing. That I'm destined to...fail." The words are glass in my throat. "But mostly, I think he doesn't want me to make the same mistakes he did."

"Which were?"

"Sacrificing a real life for the fantasy of one on the page." I straighten a book that doesn't need straightening. "My parents' marriage fell apart because my dad was always lost in his imaginary worlds instead of participating in ours. He regrets that now, I think."

Forrest is quiet for a moment, studying me with a soulfulness that makes me want to squirm. "For what it's worth," he says finally, "I think your dad's wrong. About you failing, I mean."

Something warm blooms in my chest at his words, but before I can respond, a voice over the intercom announces that the doors are opening and attendees will be entering in five minutes.

"Showtime," Daphne says buoyantly, giving my shoulder a squeeze. "You ready?"

"As I'll ever be," I mutter, smoothing my blouse and checking my lip gloss in my compact mirror.

Forrest moves to stand behind me, his hands coming to rest lightly on my shoulders. "You've got this," he assures me, warm breath tickling the shell of my ear. "They're going to love you."

I wish I could bottle the certainty in his voice and drink it when my confidence falters.

The first wave of readers enters the ballroom, a sea of excited faces clutching tote bags and book lists. I paste on my brightest smile, but as the minutes tick by, a familiar dread creeps in. People walk past my table without a second glance, their eyes scanning for the authors they came to see.

Not a single person stops.

Daphne, bless her, tries valiantly to lure people over. "Have you read Sora Cho? Her second-chance romances will make you cry in the best way!"

A few women smile politely but continue on.

I sink lower in my chair, the rejection a physical weight on my shoulders. This is what I was afraid of—being invisible in a room full of stars.

"They just don't know what they're missing," Forrest says, but even his unwavering support can't mask the pity in his voice.

After twenty excruciating minutes, I notice a commotion at the entrance. People are whispering excitedly, phones raised to capture whatever—or whoever—has just arrived.

And then I see her.

Tila Valentina sweeps into the ballroom like she owns it, her signature red hair cascading down her back, her curves poured into a skintight red dress. She's surrounded by an entourage of assistants carrying boxes of books with her face emblazoned on the side.

And she's heading straight for the empty table next to mine.

"*No*," I whisper, the blood draining from my face. "No, no, no."

Daphne's hand clamps around my wrist. "You have got to be fucking kidding me."

Forrest looks between us, confusion evident on his face. "What? Who is she?"

But there's no time to explain. Tila is setting up within range, her team efficiently arranging a display that makes mine look like a child's craft project. And already, a line is forming—snaking past my table, around the corner, out of sight.

"Oh my god, it's really her!"

"I've been following her since her BookTok days!"

"Her reviews are hilarious!"

The snippets of conversation are an onslaught of tiny daggers. Because I know exactly what made Tila Valentina famous: tearing other authors apart for entertainment.

Two years ago, desperate and naive, I borrowed money from Mom, and paid Tila to feature my book on her growing platform. Instead of the positive promotion I'd foolishly expected, she posted a vicious "honest review" that reduced my labor of love to a laughingstock. She called my writing "fluffier than a declawed kitten on Xanax" and my hero "about as sexually compelling as a damp sock."

Her followers ate it up. My reviews plummeted, everyone wanting to follow suit and throw their own rock, each pebble slowly stoning my heart to death. Tila built her empire on the backs of authors like me, using our humiliation as stepping stones to her success.

Now here she is, basking in the adoration of fans who lined up to meet the queen of mean, while I sit forgotten at the next table over.

Tila's gaze flicks to me, the briefest flash of recognition crossing her face before she turns away, dismissing me as thoroughly as she did my book years ago.

"Sora," Daphne murmurs, her eyes wide with concern. "We can leave if you want."

I shake my head, forcing a smile that feels like it might crack my face. "It's fine. I'm fine."

But I'm not fine. Especially not when readers in Tila's line start using my table as a convenient place to set down their belongings while they wait for their photo op.

"Do you mind if I leave my purse here?" a woman asks,

already dropping her designer bag on top of my carefully arranged books. "I'll just be a minute."

"Actually—" I begin, but she's already walked away.

Another woman places her stack of Tila's books on my table. "Thanks, hon. Could you watch these for me? I want to get a picture before she signs these."

Before I can answer, Forrest interjects smoothly. "I'm afraid the author needs her space. You understand."

The woman looks startled, as if noticing me for the first time. "Oh, sorry. I didn't realize... Are you an author too?"

The "too" is what does it—the casual assumption that I'm an afterthought, a nobody compared to the celebrity next door.

"Yes," I manage. "I am."

She glances at my display without interest. "Cool. Well, good luck with that!"

I sink back into my chair, mortification burning through me. This is worse than being invisible—it's being seen and dismissed.

Daphne's expression has morphed from concern to barely contained rage. "This is such bullshit," she hisses. "After what she did to you, I want to line her thongs with fire ants—"

"It's ancient history," I mutter, though the reopened wound feels fresh as ever.

Forrest glances between us, clearly trying to piece together the story, but before he can ask, I overhear a snippet of chitchat from Tila's table that turns my blood cold.

"*...so excited about my new agent. He's incredible.*" Tila's voice carries, loudly enough for me to hear. "Dane Spellman himself cold-called me to offer representation. Said my work was exactly what he's looking for."

Dane Spellman. The agent who said I was a "dime a dozen." The agent who only wanted me for access to my father, and who now apparently thinks Tila Valentina—a woman who built her career mocking authors like me—is worthy of his elite roster.

Something inside me splinters.

I stand abruptly, my chair scraping against the floor. "I need some air."

"Sora—" Forrest reaches for me, but I'm already moving, pushing past bewildered attendees, ignoring Daphne's call behind me.

I make it to the hallway before the tears start, hot and humiliating. A sob builds in my chest, but I swallow it down, ducking into the nearest restroom.

The woman in the mirror looks so pathetic—red-eyed, mascara beginning to smudge, her carefully applied lipstick bitten away. This is what rock bottom looks like: crying in a public bathroom while the woman who tried to destroy your career celebrates her success twenty feet away.

Maybe my dad was right. Maybe I should quit while I still have a shred of dignity left.

CHAPTER FOURTEEN

Forrest

Book-boyfriend bait!

"What the hell just happened?" I stare at the exit Sora disappeared through, torn between following her and giving her space. The pain on her face had been so raw, so visceral, it felt like a physical blow.

Daphne grabs my arm, her fingers digging into my bicep. "That," she says through gritted teeth, "was the aftermath of Tila-fucking-Valentina."

"I gathered that much. But why did Sora look like she'd seen a ghost?"

Daphne releases my arm to aggressively arrange and rearrange the stacks of Sora's books. Her movements are sharp, angry.

"Because Tila is the closest thing the romance community has to a professional hit woman." She lowers her voice, throwing a venomous glance toward the adjacent table where Tila is holding court, her crimson hair like fire under the ballroom lights. "Two years ago, when Sora really needed marketing help, she paid Tila to promote her book."

"Paid her?" I echo, my eyes following a young woman who casually drops her purse on our table without so much as a glance in my direction.

"Yeah, a paid collaboration. It's like Nike paying LeBron

James to show off their shoes. Tila was this rising BookTok influencer with a massive following. She'd feature indie books for a fee—supposedly to help authors get exposure." Daphne shoves the woman's purse back at her with a fake smile that doesn't reach her eyes. "Except with Sora, Tila decided to pivot her brand. Instead of promotion, she posted this vicious takedown video that went viral."

My jaw tightens. "She took Sora's money and then trashed her book?"

"Publicly eviscerated it. Called it fluffier than cotton candy in a hurricane. Said the hero had all the sex appeal of a dead fish. Made jokes about how reading it was like watching paint dry, but less exciting."

"Couldn't she file a civil suit for defamation?" I ask, my legal knowledge coming full front and center to Sora's defense.

"Ha. If only. That's not how our world works. Ruthlessness is excused for the sake of *honesty*. Except for the books Tila five-stars, which are garbage bags on fire, but of course they are written by her author besties. So frustrating." Daphne's voice cracks slightly. "Sora was devastated. Her launch tanked, her reviews plummeted, and Tila's following quadrupled overnight."

The pieces click into place—Sora's panic at seeing Tila, the way she shrunk into herself, the tears that couldn't be contained. It wasn't just professional jealousy. It was trauma.

"And now Tila's the one with the book deal," I say quietly.

"Seven figures." Daphne nods bitterly. "Built her entire career on tearing down other authors for entertainment. The publishing industry rewarded her for it."

I glance around the ballroom, taking in the scene with new eyes. Authors at every table, smiling hopefully at passersby. Some have lines; others sit alone, their expressions growing more strained with each person who walks by without stopping. It's not so different from my own line of work—the constant hustle for attention, the pressure of performance, oftentimes, the rejection.

"This whole industry is...rough, isn't it?" I muse.

Daphne barks out a humorless laugh. "You have no idea. It's like high school on steroids. There are cliques, mean girls, and popularity contests that determine whether your work ever gets seen. Forget talent—it's all about who has the most followers, who can create the most drama, who games the algorithm best."

"The algorithm?"

"Social media algorithms favor strong emotional reactions. Anger, outrage, shock—that's what gets amplified." She straightens a stack of bookmarks with precise movements. "So guess what gets rewarded? Not thoughtful, nuanced content. Not heartfelt stories. Rage rants and public takedowns. Authors and content creators battling it out, eating each other alive for clicks and likes."

I think of Sora, of her eyes lighting up when she talked about her characters, of the earnest way she described her stories. "And Sora doesn't play that game."

"She can't. It's not in her DNA." Daphne's expression softens. "That's the problem. Most authors who survive in this industry develop thick skin, or they become part of the problem—joining in the pile-ons, stirring drama for attention. But Sora..." She shakes her head. "Her heart is still so damn tender. It's my favorite thing about her, but it's also why she keeps getting her ass kicked."

Another woman approaches, already unloading her Tila Valentina books onto our table.

"Excuse me," I say, my voice harder than I intend. "This table is for Sora Cho's readers."

The woman blinks, looking around as if noticing our display for the first time. "Oh. Sorry. I didn't realize..." Her eyes slide over Sora's books without interest. "Is she new?"

"Four years, twelve books," Daphne answers tightly.

"Huh. Never heard of her." The woman gathers her books and walks away, immediately forgetting our existence.

"See what I mean?" Daphne sighs. "It's not about the quality of your work. It's about how visible you are. And in this industry, nice girls finish last."

I stare at Tila's table, at the line of eager fans clutching her books to their chests. Something cold settles in my stomach. I've spent my adult life surrounded by people who use others as stepping stones—professors who plagiarized their students' work, law partners who took credit for their associates' research, clients who treated me like a prop for their fantasies.

"I should check on her," I say, already moving toward the exit.

"Wait." Daphne catches my arm again. "Give her a minute. Sora hates for anyone to see her cry." She hesitates, then adds, "You really care about her, don't you?"

The question catches me off guard. *Do I care about Sora?* A woman I barely know, who hired me for a service I didn't even provide? But the answer comes without any doubt.

"Yeah. I do."

Daphne studies me for a moment. "How did you and Sora meet, anyway? She's been pretty vague about the details."

I pause, then decide to spin a story that feels right—one that I wish were true. "We met at a coffee shop a couple weeks ago. I was with my daughter."

"Papa Beans?" Daphne asks. "She practically lives there."

I nod, grateful for the prompt. "Yeah. I met her in line, and something about her just...caught my attention. She's clueless as to how magnetic she is." The image comes easily—I noticed a lot about Sora that day. The way she smiles with her whole face, eyes cinching shut, lips spreading wide, cheeks bunching into pink spheres. "After she selflessly gave my daughter the last kitchen sink cookie, I couldn't help myself. I asked her out right then and there."

"Cute," Daphne says with an approving nod.

"I couldn't wait, so I took her to dinner that night," I continue, the fantasy unfolding in my mind. This is how it should have been—how it would have been if I were just a normal guy who could approach a woman I found interesting. "I asked her to pick her favorite restaurant."

"Let me guess. Galbi Grill?" Daphne adds casually. "Korean BBQ."

I snap my fingers and point at her, as if she's hit the jackpot. "That's the one. She ordered for both of us—I couldn't pronounce any of the dishes, but they were incredible."

The lie feels good, like trying on a life that fits better than my own. In this version of events, I'm not an escort. I'm just a single dad who met a beautiful woman and was brave enough to ask her out. In this version, there's no money changing hands, no pretending, no complications.

Daphne smiles. "Prepare yourself. Sora always takes charge with the food. She gets it from her mom."

"I like that about her," I say, and this part, at least, is completely honest. "I like a lot of things about her."

"That's sweet." Daphne ducks her head in what seems like approval. I guess I'm passing the new-boyfriend test. "So, how long have you been in financial consulting?"

"Just a couple years."

"Oh. And does that line of work require a fancy degree?"

I assume so, but since I'm not actually a financial consultant, I don't know. I think up an excuse to satiate Daphne's curiosity. "I pivoted careers after my doctorate. I actually attended law school—Columbia."

Daphne's eyes widen. "You're shitting me. As in Columbia Law? That was my dream school."

"You're a lawyer?"

She shakes her head, a wisp of hurt crossing her face. "No, I wish. I applied after undergrad but didn't get in. Completely destroyed me at the time."

"It's competitive," I acknowledge. "But there are other good schools."

"Yeah, I know that now. But Columbia Law was on my vision board, you know?" She fiddles with a bookmark, turning it over in her hands. "But actually, I just got accepted to a program in Lincoln, Nebraska. Starting next semester."

"That's great," I say, genuinely pleased for her. "You excited?"

A shadow passes over her face. "I don't know if I'm going. I'm worried about leaving Sora. She depends on me. She asked me to move into the brownstone with her on her birthday, and I didn't have the heart to tell her I might not be here in a few months." She groans in frustration. "Or I don't know. Maybe I will be. I just can't decide."

"You can't put your life on hold forever," I say gently. "Even for the people you love."

"Easy to say. Harder to do." Her expression grows serious as she looks toward the exit door. "Sora's been through so much. Her parents' divorce, her dad's bullshit, this industry tearing her down at every turn. She puts on a brave face, but each rejection cuts deeper than she lets on." Daphne's voice cracks slightly. "I've been her rock for so long. I can't ditch her when she needs me most."

After a pause, I brush off my better judgment and reach across the table to pat her hand. "Go to law school, Daphne. I'm here now. I'll take care of Sora."

"You've been her boyfriend for exactly two minutes. I've been her best friend for more than a decade." Her voice is tinged with uncertainty.

"Whatever's happening between us is new, but..." I trail off, searching for words that won't sound hollow. "There's something about her. Something I can't walk away from. So, I'll be here. A shoulder to cry on, an ear to vent to—whatever she needs."

Daphne studies me, her gaze piercing. "You sure I can trust you with my friend's heart?"

It's a fair question. One I'm not sure I deserve to answer affirmatively, given my complicated life. But I think about how Sora looked when she talked about her books, the vulnerability in her eyes when she shared her insecurities. I think about the way my chest tightened when I saw her crying.

"I'm loyal," I say finally. "Above everything else. Ask anyone who knows me. When I care about someone, I don't bail when things get tough." I think of Dakota, of the battle I'm willing to fight for her. "If there's one thing you can trust, it's that."

Something in my tone must convince her, because Daphne

nods slowly. "Okay then. I guess Lincoln it is."

"Lincoln it is," I echo, squeezing her hand before releasing it.

A slow smile spreads across her face. "Hey, I have an idea to turn this shitshow around for Sora. Are you game to help?"

"What do you have in mind?"

Her eyes scan the ballroom, calculating. "Wait here."

Before I can ask what she's planning, Daphne darts off, weaving through the crowd with determined purpose. I watch as she approaches several other author tables, gesturing animatedly, pointing in our direction. To my surprise, the authors—all women—nod and smile, handing her various items.

She returns moments later, arms loaded down with...props?

"What's all this?" I ask as she dumps a cowboy hat, a motorcycle helmet, and a sequined bow tie onto our table.

"Our salvation." Her eyes glint with mischief. "Take off your shirt."

I blink. "I'm sorry, what?"

"You heard me. Shirt off, pants unbuttoned—but zipper up." She glances around the ballroom, then grabs a blank piece of poster board from her tote bag and a marker. "We're going to give these readers something Tila can't."

"Daphne, I don't think—"

"Look," she cuts me off, her face suddenly serious. "Sora is about to come back here, probably still crying, to an empty table while the woman who humiliated her is five feet away with a line around the block. Do you want to help her or not?"

Put like that, there's only one answer. I unbutton my shirt, ignoring the curious glances from nearby attendees. "What exactly is the plan here?"

Daphne scribbles rapidly on the poster board, her handwriting surprisingly elegant despite her speed. "We're going to use you as bait."

"Bait," I repeat flatly.

"Book-boyfriend bait," she clarifies, holding up the completed sign with a flourish: *Buy a book, take a photo with your choice of* book boyfriend! Cowboys, bikers, CEOs—we've got 'em all!"

I can't help but laugh. "You're devious."

"I prefer resourceful," she counters, arranging the props on the table. "Now, lose the shirt and give me your best smolder. We've probably got about sixty seconds before Sora comes back, and I want a line formed by then."

Shaking my head in amused disbelief, I pull my shirt overhead and toss it onto Sora's chair. Following Daphne's instructions, I unbutton my jeans, leaving them hanging low on my hips. The cowboy hat feels ridiculous perched on my head; I haven't worn one of these in years, but the small crowd already gathering suggests it's having the desired effect.

"Ladies," Daphne calls out, her voice carrying across the nearby tables. "Special promotion at Sora Cho's table! Purchase any book and get a photo with our live book-boyfriend model—your choice of theme!"

The response is immediate and shocking. Women from Tila's line begin to peel away, drawn by curiosity and, let's be honest, the novelty of a half-naked man. A group of twentysomethings giggle as they approach, pointing not-so-subtly in my direction.

"Is this for real?" one of them asks Daphne.

"One hundred percent," Daphne confirms. "Buy any book, take any photo—within reason." She gives me a wink. "Our model is very accommodating."

And just like that, they're sold. One after another, they grab copies of Sora's books, barely glancing at the covers before handing over credit cards and cash to Daphne, who's seamlessly taken on the role of cashier.

"Perfect promo idea, right?" Daphne whispers to me between sales. "Sora's boyfriend helps boost her career. That's serious relationship goals."

I nod, not trusting myself to respond. If only she knew the truth—that I'm not Sora's boyfriend, that our entire relationship is built on a lie that started with a mistaken proposition and ten thousand dollars.

By the time Sora emerges from the bathroom, red-eyed but composed, a line has formed at our table that almost rivals Tila's. The look of confused shock on her face would be comical if it weren't so heartbreaking.

"What...what's happening?" she asks, her voice small as she approaches.

"Your fanbase is growing," I respond, adjusting the ridiculous cowboy hat. "Better get signing."

To my surprise, an elderly woman thrusts a copy of Sora's book at her. "Oh my god, you're the author? Your boyfriend is hot!"

Sora blinks, then looks at me, her confusion slowly giving way to understanding. "My...boyfriend?"

"Don't be shy, sweetheart." I offer her a wink. "See? Bells on like I promised."

For a moment, I think she might be angry. Then, by a miracle of miracles, she laughs—a genuine, unexpected sound that transforms her face. The tension in my chest eases at the sight of her smile.

"Sign my book?" the woman prompts, pulling Sora's attention back.

"*Oh*. Yes, of course. Happy to!" Sora slides into her chair, careful not to disrupt my shirt, accepting the pen Daphne hands her. "Who should I make it out to?"

The next hour passes in a blur. I pose for photos with an endless stream of women—wearing the cowboy hat, the motorcycle helmet, the bow tie, sometimes combinations that make no narrative sense whatsoever. Some of the bolder ones take liberties, their hands wandering to my chest, my abs, occasionally lower before I gently redirect them.

It's not so different from my regular job, really. I'm playing a role, fulfilling a fantasy, making people feel special. The key difference is that every dollar spent, every book signed, every photo taken is helping Sora.

Between customers, I catch her looking at me—quick, furtive glances filled with something I can't quite decipher. Gratitude, certainly, but also something more. Something that makes my heart thud hard in my chest.

By the time the signing officially ends, Sora's table is completely sold out. Not a single book remains. Daphne's eleventh-hour scheme worked better than any of us could have anticipated.

As the crowds begin to disperse, Sora finally has a moment to breathe. She sinks back in her chair, exhaustion and wonder warring on her face.

"I can't believe that just happened," she murmurs, staring at the empty space where her books had been.

"Believe it," Daphne touts, counting the cash box with obvious satisfaction. "Every last book, gone. Plus pre-orders for twenty more copies of *Lonely* that I promised to ship after release."

Sora shakes her head in astonishment, then turns to me. I've put my shirt back on, though I left it unbuttoned—partly because I'm overheated from the constant photos, and partly because I like the way Sora's gaze lingers when my bare skin is on display.

"Why did you do that?" she asks quietly.

Daphne, sensing the shift in mood, mumbles something about checking on the parking validation and disappears into the thinning crowd.

I sit in the rickety chair beside Sora, suddenly very aware of how close we are. "You were upset. I wanted to help."

"By taking your clothes off and letting strange women grope you for photos?"

"It worked, didn't it?" I gesture to the empty table.

"That's not an answer." Her dark eyes search mine. "Why, Forrest? Really."

The truth rises to my lips before I can stop it. "Because I wanted to see you smile again."

Her expression softens, vulnerability replacing the wariness in her eyes. "That's...a very sweet answer."

"Maybe I'm a sweet guy." I hold her gaze, letting the implication hang between us.

She looks down at her hands, strands of dark hair coming

loose from her ponytail and curtaining her face. "You did all this for me, but you barely know me."

"I know enough."

The silence stretches, heavy with unspoken questions. Finally, she raises her head, a hint of her earlier smile returning.

"Thank you," she says simply. "For everything."

"My pleasure." I mean it more than she could possibly know.

And even though I know it can't lead anywhere—even though in two weeks I'll have Dakota full-time and my complicated life will become even more so—I can't help but savor the odd connection that's forming between us.

Maybe we're both just lonely people who recognize something in each other—something real beneath the facades we present to the world.

The crowd finally thins to empty and we begin packing up the table. I notice Sora pulls something from her tote bag.

"I saved one," she says, almost shyly. "For you."

She holds up a copy of her book with the soft pink cover—*Lovely*. "Thank you."

"You don't have to read it," she adds quickly. "It's just...a thank-you. For today."

I watch as she uncaps a pen and opens to the title page. Her handwriting is neat and small as she writes something, then signs her name. When she hands it to me, I read the inscription:

To my new friend, Forrest. Cheers to the journey.
~Sora Cho

The words echo our earlier conversation about love being a journey, not a destination. Something warm unfurls in my chest.

"I'll read it," I promise, cradling the book gently in my arms like it's a treasure.

As Sora gathers her belongings, I catch myself stealing glances at the pink cover now tucked between my bicep and rib cage.

It's clear, this is something more potent than lustful flirtation. And it's too late to forget about it. Maybe I took one step too many. I thought seeing her again would curb my interest. Like scratching an agitating itch. Instead, my intrigue has only magnified, and while I don't know what the hell I'm doing, after today, I know one thing for sure.

I'm in trouble. Complicated trouble, like I'm standing at the edge of a deep pool I'm guaranteed to drown in.

"Hey," Sora says, her bag flung around her shoulder. "I think Daphne's tired and is about to head home."

"Understandable," I say in agreement.

"But I'm not so tired. Are you? Can I take you out for a drink as a thank-you?"

I pat my new book. "*Another* thank-you?"

"A lot of women groped you today. I think I owe you a few more for exploiting you like that. I'm sorry if you were uncomfortable."

I belly-laugh at her sincerity. My whole life is getting exploited and groped by women, but she's sweet to be concerned. "A drink sounds good. But how about I pay?" I pat my wallet through my jeans. "My wallet is pretty fat these days," I tease.

Sora rolls her eyes. "Ass," she murmurs.

Laughing, I pull her tote from her shoulders and sling it around my own. Then, I collect her suitcase, light as a feather after she sold all her books. Once I'm geared up like a pack mule, I point Sora to the ballroom exit. "Come on, cookie girl..." Images of the deep, dark pool of unknown possibilities flash in my mind. "Let's dive in."

CHAPTER FIFTEEEN

Sora

Clunky, way too wet, and kind of gross. You kiss like a fish...

"When you invited me out for a drink, this wasn't exactly what I had in mind."

I look up from my boba tea to find Forrest eyeing his own cup with amused suspicion. We're seated at a tiny table by the window of Lucky Moon, my favorite twenty-four-hour boba shop in Brooklyn, just a few blocks from where the book signing was held. The place is cramped but cozy, with paper lanterns casting a warm glow over the mismatched furniture.

"You don't like it?" I ask, taking another satisfying sip through my jumbo straw.

Forrest prods at a tapioca pearl with his straw like it might suddenly spring to life. "I was picturing whiskey or bourbon, not a children's drink with weird booger things in it."

I laugh, nearly choking on my taro milk tea. "You're a grown-ass man. How have you never had boba tea?"

"Because these little balls look nuclear," he chides, uncloaked skepticism painting his whole face.

"They're tapioca pearls. And this is a legitimate beverage choice for an adult."

"If you say so." He takes a tentative sip, his eyes widening slightly when a tapioca pearl shoots up his straw. He chews thoughtfully, his expression morphing from skepticism to reluctant approval. "Huh. Chewy. Not terrible."

"High praise indeed." I roll my eyes, though I can't help the smile tugging at my lips. "Sorry, I'm not a big drinker. I'm not against it, but I don't often partake."

"I gathered that from your gummy bear adventure."

Heat creeps up my neck at the memory. "Yeah, well, I'm not big on a lot of things, honestly. Mostly just work and...more work."

"I find that hard to believe. You must have hobbies."

I shrug, avoiding his gaze. "Writing is my hobby. And my job. And pretty much my entire personality at this point."

"What about friends? You have Daphne."

I smile, thinking of my best friend's excitement as we packed up after the signing. "Yeah, she's great. I don't know what I'd do without her. She's literally my only friend. Twenty-seven years old and my social circle consists of one person...well, two if you include my mom." I bury my head in my hand when I hear the words out loud that make me sound like a forty-year-old virgin. "Damn, I'm pathetic."

"You're not pathetic," Forrest says, his voice gentle. "You're focused."

"That's a nice way of saying I have no life." I attempt a self-deprecating smile, but it feels brittle on my face.

The truth is, I've always hidden behind my work. It's safer to live in fictional worlds where I control the outcomes than to risk the messy unpredictability of real relationships. The irony of writing romance while avoiding meaningful connections isn't lost on me.

"Dakota might like this stuff," Forrest muses, poking at another tapioca pearl. "She's got a sweet tooth."

"My kind of girl. We should bring her sometime," I suggest before I can think better of it. "Most kids like the strawberry or melon flavors."

Forrest looks up, surprise evident in his expression. "You'd want to hang out with me and my kid?"

"Sure, why not?"

"Most women find that...off-putting. Especially women without kids of their own."

I shake my head, smiling. "I love kids, actually." I hesitate, then add, "My mom regularly reminds me that my biological clock is ticking. She sends me links to articles about egg-freezing and fertility declining after thirty. She's a lot of things...subtle isn't one of them."

"She wants grandchildren?" Forrest guesses.

"Oh yes. And I'm an only child, so the poor lady has one single pony in this race. Her dream is for me to put the books down, find a nice Korean boy, settle down, and start producing babies immediately. Except the closest I've gotten to a long-term relationship is Daphne." I teeter my head side to side in contemplation. "At this point, Mom's so desperate, she might actually warm up to the idea of me and Daph adopting together. Whatever puts a baby in Halmoni's arms."

"What did you just say? Hal-mornie?" Forrest asks, face screwed up in determination, but still butchering the pronunciation.

"Hal-moh-knee," I sound out for him. "Means 'grandma' in Korean."

"Ah, I see. And is that what you want?"

"A lesbian relationship with Daphne?" I tease.

"A kid, Sora." A smile tugs at his lips. *Perv.* I bet he's picturing it.

"I do want kids, eventually. When I figure out...everything else."

"Everything else being your career?"

"My life," I correct. "My purpose. Me." I trace a pattern in the condensation on my cup. "I feel like I'm still trying to figure out who I am apart from everyone else's expectations. Does that make sense?"

Forrest nods, his expression thoughtful. "More than you know."

"What about you? Did you always want kids?"

"Not particularly," he admits. "But then Dakota happened, and now I can't imagine a time when I didn't want her."

"I like the name Dakota. How did you land on that?"

He smiles, a softness entering his expression that I'm learning is reserved exclusively for discussions about his daughter. "Hannah let me choose it. I just liked how it sounded."

"Bravo," I say before taking a short swig from my straw. "You did much better than my dad. He accidentally named me after a conch shell," I blurt out, the randomness of the confession surprising even me.

Forrest's eyebrows shoot up. "What?"

"My mom wanted a Korean name for me, but she was so exhausted after labor that she told my dad to fill out the birth certificate. The dodo googled 'Asian girl names' and picked Sora, thinking it meant sky. As a fantasy writer who crafts dragons and faeries, I think it spoke to him."

"That's actually kind of sweet."

"Except he didn't bother checking what it means *in Korean*," I continue. "In Japanese, Sora means 'sky.' But in Korean, it means 'conch shell.'"

Forrest's eyes widen with delight. "You're kidding."

"Nope. There are a couple of variations in translation. According to some, my dad accidentally loosely named me after a snail." I point at my chest with a self-mocking smile. "Which, considering the pace of my career, might be shockingly apt."

He laughs, his entire face lighting up with genuine amusement. "My little conch shell, inching her way to a bestseller. There's nothing wrong with slow and steady, Sora."

The casual endearment sends a warm flutter through my chest, which I immediately try to suppress. Getting attached to Forrest is a monumentally bad idea.

"So, the signing was amazing in the end," I say, desperate to change the subject. "I've never been to an event that big. And most certainly have never sold out of books before."

"Your work deserves recognition," Forrest says with a

sincerity that makes my stomach swoop. "I saw how those readers responded to you."

"To your abs, you mean."

"To your stories," he corrects firmly. "The abs got their attention. After that, they were intrigued by *your* books."

I fiddle with my straw, not sure how to respond to such unwavering support from someone who's barely more than an acquaintance. "I still can't believe how well it worked."

"Daphne's quick thinking saved the day," Forrest agrees. "She's quite the strategist. No surprise she got into law school."

"*What*?" I gape. "What law school?"

Forrest's expression shifts, realization dawning. "Shit. That's right...she didn't tell you, yet." He hangs his head, a little color flooding his cheeks. "Any chance you can forget you heard that?"

"Let me check..." Still as a statute, I pin my eyes dangerously at him. "Nope. Now, tell me what the heck you're talking about."

His throat bobs as he swallows thickly. "She mentioned today she got accepted to a program in Lincoln, Nebraska. Starting next semester."

The news hits me like a physical blow. *Daphne's leaving? And she didn't tell me?*

"That can't be right." I shake my head. "She would have told me something that important."

Forrest's grimace tells me I'm dead wrong. "I'm sorry. I shouldn't have said anything. Wasn't my place."

My chest restricts, a familiar panic beginning to set in. Daphne is my only friend, my support system, the person who believes in me when I don't believe in myself. *And she's leaving?* I mean, of course I'm happy for her, but...this wasn't the plan.

Columbia Law was the plan. Here...*with me*, was the plan.

"Why wouldn't she tell me?" I whisper, more to myself than to Forrest. "Does she think I wouldn't be supportive?"

"Maybe she was worried about how you'd take it," he suggests gently. "Maybe she was thinking more about you than herself."

The thought stings. Am I so fragile that my best friend feels she needs to shield me from her own good news?

"I can't stop thinking about what you said earlier," I admit.

"I said a lot of things earlier." Forrest stabs at his tapioca balls beneath his orange smoothie, but keeps missing the boba. Frustration consuming him, he rips off the plastic seal and starts stabbing the little balls with the point of his straw, popping them into his mouth one by one.

"Growing on you, are they?" I smirk.

He releases a small chuckle. "What did I say earlier that's on your mind?"

"You called me out. You asked if I was writing because I love it, or to be loved."

He stops spearfishing his tapioca balls, and pushes his drink aside. Crossing his arms, he leans back in his chair. "Did you figure out an answer?"

I stare at him, amazed at his nonchalance while he zeroes in, precisely I might add, on the core of my anxiety.

"I don't think it's about love per se. Respect, maybe...from my dad."

"What do you mean?" Forrest asks. He's still like a chameleon trying to blend in with his surroundings, as if any sudden movement might scare away my confession.

I trace a new pattern in the condensation on my cup. "Growing up, I was always trying to get his attention. He was so... absent. Bored of me and my mom. Even when he was physically there, his mind was somewhere else—lost in the worlds he was creating. I used to smuggle his manuscripts from his office and read them, just to feel connected to him somehow."

Forrest's expression is thoughtful. "And now you write, hoping he'll finally see you."

I take another sip of my tea, buying time. "My dad could help me if he wanted. Think about it. Every agent, publisher, and even Hollywood studio is after J.P. Cooper's rights because they are guaranteed to turn a big profit. If he wanted to work me into a deal, he could, *easily*. But he refuses. And you know why?"

"Why?" Forrest asks.

"Because to him, I'm *that* unworthy. I don't know if it's me, or the fact I write romance, or what. But there's something about my essence that Dad thinks is so detrimentally embarrassing that he doesn't want to be attached to it. Maybe I'm trying my hardest to prove him wrong... Except all I've been doing for the past few years is proving him *right*."

"Sora—"

"You don't have to pity me or anything. I'm just trying to be honest. It's pathetic, right?" It sounds like a question, but it's not. The accuracy of my words makes my chest ache. "Twenty-seven years old and still desperate for Daddy's approval."

"Not pathetic," Forrest says firmly. "Human. I want my dad to be proud of the man he raised. It's natural for a kid."

"Is he?" I boldly ask. "Does he know what you do for a living?"

His eyes drop to his lap as the corner of his lips turn down. "No."

Forrest is a talker. It makes sense when considering that charm and charisma are two essential elements of his current job, and his almost-job as a lawyer. So, when he answers my heavy question with a single syllable, his message rings through clearer than freshly Windexed glass: *Leave it alone.*

"Anyway, I think that's why I care so much about what readers think," I continue, shifting back the focus to my skeletons instead. "If my dad won't validate me, maybe strangers on the internet will. But it's become impossible to guess what everyone wants. The right tropes, the right personalities. Too much spice, not enough spice. The things one reviewer praises, the next reviewer is disgusted by. It has sent me into a total mind spiral. I can't write lately. I second-guess every plot twist, every character arc, every word choice."

"You're writing by committee," Forrest observes. "Trying to please everyone."

"And pleasing no one in the process."

"Except you, right? Because why are you doing this if you don't love your stories?"

I bite my bottom lip to keep it from trembling. I can't keep crying in front of this man. He's going to start throwing on a rain jacket anytime I'm within arm's reach.

"Great question," I mutter. "Anyway, enough about my daddy issues. You must be bored."

"Not at all. Daddy issues pay my bills." He grins mischievously. "Or ex-husband issues, or occasionally virgin issues."

I drop my jaw, momentarily distracted from my woes. "Women hire you to take their virginity?"

He cocks a brow. "You really want me to answer that?"

I decide to change the subject before I spiral further into aggressively investigative questions about Forrest's double life. "I've spilled my guts. Now it's your turn."

"My turn?"

"Share something vulnerable," I command. "To even the score."

"You're bossing me around now?" He's looking at me like a puppy trying to roar.

"Um, if you're open to that."

"Sora, for ten thousand dollars, I'm open to a lot of things."

I point at his chest. "We're not done talking about you returning my money."

He hums with laughter. "Okay, your choice. One or the other. You want me to share something vulnerable, or you want to argue about the money you're not getting back?"

I pout, not trying to be cute, but he still looks amused. "Fine. Vulnerable. Share your secrets."

Forrest leans back in his chair, watching me for a long moment. I half expect him to deflect or offer some sanitized version of his life, the kind of story he might tell a client.

Instead, he surprises me.

"I met Hannah—Dakota's mom—in college," he begins, his voice quiet but steady. "Fell hard and fast. She came from money. Old money. The kind of wealth where you never check price tags and summer is a verb."

I nod, encouraging him to continue.

"I was supposed to go back to Wyoming after undergrad. My dad's ranch was struggling, and he needed the help. But then I got into Columbia Law, and Hannah...she had certain expectations about the kind of life we'd live." His lips twist in a self-deprecating smile. "I was young and in love. I would have done anything to make her happy."

"So you went to law school instead of going home," I say, filling in the blanks.

"A law school I couldn't afford," he confirms. "Hannah's father had connections. One of them was Sean Colt, a partner at a prestigious firm and the ex-husband of my favorite professor, Rina."

Understanding dawns. "Rina...*Rina*... Wait, you've mentioned her. Your current boss, right?"

Forrest nods. "Sean offered me a deal. The firm would pay for everything—tuition, apartment, living expenses during school—and in exchange, I'd work for them for fifteen years after graduation. The salary was insane, more than enough to give Hannah the life she wanted."

"And you signed."

"I signed." He drags a hand through his hair, a gesture I'm learning to be a sign of discomfort. "Then Hannah got pregnant during my final year of law school. It felt like confirmation I'd made the right choice."

"But something changed," I prompt, sensing the second act of his story.

"I interned at the firm that summer. Saw what they really did— who they represented. Corporations that poisoned water supplies and called it a business expense. Landlords who let children live with toxic mold and lead paint. Executives who sexually harassed employees, then threatened them into silence." His jaw tightens. "I couldn't do it. Couldn't be part of that world."

"Good for you."

That earns me a teensy smile. "I went to Rina for help. She

found a loophole: I couldn't practice law and fulfill my contract if I never took the bar exam."

I blink, putting the pieces together. "So you deliberately failed to become a lawyer?"

"I never even took the test," he confirms. "I graduated, but I walked away from the profession. Sean was furious, of course. The firm demanded repayment of everything they'd invested in me—over half a million dollars."

"Jesus," I breathe.

"Hannah was equally furious. We broke up right before Dakota was born." A shadow of hurt crosses his face. "She'd signed up for a wealthy corporate lawyer, not a…" He gestures vaguely at himself. "Whatever I am now."

"She's a money-over-love kind of girl?"

He nods. "Took me a long time to get that through my head. And when I was at my lowest, Rina threw me a lifeline. She'd started this high-end 'companion service' as a side business after her divorce from Sean. She needed male escorts who were educated, well-spoken, capable of blending in at society events. I was desperate, drowning in debt with a newborn daughter to support. The rest is history."

I try to imagine Forrest in that moment—newly graduated, dreams shattered, relationship crumbling, with a baby depending on him. The weight of it must have been crushing.

"So that's how you ended up where you are," I say. "And you're still paying off the debt to Sean's firm?"

"Every month. Plus Dakota's tuition at that ridiculously expensive prep school, plus helping my dad keep the ranch afloat." He shrugs. "The official escort work is completely legal, and pays well, but not well enough to dig out quickly. Which is why Rina turns a blind eye when me and the guys, um…offer additional services *off the books*."

"And Hannah has no clue what you do?"

"She'd try to take Dakota from me for good. Simply out of spite for destroying our relationship."

"Destroying?" I ask, incredulous. "So you make a noble decision about your life and now you're the bad guy?"

"I could've sat down, shut up, and played the part she wanted. Hannah and I would be together, we'd own a yacht, have a penthouse on the Upper East Side, Dakota would be a pretentious little punk, and I could've pretended I was okay with all of it."

"Except you couldn't."

"Right." His expression clouds. We're silent for a beat, and then he proceeds to bare his soul like we've been friends for ages. "Hannah's boyfriend, Henry, just got a job offer in Tokyo. They're moving there for at least six months, and Hannah was planning to send Dakota to boarding school while they're gone." His voice hardens. "A four-year-old. At boarding school. Alone, without her family."

"That's awful," I say, earnestly appalled.

"I put my foot down. Told her Dakota would stay with me instead."

"Good." I nod encouragingly. "You're a really great dad."

"The problem is," he continues, "my current living situation isn't ideal for full-time parenting. My roommate, Taio, is supportive, but our apartment is tiny. Two bedrooms, one bathroom, and Dakota's at the age where I shouldn't be cramming her into a bro apartment, you know?"

I nod along. "Sure, sure."

"I could move, but that would be costly. I wouldn't be able to afford her private school anymore, where she's thriving, by the way. I'd have to send her to a questionable public school where she'd be mercilessly bullied for being tiny...and admittedly, a little bit of a know-it-all."

"That's hard," I add.

"So, what I really need is a temporary living situation." Forrest leans forward, his muscular forearms sweeping the uneven table, causing it to teeter between us. "Perhaps a vacant, uninhabited brownstone that happens to be a ten-minute walk from her school."

Maybe I was too distracted, mesmerized by his razor-sharp

jawline and the gentle wafts of his sexy cologne. His eyes held mine with an intensity that stole my breath. I was so consumed by the electricity between us, I didn't realize where this was headed until he spelled it out in braille, so even a blind man could read his intentions clearly.

"You want me to give you my brownstone?" I balk.

"I want to make another deal with you."

I cackle shrilly, half out of shock, half denial. "Forrest, no offense but no way you're *that good* in bed. I'm not giving you a house worth at least eight million on the market right now. I didn't even get a happy ending from the first dumbass deal I made with you. *No.*"

It's weird how patient he is through my outburst, his expression even-keeled with just a hint of enjoyment. "First off, I don't want you to *give* me your brownstone. I'm asking if I can borrow it."

"In exchange for what?"

"I think I can help you, Sora. With your books."

"Help me how?"

"The signing went well because we tapped into something readers respond to—the book-boyfriend experience." He wets his lips, holding my gaze. "What if we expanded on that? What if I helped you explore different romance tropes firsthand so you could dive into the emotions your readers are looking for? I'll be your source of inspiration."

I blink at him, not quite following. "What are you suggesting exactly?"

"We role-play." He holds up a hand when my eyebrows create liftoff. "Not just in the bedroom sense. I mean, we create scenarios based on popular romance tropes. I play the part of different hero archetypes. You immerse yourself in those experiences and then write about them with authentic emotion. The magic touch your future bestseller needs."

That's ridiculous. Unhinged. Laughable... But wait. *Is it?* Daphne mentioned something about me writing about love, even though I've never really been in love. Is this...a solution?

"Like method acting for authors," I say slowly.

"Exactly. You said yourself you're torn between writing what you love and writing what readers want. Maybe this is a way to bridge that gap—to find inspiration that's both commercially viable and personally meaningful."

It's rapidly turning into an intriguing idea, I have to admit. And not entirely different from what I sometimes do already—putting myself in my characters' shoes, imagining how they would feel and react.

"And in exchange, I give you my new house and stay in my shitty apartment for how long?" I ask.

"It has plenty of bedrooms and four floors, Sora. Move in if you want. Koda and I only need two rooms. We'll clean up after ourselves, and do our best to stay out of your way."

I fiddle with my straw, weighing the proposal. On one hand, it makes a certain kind of sense. The brownstone is sitting empty, practically begging for a family. And I do need inspiration for my next book.

On the other hand...

"I don't know, Forrest." I rummage my brain for a plausible objection that isn't the truth—that I'm afraid of getting too attached to a man who makes his living by making women feel special. That I'm even more afraid of latching on to someone I can't keep now that I know Daphne is leaving. "There's a flaw in your plan."

"Which is?"

"It wouldn't be authentic." I swallow hard, the lie feeling bitter on my tongue. "I mean, for this to work, there would need to be actual chemistry between us. And I'm just not... I don't think you're my type."

It's possibly the least convincing lie I've ever told. Judging by the slow smile spreading across Forrest's face, he knows it too.

"Is that so?" he asks, his voice dropping to a register that sends a shiver up my spine.

"Yes," I insist, my cheeks igniting. "I mean, you're objectively attractive, to other women I suppose. But I'm not personally attracted to you."

"Objectively attractive," he repeats, amusement dancing in his eyes. "Your flattery knows no bounds."

"Don't let it go to your head." I cross my arms defensively, aware that I'm digging myself deeper with every word. "I'm simply saying, for your role-play idea to work, we'd need to simulate real feelings to spark creative inspiration. And not to mention, I don't want to get slapped with an invoice every time we kiss."

"Receipts," he teases. "You've already prepaid for quite a few kisses."

"That you still haven't delivered on," I quip back. "Can we circle back to you returning my money?"

"Nope. But I suppose we should test your theory," he says, his tone silky smooth. "To see if it could work."

Before I can process what's happening, Forrest stands, leans across our tiny table, and cups my face in his hands. His touch is gentle but firm, his eyes questioning, his pupils bouncing back and forth between mine. He's giving me a chance to pull away.

I don't take it. Mostly because I'm completely frozen in a frosty mix of intense nervousness and excitement. My heart hammers almost painfully against my lungs as he closes the remaining distance between us.

The first touch of his lips against mine is soft, tentative—a question rather than a demand. Then, as I respond with a small, involuntary gasp, his tongue slips into my mouth, deepening our kiss. His hands slide into my hair, cradling my head as he angles his lips over mine with devastating precision.

This is not the kiss of a man going through the motions. This is not a performance.

Forrest kisses like he's discovering a secret, something he's been desperately searching for. His mouth is warm and insistent against mine, coaxing me to relax into him, yet there's an underlying grisly hunger that makes my toes curl in my boots as his hand powerfully holds my cheek, preventing my head from falling right off.

I've written dozens of first kisses in my books. None of them prepared me for this reality—the heat pooling low in my belly, the way time seems to stretch and compress simultaneously, the soft groan that escapes him when my tongue meets his.

When he finally pulls back, we're both breathing heavily. The Lucky Moon café has gone utterly silent, every patron staring at our display with varying degrees of shock and appreciation. The teenage barista behind the counter gives Forrest an approving thumbs-up.

"Well," Forrest says, his voice rougher than before as he sits back down, "you're right, that was awful." At first I'm shocked until his smug, playful smile takes the stage and he continues. "Clunky, way too wet, and kind of gross. You kiss like a fish, Sora."

I blink at him, still dazed. "You jerk. You're unbelievable."

"*Thank you*," he teases. "And don't worry, we'll get you there. A few dates with me and we'll have you kissing like a pro." His eyes gleam with satisfaction. "So, do we have a deal?"

I should say no. I should absolutely, definitely say no. This man is an escort who seduces women for a living. This arrangement has "disaster" written all over it.

But my lips are still tingling from his kiss, and the memory of his hands in my hair sends another shiver through me. More than that, the promise of finding new inspiration for my writing—maybe salvaging my career—is too tempting to resist.

"Fine." I try and fail to sound reluctant. "We have a deal."

His answering grin is equal parts triumph and genuine pleasure. "You won't regret it."

I already suspect that's not true, but I'm too far gone to care.

"But I think we need some ground rules. This is strictly professional, right?"

"Of course." He nods assuredly.

"All right, so...just research. And kissing is fine, but as far as anything else...maybe we should leave that off the table."

"That's your call," he answers with pursed lips. "My only rule is we shelter Dakota from the details of this arrangement. She can't know what I do, or what we're up to."

"Agreed. Absolutely."

See? He's responsible. Considering his daughter. This is fine. This is actually a smart plan... Or maybe I'm just rationalizing a terrible decision because the man kisses like sin and looks at me like salvation.

"So, what now?" I ask. "When do we start?"

"If you want to take me back to your place and get naked, we can start research right now." He pumps his brows and is met with my narrowed eyes.

"Try again."

"Fine. How about we talk a little more about your books. What's working, what's not. We're not going to look at those bullshit reviews online, but why don't you tell me what you feel like your strengths and weaknesses are in your writing, and what we need to work on."

I tilt my head to the side, examining his sincerity. "You're genuinely trying to help me, aren't you?"

"Yes."

Dammit. I could resist a hot asshole. But this? Forrest? I'm Little Red Riding Hood, willingly leaping into the wolf's mouth.

"I'm going to need another boba tea, then." I move for my purse hanging on the back of my chair, but Forrest whips out his debit card and shoves it in my hand.

"I get the feeling book boyfriends are supposed to exclusively pay on dates. So, that's what we're going to do moving forward."

Date? Damn my stupid involuntary smile. "All right. Do you want anything?"

"I'll take whatever you recommend, my little conch shell." He sends me his signature wink before settling back into his chair.

My legs feel like jelly as I walk up to the counter to order another round of tea smoothies.

"Another taro boba for me, and a Thai tea boba for my...

friend." I look over my shoulder at Forrest, who latches on to my gaze, smiling at me like I'm walking sunshine on earth.

That settles it.

Forget playing with fire—I'm already walking through the dragon's flames, and without a doubt, I am totally, epically, and completely screwed.

Chapter 16

Forrest

Vampire fuckers, knotting, and the Vegas conundrum.

"I can't believe you're this excited about a bookstore." I laugh as Taio practically bounds ahead of us toward Turn The Page, one of Brooklyn's trendiest independent bookshops, according to Yelp.

"Man's about to cream his jeans over some paperbacks," Saylor mutters, his Australian accent adding an extra layer of mockery. "Bit sad, ain't it?"

"Fuck off," Taio calls over his shoulder, not slowing his pace. "No crime in appreciating literature."

I exchange a look with Saylor. "Did you have any idea he reads?"

"Nah, mate. You live with the guy, you didn't know about his fetish for romance books?"

"I mean, jerking off to the sex parts, sure," I answer. "But actually enjoying books? Never would've guessed."

"I can hear you dickwads," Taio retorts, pulling open the heavy glass door for us. "Mr. High-and-Mighty Columbia Law, you're not the only one who can read."

The bookstore is all exposed brick and weathered hardwood floors, with stacks stretching from floor to ceiling and the unmistakable scent of paper and coffee in the air.

"For the record," Saylor says as we step inside, "I'm not totally useless here. I once had a client who wanted me to read erotica to her while she—"

"We're in public," I cut him off, though I'm grinning despite myself. These idiots might be crude, but they're my idiots.

"What?" Saylor shrugs innocently. "I was going to say 'while she took a bubble bath.' Not everything leads to dirty, bare-ass spankings, Hawkins. Where's your sense of romance?"

Taio snorts. "Saylor, remember that baroness in London who said she just wanted you to cuddle, and then you ended up tying her up in her secret BDSM room?"

"Oh we cuddled," Saylor says. "For hours. With her hand clamped around my junk like a tire boot. I didn't think I was going to make it out of that one alive."

"Romance section," I interject loudly, pointing to the store directory. "Second floor, back corner."

"Classic," Saylor snickers, his eyes dancing with mischief. "Hide all the smut where the kiddies can't stumble on it."

"Speaking of stumbling onto smut," Taio says as we head toward the stairs, "remember that client who wanted you to dress as a lumberjack, Hawk? You had to get that glue-on beard. What was her name...Margaret? Marjorie?"

"Margot," I correct reluctantly. "And I told you that in confidence, asshole."

"Nothing's in confidence when you come home with splinters in your ass," Taio counters, earning a howl of laughter from Saylor.

"Christ, mate," Saylor wheezes, wiping actual tears from his eyes. "What were you two doing? Fucking on a log?"

"Authentic rustic furniture," I mutter, feeling my neck heat. "It was a cabin in the woods. Can you shut up about it now?"

"With authentic splinters," Taio adds helpfully.

I flip him off as we reach the second floor. "All right, focus. We're here for Sora."

"Ah, yes, the famous conch shell girl," Saylor says with exaggerated reverence. "The one who's got Hawkins all twisted up with those puppy-dog eyes." He whines and whimpers like a baby golden retriever.

"I'm not twisted up." Though the flush creeping up my neck probably tells a different story. "I'm helping her with research. In exchange for a place to stay with Dakota."

"And you brought us because...?" Taio prompts, already drifting toward the romance section with suspiciously familiar ease.

"Because of poor judgment, clearly. But seriously, I need to understand what's selling. What readers want. What Sora should be emulating." I lower my voice as we pass a cluster of browsing women. "You both deal with female fantasies for a living. I figured you might have some insights."

"Oh, I've got insights," Saylor says, waggling his eyebrows suggestively. "Women say they want a sensitive bloke who listens, but what they also want is to be bent over a couch, and after a proper pounding, for you to put your tongue right on their—"

"*Jesus, Saylor, we're in public*," I hiss, noticing a nearby shopper's scandalized expression.

"Just keeping it real." He shrugs, unrepentant. "Isn't that what you're asking for? The inside scoop on what women really want?"

"In their books," I clarify. "Not in their beds."

"Same thing, brochacho," Taio chimes in. "That's the whole appeal of romance novels. Classy girls doing really unclassy things."

I can't argue with that logic, so I don't try. Instead, I take in the romance section, which is more extensive than I expected, occupying nearly a quarter of the floor space. The shelves are organized by subgenre, with colorful, eye-catching covers facing outward.

"Fan out," I instruct, adopting what Taio calls my dad voice. "Taio, you take closed-door and paranormal. Saylor, contemporary and suspense. I'll handle fantasy and whatever 'dark romance' is."

"Uh, no, my guy. If there's no sex, I'm not reading it. Put Saylor on the fluffy cotton-ball stuff," Taio declares.

Saylor cuts him a side glance. "What is paranormal?" he asks.

"Vampire fuckers," Taio answers casually.

"Like that *Twilight* movie?" I ask, cautiously.

"Excuse me," Taio says, looking offended. "It was a book first, you caveman. And no, that stuff is for tweens. Adult paranormal is like vibrating alien dicks and werewolves knotting."

"What is knotting?" I immediately regret it when Taio opens his mouth to explain.

"It's when the hero's dick has a bulbous base that gets stuck—"

"Never mind," I interrupt hastily. "I don't want to know."

"Your loss," Taio says with a shrug, already running his fingers along the spines of books with a familiarity that's frankly disturbing. "Some of those shifter romances would blow your mind. And other parts."

As we disperse, I notice something odd. The bookstore has gone strangely quiet. Glancing around, I catch at least three women pretending not to watch us, phones angled suspiciously in our direction.

Great. Just what we need.

"Guys," I mutter under my breath, "I think we're being... documented."

Saylor, of course, immediately swivels his head, making direct eye contact with a blushing brunette who quickly pretends to be fascinated by a paperback.

"I fucking love the bookstore. It's like fishing in a tiny aquarium," Taio murmurs, deliberately flexing as he reaches for a book on a high shelf.

"Is this why you like books, Ty? Helps you get laid?" Saylor asks with genuine curiosity.

"Oh, *hell yeah.*"

Okay, now the pieces are falling into place. Taio reading to enhance his mind? *Suspicious.* Taio reading to chase tail? *Spot-on.*

"You think I could pull off damaged hero with a tragic past?" Saylor muses, striking a brooding pose. "The one who just needs the right woman to heal him."

"Please," Taio scoffs. "You're the comic-relief best friend. I'm clearly the smoldering love interest."

"You're both the comic relief," I deadpan. "Now cut the posing and focus. We're here to work."

"This is work?" Saylor sounds dubious as he pulls a book with a half-naked firefighter on the cover. "Mate, work is having to oil down a seventy-year-old widowed socialite who wanted me to—"

"Just find the bestsellers," I cut him off before he can finish that nightmare-inducing anecdote. "Look for multiple copies, special displays. Note the covers, the tropes." I run a hand through my hair, frustration mounting. "I need to help Sora figure out what's connecting with readers."

Taio, who's wandered to a table labeled "Staff Picks," whistles low. "Got ourselves a spicy one here. Listen to this: 'Olivia never expected her one-night stand to be her brother's best friend—or her new boss.' *Oh*, and judging by the blurb, Olivia has a secret," Taio adds with mock intrigue.

Saylor snorts. "She's a virgin, bet you anything. I swear brother's best friend always pairs with virgin."

"How do you know that?" I ask, surprised.

"My mum reads these by the cartload," Saylor explains, not looking up from the book he's flipping through. "Can't walk through the house without tripping over a bare-chested duke or a brooding billionaire."

"Nice," Taio says. "Bet your 'mum' has mad skills in the sheets. We should compare notes."

"I'll rip off your balls and feed 'em to your cat, mate. Leave my mum out of it."

"I don't have a cat," Taio says.

"I'll buy you one. That's how serious I am," Saylor says in a manner where I can't tell if he's kidding or trying to be menacing.

"*Sensitive*," Taio teases. "Your mom's a piece, SaySay. I'd treat her with nothing but tenderness and respect. Let this happen, man."

"She'd never go for a neanderthal who still thinks jackhammering away is what women want."

"Hey," Taio protests, "I've never had any complaints about

my technique."

"That's because they're paying you," Saylor fires back. "They're not gonna ask for a refund mid-thrust, are they?"

"Excuse me?" a soft voice interrupts their banter. "Can I help you find something?"

I turn to find a bookstore employee—petite, with a purple pixie cut and wire-rimmed glasses—regarding us with barely concealed curiosity.

"Actually, yes." I summon my most winning smile, the one that usually gets me past even the most vigilant doormen. "We're trying to understand romance subgenres. What's popular, what's trending. Any insights you could share would be great."

Her professional demeanor cracks slightly, a blush creeping up her neck. "Are you...writers?"

"Researchers," Taio supplies helpfully. "For a friend."

"A female friend," Saylor adds with a meaningful look.

"I see." Her smile widens, and she steps closer—too close for casual customer service. "Well, dark romance has been huge this year. Morally gray heroes, dubious consent scenarios."

"Dubious consent?" I repeat, alarmed.

"It's a fiction fantasy," she assures me quickly. "A safe way to explore power dynamics. Very popular with women who are tired of making decisions all day."

"What about paranormal?" Taio asks, picking up a book with what appears to be a shirtless werewolf on the cover. "Is that still poppin'?"

"Always steady," she says, turning toward him but keeping closer to me than strictly necessary. "Shifters, vampires, fated mates—those never go out of style."

"Fated mates?" I echo.

"Soulmates, essentially," she explains. "The idea that there's one perfect person for you, destined from birth. The characters often have an instant, overwhelming connection."

I nod, thinking of how Sora had described her own duet—a woman who thinks she's unlovable meeting a man determined to prove otherwise. Not fated mates exactly, but the reassurance of love finding you despite your flaws.

"What about these?" I gesture to a display of historical romances.

"*Bridgerton* effect," she says with a knowing smile. "Regency is massive again. But the modern historicals have more agency for the heroines, more explicit content."

Her hand brushes mine as she reaches for a book, the contact clearly deliberate. "This one's my personal favorite—rake reformed by the wallflower. I'm a sucker for a bad boy who changes his ways for the right woman."

She looks up at me through her lashes, the invitation unmistakable. "I can give you more detailed recommendations, if you'd like. My break's in fifteen minutes."

Out of the corner of my eye, I see Taio and Saylor exchange amused glances. The clerk—Anna, according to her name tag—is pretty, confident, and clearly interested. Six months ago, I might have taken her up on the offer. Hell, two weeks ago I might have been interested.

But all I can think about is Sora, her dark eyes wide and vulnerable as she talked about her fears, her dreams, her father's rejection.

"That's very kind," I say, taking a small step back. "But I should stick with my friends. We're actually doing this research for my girlfriend. She *is* an author. A really good one," I say proudly.

Taio makes a choking sound somewhere behind me. Anna's smile dims, but doesn't disappear entirely.

"Lucky girl," she says, recovering gracefully. "Well, if you need anything else, I'll be circulating the floor."

As she walks away, I brace myself for the inevitable onslaught.

"Girlfriend?" Taio hisses, appearing at my elbow. "Since when?"

"It's just easier than explaining," I mutter, turning back to the shelves.

"Easier than 'I'm only pretending to be her boyfriend so I

can live in her mansion while role-playing romantic fantasies that definitely won't lead to actual sex'?" Saylor asks, his tone dripping with mocking skepticism.

"It's not a mansion," I correct automatically. "It's a brownstone."

"Not the relevant part of that sentence, mate."

I ignore him, pulling a book with an illustrated cover from the shelf. It looks more sophisticated than the bare-chested models on the historical romances—a silhouette of a woman against a city skyline, the title in elegant gold script.

"Looks like chick lit," Taio says, peering over my shoulder.

"Women's fiction," corrects a female voice from the next aisle.

I turn to find a middle-aged woman with a stack of books in her arms giving Taio a stern look over her reading glasses.

"Contemporary romance with more emphasis on the heroine's journey," she continues, "including but not limited to her romantic relationships."

Taio, to his credit, looks suitably chastened. "My apologies, ma'am. Meant no disrespect."

"Hang on," Saylor says, moving to a display near the register. "What's all this 'BookTok Made Me Buy It' business?"

"TikTok recommendations," I explain, following him. "Viral videos about books. Daphne, Sora's best friend, mentioned it's a huge driver of sales these days."

"You already met her best friend?" Taio calls over, continuing his contempt for my situation.

I ignore him, scouring the display that's dominated by fantasy romance—lots of wings, horns, and mysteriously glowing eyes. But there are contemporary titles too, their covers more bold and graphic than the women's fiction I'd been examining.

"Romantasy," Taio says authoritatively. "That's the hot thing getting hotter. Romance plus fantasy elements. It's sweeping the publishing industry, the biggest return on investment for bookstores right now. That's all you see in book boxes these days."

"How do you know all that?" I inquire.

He shrugs, looking almost embarrassed. "I might have Instagram."

"You?" Saylor laughs. "Mr. 'Social Media Is for Validation-Seeking Sheep'?"

"Also for research purposes," Taio mutters. "Also for work."

"For work," Saylor repeats skeptically.

"Professional development," Taio insists with a straight face.

"Is that what we're calling it now?" Saylor snickers. "Because I've got some professional development scheduled for later tonight."

Taio smirks. "Work or play?"

"Play. A double inning if I'm feeling ambitious."

I roll my eyes at their antics. "Can we please focus on why we're here?"

"Yeah, good point. Let's focus on how Hawk is clearly falling for this writer girl," Taio counters. "Calling her your girlfriend to random bookstore clerks? That's not in Rina's escort handbook."

"Rina has a handbook?" Saylor asks, momentarily sidetracked.

"Figure of speech, dumdum."

I'm starting to regret bringing them along. "We're here to understand what Sora's up against in the market."

"Well, her books aren't here," Taio points out, gesturing around the store. "That tells you something."

The observation stings, though I know he doesn't mean it cruelly. I've been systematically scanning every shelf, every display, hoping to spot Sora's name. But there's no trace of her work in this carefully curated space.

"She's indie published," I explain, trying to ignore the sinking feeling in my gut. "Getting into physical bookstores is tough without a publisher behind you." I glance to my right and in the distance there's an entire themed display filled with her father's books. J.P. Cooper has his own section, even though it's an *indie* bookstore, and they can't leave an inch of shelf space for his daughter's work. Suddenly, I'm taking it personally.

"So she's competing with all...this"—Saylor waves a hand at

the sprawling romance section—"but without the distribution."

"Exactly."

"Rough gig," Taio comments, sliding a book back onto the shelf.

"A big publisher could get her into stores like this. What she really needs is an agent to take her on and get her some attention."

"But instead, she has you," Saylor observes. "Bit of a downgrade, I'd say."

"Thanks," I deadpan.

"No offense, mate, but you're not exactly Simon & Schuster. What do you honestly think you can do for this girl?"

"I don't know," I snap, more sharply than intended. "But I'm going to try. That's the deal."

"The deal?" Taio fixes me with a look. "Or is it something else now?"

I busy myself rearranging books, avoiding his stare. "What's that supposed to mean?"

"It means you called her your girlfriend to a bookstore clerk you'll never see again," Saylor reminds me. "That's not part of the *deal*, is it?"

"It was easier—"

"It was instinct," Taio intuits. "And we all know why."

I close my eyes briefly, exhaling through my nose. "Don't start."

"You like her," Saylor says simply. "The real kind of like, not the professional kind."

"I barely know her," I protest, but it sounds weak even to my own ears.

"Doesn't matter," Taio says. "I saw your face when you came home with that boba tea in your hand. I know that look."

"What look?"

"The 'I want this one for real' look," Saylor supplies helpfully. "Bet it's the same one you had when you met Hannah."

A jolt of alarm turns the blood pumping through my veins too hot. "This is nothing like Hannah."

"No, it's worse," Taio says. "Because with Hannah, you were just a college kid with nothing to lose. Now you've got Dakota, and debts, and a job that makes dating...complicated."

"It's not dating. It's an arrangement."

"An arrangement to live together and act out romantic fantasies," Saylor points out. "While you're clearly already halfway gone for her."

"Yeah, careful," Taio interrupts, his expression unusually serious. "You don't want to blur the lines. It takes one jilted date seeking revenge to take us all down. Don't toe that line, man." He circles his face with his finger. "You see this handsome mug? I like my job. I'm good at it. This is not the face of a man flipping burgers at Micky D's, okay? Keep it in line for all our sakes."

He's right. In our line of work, emotional entanglement is the cardinal sin. In a way, we're a brotherhood, and sticking to the rules protects all of us, and Rina. I've never tested that boundary.

Until now.

"Look," I say, dragging a hand through my hair. "I know what I'm doing. This is about Dakota. About getting her away from Hannah's fucked-up boarding school plan. The arrangement with Sora is mutually beneficial. That's all. I swear."

Neither Taio nor Saylor look convinced, but they mercifully drop the subject.

"So what have we learned?" Saylor asks, gesturing at the shelves surrounding us.

I survey the romance section, trying to organize my thoughts. "Romantasy is trending, especially with younger readers. Dark romance for the adrenaline junkies. Historical for the escapists. Contemporary for the realists."

"And tropes are key," Taio adds, unexpectedly insightful. "Brother's best friend, enemies to lovers, only one bed—readers go wild for that shit."

"One bed?" I repeat.

"You know, forced proximity," Taio explains with the air of a professor addressing particularly slow students. "Two people who have to share a space—preferably a bed—against their will. Snowstorms, power outages, booking mix-ups."

"How do you know all this?"

Taio shifts uncomfortably. "I might follow a few romance reviewers."

"A few?"

"A handful. Like...twenty."

Saylor bursts out laughing. "Closet softie."

"Shut up," Taio grumbles. "They're better company than you."

I stare at him, still genuinely surprised. In the three years we've lived together, I've never suspected Taio harbored a secret romance-novel addiction. But I'm starting to think there's a lot I don't know about my friends.

Saylor holds up a book depicting a menacing-looking octopus with a maiden in its clutches. "And how is reading books about tentacles going into places tentacles should never go, going to help your girl?"

"Jesus Christ," I mutter, pinching the bridge of my nose.

"Don't knock it till you've tried it," Taio says with a wink. "Some of the freakiest shit I've done was with the most buttoned-up clients. That corporate lawyer from last month? The one with the pearls and sensible pumps?"

"What about her?" Saylor asks, leaning in.

"Let's just say she had very specific instructions involving a ruler, hot wax, and a pair of dice."

"All right," I say loudly, checking my watch. "Let's wrap this up. I'm going to get a few of these for reference."

After some deliberation, I select six books spanning different subgenres—recommendations from both Taio and our bookstore clerk, Anna, who seems to have forgiven me for the "girlfriend" revelation. The total makes me wince, but I remind myself it's an investment in my arrangement with Sora.

"So," Saylor says as we head for the exit, shopping bag in hand, "when do we get to meet this conch shell girl? I'm dying to see who's got you all twisted up."

"You don't," I say firmly. "The last thing Sora needs is you two jackasses embarrassing me."

"Us? Embarrass you?" Taio fakes an innocent expression. "Never."

"I will literally pay you both to stay away from her," I threaten as we step onto the crowded sidewalk.

"Now, now," Taio tuts. "Is that any way to treat your support system? Your research assistants? Your—"

"Pains in my ass?" I finish for him.

"I was going to say 'voices of reason,' but sure, that works too."

As we make our way toward the subway, my phone buzzes with a text. I pull it out to find a message from Sora. It's a picture of a wall with three different paint swatches—various shades of purple.

> **Sora**
> **I'm debating painting Dakota's room. I know you said she likes purple, but which shade?**

> **The middle one. But you don't have to do all that.**

> **Sora**
> **I want to! These walls are so bland. I want her to feel at home and love her room. We should get her a new bed set too. Does she like Disney princesses?**

> **She's obsessed.**

Something in my chest squeezes tight. The thought of Sora planning for my daughter's comfort, wanting to make the brownstone feel like home for her... It hits me in a place I didn't know was so fragile.

"That her?" Taio asks, catching the look on my face.

"Maybe," I hedge, typing a quick reply.

> **Send me the swatch number. I'll pick up the paint and supplies and meet you at the brownstone. Give me a few hours.**

Sora
> **You sure? I don't want to ruin your weekend plans.**

> **I'm sure.**

Her response comes almost immediately.

Sora
> **Okay, great. It's a date.**

I jump back into my friends' conversation to hear Taio bellyaching about the cold.

"Cheapass," Taio mutters as we wait for the downtown train. "Saylor would rather have us sporting dicksickles because he's too stubborn to just pay for an Uber."

"Cab fare adds up. I don't mind the train," Saylor says.

"Couldn't agree more." I shrug, scrolling through Sora's messages one more time.

"Hey, know where it's warm? Vegas. We should fly out there this weekend for Hawk's bachelor party...since he's apparently getting married and all."

"*Not Vegas.* Do not bring up Vegas," Saylor warns, pointing an accusatory finger. "We agreed never to speak of Vegas."

Oh, city of sin. Two years ago when Saylor's mom needed

a medical procedure her insurance wouldn't cover, we booked a celebrity's bachelorette party. All three of us were hired as high-end escorts for the entire weekend. It should've been an easy cash-grab. More than enough to help Saylor's mom, except we never made it to the party. We unknowingly took a cab ride with a drug smuggler and got caught up in a major drug bust. Rina nearly had to fly down to Vegas herself to bail us out.

"Three days," Taio reminds us. "Three days of actual work we missed because we were in jail for something we didn't even do. Rina was livid."

"The casino footage cleared us eventually," I point out. "And didn't you salvage the weekend with that cute girl who carried a Yorkie in her purse at all times?" I ask Saylor.

"Yeah, but after we missed out on fifty grand in bookings," he grumbles. "That's the problem with this job, mate. The money's good when you can actually work, but the second your cock's not available for hire, you're broke."

"That's why I rarely take time off to date," Taio says, leaning against a grimy pillar. "Can't afford it. Why waste time buying dinner for some girl who might not even put out when I can get paid for the same time investment with a sure thing?"

"There's a difference between a work fuck and a fun fuck," Saylor argues. "You honestly need both to keep your sanity, mate. When's the last time you actually got laid for fun, Ty? And enjoyed it?"

Taio goes quiet, which is answer enough.

"That's what I thought. All these jokes about being a ladies' man, but all you're getting is the professional shag. That's not living."

"You're finding time for all that?" Taio asks. "Lately, I just don't see the point in casual sex outside of work. A relationship? Sure. If you find a girl who is okay with what we do and will stick with you despite it, please, clone her, or introduce us to her like-minded friends."

"That woman doesn't exist," Saylor says, suddenly serious.

"It's this job, or love. One or the other."

The train rumbles into the station, screeching against the rails, but I barely notice. Saylor's words hit too close to home.

"This is why I'm worried about you," Taio says quietly as we board the nearly empty car. "This thing with Sora...it's different. I get that. But how does this work? You're about to be roommates. You still have to work and make money, Hawk. Are you going to ask Sora to babysit Koda while you sneak out at night for a different client? How long do you think she'll put up with that before she kicks your ass out because of jealousy?"

I stay silent because I don't have an answer for that. All I can hope is that Sora doesn't feel about me the way I'm starting to feel about her. We'll both have to stay focused on the end goal of our arrangement.

She's saving my ass, putting up me and my daughter amidst Hannah's disastrous decision. The least I can do is put everything I have into helping Sora the best I can.

As the train lurches forward, carrying us back toward home, I find myself making a silent promise. Looking at the shopping bag of romance novels in my lap, thinking of Sora's books nowhere to be found on those shelves, I make a decision.

Someday, I'm going to walk into that bookstore—or one just like it—and see Sora's name on those shelves. Her books front-facing, multiple copies, pride of place. I'm going to help her make that happen, whatever it takes.

Even if it means breaking every rule in the unwritten escort handbook. Even if it means risking my heart in the process.

Because Sora deserves to be seen.

Perhaps I want to be seen too—not as the fantasy I sell, but by someone who accepts me for the man I am. I won't be an escort forever. It's a means to an end for now.

I think of the dedication Sora wrote me in her book *Lovely*.

Cheers to the journey.

Maybe she's different...maybe she doesn't mind a journey if the end destination is something real.

CHAPTER SEVENTEEN

Sora

Head... À la carte.

"I'm impressed by your handyman skills," I say, watching Forrest finish meticulously applying painter's tape along the baseboards of what will soon be Dakota's bedroom. "If I were doing this alone, it would've been a disaster. I didn't plan on taping anything."

Forrest glances up at me, a hint of amusement in his eyes. "You mean you wouldn't have taped the trim, or put plastic down on the hardwood floors before slathering purple paint all over the place? What could possibly go wrong?"

"In my defense, I've never painted a room before. It's not something I was ever taught." I adjust the bandana keeping my hair back from my forehead.

"Let me guess, your dad also never taught you to change a tire."

I snort in laughter. "That's hilarious. I don't even think my dad can change a tire. I was born and raised in Manhattan. We never had cars. Drivers, sure. But not cars."

"Ah, rich-girl problems." He smooths down a section of tape with practiced precision.

"Not exactly. We had a driver because my mom didn't like to take the subway alone, or bring a bunch of strange taxi drivers around a newborn baby. My dad was never around to help, so having a personal driver was one of the few luxuries she allotted. Otherwise, we always lived well below our means, even after Dad's fame exploded." I dip my roller in the paint tray, watching the globs drip off the brush.

"That's too much paint, Sora. Like this." Forrest puts his hand over mine and guides the brush against the clean, ribbed part of the tray, taking off the excess. "Hear that sound now? Just a little sticky—that's perfect for your best adhesion. Now, this paint has built-in primer, otherwise you would've needed a base coat. But now you can go straight to the wall. Long, smooth strokes."

"I got it now," I whisper, staring at his hand over mine. I don't flinch or pull away like I normally do. This time I let myself enjoy the warmth of his palm over the back of my hand until he releases me, proceeding to fill his own paint tray with purple paint.

"How long should the strokes be?" I pause with my brush about two inches from the wall, wondering what in the hell possessed me to think I could pull this off with no experience.

"Just do whatever you like, cookie girl." He holds up his roller brush. "I'll come around and clean up after you."

"I'll take 'cookie girl' over 'little conch shell,'" I mutter to myself, pressing the purple color into the clean white wall.

Forrest chuckles lightly to himself. "Speaking of your Korean name, what's your mom like? You seem to be a lot closer to her than your dad."

"Don't tell Daphne, but Mom's my best friend."

"What'd she say when you told her I was moving in with my daughter?"

I release a deep exhale. "I haven't told her." Since Mom's stomach bug on my birthday a couple weeks ago, I've made excuse after excuse about a reschedule. Mom thinks I'm deep in the writing cave. Truth is, I haven't written one word.

I've been distracted.

"What about your dad?" I ask, changing the subject as I carefully roll paint onto the wall. "Is that where you learned all this home-improvement stuff?"

"Yeah. Ranch life," he says, applying paint with efficient, even strokes that make my amateur attempts look pathetic. "Growing up, if something broke, you fixed it yourself. My dad wasn't the type to call in professionals unless it was absolutely necessary. Plumbing, electrical, building fences, raising and painting barns—I've done it all. Other kids played sports or started bands, but I worked after school and on weekends."

"That must have been hard as a kid."

"I must've thought that at the time. But now, I'm grateful." He shrugs, moving to another section of wall. "But it taught me to be self-sufficient. My dad worked me hard, but he was always right there beside me, showing us how to do things properly. He never asked me to do something he wouldn't do himself."

I study his profile as he works, noting the softness that enters his expression when he talks about his father. "You really admire him, don't you?"

"He's old-school. A good, simple man. Honest, hardworking. When everyone else in my life judged me for walking away from law, he just asked if I was sure about my decision. When I said yes, that was the end of it. He's supported me ever since."

"Even with your current job choice?"

Forrest's roller pauses mid-stroke. "He doesn't know the details. Just that I work in 'client services' in the city."

"That's not technically a lie."

"No, but it's not exactly the full truth either. I think he knows I'm lying, but he doesn't push. As long as my career supports Dakota, he doesn't care. Fatherhood is something he takes very seriously. If he thought I wasn't taking care of my daughter, he might get on a plane for the first time in his life, and try to belt me." He snickers as he resumes painting, his movements more deliberate now, like he's trying to get the job done.

"Speaking of your career...I've been meaning to ask you something that's been on my mind. How many women have you slept with? For work, I mean."

The silence that follows makes me regret the question

immediately. I sneak a glance at him to find him staring at me, paint roller suspended in midair.

"That's what you want to know?" he asks finally.

"If you'd rather not answer, I completely understand."

He returns to painting, though his strokes are more measured now. "I don't keep count. That would be weird."

"So a lot, then," I press, not sure why I'm torturing myself with this line of questioning.

"Not as many as you probably think," he says carefully. "A lot of clients just want company. Someone to take to an event, make an ex jealous, be arm candy at a business dinner."

"But some want more."

"Some do, yes." He looks at me directly now. "Is this going to be a problem? Because if it makes you uncomfortable thinking about what I do—"

"No," I say quickly. "I'm not judging you. I'm just curious. I'm a writer. I ask people questions, that's all."

He looks unconvinced but doesn't challenge my flimsy excuse. "It's not like I'm out there every night with a different woman."

"Do you have regulars?" I inquire.

"Only Celeste." He cocks a brow. "Which, like I told you, is strictly non-physical."

Something tight in my chest loosens at that revelation, which I immediately scold myself for. I have no right to feel relieved.

"What about you?" Forrest asks, clearly trying to turn the tables. "What's your number?"

I nearly drop my roller. "I'm not telling you that."

"Why not? You just asked me."

"And you didn't answer," I argue.

"I made an attempt. I told you, I don't keep count."

I sigh dramatically. "Fine. Three. Happy?"

"Three?" He sounds genuinely surprised. "Serial monogamist, huh?"

"Is that so surprising? Some of us actually need a connection before we jump into bed with someone."

"And yet you were ready to jump into bed with an escort you'd just met," he points out.

Heat floods my face. "I was high. And it wasn't sex, I just wanted to..." I'm not sure how to finish that sentence without making things more awkward. I just liked how he took me out of my head. He turned the worst night of my life into one of the best and I wanted to hold on to that feeling. I thought the only way he'd stay with me is if money were exchanged.

"Wanted what?" He pauses painting, and blinks at me.

"Nothing. Forget it." I focus intently on the wall in front of me.

"No, now I'm intrigued." He sets down his roller and walks over to me, paint-flecked arms crossed. "What did you want, Sora?"

"I don't know. I wanted a normal night with a normal guy." The second the words leave my mouth, I know I've messed up.

His playful expression falters slightly. "As opposed to abnormal me, the escort."

"No. That's not what I meant." I set down my roller and move closer to him.

"Isn't it?" His eyes bore into mine, searching.

"No, it's not." I reach out impulsively, touching his arm. "I'm sorry if it came out wrong. I just meant... Look, I got lost in wishful thinking. I think I was paying for an experience. It felt nice when I thought you were into me. That's all." *Oh god, I sound pathetic.*

His expression softens. "For the record, I was into you. The first time we met. That wasn't an act. I came to talk to you after your meeting. You blew me off."

For a moment, we just stare at each other, the air suddenly charged with something heavier than our usual banter.

"You liked me?" I don't even believe the words as I say them.

He grins sheepishly, breaking the tension. "But then I got to know you," he adds, "and discovered the real horror."

I gasp in mock offense. "Excuse me?"

"Your taste in paint colors." He shakes his head sadly, turning back to the wall. "It's truly tragic."

"You made the final decision. This is your travesty." I dip my fingertips in the paint can and flick them at him, splattering his shirt with tiny purple dots.

His jaw drops. "Oh, it's like that, is it?"

Before I can retreat, he's swiped his own fingers through the paint tray and is advancing on me with mischief in his eyes.

"Don't you dare," I warn, backpedaling. "This is my good painting shirt."

"As opposed to your bad painting shirt?" He lunges, and I dart around him.

We dance around the room, me trying to avoid his paint-covered hand, him trying to corner me. It's ridiculous and childish and somehow the most fun I've had in ages. I'm laughing so hard my sides hurt, and when he finally catches me around the waist, I surrender with minimal struggle.

"Okay, okay. Truce," I gasp through my laughter.

Instead of painting me, though, his fingers find my ribs, tickling mercilessly.

"Forrest," I shriek, squirming in his grasp. "Stop."

"Admit that you're attracted to me."

I squeal when he doubles his efforts. "No," I wheeze between ragged breaths. "I'm not a liar."

"Yeah, you are. We both are." His tickling intensifies even further, and I collapse against him, breathless with laughter.

"Fine, fine. You're all right," I secede, fearing I'm going to lose bladder control soon.

He immediately stops, but doesn't release me. I'm suddenly acutely aware of our position—my back pressed against his chest, his strong arms around my waist, my breathing rapid from more than just the tickling.

Heat radiates from his body, seeping through my thin T-shirt. I can feel the firmness of his chest, the tension in his muscles as he holds me. My heart pounds so loudly I'm certain he can hear it, and a delicious shiver runs up my spine when his breath tickles the sensitive skin below my ear.

"That's better," he murmurs, his voice low and close.

I turn in his arms, intending to push away, but instead find myself face to face with him, mere inches separating us. His eyes drop to my lips, then back up, a question in them. The air between us feels electric. My gaze traces the strong line of his jaw, the fullness of his lips, and I'm seized by a sudden, desperate longing to close the distance between us.

"Why are you looking at me like that?" he asks, his voice husky.

"Like what?" My own voice sounds hoarse and strange to my ears.

"Like you want me to kiss you again."

"Well, I'd ask, but you said I'm a terrible kisser."

He smiles. "I also just told you I'm a liar. And teasing you is my favorite new hobby." He runs his thumb over my cheek. "Guilty confession? It turns me on when you blush."

My heart hammers painfully. The logical part of my brain screams that this is dangerous territory, that I should laugh it off and step away. But my body has other ideas, rooting me to the spot, craving his touch like a physical ache.

"Maybe I do want you to kiss me," I whisper, surprising myself with my honesty.

A slow smile spreads across his face. "All you have to do is ask, Sora."

"I'm not good at this," I admit, trying to push him away with my palms against his strong chest. He doesn't budge, but my discomfort overcomes the tension between us.

"You're not good at what?"

"Being sexy and salacious. It's why I rarely write dirty talk. My characters kind of rush through sex with big, sweeping declarations of love. Not exactly what the readers want."

"Not that I'm complaining," Forrest says, still transfixed on my lips. "But why are you telling me this right now?"

"Because you're helping me with book inspiration, right?"

His lips turn down in a frown. "Sure."

"So, if I can't write it, what makes you think I can say it?"

I can *see* the epiphany dawn on his face. "I've been questioning my usefulness to you, but this I can do. I can teach you dirty talk. It's a second language for me."

I shake my head, my cheeks flaming. "No, thank you. I can think of nothing more awkward than you giving me a lesson in sex talk."

He pinches my side gently, but warningly. "I can. Like how awkward would it be if I tickled you until you peed yourself?"

"Forrest," I hiss. "Don't you dare."

"Tickle torture or lessons in dirty talk. Pick your poison."

"Fine. Tickle torture," I sass.

He shrugs and pulls me tighter against him. "Nope. Sorry. Dealer's choice. I'm going to demonstrate." There's a dangerous edge sharpening his tone now, and a curl of heat forms low in my belly. Forrest's eyes darken. He glances around the half-painted room, like he's come to a decision. "But not in here."

"What?"

Without warning, he scoops me up, one arm under my knees, the other supporting my back. I let out a startled rasp.

"What are you doing?"

"I'm not saying filthy things to you in my daughter's future bedroom," he explains, carrying me out into the hallway. "That would be weird."

"That's fair. Where are we going, then?"

"Your room." He navigates the staircase with impressive ease, considering he's carrying me. "The master suite, right?"

I nod mutely, suddenly nervous. But I don't tell him to put me down. I don't ask him to stop. Because deep down, beneath all my excuses about book authenticity, I want this. I want him... really bad.

My stomach flutters with a mixture of anticipation and anxiety. Flirting and banter are my native tongue. But now we're moving into Forrest's natural habitat. The land where panties melt underneath his smoldering gaze. Where women don't just ask, they beg on their knees.

What if I disappoint him? What if I'm a turn-off? Or even worse, what if all this is just another job to him? Dane's rejection is still raw in my mind... What if I'm also a "dime a dozen" to Forrest? Somehow that might hurt worse. The thoughts swirl mercilessly in my mind, but beneath them all is a singular, overwhelming and curious desire that drowns out every doubt.

He nudges open the door to my bedroom with his foot. The room is sparsely decorated; I haven't fully moved in yet. Just a massive king-sized bed with crisp white linens, a few boxes of clothes, and my laptop on the nightstand.

Forrest sets me down gently on the edge of the bed, then steps back, studying me. "You comfortable?"

I swallow hard. "Yes," I lie.

"You're blushing."

"I'm not in control of it," I say, covering my cheeks with my hands.

He doubles back, pulling my hands from my face. "Don't hide. I need to see you, and read your reactions."

"Huh?"

"I realize I'm taking you out of your comfort zone here, for the purpose of research of course," he says with a wink. "But I don't want to push you too far and upset you. I see you. I study you." He cradles my face, running his thumbs over my temples. "I know how your eyes turn down at the corners when you're about to cry. I know how the little veins above your temples flare when you're pissed but you're holding back what you really want to say. And I know you blush when you're lying. Like when you tell me you don't want me, you light up like a Christmas tree. Because you do, don't you?" He's standing between my knees, holding my head in place, looking down at me with an intensity that makes it hard to breathe. "I bet you want me almost as much as I want you."

"I don't know," I murmur, knowing without a doubt my cheeks are betraying me.

"You'd like to learn how to write good dirty talk, right, Sora?"

Call the cops and arrest this man, because the way he says my name should be illegal. "I suppose."

"Because your muse is right in front of you."

I swallow loudly, surrendering to his burning gaze without flinching. "Fine. We can talk about it."

"Just talk?" His hand comes up to my face, his thumb tracing my lower lip. "Or do you want me to show you, too?"

I nod slowly, not trusting my voice.

"Use your words," he murmurs, and the demand in his tone sends another rush of heat through me. "Tell you or show you?"

"Show me," I whisper.

His smile is predatory, and now I'm all too aware of the impatient tingling in my nipples. Without warning, he tugs the bandana from my hair. I blink in confusion as he stretches it between his hands.

"Close your eyes," he instructs.

I comply, my heart thundering like a stampede of beasts.

The soft fabric of the bandana slides over my eyes, blocking my vision completely as he ties it securely behind my head.

"Is this okay?" he asks, his voice closer now, breath warm against my ear.

I nod, then remember his instruction. "Yes."

"Good girl," he praises, and something about the simple phrase makes my insides clench with need. "Now, just listen. *Feel.* Try to get out of your head."

The bed dips as he sits beside me. I can feel the heat of him, even though we're not touching.

"The problem with dirty talk," he says, his tone conversational, as if we're discussing the morning traffic, "is that people overthink it. In writing, don't try to make it poetic or clever. Real dirty talk is raw, gritty, and above all things, it's honest. Just saying exactly what you want when you want it. No etiquette, no apologies. Simply primal. That's what drives a woman to the brink."

His hand lands on my thigh, just above my knee, and I jolt

slightly at the contact.

"Now, some women want to be praised," he continues, his hand sliding upward with agonizing slowness. "Told how beautiful they are, how good they feel. Others want to be degraded a little—called names, ordered around. The key is knowing your partner, understanding what makes them respond. All women have little tells. You have to pay attention."

"I can't exactly see my readers through the page, Forrest," I complain. "And books are written long before the reactions they elicit. So that's not exactly helpful."

He groans. "Sora, I'm trying to do a thing here. I realize my metaphors aren't perfect, but can you roll with it, killjoy?" His fingers trace maddening patterns on my inner thigh, not quite high enough to provide any real satisfaction, but enough to make me want to close my legs down on him.

"Sorry. Continue. I'll behave." I suck in a sharp breath when his hands graze an inch higher.

"Great. Back to class. So, for example"—his voice drops an octave—"right now I can tell by the way your breath hitched that you like when I touch you here." His hand skates higher, thumbs brushing dangerously close to where I'm starting to ache for him. "And I can see your nipples hardening through your shirt. You think that sassy mouth shields you, but your body is betraying you, Sora. I wish I could see into your mind, witness all the filthy things you want me to do to you right now."

I bite my lip to stifle a whimper, embarrassed by how accurate his assessment is.

"Just describe one of them," he murmurs. "I want to hear it from you. That'd be so sexy."

His other hand slides up my back, tangling in my hair. When he speaks again, his mouth is right beside my ear, his voice a low growl.

World dark behind the blindfold, I shake my head. "I...just can't. Can you please start and I'll try to pile on?"

"Sure, baby. That's fine. I have more I want to say anyway, like how I want to taste every inch of you, my sweet cookie girl. I want to run my tongue over your nipples and suck on them until they're hard enough to cut glass. I want to slide my fingers inside you and feel how wet you are for me."

If it wouldn't kill the mood, I'd grab my phone and set up an audio recording. I'd trap a little sexy Forrest essence for writing inspiration later. But the further we go, the less I'm thinking about words on the page, the more I'm thinking about Forrest's lips on my body.

I clear my throat, my mouth suddenly dry. I feel him smile against my skin.

"Are you getting a little impatient?" he encourages. "I want to dive in so bad, but I bet the teasing gets you soaked. That's how we both want it, right? You, drenched. Me, swimming laps in your sweet pussy."

I nod, beyond embarrassment now, lost in the sensation of his voice, his touch, the darkness behind the bandana heightening every feeling.

"Say it," he commands. "Tell me how you feel."

"*Wet.* My thong is wet," I whisper, the admission sending another current of desire through me. "Sorry, that's not sexy... I um, I think that's the best I can do in the way of dirty—"

"Shh, you're still in your head. Just feel, remember? I happen to think that was sexy. Such a good girl telling me your panties are wet," he praises again. "Can I see? Can I take them off?" His fingers hook into the waistband of my paint-splattered yoga pants. "Lift your hips for me."

I immediately obey, letting him peel my pants down my legs. The cool air hits my heated skin, making me shiver.

"God, look at you," he breathes, and I can hear the genuine want in his voice. "These too?" His fingers tease the edge of my underwear, and I nod frantically.

"Yes."

They join my pants somewhere on the floor, and now I'm half naked, blindfolded, trembling with anticipation.

"Lie back," he instructs, and I do, the soft bedspread cool against my back. "Spread your legs for me."

The vulnerability of the position delivers an alarm of self-consciousness into my head, but it's quickly overwhelmed by guttural need as he settles between my thighs, his breath warm against my most intimate place.

"You are so fucking beautiful," he murmurs against my skin. "Is this what you want? To come from my mouth?"

Before I can process, his tongue is on me, hot and insistent, drawing a startled cry from my throat. The initial touch is almost too much—a jolt of pure sensation that makes my thighs tense and my back arch off the bed. The blindfold heightens everything, leaving me helpless to do anything but feel.

"That's it," Forrest growls against me, his voice vibrating through my sensitive flesh. "Let me hear you."

He starts with long, deliberate strokes, mapping me with his tongue as if committing every fold and texture to memory. My hips rise involuntarily, seeking more pressure, more friction, more of everything he's giving me. His strong hands grip my thighs, holding me open, controlling my movements.

"So responsive," he purrs appreciatively. "Your body tells me exactly what it wants."

When his lips close around my clit and suck gently, a broken moan escapes me, my fingers clutching desperately at the bedspread. The dual sensation of his tongue flicking against me while his lips create perfect suction is overwhelming. My legs begin to tremble, toes curling as tension builds low in my belly.

"Forrest," I gasp, one hand reaching down to tangle in his hair. The silky strands slip through my fingers as I hold him against me, not wanting him to stop, not wanting this feeling to end.

He hums in approval, the waves of vibration dizzying me. "You taste even better than I imagined," he tells me, his breath hot against my slick flesh. "I could do this for hours."

The thought of hours under his skilled mouth nearly sends

me over the edge then and there. My breathing is wrecked, my chest heaving with each gasp and moan. I'm beyond shame now, beyond self-consciousness. There's only the climbing pressure, the exquisite tension, the relentless pursuit of release.

"Please," I whimper, though I'm not even sure what I'm begging for.

Forrest seems to know. His tempo changes, becoming more focused, more deliberate. His tongue circles my clit in tight patterns that have me writhing beneath him, my head thrashing against the pillows.

"You're so close," he observes, his voice thick with desire. "I can feel it. Your pussy is pulsing against my tongue. Am I doing a good job, baby?"

"Yes," I moan. "But faster," I beg.

"There you go. Tell me how to make you come."

Desire is a raw and visceral creature that takes over me, like a predator with eyes fixed on its prey. I don't care about anything. Not a damn thing in the world matters right now except to find my release. "Make your tongue wetter, and flick the tip against my clit. I need your fingers too."

"So. Fucking. Perfect. Your little pussy is my favorite playground. I'm going to have you singing in a minute, baby."

The vulgar words, spoken in his deep, commanding voice, pummel me with another deluge of arousal. My thighs try to close against the intensity, but his broad shoulders keep me spread open, completely at his mercy.

When he slides a finger inside me, I cry out at the sudden fullness. He works it slowly at first, getting me used to the sensation, then adds a second finger, stretching me deliciously.

"So tight," he groans, the rumble of his voice warm against my core. "You're gripping my fingers like you never want to let go."

He curls his fingers forward, finding that spot inside me that makes stars explode behind my eyelids. Combined with the relentless attention of his tongue on my clit, it's too much. The tension that's been building snaps suddenly, violently, sending waves of pleasure radiating outward from my core.

"Forrest!" His name tears from my throat as I come hard against his mouth. My body arches like a bow, every muscle taut as the orgasm crashes through me. He doesn't let up, his fingers still moving inside me, his tongue still working my clit as tremors rack my body.

Wave after wave of euphoria wash over me, each one slightly less intense than the last, until I'm pushing at his head, oversensitive and trembling. Even then, he gives me one final, gentle kiss before relenting, his fingers withdrawing slowly.

The bandana is gently untied, and I blink against the sudden light. Forrest is looking at me with a mix of satisfaction and what looks suspiciously like genuine affection.

"That," he says, wiping his mouth with the back of his hand in a gesture that should be gross but is somehow incredibly hot, "was really well done."

I let out a breathless laugh, feeling gloriously boneless. "I didn't do anything. I just lay here."

He smirks. "Well, you lay there perfectly. You did exactly what I told you to and got out of your head. Good girl."

I'm completely spent, yet the stirring begins again below my navel. "I may have a bit of a praise kink."

"I guessed that," he says with a sly smile. "It was either 'good girl' or 'my dirty little slut.'"

I narrow my eyes at him. "Don't ever call me a slut if you want this to go any further." I glance down at the bulge in his pants.

He grins, stretching out beside me on the bed. "Noted. But maybe we should pause here. Get cleaned up and finish painting?"

Reality crashes back in. *Stop? Is this rejection?* "Why? You're not into it?"

He shakes his head, looking genuinely regretful. "The opposite. Wasn't exactly planning for this when we set out to paint a kid's room. I don't have a condom on me. Do you?"

"No," I say. "We could do other stuff, though. Do you want a blowjob? It's only fair."

"Fair?" Forrest asks, absentmindedly. "Sora, you did your part. Koda and I have a home, right? I'm here so *you* can explore. You don't need to worry about what I want."

Shame presses me into the mattress like dead weight. I know he didn't mean it, but his statement makes me feel dirty and used. This wasn't an organic moment of passion. He licked me clean to earn his keep. Fuck, I slipped. For a moment it felt...so real.

I hold my palm over my clit and spread my fingers, trying to cover as much of my nakedness as possible. "I should probably..."

"Let me," he says, retrieving my underwear and pants from the floor. As I put them back on, he watches with undisguised appreciation.

"Are you all right?" he asks once I'm dressed again.

"Yeah," I mumble. "Fine."

His eyes drop to the floor, then flash back to mine. "Except you're blushing. So, you're lying."

I place my hands on my hips, childish angst pouring over me. "Out of curiosity, how much would you charge a woman to go down on her, let's say à la carte?"

His eyes harden, my question clearly pissing him off. "Why would you ask me that?"

I shrug. "Just curious what the going rate for head is."

He sucks the air between his teeth and smacks his lips, matching my haughty temper. "A grand. Maybe less for a woman like you because you came really quick." He lifts his brows. "I barely broke a sweat."

"Good to know," I snark before brushing past him toward the door.

He catches my wrist, yanking me back. "Something you want to talk about?"

"No. I think we've talked plenty." I soften my demeanor slightly and nod toward the door. "Come on, let's finish painting."

I hold his stare and mentally talk some sense into myself. It's a business arrangement, Sora. Don't fall for a man who will never, ever belong to you. This is all just research.

"If you're sure," Forrest says softly, releasing my arm.

"I'm sure."

Just business, I remind myself. If I keep saying it over and over...

Maybe eventually I'll believe it.

CHAPTER EIGHTEEN

Forrest

I've got my sea legs now.

Celeste's yacht dwarfs every other vessel in the marina—a gleaming display of wealth stretching nearly two hundred feet. From the upper deck, I watch the sunset light up the Manhattan skyline, as I try to shake the knot in my gut.

"You're brooding," Celeste observes, handing me a champagne flute. "Not a good look for your big night."

"My big night?" I ask. "I told you this was all for another client."

She gives me a knowing look. "Ah, so we're still stuck on that narrative."

I haven't seen Sora properly in three days. After what happened at the brownstone—after I tasted her, made her come apart under my tongue—she retreated behind a wall of distance. We finished painting Dakota's room in silence, ate DoorDashed burgers, without talking about anything real. We plunged into the deep end, then Sora resurfaced, sputtering and gasping, and apparently promising never to get too close to me again.

Sora's been strategically avoiding me while she can. Dakota and I move into the brownstone this weekend. I wanted to break the ice with Sora before we went from uncomfortable friends to uncomfortable roommates. So, I planned and invited her on our first role-play date—the billionaire experience.

I can't stop thinking about what might've set her off. I thought I had her. The way she trembled, those soft sounds she made, the vulnerability in her eyes. But then she followed up the affair with her question about how much I'd charge for what we'd done...

I know something triggered her.

And her question stung more than I want to admit.

"Earth to Forrest," Celeste says, snapping her fingers. "You're gone again."

"Sorry." I sip the champagne, bubbles sharp on my tongue. *Gross*. It was supposed to be a prop in my hand as I wait for Sora to arrive, yet I keep absentmindedly sipping it. "Just thinking."

"About what?" Celeste's lips curve knowingly.

"What if I admit I'm in uncharted territories?" I ask.

"Then you'd finally clue in to what the rest of us have," she answers. "But I don't really see the problem." She straightens my jacket collar, her touch efficient rather than intimate.

I shrug, scanning the horizon. "Question for you—could you ever love an escort? Accept his past, embrace his future."

Celeste's silence says it all.

"Exactly," I add bitterly. "Disregarding how I feel, is this a safe game to play? What if I do my job too well?" I had to fill Celeste in on the ruse I've cooked up for Sora, and my plight to help her career, when I asked for her help. Short of buying a big-five publisher herself and putting Sora on shelves, Celeste eagerly pulled out all the stops for this evening.

"Meaning she falls for an act and not the real you?"

"Possibly. I act so much, I don't ever remember the real me."

She studies me, head tilted. "I went out on a date with this cute younger guy, all innocent of course, and you know what he told me?"

I know damn well she's talking about me. It's why Celeste still hires me to escort her to events—she doesn't want to date right now. I doubt another suitor has miraculously appeared in the past couple weeks. "What'd he say?"

"It's never too late to start over...rewrite your story. If you're tired of the act, maybe it's time to make a change. Leave the business. You know you'd have Rina's full support." Sometimes I forget Celeste is dear friends with my boss.

"Using my words against me," I muse.

"*Inspiring* you with your own words. What's your hesitance?" Celeste asks. "You'll miss the thrill of all the different women?"

"Not remotely," I quickly answer. "I'll miss the guaranteed paycheck. There's nothing else I can do that makes this amount of money, this quickly, without requiring me to put my degree to use." Not to mention, if I so much as upload a résumé to Indeed, Sean and his firm would cook me like a sunburn. They won't let me take any type of corporate job until their debt is repaid.

"There are more important things than money," Celeste intones, surveying her luxurious yacht. "All this, and do you think I'm happy?"

"Dakota needs me to have a solid income and flexible schedule. Escorting just makes sense for now."

"But does it?"

The question hangs between us. Before I can answer, a sleek town car pulls up to the marina entrance. Through the lightly tinted windows, I catch a glimpse of long, dark hair.

"She's here," I say, my mouth suddenly dry.

Celeste follows my gaze. "Then that's my cue to disappear. The chef, servers, and captain all know the plan." She presses a quick kiss to my cheek. "Maybe tonight, try to be yourself."

"Dressed like this?" I ask, touching the lapels on my tux.

"You're in a tux these days more often than not. Maybe this is the new you."

I roll my eyes. "Thank you for this." I mean it. "I owe you."

"Consider us even if this actually works out." She winks and unburdens me of my champagne flute before she heads for the gangway.

As Celeste leaves, I watch Sora step out of the car. She pauses, looking up at the yacht with uncertainty and awe. The dress she wears—the same one I tore at the wedding, now perfectly restored by Celeste's team—hugs her curves in all the right ways. The pink fabric, veiled in black tulle, catches the fading light, making her glow against the darkening sky.

For a moment, I pretend this isn't an arrangement or research or whatever we've been telling ourselves. Right now, she's just a woman I adore, and this is just a date I've been looking forward to.

"Permission to come aboard?" Sora calls up, shielding her eyes from the setting sun. "Do people still say that?"

"No," I call back, before I hustle down the stairs to meet her. Once we're close, I extend my arm, cradling her hand with mine. I press my lips to the back of her hand. "But permission granted. You look like royalty."

Her fingers feel cool in mine, her grip light. Up close, I notice the nervous pulse at her throat, the careful makeup, the slight tremor in her smile. "Thank you. Perfect compliment, sir." She gestures at the yacht around us. "This is…a lot."

"Too much?" I ask, suddenly unsure. Maybe this was overkill. Maybe a quiet dinner somewhere would've been better. "Isn't over the top right on the nose for a billionaire romance?"

Her smile relaxes into genuine. "It's magnificent. Just unexpected. When you said we were going to research the billionaire trope, I thought we'd have to use our imaginations. But this feels…quite real."

"Go big or go home," I quip, trying to mask my nerves. "Daphne mentioned you've dabbled in billionaire romances. Does this match up to your vision?"

"Far exceeds," she answers softly.

A server approaches with champagne. I take two glasses, hand one to Sora, then dismiss him with a curt nod—channeling the impatient billionaire I'm supposed to be portraying.

"Thank you so much," Sora calls after him, her sweet, innocent etiquette unsuppressable. She turns to me, her lips morphing into a giddy-like smile. "Butlered champagne? Nice touch."

"You haven't seen anything yet." I offer my arm, which she takes after a brief pause. "Welcome aboard *Artemis*. For the next four hours, she's all ours."

Sora's eyes widen as we walk through the main salon. Mahogany walls gleam around us, custom furniture arranged perfectly. The chef and his team work silently in the galley, prepping our dinner. A string quartet plays in the corner—according to Celeste, an essential addition to the evening.

"This is incredible," Sora says, running her fingers along the polished bar. "How did you arrange all this?"

"I have my resources," I reply, deliberately vague. The powerful billionaire wouldn't explain himself.

We settle at a table on the aft deck, the Manhattan skyline providing a perfect backdrop as we cast off. The server presents our first course—tuna tartare with avocado mousse.

"To research," I say, raising my glass. "And new experiences."

Sora clinks her glass against mine, eyes never leaving my face. "To research," she echoes, though her tone suggests she's not fully buying my explanation.

As we work through the incredible courses—lobster with black truffle, wagyu beef with foie gras, a palate-cleansing sorbet—I settle into my role. I give the staff curt instructions, make decisive wine selections, and generally act like a man used to getting whatever he wants.

"You're good at this," Sora notes as they clear our main course. "Almost too good. Are you keeping secrets from me, Forrest?"

"Perhaps," I say, replacing the small sip of wine she took. I made a note to keep her glass full all night out of chivalry, but she's barely touched it.

"So, the commanding presence, the subtle arrogance. You've done your homework. Did you binge-read about a dozen romance books over the past couple days?"

"Google," I admit. "But this isn't so different from what I do with clients. I just dial up certain parts of myself and dial down others."

"Which parts are you dialing up tonight?"

I watch the candlelight play across her face. "Control. Power.

The illusion that I can have anything I want." My eyes rake across her bare collarbones. "Which is most definitely not true."

"I never understood that fantasy," she muses softly. "Women wanting a man to hand them the world."

"What appeals to you?"

She smiles sheepishly. "Taking the world for myself. Hanging my own moon. Being an important part of a team."

"I like that," I acknowledge before dropping my voice to a whisper. "But that's not what we're doing here tonight. You're supposed to feel like Cinderella. Special. Singled out and chosen by the prince who will keep your fine ass in Valentino and Louboutins until the day you die."

Something flickers in her eyes—recognition, maybe. "Is that Hannah's fantasy?"

The question comes at me from far left field. I didn't really expect her to come up tonight. Talking about Hannah pulls me out of the fantasy and right back down to earth. "Unequivocally, but at least she knows what she wants and won't settle for less. Some people would see that as an admirable quality," I say finally, biting back my unbridled thoughts about Hannah.

"You're defending her, even after she's leaving Dakota?"

I rub the back of my neck in discomfort. "Sora, I'm a country boy at heart. And I was raised by Sam Elliott's doppelganger who would spit in my face and disown me if he heard me disrespecting the mother of my child out loud. So, I don't want you to think that just because I refuse to badmouth my ex, I still have feelings for her. I don't. But I am forever grateful she gave me Dakota."

Sora blinks at me quietly for what seems like a ridiculous amount of time. She doesn't say a word and finally the quiet tension unnerves me. I have to break the ice.

"What's wrong?"

She taps her temple. "I'm just reciting that speech in my head over and over so I can remember it, because that, Forrest Hawkins, is going in my next book. Very hero-worthy. And for the record, I don't need you to talk shit about your ex to feel secure."

I smile, warm relief flooding through my chest. "What do you need to feel secure?"

"From you?" she asks. I nod, and her lips twist as she debates a reply. "Nothing. I don't think I'll ever feel secure around you."

Once again, she accidentally wounds me, inviting the elephant I thought we dismissed right onto this ship deck.

"Oh," she suddenly muses, palming her forehead with an audible smack. "You meant how to make me feel secure on a date with a billionaire?" she concludes, completely misunderstanding my intention. But I roll with it, yet another reminder that this is all just a game.

Dessert eventually arrives—a decadent chocolate soufflé with chocolate-covered strawberries on the side. I pick up one of the strawberries and hold it to Sora's lips.

"You're really taking this seriously," she murmurs, but opens her mouth anyway.

I watch as her lips close around the fruit, and her eyes flutter shut. A drop of chocolate lingers at the corner of her mouth, and I reach across to wipe it away with my thumb.

"Forrest," she says, voice slightly throaty, "are you always this attentive? Or is this just part of the billionaire act?"

"What do you think?" I counter, enjoying the flash of frustration in her eyes.

She purses her lips. "I think you're deliberately being enigmatic."

"And you're being deliberately avoidant." I lean back, studying her. "Why don't you feel secure around me, Sora?"

A server appears to refill our glasses, and Sora relaxes at the interruption. When he leaves, I wait, letting the silence build until she can't ignore my question any longer.

"Fine," she sighs. "I don't feel secure because I never know which version of you I'm getting. The escort? The devoted dad? The wannabe lawyer? The fake boyfriend?"

"Does it matter?" I ask, genuinely curious. "They're all me."

"Are they, though?" She leans forward, gaze intense. "How do

I know what's real and what's performance?"

"We agreed to this arrangement," I insist. "I didn't lie to you about being an escort. I omit details, sure, because I don't like talking about women like they're conquests. I keep intimacy private. Other than me spilling my guts about all the women I've been with, I can't for the life of me figure out what came alive and jumped up your ass after we fooled around. What is it, Sora? I keep going over it in my mind... Did I come on too strong while we were painting? Did you feel forced or pressured? Are you upset because we didn't fuck? I'm at a loss. Just talk to me."

Whatever billionaire sophistication I was harboring has gone out the window.

"That was direct," she remarks with startled eyes. "You're really not into the miscommunication trope, are you?"

My eyes pinch in confusion. "*What*?"

Before she can answer, the captain approaches to inform us we're nearing the Statue of Liberty, our turnaround point.

"Want to see the view from the upper deck?" I ask Sora.

She takes the offered escape route, standing gracefully. "Lead the way."

The night air feels cool as we climb the steps. City lights spark across the water, the stars barely visible above. The Statue of Liberty stands ahead, illuminated against the dark sky.

"It's stunning," Sora says, moving to the railing. "I've lived here my whole life and somehow never done this."

"Never taken a dinner cruise?"

"Never been on a yacht," she corrects. "Not even my dad has money like this. And even if he did, he wouldn't spend it on romance."

"I'm starting to understand why your parents didn't work out," I joke.

"You don't say," she joins in, a flicker of her usual sassy demeanor returning.

"Celeste is a special case," I offer. "All that stuff you said earlier about taking the world for yourself, hanging your own moon? Even rich women do that. Celeste, and my boss, Rina, both married into wealth. But they weren't afraid to walk away and carve their own path when love was lost and all that remained was money."

Sora nods in agreement. "I respect the hell out of that. My mom was the same. She never wanted to be with a celebrity author. She just wanted to be seen."

She leans over the railing. Her repaired dress, messengered over this morning, has little sparkles in the tulle now. It wasn't like that at the wedding. Celeste certainly knows how to enhance a gown.

"I was a jerk to you, and I'm sorry. I felt guilty, so much so, I bought Dakota a lot of new toys. I also stocked the fridge with kid-friendly things, but also healthy stuff."

I rub my palm in slow circles against her lower back. "You were a jerk to me, yet you're doting on my daughter?"

"Yeah," Sora says, eyes fixed on the water. "She's the way to your heart. Anybody who knows the real you can see that."

Knows the real me. I like how that sounds. "True. Is that what you're after? My heart?"

"No," she squeaks, whipping around. She looks scared, like I just pressed a self-destruct button and now we're waiting for the apocalypse to commence.

"What the—"

Palms in the air in surrender, Sora elaborates. "I live in my head, Forrest. Day in, day out. Creating scenarios, hopping from one mental vision board to another. And when we did what we did the other day, I think it caught me off guard because while we were playing, the pleasure was very real. I got confused for a minute, but I swear, I think I've got my sea legs now." She grins goofily, proud of her circumstance-appropriate pun.

"Your sea legs?"

"Right. I need to get lost in the moments, but not lose touch with reality. And I think I have the solution."

"Great, lay it on me."

She sucks in her lips, her gaze dropping from mine down to the hem of her dress. "We need to have sex. A lot of it. To the point we're desensitized."

Shocked, I blink at her. "While I like the 'a lot' part, I don't think desensitized sex is going to be particularly fun for either of us."

"No, not like that." She rolls her eyes and her wrist. "We can finish and stuff, I just mean we should focus on the mechanics more than the emotion. We should have sex the way you do with your other clients."

Her words hang in the air between us, the casual suggestion at odds with the way her voice trembles slightly. The night breeze picks up, sending a tendril of her hair across her face. I tuck it behind her ear, letting my fingertips linger against her skin.

"Is that what you think I do with my clients? Have emotionless sex?"

She shrugs, aiming for nonchalance but missing by a mile. "Isn't that the point? It's a transaction, not a connection."

I step closer, forcing her to tilt her head back to maintain eye contact. "You really think you can separate the physical from the emotional so cleanly? That you can compartmentalize like that? It's not that easy."

"Of course I can," she answers too quickly. "I'm an adult. I understand the arrangement and the end goal."

Her chin lifts in that stubborn way I'm starting to recognize, but her eyes betray her—wide and uncertain, like she's trying to convince herself more than me.

"Sora." I keep my voice low, intimate. "You're a romance writer. You literally make your living writing about emotional connections. And you're telling me you can have meaningless sex for the sake of research?"

"Yes." Her answer is firm, but her fingers fidget with the fabric of her dress.

I study her face, searching for the truth behind her bravado. "You don't believe that."

"I do," she insists, crossing her arms like armor against her chest. "I have to believe that or this won't work. Us, too entangled... doesn't work."

There's logic in her words, but her eyes tell a different story. They've always been her tell—those expressive dark eyes that reveal every emotion she tries to hide.

"All right," I say finally. "Let's test your theory."

Her brows furrow in confusion. "What do you mean?"

I move closer, until there's barely a breath between us. "If you can have emotionless sex, then surely you can handle an emotionless kiss."

Her breathing quickens visibly, her lips parting slightly. "Right, right. Of course."

I tilt her chin up with one finger. "Unless you're afraid I might prove you wrong."

"I'm not afraid," she says, the defiance in her voice betrayed by the flush spreading across her cheeks.

"Then close your eyes."

For a moment, I think she'll refuse. Then, with a small exhale of surrender, her eyelids flutter shut.

I take my time, studying the delicate lines of her face in the moonlight—the curve of her cheekbones, the slight wrinkle between her brows, the nervous tremble of her full lips. I've kissed her before, but not like this, never with this strange mixture of hope and fear twisting in my chest. I'm so desperate to prove her wrong.

When I finally lean in, I brush my lips against hers with exquisite gentleness—a whisper, a question, a beginning. She remains perfectly still, as if afraid to shatter whatever fragile thing is building between us. I trace the seam of her lips with my tongue, coaxing rather than demanding, and feel the small gasp she tries to contain.

Her hands come up hesitantly, fingers splaying across my chest, neither pushing away nor pulling closer. I deepen the kiss gradually, my hands framing her face, thumbs stroking the soft skin of her cheeks. There's no rush, no urgency—just a slow, deliberate exploration that feels more intimate than any passionate embrace.

When her lips part beneath mine, the kiss transforms. What began as tender becomes something far richer. Her hands slide up to my shoulders, then to the nape of my neck, fingers threading through my hair. I taste the chocolate dessert we shared, the wine she barely sipped, and something uniquely Sora that makes my pulse thump like an eight-oh-eight drum.

I kiss her like I mean it—because I do.

Like she matters—because she does.

I kiss her like a man who's discovering something precious rather than performing a service. And when she makes that small, broken sound in the back of her throat, I know I've won this particular battle.

When I pull back, her eyes remain closed, her lips still slightly parted. For several heartbeats, she doesn't move, as if caught in a spell she can't quite break.

"Sora," I whisper.

Her eyes open slowly, dazed and vulnerable in a way that makes my chest tighten. I watch the awareness return, watch her rebuild the walls I just managed to breach.

"Did you feel anything?" I ask, already knowing the answer but needing to hear her admit it.

She swallows hard, then forces a careless smile that doesn't reach her eyes. "Nope," she lies smoothly. "Completely immune. See? I told you I could compartmentalize."

It's such an obvious untruth that I almost laugh. Instead, I sweep my thumb across her lower lip, noting how it flinches at my touch. Her cheeks deepen in a familiar red that gives her away so easily.

"Liar," I murmur, but there's no heat in the accusation.

She steps back, creating space between us, her smile fixed in place. "It was a nice kiss. A little sloppy, but don't worry—we'll get you there."

I belt out in laughter as the yacht begins its final turn back toward the marina, the city lights growing clearer as we approach.

"This was so lovely," Sora says, pairing it with a sigh. "I can't believe it's already over."

"Over?" I wrap my arms around her, pecking her cheek as we look out at the dark water, New York City lights sparkling across the surface. "I still have a few tricks up my sleeve."

CHAPTER NINETEEN

Sora

This reckless fucker is trying to make me fall in love with him.

Who kisses like that on accident?

The thought blazes through my mind like a comet, bright and terrifying and impossible to ignore as I stare into Forrest's eyes. We're standing on the upper deck of this ridiculous yacht—this floating palace that puts even my father's extravagant brownstone to shame—with Manhattan's skyline glittering behind us like someone scattered diamonds across black velvet.

"I still have a few tricks up my sleeve," he just said, and the promise in his voice is still making my stomach do flips.

I claimed to be immune to his charm. But standing here in my repaired dress with its new Swarovski crystals catching the first hint of moonlight, with his arms around me, and the lingering taste of chocolate and *him* on my lips, I'm losing my grip on reality.

"What surprises?" I ask, forcing my voice to remain steady, unaffected. Like he didn't just kiss me senseless. Like I didn't just lie through my teeth about feeling nothing.

His smile is slow, confident, a billionaire's smile that says he owns the world. But there's something softer in his eyes, something that makes me wonder which Forrest I'm seeing right now—the escort playing a role, or the man underneath.

"Dance with me," he says, holding out his hand.

More romantic dancing? What the hell? This reckless fucker

is trying to make me fall in love with him.

The string quartet we passed earlier has relocated to the upper deck, settling in a corner with their instruments. At some invisible signal from Forrest, they begin to play.

"Oh," I breathe as the first notes drift across the deck. "This is..."

"Dido," he finishes for me. "The pretzel cart. The sidewalk. You remember?"

As if I could forget. The memory of our first dance is etched into my mind like an engraving—the night air, the pretzel vendor's cheap speakers, Forrest's arms steady around me as my world spun from those accidental edibles.

The melody of "White Flag" floats around us, carried on the sea breeze. I place my hand in his, letting him draw me close. His palm is warm against the small of my back, and I can feel the strength in his shoulders beneath my fingertips.

"I remember you explaining the song to me," I say, following his lead as we begin to sway. "About surrender and going down with the ship."

"About choosing love even when it's messy," he adds, his voice low near my ear. "About refusing to give up."

I close my eyes, letting the music wash over me. This is dangerous territory. This whole evening has been strategically designed to make me feel things—to give me authentic emotional material for my writing. But the problem is, it's working too well.

The yacht rocks gently beneath us, a subtle reminder that we're floating, untethered to the real world. It would be so easy to get lost in this scene—to believe this is my life, that I'm the kind of woman who has five-course dinners on private yachts, who dances under the stars with a man who looks at me like I'm the center of his universe.

"Did I do all right?" Forrest asks after a moment, his mouth plush against my temple. "The whole point of these dates is to spark your creativity. I did a lot of billionaire romance tropes research, trying to get it right. How'd it land?"

I pull back just enough to look at him and smirk. "Google steered you right."

He spins me in a slow circle before drawing me back to his chest. "My roommate, Taio, was surprisingly helpful—turns out he's secretly addicted to romance novels. Who knew?"

The image of Forrest's roommate—all muscle and swagger—devouring romance books is so incongruous that I can't help but laugh. "Seriously?"

"Even I was surprised. Taio is all macho and bro-ish, I had no idea he was obsessed."

"A guy who reads romance books...*that's hot*."

Forrest abruptly halts. "Watch it," he growls against my ear.

Seizing an opportunity to unnerve him, I continue, "Is Taio an Asian name?"

He blinks at me, very unimpressed. He barely musters a response. "His mother is Japanese."

"Asian American *and* loves romance books? We have so much in common already. So, when do I get to meet this...*Taio*?"

"Never," Forrest grunts, moving his feet again. "He's an escort too, so don't get your hopes up."

Ha, nice try. Apparently that vocation doesn't deter me. "Clearly you've never heard of why choose," I mumble.

"I haven't, but I can guess. And *no*. I won't be sharing you with anyone. You're mine."

"We said this was strictly business. No strings attached."

"You're at least mine for this dance, so let's drop the dirty thoughts about my dumbass best friend, okay?"

I can't help but poke the bear one more time. Mostly because it's fun. But partly because jealous Forrest is doing things to my insides again. "I bet he's tall," I daydream. "What's *his* going rate?"

He yanks me tighter against his body, winding me. "Really, pipsqueak? Six foot two isn't enough for you? You know I nearly break my back every time I have to lean down to kiss you."

"Mhm, your outrage is only telling me one thing. Taio is taller than you, isn't he?"

"Six foot four," he begrudgingly provides. "You done?" He swats my backside rather firmly as I giggle against his chest.

"That's what you get for telling me I kiss like a fish."

"Have you ever kissed a fish?" he asks. "Maybe that was a compliment."

"Gross," I grumble.

He kisses the top of my head. "You are by far the best I've ever had, my little conch shell. A kiss I'll remember until my dying day."

"Aaand back in character."

His chest lifts as he sighs heavily, but he doesn't say anything. We just continue to dance until the song fades.

"This billionaire date was executed perfectly, but I think I've had a revelation."

"Being?" Forrest prompts, intrigue lining his voice.

"I'm not so into it."

He scoffs. "Good to know."

"No, no," I say, cuddling closer into him. "I mean it's not the luxury that makes this night magical. It's all the effort you put in. That's the secret sauce. I think I could do that with a different genre."

"So no billionaires for your bestseller?"

I shake my head. "I don't think so. I'd be chasing trends, forcing it. It's the eternal struggle—write for the market or write for yourself."

"Sounds familiar," he murmurs. "Do what pays the bills or do what feels right."

The parallel isn't lost on me—his escorting versus the legal career he walked away from. We're both compromising in our own ways, both trying to find our paths.

"Write what you love. It'll work out, Sora. Don't worry too much. I got you."

We fall into a comfortable silence, still moving together beneath the stars. The yacht rocks gently beneath our feet, the lights of passing boats reflecting on the dark water. A server appears briefly with champagne flutes, but Forrest waves him away. Everything falls away.

"So I had one more thing planned for this evening, but now I don't know if I should do it, since you're over billionaires and all."

"Try me," I hum out.

He guides me toward one of the plush sofas that line the deck.

I sit down, arranging my dress carefully around me. The fabric shimmers under the deck lights and I'm distracted like a fish by my own shininess. I can see my breath, the evening air chilly, but I don't tell Forrest that. He'd offer me his coat, and I don't want my ensemble disturbed. I feel like a princess tonight, done up like I'm Cinderella headed to the ball. I only have a few more minutes until the clock strikes twelve. I'll let him go, I swear. But right now I'm savoring every second.

Forrest stands in front of me, looking uncomfortable.

"What's wrong?" I ask.

"From what I learned, a lot of billionaire romance books have that big proposal moment—the girl softens the bosshole, he has some big, sappy declaration of love, and then of course, that fat diamond he gives her after promising he'll take care of her forever."

"Oh yes, painfully cliché, and the ring is always the size of her fist, even though she's not into money of course." I clutch my fingers together in a tight ball proving my point.

"This one isn't quite the size of a fist."

"What?" I ask, my voice coming out higher than intended.

His eyes lock with mine as he reaches into his pocket and pulls out a small velvet box. My heart stops, then restarts at double speed.

"I wanted to give you that big movie moment—is this going too far?"

Yes, I think. "No," I say, desperately. "Just do it."

"Nike style, I like it," he says with a grin, then his smile disappears. Clearing his throat, he drops right back into character. "Sora, little conch shell, Cho-Cooper," he begins, opening the box to reveal a ring that catches the light like a miniature sun. "I know this might seem sudden, but in my experience, love only happens when you truly let it. For a man like me, who has everything money can buy, I knew I had absolutely nothing worth keeping until the moment you walked into my life."

I stare at him, unable to breathe. I'm well aware these are theatrics, so why is my treacherous heart still pounding like it might explode?

"You challenge me," he continues, "you inspire me, you make me see the world differently," he continues. "And for fuck's sake... your tight little pussy—"

"Don't ruin it," I hiss.

He laughs, a rumble from deep within his belly. "My point is, I will wake up every single day for the rest of my life grateful to be alive as long as you're beside me. Will you marry me?"

"Did you ask my dad?" I bumble out, trying to be funny, even though my watering eyes are quite real.

"Definitely not."

"Then the answer is yes. *Yes*. A thousand times yes."

He slides the ring onto my finger—a perfect fit, which seems impossible—and leans close to whisper in my ear, "Unfortunately, we'll have to give the ring back."

"*Nooope*. Not happening. It's stunning," I say, admiring how the diamond catches the light. The band is platinum, I think, with smaller diamonds flanking the center stone. It looks antique, with delicate filigree work that speaks of craftmanship and history.

"Sora, I could go to jail if you ran off with something like this."

"A risk I'm willing to take," I tease. "How much is something like this worth?"

"Two of your brownstones," Forrest answers without missing a beat.

"Jesus," I breathe. "That's obscene."

"That's billionaire romance," he counters with a smirk.

He joins me on the sofa, his arm stretching casually along the back behind me. His fingers are close enough to my bare shoulder that I can feel their warmth, but he doesn't quite touch me.

"So, what do you think? Did it give you butterflies?" he asks, adorably eager.

I twist the ring on my finger, watching the play of light across its facets. The weight of it is both foreign and oddly satisfying. I've never been the kind of girl who spent hours dreaming about engagement rings, but I have to admit, this one is breathtaking.

"An entire butterfly garden," I tell him. "The yacht, the private chef, the string quartet, the proposal under the stars...it's textbook perfection. But like I said, not for me."

His fingers brush against my shoulder, sending a small shiver along my back. "What would win you over, then? If not wealth and luxury?"

The question feels weighted with layers of meaning neither of us is ready to acknowledge.

"I don't know yet. But it needs to be real and honest. Not like this. Not the things you and I can't have."

The moment the words leave my mouth, I regret them. Hurt pinches Forrest's face before he can mask it, and I wish I could take it back.

"I'm sorry—"

"Don't be," he says. "You're right. This isn't real."

A heaviness settles over us, a shared recognition of the boundaries we've established and the pretense that keeps us safe. The string quartet has begun playing again, something slow and melancholy that matches the sudden shift in mood.

I find myself staring at the ring again, imagining a version of reality where it isn't borrowed, where Forrest isn't playing a part, where I'm not just gathering material for a book.

"I used to pretend I was engaged when I was little," I confess, the words slipping out unbidden. "I'd wrap a piece of yarn around my finger and make up elaborate stories about my 'fiancé' for my stuffed animals. They were very impressed."

Forrest's smile returns, softer now. "What was he like? Your imaginary fiancé?"

"Strong. Kind." I laugh a little, embarrassed. "He had a horse named Lightning."

"Of course he did." Forrest chuckles. "Every good fiancé needs a trusty steed."

"What about you?" I ask, genuinely curious. "Did you ever imagine your future spouse when you were younger?"

He's quiet for a moment, considering. "I can honestly say I don't ever think about love until I'm somehow already in it."

We sit in silence for a moment, the distant hum of the yacht's engines and the gentle lapping of water against the hull the only sounds. The city is growing closer as we make our way back to the marina, the night drawing to a close.

Forrest stands, holding out his hand once more. "One more dance?"

I accept his hand, letting him pull me to my feet. This time when he holds me, there's a reverence to his touch, as if I'm something precious and fragile.

I close my eyes, surrendering to the fantasy. For these few stolen moments, I allow myself to believe that this is my life—that I'm a woman newly engaged to a man who adores me, that we're celebrating our love beneath the stars, that our future stretches before us, bright with promise.

"Just for tonight," I whisper, almost incoherently.

The music envelops us, and I try to memorize every detail—the feel of his arms around me, the scent of his cologne, the steady rhythm of his heartbeat beneath my cheek. I want to capture it all, preserve it for when this night is just a memory.

"Don't be mad at me," Forrest says suddenly.

"It would be impossible right now." I nuzzle deeper into his chest.

"When you said earlier that we should have a lot of sex, what exactly does that mean? How much sex is a lot for you?"

I chuckle. "Worried I'm going to wear you out?"

"Answer the question, Sora," he breathes out, not matching my humor, too focused on the answer.

"I don't know, like twice a week? Or is that excessive? What's a lot of sex to you?"

His Adam's apple leaps, then falls as he swallows heavily. "Um, yeah. Same. Twice a...week."

He's normally a fantastic liar. Right now, not so much. And the rock-hard cylinder suddenly pressed against my stomach tells me what's definitely on his mind. "Soon. Not tonight though. Tonight, I want the night to end exactly like this," I confirm.

Stars in the sky. Stars in my eyes.

But the brightest star nestled on my left hand for now.

CHAPTER TWENTY

Forrest

You really are a country boy, aren't you?

"Daddy, are we there yet?"

Dakota's voice pipes up from the back seat for the fourth time in fifteen minutes. I glance at her in the rearview mirror, her tiny legs swinging impatiently, barely reaching the edge of the car seat. Her favorite stuffed bunny, Mr. Flops, is clutched tightly in her arms.

"Almost, Koda. Just a few more blocks."

I check the time on the dashboard. We're running about twenty minutes behind schedule, but that's to be expected when you're moving with a four-year-old. The morning had been chaos—Dakota insisting on packing her toys herself, which meant unpacking and repacking her princess suitcase three times; the unexpected phone call from Rina about a client cancelation; Taio making a last-ditch effort to convince me that moving is a mistake.

"You're blurring lines, man," he warned as he helped load the last of our boxes into the rental SUV. *"Playing house with a client won't end well."*

I reminded him that Sora wasn't technically a client, which earned me an eye roll and a muttered, *"Whatever helps you sleep at night, my guy."*

But now, with Dakota fidgeting excitedly in the back seat and the brownstone just minutes away, I'm not second-guessing my decision. This arrangement with Sora is the best solution for everyone involved—Dakota gets to stay in her school, I get more time with my daughter, and Sora gets...well, whatever it is I'm giving her.

Three days have passed since our night on the yacht, and my thoughts keep drifting back to the weight of her in my arms as we swayed beneath the stars, the whispered "what-if" that hung between us like a fragile promise. I'm still not sure what to make of that moment. Because when I saw the ring on her finger, it messed me up a little.

Knowing I'd never, ever be able to afford something like that for her. Unless maybe I worked triple-time as an escort, but therein lies the problem. What woman would want to marry an escort? Even when I leave this all behind, I can't lie to my future wife. Who would accept my messy past?

"Daddy, is Sora nice?" Dakota's question pulls me from my thoughts.

"Very nice," I assure her, turning onto Sora's tree-lined street. "You met her before, remember? At the coffee shop?"

"The lady who gave me the cookie?" Her face lights up with recognition.

"That's right."

"I like her," Dakota declares with the absolute certainty only a child can muster. "Does she have toys?"

I chuckle. "You brought your own toys, Koda. But she painted your room purple, just like you like."

Dakota gasps, her eyes widening. "My *very own* purple room?"

"Yep. With space for all your stuffed animals and your books."

She hugs Mr. Flops tighter, whispering something in his floppy ear that I can't quite catch. Probably updating him on their new living arrangements.

As we pull up to the brownstone, I spot Sora waiting on the steps, wearing jeans and a soft-looking sweater, her dark hair falling loose around her shoulders. My heart does a stupid little skip at the sight of her.

For a moment, I feel an almost overwhelming urge to kiss her hello—to feel her lips against mine, to pull her close and breathe in the scent of her hair. I have to physically restrain myself, gripping the steering wheel a bit tighter. What am I thinking? Dakota's right here, and besides, Sora and I aren't...whatever my traitorous heart seems to think we are. Our situation is complicated enough without adding more confusion.

God, what is wrong with me? I'm acting like a teenager with his first crush, not a grown man with a complicated life.

"Is that her?" Dakota asks, pressing her face against the window.

"Yes, that's Sora." I park the SUV and turn to look at my daughter. "Remember what we talked about? We're going to be staying with Sora for a while because Mommy had to go on a trip."

Dakota nods solemnly. "And Mommy wants us to have qualipy time together."

"Quality time, sweetheart," I correct. "With a 't' like for tiger. But that's right. We're going to spend a lot of time together now, thanks to Mommy." I swallow the bitterness that rises whenever I think about Hannah's Tokyo plans. I've been careful not to let any of my anger toward Hannah slip in front of Dakota. Whatever my feelings about her mother, Dakota doesn't need to hear them.

"Okay. Can I show Sora Mr. Flops?"

"I bet she'd love that."

Dakota unbuckles her seat belt with impressive dexterity for her age, bouncing in her seat as I come around the black SUV to open her door. The moment her feet hit the pavement, she's off, racing toward Sora with Mr. Flops dangling from one hand.

"Hi! I'm Dakota! This is Mr. Flops! He's a bunny! Do you like bunnies?"

Sora looks momentarily startled by the tiny whirlwind barreling toward her, but recovers quickly, crouching down to Dakota's level.

"I love bunnies," she says seriously, extending a hand to the stuffed animal. "It's very nice to meet you, Mr. Flops. And you too, Dakota. I'm Sora."

"I know. Daddy told me. He said you're very nice and that you painted my room purple!"

Sora glances up at me, a smile tugging at her lips. "Did he now?"

"I may have mentioned it," I say, approaching with Dakota's princess suitcase in one hand and a box of her books in the other. "We're running a little late. Sorry about that."

"No problem." Sora stands, tucking her hair behind her ear in a nervous gesture. "I was just enjoying the sunshine. It's a beautiful day for a move."

Our eyes meet, and for a moment, I'm back on that yacht, holding her close as we danced beneath the stars. Then Dakota tugs at my pants leg, breaking the spell.

"Can I see my room now? Please?"

Sora laughs, the sound bright and genuine. "Of course. Let me help your dad with your things first."

"I've got it," I say. "There's more in the car, but we can get that later. Let's give Koda the grand tour first."

Sora nods, leading the way up the steps. Dakota follows, practically vibrating with excitement, Mr. Flops clutched tight against her chest.

The brownstone is even more impressive in daylight than it was when I first visited. High ceilings, hardwood floors, tasteful art on the walls—it's the kind of place I would have dreamed of providing for my family if life had gone according to plan.

"Wow," Dakota breathes, spinning in a slow circle in the entryway, taking it all in. "This is like a princess castle."

Sora smiles, clearly pleased by her reaction. "Would the princess like to see her royal chambers?"

Dakota's eyes glisten. "Yes!" She looks at me, reads my expression, then quickly adds, "*Please*."

"Good job," I say. "Mind your manners, lil miss."

Sora shoots me an amused glance. "You really are a country

boy, aren't you?"

I pretend to tip a hat at her.

"This way, Your Highness." Sora offers a little curtsy, then leads us upstairs.

I follow, watching the easy way Sora interacts with my daughter. No awkwardness, no forced enthusiasm—just a natural warmth that has Dakota already reaching for her hand as they ascend the staircase.

The purple room is on the third floor, across from what will be my bedroom. The door is closed, but there's a paper sign taped to it with "Princess Dakota's Royal Chambers" written in elegant calligraphy. There are little stars and hearts drawn around the words, and a crown at the top of the sign.

"Did you make this?" I ask Sora.

She nods, suddenly looking shy. "I thought it might help her feel welcome."

Something warm unfurls in my chest. I didn't expect her to go to such lengths.

"Can I open it?" Dakota is practically dancing with anticipation.

"Go ahead," Sora says.

Dakota turns the knob and pushes the door open, then freezes in the doorway, her mouth forming a perfect O of amazement.

The room is magical. The walls are a soft lavender, just as we'd painted them, but Sora has added so much more. Sheer white curtains frame the windows, twinkle lights woven through them. A canopy of gauzy purple fabric hangs over the new twin bed, which is covered in a fluffy comforter adorned with stars. There's a small bookshelf already filled with children's books, a toy chest with Dakota's name painted on the lid, and a little table and chairs set up for tea parties.

"Is this...mine?" Dakota whispers, as if afraid speaking too loudly might make it all disappear.

"All yours," Sora confirms. "Do you like it?"

Dakota turns, her face alight with joy, and launches herself at

Sora, wrapping her arms around her legs. "It's the most beautiful room in the whole wide world! Thank you, thank you, *thank you*."

Sora looks momentarily startled by the display of affection, but then gently pats Dakota's back. "You're very welcome. I'm glad you like it."

I set down the suitcase and box, unable to tear my eyes away from the scene. This room must have cost a fortune to set up, not to mention the time and thought that went into it. All for a little girl she barely knows.

"Sora, this is incredible," I say, my voice rough with emotion. "You didn't have to do all this."

Her fingers play with the hem of her T-shirt, seeming embarrassed by my gratitude. "It was nothing, really. I had fun with it."

"Daddy, look!" Dakota has already moved on to exploring, pulling open drawers and exclaiming over each new discovery. "There are fairy lights! And look, she got me princess books! And a tea set!"

I meet Sora's gaze over Dakota's head. *Thank you*, I mouth silently.

She just smiles, a hint of color rising in her cheeks.

"Can I stay here forever?" Dakota asks, flopping backward onto the bed, arms spread wide. "It's way nicer than my room at Mommy's."

I wince at the comparison. "Different, not better," I correct automatically. The last thing I need is Dakota going back to Hannah with tales of how much "nicer" things are at Dad's place. "And we'll be here for a while, but not forever."

Sora's smile falters slightly at my words, and I realize how they might have sounded—like I'm already planning our exit, already thinking of this as temporary.

Which it is, I remind myself. This arrangement is a stopgap, a solution to an immediate problem, not a forever kind of deal.

So why does the thought of goodbye already have me feeling so hollow?

Sora kneels beside the bed, looking at Dakota with earnest curiosity. "I'm surprised you like this room so much. Your mom and Henry have a beautiful home, don't they?"

Dakota nods. "It's pretty." Her knobby little shoulders rise and then slump. "But everything is white. White walls, white couches, white rugs. Mommy says my toys have to match the house, so I have white stuffed animals and silver blocks." She looks around the purple room with renewed fascination. "I don't have colorful things like this there."

Something sharp twists in my chest. I knew Hannah was particular about her home's appearance, but I hadn't realized she'd extended those restrictions to Dakota's toys and personal space.

"That must be hard," Sora says softly, not a hint of judgment in her voice, though I can see the concern in her eyes.

"Yeah," Dakota agrees. "And I'm not allowed to play in the living room because I might mess it up. But I like this better." She bounces on her knees on the bed, beaming. "It's pretty and fun!"

I turn away, needing a moment to compose myself. The image of my daughter playing quietly with white toys in a white room, careful not to disturb the perfect staging of Hannah's showcase apartment, makes me want to punch a wall. But that won't help anyone, least of all Dakota.

"Why don't you help Dakota get settled?" Sora suggests, noticing my demeanor. "I'll make some lunch. Are sandwiches okay?"

"Sandwiches sound great," I say, grateful for the change of subject. "What kind were you thinking?"

"I was going to make peanut butter and jelly, but..." She makes a face, looking slightly embarrassed. "I'm not exactly a gourmet chef. Grilled cheese is pretty much the peak of my culinary skills."

"Grilled cheese!" Dakota exclaims happily. "With the cheese all melty and gooey?"

Sora laughs. "That's the plan. With tomato soup...from a can?"

"Perfect," I say. "We'll be down soon to get the rest of the things from the car."

Sora nods and heads downstairs, leaving me alone with Dakota, who is now carefully arranging Mr. Flops on his new throne—the center of the purple comforter.

"I like her, Daddy," Dakota announces, smoothing the bunny's ears. "She made my room pretty."

"She's very nice," I agree, sitting on the edge of the bed.

"Is she your girlfriend?"

Like a lasso, the question wraps me up and drags me back to reality. "No, Koda. She's just a friend who's letting us stay with her."

Dakota fixes me with a look that's eerily reminiscent of Hannah at her most skeptical. "But you like her."

It's not a question. My four-year-old is stating a fact that I've been trying to dance around for weeks.

"I do like her," I admit. "She's a good friend."

Dakota seems satisfied with this answer, turning her attention back to arranging her stuffed animals on the bed. I watch her for a moment, marveling at how resilient kids can be. Just two weeks ago, her mother was planning to ship her off to boarding school across the country. Now she's settling into a new home with barely a hiccup.

"Daddy?"

"Yes, Koda?"

"If you marry Sora, will she be my new mommy?"

"No one's getting married," I say firmly. "And you already have a mommy who loves you very much. Remember what we talked about? Mommy's on a trip, but she'll be back."

Dakota nods, but she doesn't look entirely convinced. "I know. But Mommy doesn't make pretty rooms like Sora."

I have to bite back a laugh at that. Hannah's aesthetic runs more toward minimalist luxury—lots of white furniture and abstract art that costs more than most people's cars. Not exactly a little girl's dream.

"Everyone's good at different things," I tell her. "Mommy's

good at...other stuff."

Nothing comes to mind at the moment. *No.* I shut that thought down hard. I promised myself I wouldn't badmouth Hannah to Dakota, no matter how much it feels warranted in the moment.

"Come on," I say, standing up and holding out my hand. "Let's go help Sora with lunch, then we can bring in the rest of your things."

Dakota hops off the bed, taking my hand. "Okay. Can I show Sora my princess dresses? Do you think she'll like them?"

"I'm sure she will," I say, guiding her toward the door.

"And my puzzles? And my tiara? And my—"

"One thing at a time, Koda." I lead her down the stairs. "Try not to bother Sora too much, okay? If you need something like a snack or water, come find me. Sora isn't at your beck and call."

"What's a beckett-call?" she asks, dead serious.

"Never mind, sweetheart. Just ask me first whenever you need anything."

We find Sora in the kitchen, slicing cheese for the sandwiches. The domesticity of the scene hits me square in the chest—Sora at the counter, preparing lunch for my daughter, the three of us about to sit down for a meal together like...like a family. The one I never got. But damn, this version looks even better. I try to shove the thought down. But it lingers, a warm ember refusing to be extinguished.

"Can I help?" Dakota asks, already dragging a chair toward the counter.

Sora looks over, surprised but pleased. "Sure. Want to butter the bread for me?"

"I'm very good at buttering," Dakota loftily informs her. "Daddy lets me do it all the time."

This is news to me, but I keep my mouth shut, watching as Dakota clambers onto the chair and accepts the butter knife Sora hands her with all the gravity of a knight receiving a sword.

"Careful," I warn, moving closer. "Need me to help?"

"I got it, Daddy," Dakota says with the exasperated tone of

someone who has been doing this for decades, not seconds.

Sora catches my eye over Dakota's head, her lips twitching with suppressed laughter. I shrug, silently communicating my surrender.

As Dakota dutifully—and somewhat haphazardly—butters the bread, Sora turns to me. "There's fresh coffee in the pot if you want some. Mugs are in the cabinet to the left of the sink."

"Thanks." I move toward the coffee maker, all too aware of the brush of her arm against mine as I pass. The kitchen suddenly feels much smaller than it is.

We work in companionable silence for a few minutes—Sora supervising Dakota's buttering efforts, me pouring coffee and then setting the table, all of us moving around each other in a dance that feels surprisingly natural for people who aren't used to sharing space.

"So," Sora says eventually, "I was thinking we could have a housewarming dinner tonight. Nothing fancy, just the three of us. We could order in? My treat."

"I like pasta!" Dakota votes enthusiastically, nearly dropping the butter knife in her excitement.

"Pasta it is," Sora says, smiling at her. "Forrest?"

"Sounds great," I agree. "But you know our deal. *My treat.*"

The sandwiches are ready a few minutes later, perfectly golden and oozing cheese. Dakota takes her first bite and declares it "the bestest grilled cheese ever," which earns Sora a beaming smile.

Watching them together, something shifts inside me—a settling, like puzzle pieces finally clicking into place. It's both terrifying and exhilarating, this sense that something important is happening here, something I didn't plan for but desperately want.

After lunch, we bring in the rest of our things from the car. It doesn't take long—most of my possessions are still at the apartment, waiting to be moved over the weekend. Today was just the essentials: clothes, Dakota's favorite toys, and a few personal items.

Dakota insists on giving Mr. Flops a tour of every room in the brownstone, with Sora as their patient guide. I hang back, ostensibly unpacking but really just watching the two of them together—my daughter's hand tucked trustingly in Sora's, Sora pointing out features of each room with the same enthusiasm she might use for a real museum tour.

"And my room is all the way at the top," Sora explains as they reach the third floor. "On the highest floor."

Dakota gasps. "Like where the dragon keeps the princess? Can we see?" Dakota asks eagerly.

"Maybe another time," Sora says. "It's a bit messy right now. I wasn't expecting royal visitors."

Dakota giggles at that, delighted to be treated like royalty. It's perfect. *Too perfect.*

My phone vibrates in my pocket. I pull it out to find a text from Rina.

Rina

I have a job for tomorrow night. Available?

Where? I have Dakota full-time starting today. Can't travel.

Rina

It's in Jersey. You'd just need a sitter for the night. From the sound of it, it'll be quick. She's only after one thing.

Reality comes crashing back. All I feel is guilt. How can I agree to sleep with another woman with Sora this close?

I'll pass.

> **Rina**
> Hawkins, you've turned down the last three gigs. What gives? Did the money tree you planted finally sprout?

> I wish.

> **Rina**
> Then get back to work. I know you're going through a lot. If you need a good nanny, I can make some calls. But if you keep turning down jobs, I'm going to stop offering.

> Fine. I hear you. I'll book the next one, promise.

I put the phone away, my good mood dampened. When I look up, Sora is standing in the doorway, watching me.

"Everything okay?"

"Yeah," I lie. "Just a work thing."

She nods, not pressing for details, which only makes me feel worse about keeping secrets. I know she understands what I do for a living—she's hired me herself, after all—but we haven't discussed how this will work now that we're living together. With Dakota around, the conversation becomes even more complicated.

As if on cue, Dakota bounds up behind Sora, already in the princess dress she insisted on changing into after lunch.

"Daddy, Sora said we can have ice cream after dinner!"

"Did she now?" I raise an eyebrow at Sora, who has the grace to look slightly sheepish.

"I may have mentioned I have some cookie dough in the

freezer," she admits. "But I said only if it's okay with your dad."

"Please, Daddy? Pretty please with a cherry on top?"

How am I supposed to say no to that face? "We'll see," I say, the universal parent code for "probably yes, but I'm not committing yet."

Dakota seems to accept this, spinning away to continue her exploration of the house. Sora lingers in the doorway, a slight furrow between her brows.

"I should have asked first," she says. "About the ice cream."

"It's fine," I assure her. "Really. I'm not that strict about desserts."

"I just don't want to step on your toes. I know how you get with rogue cookies." She waggles her brows at me. "I want to be respectful. I'm new to living with a child, especially when decisions aren't mine to make. Was her room too much?"

"Not at all. You're doing great," I tell her, and I mean it. "Dakota already adores you."

The furrow between her brows eases, replaced by a pleased smile. "She's pretty easy to adore back."

"Yeah, she is," I agree, feeling a familiar surge of love and pride.

An awkward silence lies over us. There's so much I want to say, so many questions I want to ask. About the yacht, about the kiss, about other things. But the words stick in my throat.

"So," Sora says finally.

"So?" I ask back. "Something on your mind?"

"Do you have ideas for our next...research date?"

"Oh shit," I breathe out, dragging my hand over my face. "I'm sorry. I meant to get some ideas from Taio, but I've been distracted with Dakota and trying to make this whole big change for her easy and—"

"Oh, hey now, *of course*. Don't worry about it. Forget it. You have bigger fish to fry."

"Sora, you're just as big a fish as any in my life. I don't mean like that... I mean clients. Shit, no, I mean *yes*, you are a client. An important one. I just mean..." I lift one brow. "Can you save me, here? You know what I'm trying to say."

She scrunches her nose and clamps her eyes shut. "But you're so cute when you're uncomfortable and squirmy."

"I already miss Taio," I deadpan.

She belts out in laughter. "Hey, know what I was thinking? What if we called this whole deal off?"

"Sora," I plead. "We just got here, please don't—"

"*No*, I don't mean for you to leave, Forrest. I'm saying, just pay me what you can in rent, and if that's simply returning my ten thousand dollars, that's fine." She flashes me a toothy grin. "You guys can squat here as long as you like, no pressure. We can be actual friends." She holds out her hand and wiggles her fingers. "*Just friends.*"

I shake her hand, pretending like I'm on board with her suggestion, but when she's least expecting it, I tug her in close against my body. I scan the room to ensure Dakota isn't lurking, then when I'm satisfied the coast is clear, I smack Sora's ass, firmly. She yelps in surprise.

"Have you been writing?" I ask in her ear.

"Blocked as ever," she croaks out, her breath growing ragged the way it does whenever I touch her like this.

"Then my job isn't done. We're not calling anything off. Give me a little time, I'm going to plan something great, I promise."

"Something that involves me getting that ring back?" she asks, fluttering her lashes at me.

Not likely. I swear my ass cheeks were clenched in anxiety until I handed that thing back to Celeste. It's from a rare collector's line, and quite literally would've cost my life if I lost it.

"Excuse me, J.Lo, I thought you said your love don't cost a thing. Aren't we moving past the billionaire trope?"

She nods, a hint of color rising in her cheeks. "Maybe something with more edge? The dark, dangerous hero. The masked stranger. That whole thing?"

I can't help the slow smile that spreads across my face. "Sora

Cho, are you asking me to play the villain?"

"Not the villain," she corrects quickly. "Just not the golden retriever. The anti-hero. The morally gray love interest."

"I can do that," I say, putting my hand back on her ass, shamelessly exploring as much as she allows me to. "Sometimes I'm not a good guy."

"Daddy, I need a snack," Dakota says, reappearing.

Sora leaps away from me like an antelope that just realized it mistook an alligator for a rock. She catches actual air in her determination to put as much space between our bodies as possible after the reemergence of my daughter.

"Baby, you just ate. You're hungry again?"

Koda nods at me, her big, sad blue eyes growing huge. She presses her hands against her stomach and grimaces. *So hungry.*

I exhale. "Bottomless pit at this age, I swear," I say to Sora.

"Dakota, I have grapes, strawberries, blueberries, and vanilla yogurt in the fridge. Does any of that sound yummy?" Sora sweetly asks.

"Grapes and strawberries," Koda answers, then shoots me a look. "Please."

"Coming right up, lil lady." Sora bustles to the fridge. I follow behind, trying to make myself useful by grabbing a bowl.

"You keep a healthy fridge," I say.

She snorts in laughter. "I was just trying to impress you. The fridge in my apartment only has spicy pickles, old birthday cake, Coke Zero, and Flamin' Hot Cheetos."

"You put Cheetos in the fridge?"

Sora proceeds to rinse a cluster of green grapes. "You've never tried that?"

"No. Because it's weird. Also, I don't like spicy food."

She stops rinsing, sets the grapes on the counter on top of a stack of paper towels, then presses her palm against her heart like she's in pain.

"Are you okay?" I ask, filling with concern.

"You said you don't like spicy food. I'm just mourning the

death of our friendship."

I laugh. "You kook. Rinse me some grapes too, please?"

She winks. "You got it."

It's wonderful and terrifying how natural this feels. Just a couple hours after stepping foot into the brownstone, it already feels like...

Home, I realize with a start.

Not the brownstone itself, impressive as it is, but *her*. It's way too fast, way too much, but it's undeniable.

Home is where she is.

In the span of a month, Sora has somehow worked her way in and become the other center of my world. The two people who collectively consume all of my thoughts, in one space together.

I know it can't work between us.

But also...

How can it not?

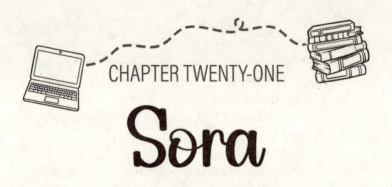

CHAPTER TWENTY-ONE

Sora

Not bad for a damsel liability...

"Is she actually coming?" a man who I'm assuming is Taio asks Forrest, fidgeting with his paintball mask's chin strap. "From everything you've said, she seems more 'afternoon tea at the Ritz' than 'mud-crawling commando.'"

I can't help smirking as I emerge from the women's changing room at Extreme Paint Warriors. The facility, just outside the city, sprawls before us—a massive compound with terrain that ranges from mock urban landscapes to dense woodland areas strewn with bunkers. Forrest and I left home separately, as he and his friends apparently needed to pick up new gear and ammo for the match today.

"How ridiculous do I look?" I gesture to my outfit—camo overalls with a tight black tank top underneath, my hair pulled back in a sleek ponytail. The ensemble is surprisingly comfortable, with the exception of my clunky black combat boots.

Forrest turns, his face lighting up in that spontaneous way that always catches my heart in a chokehold. His eyes perform a quick evaluation, idling on the way the tank hugs my curves, and despite the decidedly un-glamorous setting, I feel a flush spreading across my chest.

"Not ridiculous at all. You look ready for battle," he says, his voice warm with approval.

Taio pivots toward me, and my first thought is that Forrest seriously undersold his roommate's height. The man is a skyscraper, broad-shouldered with an easy confidence that explains his success in their line of work. Behind him stands a tall, but more compact, muscular blond man wearing a weathered Australian flag patch like a badge of honor.

"The infamous Sora in the flesh," Taio says with an appreciative whistle. "The brownstone bandit who stole Forrest's bedroom slippers and his..." He drops his voice dramatically. "...let's say, *concentration*."

I shake his extended hand. "Guilty as charged. Though I have yet to see Forrest wear bedroom slippers."

"Really? You can't miss them. They are pink, fluffy, with little Hello Kitty charms on the front. Koda-cakes has a matching pair," Taio says, teasing his friend.

Yet Forrest seems unfazed. "Is that supposed to embarrass me? Because I'd have no qualms matching slippers with my kid." Forrest returns his attention to me and nods toward the blond. "Meanwhile, this kangaroo wrangler is Saylor."

Saylor offers an irreverent two-finger salute. "A pleasure to finally meet the woman Forrest's been drafting text messages to for twenty minutes before sending."

That got him. Forrest narrows his eyes at Saylor. "Inaccurate."

"I've got receipts, mate," Saylor stage-whispers to me. "He's become a walking thesaurus trying to impress you."

"So," I say, enjoying the color rising in Forrest's cheeks, "thanks for letting me crash your guys' day. Though I'm still not clear how paintball relates to this 'touch her and die' trope we're supposedly reenacting." I make air quotes around the words. "Seems like a stretch."

Taio lifts an eyebrow. "Who says it's a stretch? Paintball is the perfect theater for primal possessiveness. Add some danger, a damsel, a hero—"

"Whoa, hey now. I'm nobody's damsel. I'm here to be a helpful fourth," I interject, jabbing a finger into his chest.

"Well, good. Because no pressure, but we have a league reputation to protect," Taio says with utmost seriousness. "And today we're up against the Slaughterhouse Four."

My posture stiffens. "Slaughterhouse? Why does that sound so murderous? I thought this was a fun paintball game. Like... children play here, right?"

"Not on Saturdays," Saylor remarks. "No knives, no eye-gouging, and no boots to the back of the head, but other than that, pretty much anything goes, love."

Forrest reads my petrified expression. "It can get a little intense sometimes, but Slaughterhouse knows we have a newbie today. They won't give you a hard time."

"See that look on Hawk's face, Sora?"

"Mhm," I murmur, staring into Forrest's sweet smile.

"Remember that look. That's how you'll know he's serving up a heaping pile of bullshit. Slaughterhouse will not only show you no mercy, they'll specifically target the weak link."

"Don't scare her," Forrest barks at Taio, before turning back to me. "I'll admit, we've had a bit of an unfriendly rivalry, but that doesn't apply to you."

"They're here." Saylor perks up, suddenly alert. "Randy, Trevor, Brody, and looks like Jax is their fourth today? *Shit*."

"Fuck. They brought in their sniper," Taio says bitterly, his expression grave. "They're looking for blood after what happened last match."

"What happened last match?" I can't help asking.

The three men exchange glances loaded with unspoken history.

"We might have ambushed them in the locker room with leftover paint," Saylor admits.

"While they were showering," Taio adds.

"And livestreamed it on Say's socials," Forrest finishes.

I burst out laughing, unable to picture buttoned-up Forrest participating in such juvenile revenge. "Oh my god, so whatever you have coming today, you deserve it."

Taio wraps his arm around my shoulders, squeezing me tightly. "No, no, teammate. *We* deserve it. You're one of us now, and shit's about to get gnarly. You ready?"

I sniff twice. "You smell so familiar," I tell Taio. "What is that?"

"Elixir by Dior," Taio says proudly. "Little pricey, but it was a gift from a client."

"Oh, yes. *Elixir*. My mom's ex-boyfriend wore the same cologne. I was always fond of it. Such a nice smell."

Taio winks at me. "I wear it better than your mom's ex, right?"

I duck my head in a deep nod. "Of course you do."

"Hey, Ty? You fond of that hand?" Forrest asks.

"I guess?" Taio answers, confused.

"Then remove it from Sora's body before I remove it from yours," he says through gritted teeth.

Taio cackles in glee at Forrest's discomfort. Instead of removing his hand, he holds me tighter, and I swear Forrest is about to lunge, until our guests of the hour circle around us.

A tall man with a meticulously trimmed beard approaches, flanked by three equally athletic-looking men. His smile doesn't reach his eyes, which flick dismissively over our group before settling on me with sudden interest. "Hawk, Ty, the Aussie, and... what's this? Fresh meat?"

"Randy," Forrest acknowledges stiffly.

"Who's the pretty lady?" Randy asks, his gaze stalling on me a beat too long.

"Sora Cho," I introduce myself before Forrest can answer. "Nice to meet you."

Randy's grin widens. "Charmed. So are you the ringer or just eye candy for the game?"

"We'll see," I reply mock-sweetly.

"Randy, back the fuck off, all right? It's Sora's first time here, she's not a regular, so I expect you neanderthals to find some manners before the game."

Trevor, a lanky guy with intense eyes, lets out a derisive snort.

"Touchy, touchy. Clearly she belongs to Hawk."

"She doesn't belong to anybody, you misogynistic prick," Taio growls out. "Quit your clucking. Let's lay the terms."

"Same terms as always," counters a shorter, stocky guy who I assume is Brody.

"Or, how about we make this interesting?" Randy suggests, his eyes gleaming with challenge. "Losers buy drinks for the entire winning team at McGinty's. Plus, a public admission of our superior skill, recorded for posterity. *And*, losers have to stay out of this arena for an entire year."

"A year?" Saylor balks. "The only other arena nearby is in Jersey and it looks like something you'd find on Blippi."

"Done," Forrest agrees without hesitation, extending his hand.

"Hawk!" Saylor gripes. "Did you not hear me say *Jersey*?"

Randy shakes it, then winks at me. "See you on the battlefield, Sora. Try not to get too much paint on that pretty face."

As the Slaughterhouse Four strut away, I turn to Forrest. "That was intense."

He shrugs. "As far as encounters with Slaughterhouse goes, that was pretty tame."

I gulp. "So, what's our strategy?"

"Have you ever shot a paintball or airsoft gun before?"

I shake my head.

"Have you ever been *shot by* a paintball or airsoft gun before?"

"No...does it hurt?"

Forrest winces. "It stings a little in close proximity."

I inhale, then blow out a deep breath. "It's fine. I can take it. I survived laser hair removal, so this should be a cinch. I'm ready for battle against those creeps."

"Easy there, Braveheart," Forrest says, smiling. "You have no experience and I'm not going to risk you getting hurt. The strategy is simple. You stay behind me at all times."

I roll my eyes. "Is that the 'touch her and die' skit? I follow you around like a scared puppy and try not to trip?"

"No," Forrest says, adjusting his protective vest, "the 'touch her and die' skit is the overprotective hero who loses his mind if anyone threatens his woman."

"His woman? So I'm just a prop in this game?" I comment, but there's something undeniably appealing about the intensity in his gaze.

Half a smile tugs at the corner of his lips. "Perhaps. But you're the prettiest prop the world's ever seen."

Thirty minutes later, I'm crouched behind a stack of wooden pallets, heart pounding, adrenaline pumping fire through my veins. The playing field is a sprawling urban warfare setup—abandoned buildings, junked cars, and makeshift barriers creating a labyrinth of potential hiding spots and ambush points.

Our team's strategy was simple: stick together, watch each other's backs, and don't let the other team separate us. So naturally, within the first five minutes, we were completely scattered.

A paintball whizzes over my head, splattering against the wall behind me. I swallow a yelp and duck lower. From my earpiece, I hear Taio yelling coordinates, Saylor cursing in such a thick Australian accent it sounds like a different language, and Forrest repeatedly asking where I am.

"I'm behind the pallets near the blue building," I whisper into my mic. "Someone's got me pinned down."

"Hang tight," Forrest's voice crackles through the earpiece. "I'm coming for you."

"Or," Taio interjects, "you could flank him. Three o'clock from your position, there's a rusted car. If you can make it there, you'll have a clear shot at whoever's shooting at you."

I peer around the edge of my shelter. Sure enough, about fifteen feet away sits a hollowed-out sedan, offering perfect cover and a strategic vantage point.

"No," Forrest cuts in. "It's too exposed. Stay put, Sora. I'm coming."

Something in his tone—a touch too commanding, a hint too controlling—makes my competitive streak flare.

"I'm going for it."

"Sora, wait—"

But I'm already moving, darting from my hiding spot in a zigzag pattern like I've seen in movies. Paintballs explode around me, miraculously missing as I dive behind the car.

Panting, I peer through the empty window frame and spot my attacker—Jax, perched atop a stack of tires. Without overthinking it, I raise my paintball gun, aim, and squeeze the trigger.

To my utter astonishment, the paintball hits him square in the chest.

"I got one!" I whoop into my mic. "I actually hit him!"

"That's my girl!" Taio cheers.

My enthusiasm is quickly curbed when I see the paintball didn't burst. I heard the impact, but there's no evidence of my shot. "Dang it. The paintball was a dud," I say defeatedly, watching Jax disappear from his perch, still in the game.

"That's okay. Still a nice shot, conch shell," Saylor adds, my nickname giving away the fact that Forrest does indeed talk about me to his friends.

But now, even after my triumphant shot, Forrest is suspiciously silent.

I don't have time to overthink it because suddenly, I hear footsteps approaching from behind. I spin around, paintball gun raised, only to find Forrest standing there, his own weapon lowered.

"You were supposed to wait for me," he grits out, voice tight beneath his mask.

"I had an opening." I shrug. "And it almost worked." *Stupid faulty equipment.*

Before he can argue, a barrage of paintballs pelts the car, forcing us both to duck.

"Trevor and Brody, ten o'clock," Forrest mutters. "We're

surrounded."

Just then, Taio's voice crackles through our earpieces. "Saylor's down. They got him in the back."

"Bloody cheap shot," Saylor grumbles.

"Where are you guys?" I ask.

"North corner, by the tower," Taio says. "Randy's hunting me."

"We need to regroup," Forrest decides. "Sora, stay behind me. We're going to make a run for the central building."

I nod, my hands shaking from adrenaline. This is supposed to be just a game, but the fervor in Forrest's eyes tells me he's taking the protective hero role very seriously.

We move together through the maze of obstacles, Forrest shielding me with his body at every turn. Despite the bulky gear and masks, there's something undeniably intimate about the way he keeps me close, his hand occasionally brushing mine.

"Almost there," he murmurs as the dilapidated central structure comes into view. "Just a few more— *Ah! Fuck!*"

A paintball explodes right above his shoulder, the bright blue dusting his protective vest.

"Sniper!" he yells, pushing me behind a concrete barrier. "From the tower!"

I peek around the edge and spot Jax, perched in the watchtower, reloading his weapon.

"It's Jax," Forrest confirms. "He's got the high ground."

"Dammit," Taio mutters. "And Trevor and Brody are guarding the entrance to the building. We're cut off. Any bright ideas?"

Forrest thinks for a moment. "We need a distraction. Something to draw them out of position."

"I have an idea. Sora, remember how we got separated at the beginning?" Taio asks.

"Yeah?"

"That wasn't an accident. They're using a divide-and-conquer strategy. But we can turn it against them."

"How?" Forrest asks.

"Let them capture Sora."

"What?" Forrest's voice rises in disbelief. "No way in hell."

"Think about it," Taio continues. "They've been targeting her to fuck with you, Hawk. If they 'capture' her, they'll relax and lower their guard. They'll think they've won."

"And then what?" I ask, oddly intrigued by the plan.

"Then we launch a counterattack while they're celebrating. Classic Trojan horse."

"I don't like it," Forrest says stubbornly. "Using Sora as bait is exactly what they want."

"I can handle myself," I insist. "Besides, isn't this whole day about the 'touch her and die' trope? What better setup than a rescue mission?"

Forrest is quiet for a moment, then sighs. "Fine. But at the first sign of trouble, abort."

"Not your rodeo anymore, cowboy. I'm taking over the offensive strategy now," Taio says. "Sora, make it look convincing. Let them capture you and take you to their base in the tower. I'll be right behind you."

I take a deep breath. "Okay. Here goes nothing."

Before Forrest can protest further, I stand up, hands raised, and step out from behind our cover.

"Don't shoot!" I call out, trying to sound appropriately defeated. "I surrender!"

The paintball field goes quiet for a moment. Then Randy's voice rings out from the tower: "Well, well. Look who's all alone." He gestures to someone out of my sight. "Brody, escort our guest to the tower."

Brody emerges from behind a barricade, paintball gun trained on me.

"Don't," I plead.

"Don't what?" he grunts.

"Shoot me," I say. "I've never been hit before. Does it hurt really bad?"

The dumbass falls right into the trap. "Aw, is that why you

surrendered? You don't want to get shot? Calm down, Barbie. I'm not going to hurt you."

I comply, casting one last glance at Forrest's hiding spot. I can't see him, but I can practically feel his tension radiating from here.

As Brody marches me toward the tower, I secretly assess my surroundings, noting potential escape routes and cover points. The tower is a three-story structure with a spiral staircase leading to a platform at the top. Randy waits there, looking smugly triumphant as Brody pushes me onto the landing.

"Welcome to our humble fortress," Randy says with a mock bow. "Where are your friends hiding?"

I shrug innocently. "No idea. We got separated."

"Right," he scoffs. "Taio! Forrest!" he hollers out. "We've got your girl! Surrender now, and maybe we'll go easy on you!"

Silence answers him.

"They're probably regrouping," Brody suggests.

"Or they abandoned her," Trevor says, appearing at the top of the stairs. "Not that I blame them. She's deadweight."

I bite my tongue, reminding myself it's just a game and these are boys being boys, but come on. *Deadweight?* Rude.

"Jax is keeping watch on his perch," Trevor continues. "No sign of movement."

Randy nods, satisfied. "Perfect. Once we pick off Taio, Hawk will be easy. He's too busy worrying about his girlfriend to make any forward moves." He whirls on me with a condescending smile. "No offense, sweetie, but you're a liability out there."

"None taken," I reply cordially. "But I am curious about one thing."

"What's that?"

"Do you reserve hotel rooms or are you perfectly comfortable bringing women home to your mama's basement?"

Trevor snorts with unexpected laughter, which he quickly disguises as a cough when Randy glares at him.

"Funny," Randy says flatly.

"Oh my god, I was kidding, but it's true isn't it?" I cackle mercilessly. "You live with your mom?"

"You won't be laughing when your team is doing their walk of shame on camera," Randy sneers.

"Speaking of cameras," Brody says, pulling out his phone, "let's document this moment." He points the camera at me. "Feel free to unclasp those overalls and show a little more skin, honey. We'll be sending this to your boyfriend."

He's lowered his paintball gun to hold his phone. How interesting. Trevor, too, has relaxed his stance, as if I'm clearly not a threat. Even Randy has turned partially away, scanning the field below for signs of Forrest and Taio.

Silly rabbits. Full of tricks today.

In one fluid motion, I drop to the floor, roll, and come up with my weapon aimed squarely at Brody. I fire before he can react, hitting him point-blank in the chest.

"What the—" Randy spins around just as I swing my aim toward him, firing again. The paintball catches him on the shoulder, bright yellow against his black gear.

Trevor raises his weapon, but he's too slow. My third shot hits him on the mask, temporarily blinding him as paint splatters across his visor.

"Sorry, boys," I murmur, backing toward the stairs. "Liability, hmm?"

Randy wipes furiously at his shoulder, his face contorted with disbelief. "You conniving little—"

"I dare you to finish that sentence," Forrest's voice booms from behind me. He stands at the top of the stairs, paintball gun raised, Taio right behind him.

"Looks like our damsel rescued herself," Taio observes with obvious delight.

Randy looks from me to Forrest and back again, his expression slowly morphing from shock to grudging respect. "Well played. But Jax is still out there, and this game isn't over until—"

A loud whistle cuts him off. Below, a referee waves a blue flag.

"Game over! Home team wins by elimination!"

"What?" Randy rushes to the railing. "That's impossible."

"Oh, did I forget to mention, mates?" Saylor's voice comes through our earpieces, dripping with satisfaction. "I was never really out. Played dead, then circled around and got Jax while you lot were busy with your hostage situation."

Forrest lifts up his visor, breaking into a wide grin shadowed beneath his helmet, beaming at me.

"Not bad for an 'afternoon tea at the Ritz' girl, huh?" I call over my shoulder, breathless from the adrenaline and his proximity.

"Not bad at all," he agrees, his voice dropping to a lower register that sends a shiver up my spine. He very obviously looks me up and down. "In fact, that was...incredibly sexy."

Taio clears his throat. "If you two are done having a moment, we have a victory dance to perform and some very public humiliation to witness."

As we exit the tower, the humid air thick with the smell of paint and sweat, that familiar post-victory euphoria hits me good and hard. My pulse races; my hands still tremble from the rush. Without thinking, I grab Forrest's wrist and tow him toward a small equipment shed half-hidden by overgrown bushes near the edge of the playing field.

"What are you—"

I silence him with a look.

"Taio and Saylor can handle the victory formalities," I whisper, tugging him into the shed and closing the door behind us. The space is tiny—barely six by six, with shelves of paintball supplies lining the walls. Dust motes dance in the shafts of afternoon light filtering through cracks in the wooden slats.

Forrest's eyes darken as he realizes my intent. "Sora..."

"I must be on an adrenaline high or something," I confess, my voice raspy as I press against him. "I never do things like this. Ever. But there's something about you that makes me..." I gulp, unable to articulate the whirlwind of desire that's been knocking around my insides since the moment I met him.

"Makes you what?" he prompts, giving me a long, molten look.

"Different," I whisper. "You make me want to live a little."

He quirks an eyebrow. "Fooling around in an equipment shed is living a little?"

I lift up on tiptoe and press my mouth to his, tasting the salt of sweat on his upper lip. His helmet dangles from his hand as he drops it to the ground, wrapping his arms around me. The protective gear makes intimate contact nearly impossible, layers of padding keeping our bodies frustratingly apart.

"Off," I command, fumbling with the straps of my vest. "Too many...obstacles."

"Are you sure?" Forrest asks, even as his fingers assist mine, tugging at buckles and fastenings.

"We've been dancing around this for weeks," I say raggedly. "I keep waiting for you to... Anyway, I'm done waiting."

His chuckle is low and rough. "I was trying to do something special for you. A nice date first, or—"

"I don't want special. I want *now*." I unsnap the straps of my camo overalls. They fall to my waist, leaving me in only the tight black tank that *still* feels like too much fabric between us.

Forrest's gaze travels hungrily over my body. It might as well be a physical touch, leaving trails of heat wherever it lands. "Someone could walk in."

"Then you better be quick."

That's all the invitation he needs. All at once he backs me against the wall, his mouth finding mine in a bruising kiss that's nothing like the careful, tentative ones we've shared before. This is raw and desperate, his tongue demanding entry, teeth grazing my lower lip. I match his energy, fingers tangling in his hair, pulling him closer.

The shed is stifling, the air heavy with dust and the scent of paint and our mingled sweat. The wooden wall is rough against my back, but I barely register it, too consumed by the heat of Forrest's body against mine. His hands are everywhere—sliding up my sides, thumbs brushing the underside of my breasts, fingertips digging into my hips.

"I've thought about this," he murmurs against my neck, teeth grazing the sensitive spot below my ear. "Every night since I moved in. It's fucking torture, lying in bed, knowing you're right above me. Wondering if I'm also on your mind...maybe touching yourself, thinking about me."

His hand goes exploring beneath my tank top, palm hot against my skin as he cups my breast. Even through my sports bra, my nipple hardens against his touch. His thumb circles it, the friction of the fabric creating a delicious tension that has me arching into his hand.

"Forrest," I gasp, my head falling back against the wall as he pushes the tank up, mouth replacing fingers. The wet heat of his tongue through the thin fabric of my bra delivers shockwaves straight to my core.

My hands go on their own little quest, tracing the hard planes of his chest beneath his shirt, marveling at the contrast of smooth skin and taut muscle. I tug impatiently at the hem, needing to feel him, all of him. He pulls back just long enough to strip it off, then returns to me, skin against skin as I rake my nails lightly down his back.

He groans when I palm him through his pants, already hard and straining. "We don't have much time."

"I'll take what I can get," I whisper, my voice unrecognizable even to myself—breathy, demanding, shameless.

He turns me around to face the wall, the sudden movement making me inhale sharply. His chest presses against my back, one strong arm wrapping around my waist while his other hand slides beneath the waistband of my leggings, fingers dipping into my underwear.

"Already so wet," he murmurs against my ear, the wonder in his voice sending a fresh surge of arousal through me. His fingers find me slick and ready, the first touch making my knees buckle.

I bite back a moan as his middle finger circles my clit, teasing at first, then with growing pressure. His other hand covers my mouth, muffling the sounds I can't help making as he glides one finger inside me, then two, deepening his reach to hit the spot that makes me see stars.

"Shh," he whispers, his mouth open and hot against my neck. "Unless you want the whole paintball field to hear you come."

The thought of being discovered only heightens every sensation—his fingers pumping inside me, his thumb working my clit, his erection pressed hard against my ass through our clothes. I rock back against him, chasing the building pressure, lost in the dual sensations of fullness and friction.

"That's it," he encourages, his voice hewn with desire. "Don't fight it. Let go for me."

The cords of his forearm flex with his movements, his wrist twisting slightly to adjust the angle. His palm molds to my pubic bone, creating counter pressure with the rhythm of his fingers inside me that's making me mindless, and my inner walls clench hard around him.

As if inspired, Forrest's thumb presses more firmly, making tight circles around my clit as his fingertips curl upward, hitting that perfect spot with every thrust. The combination is overwhelming, sending floods of sensation that capsize me. I moan and whimper, issuing sounds I don't recognize. My thighs begin to tremble, my body tensing as the orgasm builds.

When his teeth scrape the sensitive skin where my neck meets my shoulder, I shatter. The orgasm hits me with sudden force, my walls clamping down around his fingers as the burst of pleasure radiates. What I could *not* have prepared for is the intense release that follows, a small rush of wetness soaking his hand and the inside of my underwear.

"Sora," Forrest whispers, sounding awed. "Do you always do that?"

I shake my head, too stunned to speak, my legs quivering so badly I'd collapse if not for his arm around my waist. "Sorry, sorry," I murmur, breathlessly. "I've never...not like *that*—"

"Just for me? Fuck, I love that so much. *Good girl*," he growls. "From now on you only come for me."

"Yes, okay. *Yes*." My lungs are all but collapsed, my skin hypersensitive as aftershocks ripple through me.

When I can finally move again, I turn in his arms, dropping to my knees on the dusty floor. His head rears back as I reach for his waistband, then work the button of his pants with newfound determination.

"Your turn," I offer, peering up at him through my lashes. My hair has come loose from its ponytail, falling in waves around my face.

"You don't have to—" he begins, but stops when I press my palm committedly to the large bulge in his pants.

"I want to." I free his cock, wrapping my hand around the impressive length. My thumb and middle finger can barely connect around his girth. It might be more than I can handle, but lust obliterates my hesitance. He's pulsing and hot in my palm, the skin like velvet over steel, already leaking from the tip. "I've pictured this for weeks."

"Does it measure up to your fantasy?" His voice is shredded and strained.

"Far exceeds." As I lap at the smooth crown of his sex.

The shed's dim lighting casts shadows across his face, but I can still see the way his pupils dilate, the way his jaw clenches with restraint. His hand comes to rest on my cheek, thumb brushing my bottom lip in a gesture that's surprisingly tender given the urgency of the moment.

His head falls back against the wall as I take him into my mouth, my tongue swirling around the head before I take him deeper. The taste of him is salt and musk, distinctly male, distinctly Forrest. His fingers twine in my hair, not guiding, just holding on as I set my own pace.

I hollow my cheeks, sucking as I pull back, then swallow him deeper. My hand works what my mouth can't reach, twisting slightly on the upstroke. I can feel the tautness in his thighs, the restraint it takes for him not to thrust.

"Fuck's sake," he groans when I use my free hand to cup him, gently rolling his balls between my fingers. "You're going to be the death of me."

I hum in agreement, the vibration eliciting a curse under his breath. His hips start to move in small, controlled thrusts, careful not to go too deep. Always considerate, even when he's losing control.

The power I feel is intoxicating—this strong, gorgeous man coming undone by my touch, by my mouth. I've never felt so desirable, so feminine, so connected to someone during an act that's always felt more mechanical than intimate before.

"I'm close," he cautions me after a few minutes, trying to pull away. "Sora, move—"

I ignore his warning, redoubling my efforts. I take him as deep as I can, relaxing my throat around him, feeling him swell against my tongue. With a strangled groan, he comes, his release hot, so deep against the back of my throat, I have no choice but to swallow. I do so without hesitation, reveling in the carnal intimacy of knowing him *like this*—the taste of him. My breath slows. I hold his eye contact as I lick my lips.

For a moment, we're locked in time—him leaning against the wall, me kneeling before him, both of us breathing hard. Then reality starts to filter back in. The sounds of the paintball field outside, voices calling for us, the uncomfortable awareness of our surroundings.

"That was…" Forrest starts, helping me to my feet.

"Overdue," I complete, adjusting my clothes. "We're behind on our research, Forrest. Time to catch up."

He chuckles, tucking himself back into his pants. "I fucking love school."

CHAPTER TWENTY-TWO

Sora

And then my heart falls right out of my ass.

"To Sora!" Taio raises his beer high. "The stealthiest double agent in paintball history!"

"*To Sora!*" Saylor and Forrest echo, clinking their glasses against mine.

An hour after our paintball victory, we're seated in a corner booth at McGinty's, the local pub near the paintball facility. The Slaughterhouse Four occupy a table across the space, looking markedly less cheerful as they nurse the beers we bought them out of pity. We spared them from buying our drinks but still forced them into the reluctant video testimonial, declaring us "the superior paintball team in every way, now and forever."

I'm still riding the high of our victory, my body humming with leftover adrenaline and the pleasant buzz of the hard cider Saylor insisted I try. My hair is damp from the shower I took at the facility, and my skin still bears faint marks—almost hickeys—where Forrest sucked on my skin in the equipment shed.

"I still can't believe you took out all three of them," Saylor says, shaking his head in disbelief. "Where'd you learn to shoot like that?"

"Beginner's luck," I say with a pop of my shoulders.

"Bullshit," Taio counters with a knowing smirk. "You're a natural-born killer."

"Hardly." I laugh. "But I did grow up playing a lot of arcade games with my dad when he was actually around. When I was little, he used to take me to Pewter's, which is like a Dave & Busters. We liked that hunting game."

"Your dad playing Big Buck Hunter," Forrest muses, taking a swig of his beer. "Now there's an image."

"He was terrible at it," I admit. "But he tried. It was one of the few childhood memories I have of us together."

An awkward silence falls over the table at the mention of my father, and I mentally kick myself for bringing down the mood. I've noticed both Taio and Saylor are careful to avoid the subject of Forrest's escort work, and in return, I should probably be more careful about my own familial baggage.

"So," I say, eager to change the subject, "how's Dakota doing at her grandparents'? Have you heard from her?" I direct the question at Forrest, who's been checking his phone periodically throughout the evening.

His expression softens at the mention of his daughter. "She's good. Hannah's mom sent me a photo of Koda in her new princess floaties."

"That's sweet of her."

He must sense the curiosity in my tone, because he elaborates. "Hannah's parents have always been good to me. They weren't thrilled when we split, but they've made an effort to stay in Dakota's life—and by extension, mine."

"Unlike Hannah herself," Taio mutters under his breath, earning a warning look from Forrest.

"Speaking of family," Saylor interjects smoothly, "Forrest tells us you're a hotshot romance writer. We were at Turn The Page the other day looking for your books."

"Yeah...my books aren't there," I say, forcing a small smile. "I'm an indie romance author."

"It's an independent bookstore," Taio adds.

"Yeah, well, I inquired a few times. Never heard back. They don't like to stock inventory they don't think they can sell." I feel my face flush. "I'll never be a big-name author like my dad or anything, I'm just trying to keep my head above water." My default is to humbly accept defeat, but the words taste bad as I say them. Not because they're self-deprecating, but because they are the truth. I'm chasing a dream I know I'll never have.

"Hey, chin up, damsel," Taio perks up. "You just started, right? You have time to make your name."

"Four years, twelve books." I sigh. "Not one has ever turned a decent profit."

Here's something interesting about escorts, or at least *these* escorts, they are emotionally intuitive. They all exchange small, piteous glances.

"Real talk—do you suck at it, love?" Saylor asks right before he catches Forrest's balled-up fist right in the sternum.

He's still wheezing when Forrest cuts in. "Don't be an ass. She's phenomenal. But the book industry is a lot like Hollywood. It's luck, lottery, and all about who you know."

"Doesn't she have connections though? Forrest told us your dad is—"

"J.P. Cooper, yes," I confirm. "Wow, Forrest." I flash him a look. "How many of my secrets have you shared with your little cohort, hm?"

"Just your nicknames, your deep insecurities as an author, your strained relationship with your dad, and all the wild monkey sex you two have," Taio helpfully supplies.

I widen my eyes at Forrest. "So, just surface-level stuff, then."

Forrest hangs his head in shame. "I'm sorry. I only shared our situation so they could help. They were supposed to be helping me plot book-themed dates"—he glares at Saylor, then Taio—"not opening their fucking mouths and swallowing their feet whole."

"Sora, ignore his temper tantrum," Taio says, taking another big swig of his lager. "Consider us your support crew. I don't care if we have to strap your books around our chest and step out on Broadway, naked. We're all here to help you. If Forrest has a mission, that means we do too."

"Aw, that's so sweet. You guys are good friends." I nudge Forrest's stiff shoulder. He's still staring maniacally at Saylor.

"So what's your next book about? The upcoming release—second part of the duet, right?"

I flash Forrest another look. "*Jesus.* Do they know my bra size as well?" He stays silent, avoiding my gaze. "It's…" I hesitate, suddenly self-conscious. "It's a second-chance romance about high school sweethearts who reconnect at their ten-year reunion. The first book was from her perspective. They broke up because of circumstances at the end of book one, and now book two is from his perspective and how he wins her back. I don't think it's going to do well. I thought it was clever—something out of the norm to write an entire romance book from the hero's POV, but I'm convinced it's going to be yet another flop."

"Nah, that's kind of cool. Good representation. I'll read it. Every single page." Taio nods approvingly. "Does it have the big grovel?"

"The what?" Forrest asks.

"The grovel," Taio explains with the patience of a professor. "When the hero has to beg for forgiveness, usually in some grand, public gesture that proves he's grown and changed."

I stare at him, momentarily speechless. "You really do read romance."

Taio shrugs. "I contain multitudes."

"He's also surprisingly good at braiding hair," Saylor adds. "Does a mean French braid for Koda when he's not being a complete tool."

"Hidden depths," I murmur, glancing at Forrest, who's watching our exchange with an unreadable expression. "Always a good quality in a hero."

After another round of drinks, I check my watch and realize how late it's gotten. "I should probably get going. It's been a long day."

"I'll grab the tab and call a ride," Forrest says, his hand finding mine under the table.

"No, stay," I insist. "I've already hijacked enough of your boys' day. You deserve some time with your friends."

"I'm sick of these fools. I'd rather be with you," Forrest says playfully. Then with his voice low enough that only I can hear, "We have some unfinished business, yeah?" The heat in his gaze is palpable, memories of the shed still vivid in my mind.

"Is that so?" I lean closer.

"Absolutely."

"Special plans?" I tease.

Forrest shoots me a wink. "Let me take you to dinner."

"A dinner date isn't particularly tropey," I muse. "What would we be researching?"

"No, just dinner. No research tonight. Just me and you, breaking bread. Anywhere you want."

The sincerity in his voice catches me off guard. This isn't Forrest the escort, fulfilling a contract. This is just...Forrest. Asking me out. Like a normal guy.

"Are you sure?"

"Positive," he says. "We practically live together, but we've never been on a proper date. I want to fix that."

My heart does a little flip. "Well, in that case, I know just the place."

After saying our goodbyes to Taio and Saylor, Forrest and I head out into the crisp pre-evening air.

"So, where are we going?" he asks as we walk to the cab. "Gotta let the driver know."

"Anywhere I want?"

He nods.

"Galbi Grill," I tell him. "Best Korean BBQ in the city. My mom practically raised me on their food."

"Perfect." He opens the passenger door for me. "I've been craving Korean."

I chuckle at the obvious innuendo.

An hour later, after a flirty cab ride, we enter one of my favorite places on earth. The restaurant is bustling, filled with the sizzle of meat on hot plates and the rich aroma of garlic and ginger.

"This place looks...intimidating," Forrest observes, his eyes darting left and right.

"Two, please," I say to the hostess. "In a tatami room. Is that okay?" I ask Forrest.

"Sure? What does that mean?"

"Traditional Korean dining. It's a low table and we sit on the floor on big cushions. But they have regular tables if you prefer."

"No, tatami it is," Forrest says eagerly, a wide smile on his face. "Whatever makes you happy."

The hostess checks her seating map, and beams. "It looks like we have space in Seoul." She looks at Forrest to clarify, recognizing him as a first-timer. "All the tatami rooms are named after major South Korean cities—Seoul, Busan, Daegu, Incheon. Everything is full with reservations tonight, but there's only one other couple dining in Seoul, we just seated them. We have another barbeque table open."

"Great," he answers, still looking a touch overwhelmed.

The hostess fetches two large menus and leads us to the back of the restaurant. She slides open the partition to the private room, and apologizes to the couple already seated for disrupting them.

My heart sinks when I see who we're dining with tonight.

"Soraya?" my mom asks, saying my name Korean-style, the accent she normally suppresses barreling through. Her eyes pop in surprise, then latch on to my hand which is weaved in Forrest's.

Shit, that would've been uncomfortable enough, but then the gentleman she's with turns his head, and my heart falls right out of my ass.

"Dad?" I ask in shock.

"Your dad," Forrest echoes, nearly choking on the words. "Well," he murmurs under his breath, "this should be interesting."

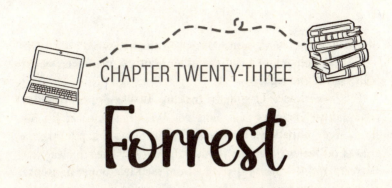

CHAPTER TWENTY-THREE

Forrest

She might as well be Eloise at The Plaza.

The moment my eyes lock with J.P. Cooper's, I feel like I've been hit by a freight train—if freight trains wore designer glasses and had perfect salt-and-pepper hair. Here I am, an escort with a law degree, standing in front of one of the world's most celebrated authors, who also happens to be my fake girlfriend's father.

A fake girlfriend who is currently staring at her parents—together—with her mouth hanging open so wide you could park a small aircraft carrier in it.

"Mom? Dad?" Sora squeaks, still clutching my hand like it's the last life vest on the Titanic. "What are you doing here? Together?"

Jennifer Cho recovers first, smoothing her elegant silk blouse with a practiced calm that reminds me of Sora whenever she's flustered. "What a lovely surprise, Sora," she says, switching seamlessly back to a dialect devoid of an accent. "And who is this handsome man?"

I gather my wits and extend my hand, trying not to look like someone who gets paid to take his clothes off for a living. "Forrest Hawkins, ma'am. It's a pleasure to meet you."

J.P. Cooper doesn't rise to shake my hand. Instead, he studies me with the unnerving intensity of someone who makes a living dissecting human nature—or possibly dissecting frogs in his spare time. "Pleasure," he says, his voice deep and measured.

"Dad, remember how you like me to tell you when you're being rude?" Sora warns.

"Sorry. Soju and gravity making me lazy," he grumbles, thoroughly chastised by his daughter. He rises to his feet, his full frame more burly than I expected. Disguised as a handshake, he tries to pulverize the bones in my hand to ash. "Nice to meet you, Forrest. I'm J.P.—please spare me from the Mr. Cooper nonsense. How about you two join us for dinner?"

Sora, satisfied at the greeting, finally releases my other hand to slide onto the cushion across from her parents. I follow, peeved at the low table that won't hide my jittery legs. I've met plenty of clients' parents and family members before. Endless weddings, bah mitzvahs, anniversaries, pretending to be in love with a client I barely knew, but this? It's different. Because I want to give an actual good impression.

And the only thing I've done today to prepare for this big moment in Sora's and my weird relationship is finger-fuck her until she was sated in a dirty paintball equipment shed. Not ideal.

"So, Dad, when did you get into town?" Sora asks nonchalantly.

"Yesterday, actually. I swung by the brownstone to see you today, but there was no answer," J.P. says so casually.

"You didn't just go in?" Sora asks, the color slowly draining from her face.

"No, it's your home now. Why would I do that?"

"Forrest is living with me at the brownstone," she blurts out in a hurry, abandoning any prior sense of cool. She clasps her hands over her face, like she can cover her guilty confession. "And his little daughter," she murmurs between split fingers.

We're momentarily saved by our waitress returning with two small glasses of ice water with lemon. She asks if we want any alcoholic beverages and our answers couldn't be more different.

"No, thank you," Sora says, "but a Coke Zero, please?"

"And for you, sir? The same?" the waitress asks me. I catch her eyes, flashing her a pleading look that says: *Save me.*

"Oh, no. Bring me alcohol, please."

"What kind?" she asks.

I shrug, evidence of my discomfort visible all over my face. "Doesn't even matter. Surprise me."

She laughs and then turns her attention to Sora's parents. Her mother proceeds to ask about chef specials, and I steal a momentarily private audience with Sora.

"Really? Just jumped in with the admission?" I ask under my breath. "Couldn't let me warm up the crowd first?"

"Sorry," she mutters. "My mom is a human lie detector test. It's better to be up-front."

"Even so, I think there are some things we need to keep to ourselves tonight, yeah?" I widen my eyes at her.

She nods, visibly shaken.

"Do you mind if I order for the table? J.P. doesn't know his favorites, but I do," Ms. Cho says, addressing me and Sora, but her gaze is on me.

"Not at all."

Ms. Cho starts ordering in fluent Korean, way too much food. The only thing I can understand is when she finishes by requesting a round of apple soju.

"It's sweet, you'll like it," Sora assures me.

There's pretty much just uncomfortable silence until the waitress returns with the first round of drinks.

"One won't kill you, Sora," Ms. Cho urges, grabbing the green glass bottle and pouring the clear liquid into four shot glasses. "Come on, we're celebrating."

"Celebrating what, exactly?" Sora asks, pointing between her parents. "Last I heard you weren't returning Dad's texts. Now he's visiting again, and you two are on a date?"

"Right, good assist with that, kiddo," J.P. mutters.

Sora blushes. "I was going to talk to her for you, Dad. I got distracted."

J.P. lifts a brow. "Distracted? And here I thought his name was Forrest." He smirks at his not-that-funny joke. "Anyway, I flew in because we're celebrating your mom's recent promotion." He raises his shot glass and tips it at each of us, before falling into a speech. "This woman is an enigma. Graceful, tender, soft, warm, yet fierce like a knight in the face of battle. Battle being the sexist pigs at her office, determined to keep their glass ceilings in place. Nonetheless, with wit, charm, and the most beautiful soul, she crashes through their crystal walls, every single time. Jennifer—*Cho, Min-Ja*—cheers to finally getting the recognition that is so long overdue for you, my sweetheart."

Following J.P.'s lead, I throw back the shot, expecting something akin to the smoothness of vodka. Instead, it's sweet and deceptively mild—the kind of drink that'll have you on the floor before you realize what's happening.

I turn to Sora. "That was really good. I think—" I stop short when I see her bewildered expression, her shot glass still full, teetering between her fingers. "What's wrong?" I ask.

"What the hell kind of speech was that?" she asks accusingly, looking between her mother and father.

"I thought it was quite nice," her mother chimes in.

"Yeah, *too nice*. Is no one else concerned that an alien parasite might be safe-harboring in Dad's body right now?"

Ms. Cho shrugs. "It's crossed my mind, but I prefer the parasite to the old version of your dad." She proceeds to fill her glass again, a playful grin on her face as she refills the other empty soju glasses, mine included. "Drink up. It's bad luck to leave it on the table," she tells her daughter.

Begrudgingly, Sora throws back her shot like it's water, not reminiscent of a girl who rarely drinks.

"So," J.P. strikes up, setting down his glass with deliberate precision, "you're living with my daughter at my house?"

"Dad, I thought you just said it was *my* house now?" Sora warns. "And it's not like that."

"On the contrary, it's exactly like that," he counters. "You share a residence. That's the definition of living together."

I clear my throat. "Sir, I should explain. Sora has been

kind enough to let me and my daughter, Dakota, stay with her temporarily. My ex left the country—"

"Left her four-year-old daughter behind," Sora adds.

"—and Sora offered her home as an alternative. My old apartment isn't suitable now that I have my daughter full-time. And you know how real estate is in New York City." I run a hand through my hair, painfully aware of J.P.'s penetrating stare. "It's been a tremendous help. But it won't be forever. I realize how that sounds, taking advantage of Sora's generosity, but—"

"Son, calm down," J.P. interrupts. "You're not on trial. We're glad Sora's making new...friends. Daphne is a bit much, even in small doses."

"You've met her like four times ever," Sora grumbles.

"Case in point," he sasses back. "Anyway, Mr. Hawkins, what do you do for work?"

The million-dollar question. I feel Sora tense beside me.

"Financial consulting," I answer smoothly. "Mostly private clients."

"Private clients," J.P. repeats, turning the phrase over like he's examining a suspicious object. "Must be lucrative. You and Jennifer have a lot in common. Same field."

My face fills with heat. Oh shit. Sora didn't tell me her mom's profession is my fake one. I scramble, racking my brain for any finance jargon I can pull out of my ass in a hurry.

"It pays the bills," I say, keeping my expression neutral despite the sudden warmth crawling up my neck.

Luckily the conversation steers to Dakota, which is an easy topic for me. Ms. Cho asks questions about Dakota's milestones, her hobbies and interests, enthused, like she's her own grandchild. Conversation flows easily until the first round of food arrives. *Banchan* as Ms. Cho explains it—small side dishes that precede the main meal. She immediately begins describing each one, her hospitality overshadowing her ex-husband's somewhat grumpy demeanor.

"This is kimchi, fermented cabbage. And here we have

japchae, sweet potato noodles. This one is quite tasty," she exclaims, pointing to a vibrant red dish.

"Forrest doesn't like spicy food," Sora interjects, trying to come to my rescue as her mom pushes little silver bowl after bowl my way.

Ms. Cho balks, shock filling her face like she's a touch offended. "Kimchi isn't spicy. Galbi Grill has the best banchan. Very mild."

Sora groans. "She's lying to you, Forrest. Run from kimchi."

"It's fine. I like spicy food, I just eat it sparingly," I lie with conviction, reaching for exactly what she warned against. "I'd love to try it." I take a generous bite, and immediately feel like I've swallowed molten lava. My eyes water, my sinuses clear instantly, and I'm fairly certain my tongue is filing for divorce from the rest of my body. For some stupid reason, I take another bite.

"Mmm," I manage, giving a thumbs-up as tears stream down my face.

Ms. Cho looks impressed. "See? Good, right? Eat up, honey. We can order more."

Sora looks horrified. "Are you dying?" she whispers.

"I'm fine," I croak, reaching for water, which only spreads the fire.

J.P. smirks. "The soju helps," he suggests, filling my shot glass again.

I gulp it down gratefully, the relief immediate, as the taste of sweet apple replaces the burning flames.

"So, Ms. Cho," I say once I can speak again, "Sora's dad mentioned you also work in finance?"

"Jennifer, please," she insists. My country-boy heart struggles with this. I'll call them what they prefer but it's painful not to address my girlfriend's parents as anything other than Mr. and Ms.

"Thank you, Ms. Jennifer," I respond, finding a happy compromise.

"Such a gentleman," she coos. "And yes, I work in wealth

management for a private bank. Nothing as riveting as what you probably do. I'm assuming your clients are more invested in stocks? Personal wealth? We work more with venture capitalists."

"Spot-on," I say flatly, not knowing if that's true.

"Now what's the likelihood of you getting Sora a job?"

"Sora has a job," I respond, a little sharper than I intend.

"Mom thinks writing romance novels is ridiculous," Sora explains, a trace of old hurt in her voice.

"I said frivolous, not ridiculous," Jennifer protests. "I said it's difficult to make a living at it. There's a difference. How many writers do you know can feed their families off their income?"

"Besides Dad?" There's challenge in Sora's eyes, addressing the obvious truth we're all privy to. J.P. Cooper is a do-as-I-say, not-as-I-do kind of father.

The table falls silent. Even the sizzling grill seems to quiet.

"For clarity, I'm also an author, Forrest," J.P. echoes.

"Oh, I know. You're a legend, sir. And it's nice to see that the apple doesn't fall far from the tree." I wrap my arm around Sora's shoulders, giving her a little squeeze. "If we ever have children, I hope they are creative and brave enough to follow in your guys' footsteps."

J.P.'s jaw hardens, and his eyes go flat. "I've been trying to kick the apple clear off the orchard for years now. But Sora's a stubborn one."

"Lovely, Dad, thanks," Sora grumbles, further deflating.

"I think it's admirable." I place a hand on Sora's knee and squeeze, like I'm trying to hold her together. "Following your passion takes courage."

"It takes something," J.P. mutters. "Not sure it's courage."

"J.P.," Jennifer warns quietly.

"What? We're all adults here." He fixes Sora with a penetrating stare. "How much was your last royalty check? Enough to cover rent? Groceries?"

"Dad—"

"Because if not, you're not following your passion. You're

indulging a hobby at the expense of a real career."

Sora's shoulders slump, and something coiled up in me finally unravels, then snaps.

"With all due respect, sir," I say, my voice calm but firm, "your daughter is incredibly talented. And resilient. She works harder than anyone I know."

J.P.'s eyebrows shoot up. "Is that right?"

"Yes, it is." I meet his gaze. "Not everyone's path to success looks the same. And not everyone measures success by the size of their bank account."

"Easy to say when you have one," J.P. counters.

"I know struggle," I reply, thinking of the endless days and nights of my childhood on the ranch, working to make ends meet. How my dad got up every day, not knowing if the lights would stay on, but he laced up his boots and put on his hat just the same. "And I know what it takes to keep going when the odds are stacked against you."

I look over at Sora, her eyes wide with surprise. "You know what I hope? I hope that one day Dakota grows up to be as brave and determined as you. I hope she finds something she loves as much as you love writing. And I can promise you this—no matter what her passion is, I'll be cheering her on every step of the way, not trying to snuff out her dream."

J.P.'s face darkens. "That's because you're still a young father. You don't understand your purpose yet."

"My purpose?" I ask, turning back to his stoic expression.

"Mothers nurture. They care for their children, build them up." He gestures to Jennifer. "A father's job is to teach their children not to need them. We prepare them for the real world."

"By crushing their spirits?" I challenge.

"By being honest." J.P. leans forward. "The way Sora's going, the only way she keeps her head above water is because of constant money transfers, gifted housing, and the princess lifestyle I've provided. No way she could fend for herself in New York City without my help. Now, I'm not saying my daughter is greedy. She's a lovely girl with a beautiful heart, all thanks to her mother, but with the way she's making life decisions, she might as well be Eloise at The Plaza. Living in the clouds, never afraid of falling because Daddy's wallet will always be her safety net."

Sora flinches like she's been slapped.

"If I'm bitter," the man continues, "it's because I'm mad at myself. I've failed as a father. My daughter is twenty-seven years old and still can't take care of herself like an adult because she's busy chasing something that is almost guaranteed not to work out." He looks at Sora, his expression softening slightly. "It's a tough realization, but it's true."

Sora's eyes fill with tears. She places her napkin on the table with wobbly hands. "Excuse me," she whispers, her voice breaking. "I need the restroom."

She rises and hurries out of the private dining room, shoulders hunched against the weight of her father's words.

Jennifer turns to her ex-husband, fury in her normally gentle eyes. "Did you have to do that? Today of all days?"

"It's out of love," J.P. insists, though he has the decency to look uncomfortable. "We've coddled her for so long. She needs to hear the truth."

"Your version of the truth," Jennifer corrects sharply. "You're so determined to protect her from failure that you won't even let her try."

"I thought we were in agreement it's time for her to grow up?"

"When she's ready. *She's still a baby*!"

"She is *not*, Jennifer. When we were her age—"

"Oh, what do you remember about when we were her age? Hm?" Jennifer taps her temple furiously. "You were there, but you *weren't there*, J.P."

They continue to argue as if I've disappeared into the background. I hate the way they're talking about Sora. Their narrative leaves out the most crucial parts of her story. *A princess?* Please. I've never met anyone more humble than Sora. *Head in the clouds?* Every day I have to help Sora fight the urge to quit amidst the tough reality of her stalled career. I'm here to remind my cookie girl that she's good enough, more than good enough—she's worthy.

As for all the financial help J.P.'s giving her—which Sora wasn't exactly forthcoming about—who the fuck cares? Sora clearly only takes what she absolutely needs. The only designer thing I've ever seen her with is that dress, which let's be honest, she's probably had since high school. We're all just trying to survive. He should be thrilled his wealth can serve a noble purpose like giving his child a beautiful life.

I can't take this shit anymore.

I reach into my pocket, pull out several hundred-dollar bills, and place them on the table.

"Dinner's on me," I say, interrupting their conversation.

J.P. looks up, surprised. "That's not necessary—"

"I think it is." I meet his gaze once more. "You know, Mr. Cooper, I'm starting to understand why there's so much turmoil between you and Sora. You might be speaking what you believe is truth, but your delivery...it needs work."

"Excuse me?"

"You know what Sora's biggest dream is? It's not to be a famous author with her name in lights. It's just for you to be proud of her." I stand up slowly, "So yeah, I guess you're right. She is doomed to fail at her dreams."

J.P. stares at me, eyes narrow, his expression warring between anger and shock.

"It was nice meeting you, Ms. Jennifer," I say, nodding respectfully to Sora's mom. "Thank you for your hospitality."

Jennifer gives me a small smile. "I'm sorry, Forrest. We're not usually this...animated."

Bullshit, I think to myself.

I head toward the restrooms, leaving J.P. to absorb my words. In the corridor, I nearly collide with Sora, her eyes red-rimmed but dry. She's pulled herself together, preparing to return to the table with her dignity intact.

"Hey," I say softly, taking her hands in mine. "You okay?"

She nods stiffly. "I'm fine. I'm so sorry I ditched you. I'm ready to go back—"

"No." I squeeze her hands. "Let's go home."

"But my parents—"

"Will understand." I brush a strand of hair from her face. "Or they won't. Either way, you don't need to sit through more of that tonight."

"He's right, though," she whimpers, looking down. "I'm not making it on my own. I'm failing. But I promise you, I'm not some rich, irresponsible, spoiled brat. Yes, my dad has helped me through some—"

"Sora, I am tired of your dad for the evening. And I don't give a fuck if you sucked his bank account dry. It doesn't change what I know about you and your heart." I tilt her chin up, so she meets my gaze. "Listen to me. Even if I'm the last man standing, I will always be in your corner. Always supporting you. Always cheering you on."

Her eyes search mine, looking for the truth.

"No matter what happens," I continue, "you better not give up. Not on your writing, not on yourself."

Something shifts in her expression—a flicker of hope rekindling. "We should go back to the table," she says, but there's no conviction in her tone.

"Or I could take you home," I suggest quietly. "Our home."

The word hangs between us, weighted with meaning. For a moment, we're not pretending. Not playing roles. Just two people, standing in the dim corridor of a Korean restaurant, holding on to each other like lifelines.

"Our home," she repeats, and there's a smile in her voice even as fresh tears shine in her eyes. "Yes. Let's go there."

I place my hand at the small of her back, guiding her toward the exit. We don't look back at the tatami room where her parents sit. Tonight isn't about them. It's about Sora reclaiming her worth, her dignity—and me, realizing just how far I've fallen.

As we step outside into the cool evening air, Sora leans into me, her body warm against mine despite the chill. I wrap my arm around her shoulders, drawing her closer.

She giggles softly out of the blue.

"What?" I ask.

"You always say daddy issues are your bread and butter." She smiles up at me. "Now you see mine clear as crystal. I'm so glad Dakota will never, ever feel like this, Forrest. You're a really good dad. The times you doubt yourself, don't forget that. You're great at the thing that matters most."

The simple statement hits me like a punch to the chest—unexpected and powerful. Before I can respond, she rises on her tiptoes and presses a gentle kiss to my jaw.

"Thank you," she whispers. "For defending me."

"Always," I promise, as serious as a vow.

Our rideshare pulls up to the curb, and as we slide into the back seat, I can't help but think about how quickly this arrangement has become something real. Something I don't want to lose.

Sora settles against my shoulder, her familiar scent—peaches and vanilla—filling my senses. Her fingers find mine in the darkness, intertwining with a certainty that belies her father's doubts.

And as Sora's breathing steadies against me, I make a silent promise. Even if we can't last, even if this is just a story, for her sake, I'm going to make damn sure it has a happy ending.

CHAPTER TWENTY-FOUR

Forrest

Lean into the mess.

I started on the six-pack before I even knocked on Taio's door—my old door, technically. The hallway is still the same uninspiring beige, the flickering light above the apartment number still needs fixing, the Indian lady from 6B is still cooking something that makes the entire floor smell like heaven.

Home sweet former home.

When Taio finally opens up, he's wearing nothing but basketball shorts and a confused expression. He leans against the doorframe, crosses his arms, and gives me a once-over.

"You're lost, bro. You no longer live here," he says, barely suppressing a grin. "Go back to your princess castle."

I hold up the remaining beers, the cardboard handle of the carrier lazily looped around my fingers. "I need to talk."

"Must be serious if you're sharing the good stuff. And by good stuff, I mean this bargain-basement piss you call beer."

"Shut up. My pockets are a little light these days." Truth is, I haven't been working. Because I'm scared of what that'll do to me and Sora.

Taio steps aside to let me in. The apartment looks exactly the same, except for the new addition of about seventeen sneaker boxes stacked precariously in one corner. Taio's latest obsession—limited-edition Jordans he'll probably never wear. Meanwhile, I'm not working, but clearly Taio's hustling hard.

"Make yourself at home," he says, grabbing one of the beers. "Oh wait, this actually was your home before you abandoned me for a mansion."

"It's a brownstone, not a mansion," I correct him, falling into our familiar routine. "And the bathroom no longer smells like your rancid protein drinks, so I consider that an upgrade."

"My protein drinks smell like success, asshole." He flops onto the couch, propping his feet on the coffee table. "So what brings you back to the peasant quarters? Dakota still with her Stepford family?"

"She's with Hannah's parents for the whole weekend." I settle in next to him, the familiar grooves of our secondhand couch enveloping me like an old friend. "They wanted some grandparent time."

Taio takes a long pull from his beer. "How was dinner? Why are you here? I thought you and Sora would be pounding energy drinks, getting ready for round eighteen."

"We went to dinner, and accidentally ran into her parents."

Taio's eyes bulge. "As in you met J.P. Cooper?"

"In the flesh."

"*Damn.* What's your new pops like?"

I roll my eyes. "My *pops* lives in Wyoming. And J.P. Cooper is a massive dick...especially to his daughter."

"That bad?"

"Worse." I pop open my beer and catch up with him. "Right in front of me and her mom, the man basically told Sora she's a failure because her daddy still pays her bills. Said she should've gone into finance like her mom. Real heartwarming stuff. She bolted from the dinner table, crying. God, I wanted to clock him right then and there."

"You should've. What an asshole." Taio takes another long swig, then swivels the remnants in the bottle, making a whirlpool.

"Worst part? He's probably right."

Taio whistles low. "Damn, Hawk. Did not see that coming.

Since when are you on Team Dream Crusher?"

"I'm not," I snap. "Nobody wants this for Sora more than me. Except maybe Daphne. But look, Sora's talented. Really talented. But the odds of making it as an author? I'm learning it's like winning the lottery."

"So? People win the lottery every day."

"And millions don't," I add.

"You know what surprises me most about this conversation?" Taio asks, reaching for beer number two.

"What?"

"That you keep saying she's amazing and talented, but you haven't read her books."

I shrug, suddenly self-conscious. "Your point?"

"Why not?"

"I don't know," I mumble before polishing off the bottle.

"I know why," he says.

"Do I want to hear your reasoning?" I gaze at the wall, acting aloof, but knowing we're on the cusp of a difficult conversation. I toss the empty bottle and grab another.

"Probably not, but I'm going to drop a truth bomb on you anyway."

I let out a low grumble of annoyance mixed with curiosity. "Fine. Lay it on me."

"You're afraid she isn't a good writer. Or maybe she's a good writer, but doesn't have good story ideas. You're probably thinking that if you dig too deep into the truth, you might be peddling the same bullshit her dad is." He curls up on the couch in a defensive position, arms blocking his head. "Go ahead and hit me. I'll let you have one good lick, just not in my money maker."

"I don't want to hit you," I murmur, staring at the peeling label on my beer, buying time. "You're right. I don't know. I just...I don't want to see her hurt. But all she does is cry."

"That's not true," Taio says, relaxing again, stretching out his legs once more. "She had a blast at paintball today. She had *fun* and let loose. It's obvious she doesn't do that often. She was laughing and joking with a smug little smile, all proud of her badass antics. It was cute. You did that for her, man."

"Did I?" I muse quietly.

For a moment, it's just the sound of us slurping down our beers, allowing the calm silence to settle between us.

"I read her book," Taio finally says.

"Which one?" I sit up straight, intrigue piqued. "How was it?"

"Binged a few, actually. Just wrapped up *Lovely* when I got home. Dominated at paintball. Got tipsy at the pub. Came home, read, shed a few tears. Perfect day, my guy."

"Focus. How was the book, Ty?" I rush out.

"Really good. The way she writes about people feeling like they're unlovable—it's like she gets it, you know? Like she understands what it's like to always be on the outside looking in. But I think that's her big problem."

"What is?"

Taio eyes me over his beer. "Sora writes for a certain type of reader. Someone with depth who wants to learn a little emotional intelligence." He spans his pitcher's mitt of a hand over his chest. "Obviously, as a refined man, I get it. But other readers? As far as escapism goes, I think most want pure entertainment. Not a lesson in love."

"I'm not surprised she has trouble connecting with the masses, because she's so unique, you know?" I tell him. "Like she's sassy, but also sweet. Hilariously snarky, but so polite and tender too. A total amateur at some things, but a professor at others. She's the kind of girl that gives you whiplash in the best way."

Taio stares at me like he's disgusted. "Damn, you're already in deep."

I exhale slowly. "Fine. I think I'm in over my head. And I have no damn clue what to do about it."

"What's to do? You like her, she likes you. Seems pretty straightforward."

I sigh. "Yeah, there's just the small matter of me needing to fuck other women for a paycheck. I've been dodging Rina's calls best I can, but she's getting pissy. I haven't seen a client since the first night I stayed with Sora. She's been giving away all my jobs."

Taio slams his beer down on the coffee table. "So you're the reason I'm working every other night, and my dick is cooked like an overdone bratwurst." He adjusts himself for emphasis. "I had to use cream for the *chafing*, man."

I laugh, choking on my beer. "Sorry about that."

"Don't be. Money's good." He leans forward, suddenly serious. "But what's your endgame here, Hawk? You can't avoid Rina forever."

"I know," I groan, rubbing my face. "But working suddenly feels like betraying Sora. I'm not saying I'm the best at relationships, but I'm pretty sure cheating on her wouldn't bode well."

"Cheating? That's bold. She knows what you do for a living. It's not emotional, just a job. Even porn stars get into relationships. They figure it out without the jealousy."

I cut him a sideways glance. "You can split hairs all you want. But if it feels like cheating, *it's cheating*."

"Fine. So what's your endgame, then?"

"I've got no endgame here," I confess, slumping back into the couch. "I'm just...winging it."

Taio snorts. "That's a first. Mr. Plan-Everything-to-Death has no strategy."

"Look where all my careful planning got me." I gesture vaguely around us. "Debt up to my eyeballs. Dakota's pretty much estranged from her grandpa, all because I'm ashamed to face my dad while I'm selling my body to pay the bills."

"Silver lining—you're living in a multimillion-dollar brownstone with a hot author who looks at you like you hung the moon," Taio adds dryly. "Real tragedy."

I laugh despite myself. "Temporarily."

Taio shifts, turning to face me fully. "You know what's ironic? You're telling Sora to get out of her head. To live a little. To stop overthinking everything and just enjoy the ride."

"So?"

"So maybe you should take your own advice, genius." He tips his beer in my direction. "Sometimes you have to stop planning and lean into the mess. That's life, man."

I comb a hand through my hair, tugging slightly at the roots. "It's not that simple."

"It never is. But all those choices you're beating yourself up about? They brought you to where you are now. To her."

"Real astute, Ty," I bellyache.

He drains his beer, then sets the empty bottle on the coffee table with a definitive thud. "Why haven't you two sealed the deal yet?"

I stare at him. "What makes you think that?"

"Please. If you'd gone all the way, you wouldn't be sitting on my couch right now pouting like someone smacked your puppy. Koda's away tonight, right?"

"Two more nights. Mrs. Novak is dropping her off at school on Monday, then I'll pick her up at three like usual."

"Great. So go home. You should be back at that brownstone, making memories with Sora's thighs clamped around your face."

"You're a perv."

"As advertised," he sasses with a knowing smirk.

I sigh heavily. "Fine. You're right. We haven't. We've done other things. But not that."

"Why not? You're obviously both into each other. Living in the same house. What's the holdup?"

I stare at the label on my beer bottle, picking at the edge until it peels some more. "Because I know what happens if we cross that line."

Taio nods with sincerity. "I completely get it."

"You do?"

"Yeah, you're so pent up you're afraid when you finally cross that line, you're going to erupt like a geyser in Yellowstone minuteman-style. It's a legitimate concern."

This fucking guy. "Would it kill you to be serious for once?"

"It might."

"That's it." I stand up. "I'm going to Saylor's." It's an empty threat. We both know that's a demotion in conversation. Unless his mom's awake, and then maybe I could get some sound advice.

"All right, all right. Want my advice for real?"

"Two beers ago," I snark.

"Have sex with her," he says simply, like he's suggesting I try a new brand of protein powder. "But without all the pressure."

"What pressure?"

"The pressure you're putting on it. Stop building it up like it's going to be this life-altering, cosmic event. Don't make it epically romantic or some shit. Keep it hot and to the point."

I laugh incredulously. "That's your great advice? 'Hey, Sora, let's bone, but don't worry, it won't be special'?"

"I'm saying, you guys are overthinking it. Just get it out of the way so you can get to the good stuff."

"Poetic," I deadpan.

"My guy, you're trying to make sex some big declaration of your love. Yet, you're not ready to declare shit. So stop focusing on what sex promises, and start focusing on the point—you're just connecting. The rest will unfold as it should in time." Taio pats my shoulder.

"Um..."

"What?" he asks, looking puzzled.

"Sorry, that threw me off because it was actually helpful. Wasn't expecting that from you."

He scowls. "I hope my future roommate is nicer to me."

I chuckle. "Me too."

Taio holds up a finger. "Since we're on the subject, I've got something for you." He pushes himself off the couch and disappears down the hallway to his bedroom.

When he returns, he's holding a dog-eared paperback. The cover shows a shirtless man with a mask, his muscular arm wrapped possessively around a woman in a red dress. The title reads, *Midnight Captor*.

"What the hell is this?" I ask as he tosses it onto my lap.

"Research," Taio says smugly. "Dark romance. It's what all the cool kids are reading these days."

I flip through the pages, noticing colored tabs sticking out from various sections. "You color-coded it?"

"For your convenience," he says with exaggerated formality. "Red tabs—don't even think about it unless you want to do hard time in prison. Orange tabs—proceed with extreme caution, and get her consent in writing first. Yellow tabs—go forth and conquer, my friend."

"Christ." I skim one of the yellow-tabbed pages and feel my eyes widen. "Women read this?"

"No, they inhale it," Taio confirms, looking entirely too pleased with himself. "With dark romance, it's all about the pulse. Keeping her adrenaline flowing."

"By scaring the shit out of her?"

"By keeping her on edge. A little scared, a lot turned on. Make her feel like if she submits to your power, you'll protect her always. It's primal, man."

Despite myself, I keep reading, oddly captivated. "This is... not what I expected. All the sex scenes are this intense?"

"Yeah, so the general gist is you can do whatever you want to her as long as she orgasms first." Taio pops his brows high. "*In fiction only*. I'm serious, brochacho, do not attempt those red tabs. You're too pretty for prison."

"Noted," I grumble distractedly. The dirty scene on the page is stuck to my eyeballs like bubblegum.

"You know what would be perfect?" Taio says suddenly. "There's this year-round haunted house upstate. Hellfire or Hell's Manor or some shit. Apparently, it's legitimately terrifying."

The gears in my head start turning. "A haunted house?"

"Think about it," Taio continues, warming to his theme. "Dark, creepy setting. Adrenaline pumping. Her clinging to you for protection. Then you whisk her away to some cabin in the woods afterward..."

"Where nobody can hear her scream?" I joke, but I'm actually considering it. The masked man trope. The danger, the rescue, the release of tension. I toss the book back to him. "Why are you so invested in helping me and Sora anyway? Trying to get in on the ground floor with a future famous author?"

He catches the book, laughing. "Yeah, that's it. I'm playing the long game. Gonna ask her to name me in her acknowledgments when she hits the bestseller list."

"Seriously, though."

Taio's smile fades, replaced by something more genuine. "Honestly? I haven't seen you like this, maybe ever."

"Like what?"

He looks right at me, no trace of his usual smartassery. "Falling in love, man."

The word feels weighty and undeniable. I open my mouth to argue, to downplay it, to make some joke about how I'm just horny or bored or lonely. But nothing comes out.

Because he's right.

I'm falling hard for Sora Cho, and there's not a damn thing I can do about it except lean into the mess.

Chapter 25

Sora

Lady, you're asking to be featured on an episode of Dateline.

The rideshare driver slows to a stop in front of imposing black iron gates that are easily twelve feet tall. I peer through the window, my eyes following the winding path up the hill to what appears to be a Victorian mansion silhouetted against the twilight sky. Ominous shadows dance across the moonlit clouds, and I swear the place is straight out of a horror movie poster.

"Are you sure this is where you meant to end up?" the driver asks, skepticism heavy in his voice.

I double-check my phone. "Yep. Blackwood Manor, 1313 Raven Hill Road."

A hand-painted wooden sign hangs crookedly on the gates: *Pre-booked admission only. No refunds. Enter at your own risk.*

Below it, a smaller sign reads: *Management is not responsible for heart attacks, panic disorders, or changes to undergarments.*

Is that supposed to be funny? Or just the most obnoxious fine print I've ever read?

"Yeah, this is definitely it," I mutter.

The driver shifts nervously in his seat. "So...do you need me to wait or something? Because this place gives me serious heebie-jeebies."

"No need. My date said he'd be inside waiting for me." I gather my purse, trying to project more confidence than I feel.

"Apparently my name should be on some kind of list."

"A date? Here?" The driver gives me a look through the rearview mirror that indicates he's questioning my life choices. "Lady, you're asking to be featured on an episode of *Dateline*."

"It's complicated," I reply with a weak laugh. How do I explain to him that for my adventure into dark romance with Forrest, the creepier, the better?

As I reach for the door handle, the driver turns around fully. "I don't normally do this, but I feel like I should wait until I see your date and confirm you're safe. This whole setup is giving me major slasher-film vibes."

"Thanks, but I'll be fine. I promise." I step out of the car, the crisp autumn air immediately raising goose bumps on my arms. "My boyfriend is inside, blending in as part of the cast." I hold up my phone, waving it in the air as if the driver could read my text conversation with Forrest. "He's apparently dressed as Ghostface, in a Scream mask. It's a whole thing."

"That's not as reassuring as you think it is." The driver shakes his head. "Good luck, lady."

With that ominous send-off, I watch as he speeds away, tires crunching on the gravel road. Great. Even Uber drivers think I've lost my mind.

I approach a small ticket booth beside the gates where a bored-looking guard sits scrolling through his phone. His face is half-hidden by the brim of a dusty cap, but I can see the scraggly beard underneath.

"Hi. Um, I'm supposed to meet someone here? Sora Cho. The name should be on the list."

Without looking up, he taps something on his screen, then reaches over to press a button. The gates creak open with an ominous groan that feels entirely too theatrical.

"Enjoy your evening," he says in a monotone that suggests enjoyment is the furthest thing from what awaits me.

I step through the gates, my heart already racing even though nothing remotely scary has happened yet. The path before me is lined with flickering lanterns that cast just enough light to prevent me from tripping but not enough to dispel the shadows lurking at the edges. Dead trees twist toward the sky like gnarled fingers, and somewhere in the distance, an owl hoots mournfully. This is comically right on the nose of every bad horror film Daphne's ever made me sit through.

"Research, my ass." I hug myself as I begin the trek up the hill. "I would've preferred a date in the library *reading* about this shit, instead."

As I walk, my mind drifts to what I really want to talk to Forrest about tonight. After yesterday's dinner fiasco with my parents, something shifted between us. The way he defended me to my father, not just politely disagreeing, but genuinely standing up for me, for my dreams—no one's ever done that before.

And that's the problem, isn't it? I'm falling for a professional escort who makes his living by making women feel special. How could I possibly know what's real and what's performance?

I kick a pebble in frustration, watching it skitter down the path. Could I handle Forrest continuing his current job if we tried to make this real? The answer is a resounding, emphatic, neon-flashing, *no*. The thought of him with other women makes my stomach twist into pretzel shapes.

But is it fair for me to ask him to find a new job? What kind of selfish person demands someone give up their livelihood? I'm barely making enough to support myself, especially because as of last night, I've vowed never to ask Dad for another handout again, or accept one for that matter. Unless my books start selling, how can I contribute meaningfully to family and household expenses, especially with Dakota in the picture? It seems like either Forrest needs a new job...or I do.

The temperature drops as I climb higher, or maybe it's just my nerves making me shiver. A thin mist has begun to gather around my ankles, curling upward like ghostly tendrils. The lanterns flicker more aggressively now, some extinguishing entirely as I pass, plunging sections of the path into momentary darkness before the next light source reveals itself.

In the distance, the mansion looms larger with each step. The windows are mostly dark except for occasional flashes of colored light that suggest activity within. The architecture is impressive really, a nightmarish blend of Victorian and Gothic influences—turrets spiral toward the sky, gargoyles perch on ledges, and the roof seems to be intentionally uneven, as if the house itself is off-balance. If this were a horror movie, even the ditzy girl who usually dies first would know better than to enter this place.

I'm so lost in these observations that I don't immediately register that I've reached the mansion's front steps.

"Here we go," I mutter, reaching for the knocker.

Before I can touch it, the door swings open with a dramatic creak. Inside is a dimly lit foyer with peeling wallpaper, dusty chandeliers, and a grand staircase that looks one step away from collapse. I pause in front of the cobweb-dusted sign on the entryway table which reads: *Follow the screams. Or don't. We get paid either way.*

Again, their attempts at humor are very lost on me.

I take a deep breath and step inside. "Forrest?" I call out, my voice echoing in the empty foyer.

No response.

Right. He's playing the masked villain. I remember his text: *I'll be waiting in a Scream mask. Don't be scared when you see me.* As if a text like that wouldn't make me more scared.

I wander through the first floor, passing rooms designed to replicate various horror scenarios—a blood-splattered kitchen with a butcher's table, a nursery with creepy dolls that seem to follow my movements with their glass eyes, a library where books occasionally fly off the shelves thanks to some hidden mechanism.

"This is ridiculous," I announce to no one in particular as I dodge a rubber bat on a string. "Who enjoys this? How is this a fantasy for anyone?"

Dark romance has never been my thing. Give me sunshine, flowers, and meet-cutes over stalking, blood, and terror any day.

Yet apparently thousands of readers disagree with me, based on the bestseller lists.

The floorboards groan beneath my feet as I move deeper into the house. The air grows heavier, thicker somehow, carrying the scent of dust, aged wood, and something metallic that I refuse to believe is actual blood. The walls themselves seem to pulse with an eerie energy, and I could swear I hear whispers following me, always just behind my right ear, never quite distinct enough to make out the words.

I push open a heavy door and find myself in what appears to be a dimly lit throne room. Somewhere you'd stow an evil, two-headed dragon. Candles flicker in wall sconces, casting long shadows across the stone floor. And there, standing beside a massive throne carved with skulls, is a figure in a Scream mask, dressed all in black, holding what appears to be a very realistic executioner's blade.

My pulse skips, but then I relax.

"There you are," I say, stepping farther into the room. "I was beginning to think you'd set me up. Do they know you're lurking around, posing as a cast member?"

The figure doesn't move or speak.

"Really committing to this whole silent stalker vibe, huh?" I laugh nervously, moving closer.

Still nothing.

"Okay, you've done your job. I'm thoroughly scared," I mock, although there's truth behind my words. I cross my arms, leaning against the wall. "Are you just going to stand there all night? Because I had some things I wanted to talk about. Are you ready to go?"

The figure tilts its head slightly but remains silent.

"Fine. Here, then. I'll talk, you can listen." I take a deep breath. "Yesterday got me thinking, after the whole dinner-with-my-parents thing. The way you defended me...it wasn't just what you said, but how you said it. Like you really care from your very core."

The figure shifts its weight but doesn't respond.

"I know this started as an arrangement. A deal. But it doesn't feel like that anymore, at least not to me." My heart is pounding now, confessing to a silent mask. But maybe that makes it easier. "I'm just going to say it. It's probably no surprise, but I have real feelings for you, Forrest. And I'm scared because I don't know if what I'm feeling is real, or if this is just the 'Forrest effect' if that makes sense?"

The masked figure straightens, gripping the executioner's blade tighter.

"And I'm not trying to come on too strong, but the thing is, I see you. *The real you.* Not the escort, not the performance. I see the incredible father who'd do anything for his daughter. The good man who stands up for what's right. The person with the best heart I've ever gotten to know." I'm on a roll now, all my thoughts spilling out. "I know it's a long shot, but I think if we figure some stuff out, we could have something real. But...only if you want that too."

The silence stretches between us, but somehow it doesn't feel awkward. It feels like he's really listening.

"Okay, so you're going to stay in character. That's fine." I push off from the wall, walking toward him. "But just know this next kiss isn't for research, okay? It's just a girl kissing the guy she's falling for."

I reach up, carefully lifting the bottom of the Scream mask just enough to reveal a pair of lips. Without hesitation, I press my mouth to his, but something feels...off. These aren't the lips I've come to know so well. They're thinner, stiffer, and they taste like chew tobacco masked by cinnamint gum.

Forrest doesn't dip. And I've only ever tasted spearmint on his breath.

Before I can process what's happening, the doors burst open with a thunderous bang.

"What the *fuck* is going on, Sora?"

I whirl around to see Forrest—*the real Forrest*—standing

in the doorway, in dark jeans, a hoodie, and leather jacket on top, holding a different mask in his hand. His face is a storm of emotions.

Oh, shitastic hell.

I leap away from the masked stranger as if he's suddenly burst into flames. "*Forrest!* You said you'd be in a Scream mask. I thought I was kissing you," I blubber up, overly defensive, before I narrow my eyes at the Ghostface in front of me. "What the actual hell, dude? You didn't stop me?"

The stranger slowly reaches up and pulls off his mask, revealing a sheepish young man who can't be older than twenty. "I'm just an actor, ma'am. I'm supposed to stay still. Part of the haunted house experience."

"You can't even break character to let a woman know she's kissing the wrong guy?"

He shrugs innocently. "I mean…you're hot, and I'm interested. What's the problem?"

"I'm your problem, fucker," Forrest growls out as he storms across the room, his eyes blazing.

I catch him by the wrist before he can buck up on Ghostface. "What happened?" I ask.

"I found a cooler mask." He holds up a black mask with red exes for eyes and a smile made of stitches, proving his point. "I thought I'd surprise you. I didn't realize I'd have to worry about you making out with the first Ghostface you came across."

"Don't you victim-shame me, sir." I throw my hands up in exasperation.

"*Victim?*" the actor grumbles out.

Ignoring him, I point my finger at Forrest's chest. "You said, *and I quote*, 'Look for me in a Scream mask.' This guy"—I point accusingly at the now-unmasked actor—"is wearing a Scream mask!"

"I'm just gonna…" the actor mumbles, his eyes fixed on Forrest's balled-up fist. He edges toward a side door. "I have other rooms to haunt. Sorry for the confusion."

"Don't you dare move," Forrest growls, but the actor slips through the door before Forrest can stop him. "Coward."

"Calm down," I say, though I'm fighting a ridiculous urge to laugh at the absurdity of the situation. "This is your fault for not updating me on the costume change."

"My fault?" Forrest rakes a hand through his hair, making it stand on end. "I turn my back for two seconds and you're kissing another man?"

"I thought it was you. How much did you see?"

"Enough," he bites out.

A rush of heat burns my cheeks. "So you didn't *hear* anything?"

"No, hear what?" His voice drops, the anger giving way to something more vulnerable. "What did you say to him?"

The humor of the moment dissipates, replaced by the weight of my heartfelt confession that's now lost with the whispers of this hell house. "Nothing."

Forrest takes a step closer, his eyes never leaving mine. "Are you mad at me?"

"For the mask mix-up? No." I shrug. "Hard to stay mad when you're this hilariously jealous."

"I'm not jealous."

"You just scared off a minimum-wage haunted house employee because he got a peck on the lips."

"It was more than a peck," Forrest barks out, closing the distance between us. "And fine, yes, the thought of anyone else touching you, even by mistake, quite frankly pisses me off. But is that fair? I don't own you."

"Since when have you played fair?" I whisper.

"What's that supposed to mean?"

I hold his gaze, then pump my brows suggestively. "It means you can own me a little if you want."

Something changes in his demeanor then. The playfulness vanishes, replaced by something darker, more intense. "Is that what you want?"

I nod slowly, convincing myself while I try to persuade him.

His eyes harden, and when he speaks again, his voice is dangerously soft.

"Run."

I blink, not sure I heard him correctly. "What?"

He reaches into his pocket and pulls out a pair of handcuffs that glint in the candlelight. "I said run, Sora. Because if I catch you, I'll actually own your ass and do whatever the hell I want to you."

A thrill shoots through me, part fear, part anticipation. "Are you kidding?"

"Do I look like I'm kidding?" His face is deadly serious. "You have a thirty-second head start. I suggest you use it wisely."

Something clicks in my brain, and suddenly dark romance makes more sense. It's not about the horror or the fear—it's about the edge. The suspense. The delicious uncertainty of being pursued by someone who awakens both your flight and your fight responses simultaneously.

I don't need to be told twice. I bolt for the door, excitement surging through my veins as I sprint down the corridor, through the foyer, and out the front door into the cool night air. Behind me, I can hear Forrest counting loudly.

"Twenty-eight...twenty-nine...thirty. And now you're mine, cookie girl."

The grounds outside the mansion include a sprawling garden and, beyond that, a small wooded area. I head for the trees, heart pounding in my ears, a ridiculous smile plastered across my face despite my breathlessness. He's unhinged. This is thrilling. This is the most alive I've felt in years.

The night air is crisp against my flushed skin, carrying the scent of damp earth. My exhales are visible puffs, clouds of vapor betraying my location. Not to mention I'm breathing loudly enough he could hear me over a parade.

I duck behind a wide oak tree, clamping my hand over my mouth as I inhale through my nose. The rough bark presses against my back, tiny pieces flaking off and catching in my hair.

My pulse is thick in my throat, a rapid staccato beating in time with the distant sound of what might be footsteps—or just my imagination.

In the distance, I can hear Forrest calling my name, his voice carrying through the night.

"Sora...where are you hiding?" His tone is playful but cut with something primal. "Bet you're tired, baby. Is it time to stop running and face your fate?"

The forest floor is carpeted with fallen leaves that crunch beneath my feet, no matter how carefully I try to step. Each sound seems amplified in the quiet darkness, announcing my position like a beacon. The temperature has dropped further, and goose bumps pebble across my arms—not just from the cold, but from my twisted eagerness to be found.

I peer around the tree trunk, trying to spot him. Nothing. I decide to make a break for a denser patch of woods to my right, but as I step out from my hiding place, a twig snaps under my foot.

"Got you."

Forrest appears seemingly from nowhere, his hand clamping around my wrist like a bear trap. His eyes glint in the moonlight, predatory and fierce.

"That wasn't much of a chase," I manage to say, my breath coming out in short pants again, now for a different reason.

"You were never going to outrun me." He tugs me closer, his free hand still clutching the handcuffs. "That was never the point."

"What was the point, then?" I ask, though I already know the answer.

"The hunt." His gaze descends to my lips. "And the capture."

He backs me up against the oak tree, one hand pinning my wrists above my head, the other cupping my face. "Is this what you want? To be shown you're mine?"

The weight of the question hovers between us. This isn't part of the game anymore. This is real.

"Yes," I whisper, surprised by my own boldness. "I want to be yours. *Only yours.*"

"Good girl. Don't ever do that again. If I catch another man kissing any part of you, I'll rip his lips right off. You got it?" Something flares in his eyes—desire, possession, need. I think he's acting, but I wouldn't mind if it were real.

I nod, unable to find my voice.

"Say it," he demands, his thumb dragging across my lower lip. "I need to hear you say you understand."

"I understand." I swallow hard. "I only want...you."

That's all it takes to unleash him. His mouth crashes down on mine, hungry and demanding. There's nothing gentle about this kiss—it's all teeth and tongue and desperation. I arch into him, matching his intensity, letting myself surrender to the sheer force of what's between us.

With graceful ease, he spins me around to face the tree, my cheek pressed against the rough bark. I hear the metallic clink of a belt buckle being undone, then the rustle of fabric. His hands slide down my sides, peeling off my tight leggings. Abandoning his grisly demeanor for a minute, he carefully helps me kick off my boots and pull off my bottoms.

For a moment, I thought he forgot about my underwear, or maybe he doesn't want this to go as far as I do. But then I'm pushed back against the tree in my previous position, him pressing against me from behind. "These are in my way," he complains, his breath hot against my ear. Without warning, he hooks his fingers into the waistband and tears the delicate fabric apart.

I gasp at the sudden exposure to the cool night air, but the chill is immediately replaced by the heat of his palm against my bare skin, exploring, teasing. "Forrest, someone could see."

"It turns me on," he answers promptly. "Let them watch. Get a glimpse of what's all mine, and what they can never, ever have."

The way he's talking makes me swell with need. We're alone, not a living soul in sight, but what's more concerning...even if there were, I don't know if we could stop.

"You're so wet. Tell me, baby, do you get wet for me or *stay* wet for me?" he growls, his fingers finding proof of my arousal.

"Bet you dream about my hard cock all day, don't you? Is that why you're such a good girl? You want to be rewarded?"

In one fluid motion, he drops to his knees behind me, hands gripping my hips to steady me. I barely have time to process what's happening before I feel his mouth on me, his tongue exploring my most intimate places with devastating precision.

"Oh sweet hell," I moan, my fingers grappling at the tree bark.

The sensation of his mouth against me is overwhelming—hot and insistent, his tongue flicking and circling with expert knowledge of what will drive me to the edge. His hands knead the flesh of my ass, spreading me wider for his ministrations. The cool night air contrasts with the heat of his breath, creating a cascade of sensations that makes my knees buckle.

He devours me like a man starved, his tongue circling my clit in exquisite, deliberate patterns that have me seeing stars. When he adds suction, I cry out involuntarily, the sound echoing through the trees. Birds scatter from a nearby branch, startled by my vocalization.

My legs begin to tremble, and just when I think they might give out, he slides two fingers inside me, curving them in a "come hither" motion that hits exactly the right spot. The dual sensation—his tongue relentless against my clit, his fingers delving inside me—sends waves of pleasure radiating from my core.

"*Oh god,*" I pant, the tension building low in my belly. "I'm going to—"

"Not yet," he commands, suddenly withdrawing. Before I can protest the loss, he's standing again, spinning me to face him. "Hands," he says, holding up the handcuffs.

I extend my wrists without hesitation, watching as he secures the metal around them. The cuffs aren't tight enough to hurt but snug enough that I can't slip free. The constraint is deliciously erotic, as we fall into something more intimate than anything we've done before. *His control. My surrender.*

The metal is cold against my skin, the weight unfamiliar but not unpleasant. Each tiny movement causes the chain connecting the cuffs to jingle softly, a constant reminder of my willing captivity. I test their strength, pulling slightly, and feel a thrill at the unyielding resistance.

"Put your arms around my neck," he instructs, and I comply, the cuffs forcing my arms to remain together as they encircle him.

With my arms raised, he takes the opportunity to yank up the top of my chunky cream sweater and wireless bra, exposing my breasts to the moonlight. His eyes darken as he takes in the sight.

"Perfect," he admires, before lowering his head to take one nipple into his mouth. The wet heat of his tongue sends electricity coursing through me, and I arch into the feeling, my bound hands pulling him closer.

The contrast of sensations is unnerving—the cool metal of the handcuffs, the rough texture of the tree bark against my back, and the hot pressure of his mouth on my sensitive flesh. He alternates between gentle suction and the sharpness of his teeth, bringing me to the razor's edge between pleasure and pain.

While his mouth works its magic on my breast, his hand scopes back between my legs, resuming its earlier rhythm. His fingers find me slick and ready, circling my entrance before plunging back inside. The dual sensation is mind-blowing, and I find myself racing toward the edge again.

"Please," I beg, not entirely sure what I'm asking for.

Forrest understands. He withdraws long enough to undo his pants fully, freeing himself. Even in the dim moonlight, I can see how hard he is, how ready. The sight of him—powerful, aroused, barely controlled—sends another rush of heat through me.

"Are you on birth control?" he asks, the question so practical amidst our primal encounter that I almost laugh.

"Yes," I confirm.

"I don't have a condom, Sora. If we're going to do this, it's just us and trust. You want it, or you want to stop?"

"Don't you dare stop," I say, pouting. "Us and trust. *I want it.*"

With that logistical hurdle cleared, he lifts me effortlessly, my back pressed against the tree for leverage. I wrap my legs around his waist, the position opening me up to him perfectly. The bark scrapes against my exposed skin, a rough counterpoint to the smoothness of his body against mine.

"Look at me," he demands as he positions himself at my entrance. "I want to see your eyes when I fill you for the first time."

I obey, locking my gaze with his as he pushes forward in one long, slow thrust that steals the breath from my lungs. The stretch is delicious, my body too tense at first, then slowly adjusting to accommodate his size. I can feel every inch of him, hot and hard.

"Fuck," he groans when he's fully seated. "You feel incredible."

For a moment, neither of us moves, savoring the connection. I can feel his heartbeat through our joined bodies, racing in time with my own. The night seems to have gone completely silent around us, as if nature itself is holding its breath.

Then he begins to withdraw almost completely before driving back in, establishing a rhythm that has me wincing in pleasure with each thrust. The sensation is...too much, and not enough. The fullness, the friction, the knowledge that it's him inside me, claiming me in the most animalistic way possible.

"Harder," I beg, tightening my legs around him. *"Please, fuck. Yes, I need—"* I stop, unable to finish my thought. I don't know what I need except for this to never end.

He responds by doubling his efforts, his hips snapping against mine with increasing force. The bark of the tree scratches against my back, but the slight discomfort only enhances the pleasure, grounding me in the reality of the moment. The sound of our bodies coming together, skin against skin, fills the clearing, punctuated by our ragged breathing.

"All fucking mine," he growls against my neck, underscoring the declaration with a particularly deep thrust. "Say it."

"I'm yours," I gasp, the words feeling like both surrender and victory.

He shifts his angle slightly, and suddenly he's hitting a spot inside me that fires electricity up my spine. I cry out, my bound hands clutching desperately at his shoulders, nails digging into his flesh through his shirt.

"That's it," he encourages, maintaining the new angle. "Now, baby. Come for me. Coat me."

The tension builds to an almost unbearable peak, and then I'm falling, crashing over the edge with an intensity that has me singing his name in worship like a hymn. Wave after wave of pleasure rolls through me, until I'm left trembling and boneless in his arms.

Forrest doesn't slow his pace, chasing his own release. Overly satiated, I'm a rag doll in his hands, and he has no problem using me. His rhythm becomes more erratic, his breathing harsh against my skin. His hands grip my thighs, fingers digging into the soft flesh, probably leaving marks that I'll discover tomorrow with secret satisfaction.

"Inside or out?" he manages to ask, ever the gentleman even in the midst of our feral encounter.

"Inside," I whisper, wanting to claim him in a way of my own.

With a final, powerful thrust, he buries himself to the hilt and finds his release, his body shuddering against mine. I feel the hot pulse of him deep inside, marking me in the most intimate way possible. His forehead drops to my shoulder, his breath coming in ragged gasps against my skin.

For several moments, we stay locked together, both of us breathing hard, coming down from the height of pleasure. The night air cools our overheated skin, raising goose bumps along my exposed flesh. The distant hoot of an owl reminds me that we're outdoors, exposed, vulnerable—yet I've never felt safer than in his arms.

Slowly, carefully, he lowers my feet back to the ground, supporting me until he's sure my legs will hold. They feel like liquid, barely capable of supporting my weight, and I lean heavily against him as he zips and buckles, righting himself.

The shift in his demeanor is immediate and striking. Gone is the dominant, possessive lover, replaced by tender concern as he gently removes the handcuffs.

"Are you okay?" he asks, his voice soft as he massages my wrists where the metal had rested. "I didn't hurt you, did I?"

I shake my head, still too breathless for words. My mind feels pleasantly fuzzy, my body humming with satisfied energy.

He helps me back into my leggings, covering my exposed skin with careful attention. His fingers linger, almost reverent, as they roll the stretchy fabric back into place. Then he reaches into his pocket, pulling out the remnants of my underwear.

"Souvenir," he says with a slight smirk, tucking the torn fabric away. "Sorry about that."

"No, you're not." I laugh, finally finding my voice.

"You're right, I'm not." He kisses my forehead, gentle now. "But I am sorry if I got carried away."

"Don't be. That was..." I search for the right word. "Enlightening."

His chuckle is low and warm, vibrating through his chest against my cheek. "Enlightening? Sure."

"It was," I defend, feeling my strength returning gradually. "I finally understand the appeal of dark romance. It's not about the fear itself—it's about the surrender, the trust. It's about knowing someone could hurt you, but trusting they won't. About giving up control and finding freedom in that release."

"The surrender," he echoes, his fingers tracing the curve of my cheek. "I like that."

Before I can say more, he scoops me up into his arms, cradling me against his chest. Dipping back down, he tells me to collect my boots in my hands. "I rented a car for the day. I'm carrying you back to the parking lot. Don't argue."

"Wasn't going to argue," I mumble, resting my head against his shoulder. The steady rhythm of his heartbeat is comforting, and I find myself relaxing completely in his embrace.

His arms around me feel like sanctuary—strong, secure, safe. The night has taken on a dreamlike quality, the haunted house and its manufactured fears seeming distant and inconsequential compared to the raw, real emotion between us.

As he carries me down the path, away from the haunted mansion and back toward reality, I can't help but reflect on what just happened. On what it means for us. On the sharp distinction between the terror I was meant to feel in that house versus the exhilaration I experienced in his arms.

"You know," I say into the comfortable silence, "I don't think I could pull off writing dark romance. But I definitely want to see this version of you again sometime. In the bedroom."

He laughs, the sound rumbling through his chest beneath my ear. "Sora, you can have any version of me you want, whenever you want it."

The implication hangs in the air—*versions* or *acts*? Moments that won't last? Promises he can't keep? I'm too tired to offer a coherent response right now, so I let it go.

The path winds downhill, illuminated now by the full moon that has emerged from behind the clouds. The mansion looms behind us, its windows like watchful eyes tracking our departure. But its manufactured horrors hold no power over me now—it looks more comical than anything, me leaving with exactly what I came here for. A revelation.

Forrest's car comes into view, a sleek SUV rental parked at the base of the hill. He shifts me carefully in his arms to reach his keys, but doesn't put me down until he's opened the passenger door and can gently place me on the seat.

"I'm not made of glass, you know," I say as he buckles my seat belt for me, treating me with exaggerated care. "I won't break."

"I know," he says, brushing the wayward hair from my face. "Miss Independent, tough-as-nails, hangs-your-own-moon." He smiles at me sweetly. "I know you can take care of yourself. But I like to pretend you need me."

I do need you. I think it; I dare not say it.

He circles to the driver's side, slides in beside me, and starts the engine. As we pull away from Hellfire Manor, I reach across the console to take his hand, lacing my fingers through his.

For once, I'm not overthinking. I'm not planning or projecting or anticipating failure. I'm just here, in his car, feeling the cool night air from the vents on my face and the warmth of his hand in mine.

And for now, it feels like, *The End*.

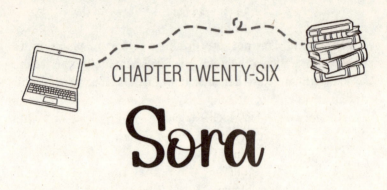

CHAPTER TWENTY-SIX

Sora

Did you just call me Mommy?

The bitter chill of late fall seeps through the brownstone windows. The last few withered leaves skitter across the city sidewalks, as the frost-dust begins to take over the concrete.

I've always loved this transitional time in New York—when autumn reluctantly surrenders to winter, when the city wraps itself in twinkle lights and promises of snow. The air carries the specific perfume of change: decaying leaves, chimney smoke, and that indefinable edge that whispers of holidays nearing.

I wrap my cardigan tighter around myself, the soft wool inadequate against the growing cold outside. But the brownstone feels warmer than it ever has before, which has nothing to do with the electric fireplace. It's something else, something I'm still getting used to—the sound of small feet patting across hardwood floors, a little girl's laughter echoing in spaces that used to be meaningless. Over the past few weeks, Dakota has made this house into a home.

The front door opens with a decisive thud, followed by the telltale rustling of paper grocery bags. Dakota's excited squeal echoes through the house as she abandons her coloring book on the coffee table and dashes toward the entryway, her socked feet slipping slightly on the polished wood.

"Daddy's home!" she chirps, her voice pitched high with excitement.

I wipe my hands on a kitchen towel, breathing in the comforting vanilla scent of the cookie dough I've started prepping, and follow her at a more measured pace. My heart does that ridiculous little flutter it always does now when Forrest comes home. *Home.* Was this ever really a home before Forrest and Dakota invaded in the best way possible?

Taking in the sight of Forrest juggling several overstuffed paper bags while Dakota tugs at his jacket, I can't help but smile. His dark hair is windblown, cheeks flushed from the chill outside, and there's that crooked half-smile that still makes my stomach perform gymnastic routines that would score ten out of ten with Olympic judges.

"Let me help," I offer, stepping forward to relieve him of a bag that looks dangerously close to tearing, the paper already damp at the corners from the light drizzle outside. Our fingers brush during the exchange, and the jolt that courses through me is anything but accidental. Three weeks of crossing lines that shouldn't be crossed, and still every touch feels electric.

"Did you get everything on the list?" I ask, peering into the bag I've claimed, catching whiffs of chocolate and sugar and possibility. "Even the mini M&M's and toffee bits?"

"No, I completely ignored your detailed, color-coded, alphabetized shopping list and just grabbed whatever shiny objects caught my attention," he deadpans, shaking snowflakes from his hair like a retriever coming in from a frigid pond.

I narrow my eyes at him. "You're wildly exaggerating."

"Not wildly," he answers, setting the remaining bags on the kitchen counter with a satisfying thud. I may have listed what I wanted, and then two to three alternates per each ingredient, in case the local bodega was out. "And yes, I got your twelve different kinds of sugar. And the pretzel pieces, and the three types of chocolate chips, an assortment of candy, and something called 'candy melts' which seems like it's more chocolate."

I find myself watching Dakota as she eagerly inspects the grocery bags, her face a picture of childhood excitement. It strikes me suddenly, how full her early memories will be. How present Forrest is in her life, despite everything else.

"You know," I say, keeping my voice light, though the thought feels heavy, "Dakota is so lucky."

Forrest looks up, surprised. "How so?"

"You're so present with her," I explain, clearing my throat to carefully hide the unexpected emotion tightening me up. "Early memories of my dad are so few and far between. He was never available, even if he was physically around. But Dakota's childhood album will be filled with moments like this—with you making her the center of your universe. I love that so much for her."

Forrest's expression softens, his eyes searching my face. "J.P. really missed out." He opens his mouth like he wants to say more, but the words seem to escape him.

"Oven's preheated. Time to roll," I say, sparing him from the deepening conversation. Too deep for sweets. We're supposed to be having lighthearted fun right now.

He proceeds to dramatically pull items from the bags, holding each one up like a game show host presenting prizes. "See? Got 'em all. I think I deserve some kind of medal."

"Your medal is getting to eat the cookies when they're done," I say primly, sorting through the ingredients with a satisfied nod.

Forrest steps closer, lowering his voice. "If I forgo the cookies, can I have a different kind of reward?" he asks, his breath warm against my ear, carrying the faint scent of mint.

The heat rises in my cheeks embarrassingly fast. I glance pointedly at Dakota, who's now rummaging through one of the bags with singular focus. "Is there only one thing on your mind these days?" I whisper back.

Since we broke the seal at the haunted mansion, Forrest and I have been sexing like a pop hit on repeat. Nonstop. Every day. Anytime we're alone, we're naked. It's never enough. We toggle between surprise shower quickies, christening every room of the brownstone while Dakota's at school, and then slow, tender touches under the sheets after his daughter's gone to bed. And now

I truly understand the definition of "a lot of sex." *Twice a week?* Ha! Seems laughable now.

"You like that it's always on my mind," he counters softly, letting his lips linger a moment too long on my neck.

"Hush, you," I warn with mock sternness, stepping away before I do something ridiculous like kiss him right here in the kitchen with his daughter three feet away. "Dakota and I are busy making a very special treat tonight."

Dakota bounces on her toes, clapping her small hands together. The sound reminds me of rain on a tin roof—light, steady, joyful. "Can I tell Daddy the surprise now?"

I nod fervently. "Have at it, sweetie."

"We're making kitchen sink cookies!" she announces proudly, her blue eyes wide with excitement. "Like the ones from Papa Beans. *Surprise*! I've never baked before but Sora's going to show me how."

Forrest slides me a teasing sideways glance. "Well, isn't that the blind leading the blind?"

"Shut it. We're doing just fine. And my cooking skills are greatly improving."

"That they are," Forrest says. "You cook Top Ramen in the microwave like a Michelin-star chef."

"I'm choosing to ignore you now," I snark at a chuckling Forrest before turning my attention back to Dakota. "Kitchen sink cookies are special," I continue, helping her climb onto the step stool I've positioned at the counter. The wooden stool wobbles slightly, and I steady it with my hand instinctually. Parenting is a minefield of potential disasters I never had to navigate before. But I'm getting better at it. "They're made up of little bits and pieces that represent different things. The base is always the same, but what makes them special is how you customize them to match your own personality."

"That's why we need all this stuff," Dakota adds seriously, gesturing to the array of ingredients now scattered across the counter, her small hand sweeping through the air with impressive authority. "Because we all get to put in the things we like best! Our cookies are all going to be different, Daddy."

"Why's that?" Forrest asks with an uninterruptible focus on his daughter.

"Because Sora says...she told me that..." Dakota scrunches up her little face, trying to remember my cookie lesson from before. Lost for words, she looks at me for an assist.

"We talked about how these cookies are like people." I scoot the bowl of cookie dough close to her. "The base is the same. We're all made of the same stuff." I gesture to the cornucopia of cookie fill-ins displayed across the kitchen island. "But it's the little pieces we add to ourselves that make us beautifully unique. No two cookies ever come out exactly the same."

He leans against the refrigerator door, his gaze peeling away from his daughter and landing on me. "Your cookie parables are surprisingly poetic."

"What are par-y-bles?" Dakota asks half-heartedly. She's licking her lips, gaze deadlocked on the bag of gummy worms. *Me too, friend.* This kid is my spirit animal.

"I'll explain later, smarty-pants," Forrest says. "Now, how can I help?"

I turn to Forrest and place a gentle hand on his arm, feeling the solid warmth of him through his shirtsleeve before I give him a little nudge. "You, *out*. You did your job. Thank you for the groceries. Dakota and I've got this covered. We're bonding."

He lights up like Vegas at night, flashing me a smile that makes me think I just conquered my first marathon—so proud. So impressed. "Careful, cookie girl. Keep all this up and I'm never going to be able to let you go."

"Who's asking you to?" I give him a gentle push toward the living room. "Grab a beer, and go put your feet up. There's a game on, I think."

Forrest hesitates, glancing between Dakota and me with an unreadable expression. His eyes, the exact shade of a summer sky, search my face. "Are you sure all this is okay with you?" he asks quietly, his voice dropping so only I can hear.

I understand immediately what he's asking. It's the same question that's been unspoken but palpable for weeks now, as persistent and inescapable as the scent of his cologne that clings to my pillowcases. The acknowledgment of what's developing here—the tentative family unit we're becoming, despite all our initial intentions.

"What do you mean?" As if I don't know exactly what he means. My fingers toy with the hem of my sweater.

He runs a hand through his hair, the dark strands standing up at odd angles afterward, making him look younger, more vulnerable. "This is a lot, very fast. Me sneaking into your room at night, then having to wake up early to get back to my bed before Dakota wakes up. Friday nights at home, making cookies instead of going out. It's so domestic. We're taking over your whole life."

What life? Before Forrest, was I living? Or just writing about living?

"With or without you guys, I'd be in on a Friday night making cookies by myself. It feels good not to feel so alone anymore," I say softly, meaning it more than I should. The weight of that admission takes up residence between us, heavier than it has any right to be.

"The more time I spend with Dakota here, the more I'm convinced I want full custody. I finally feel fulfilled, you know? But that means..." His eyes ping toward his daughter, who's now carefully organizing chocolate chips by size, her tongue caught between her teeth in concentration.

"A kid-centered life," I finish for him. "I understand." And I do, surprisingly. I, who months ago declared to my mother that children were not part of my five-year plan. I, who thought finding success should precede starting a family. Yet here I am, with step stools and juice boxes in my kitchen, and it doesn't feel like an invasion or interruption.

It simply feels...right.

"Does that make you want to run for the hills?"

"Perhaps...if it's dark and you're chasing me." I wink at him.

He smirks before lowering his rough-hewn voice even more. "New kink unlocked, hmm?"

There's a lot to talk about...a lot to unpack. And it all starts with Forrest finding a new job. But I'm not sure if we're ready to have that conversation. All I can think about now is how perfect tonight is and how I'm not interested in heavy conversations ruining our sense of peace.

"We don't have to figure out everything right now, okay? Tonight is just about *this*." I gesture to the cozy kitchen scene, the ingredients strewn across the counter, Dakota humming tunelessly as she sorts through sprinkles.

He forces a smile. "Okay. Just this, then."

I turn back to the counter, willing my chest to feel less tight, my thoughts to untangle. "What do you want in your kitchen sink cookies, by the way?"

His answering grin is soft and intimate. "I want the exact cookie that brought you into my life."

How does he do that? How does he manage to say *the* right thing to make me forget all my misgivings and throw caution to the wind?

"Coming right up," I promise, trying to ignore the dangerous fluttering in my chest, the little voice that whispers I'm already in way, way too deep.

Forrest retrieves a beer from the fridge, pops the cap with a satisfying hiss, and leans against the counter, watching us. His eyes are glazed over, his mind clearly elsewhere as he takes turns surveying his daughter, then me.

"Dakota, can you fetch the big mixing spoon from the drawer?" I ask, and she scurries to comply, clearly thrilled to be my official sous-chef. Her footsteps patter across the tile, like an eager little mouse.

A loud ring cuts through the bustle of cookie-making. Forrest checks the caller ID of my phone on the kitchen counter. "It's your dad," he mentions casually, causing me to swivel around. "You want to answer?"

I shake my head. "Not tonight." It's an unwelcome reminder of our dinner a couple weeks ago. The bitter taste of that evening is still swimming in my mouth like an aftertaste that won't dissipate.

"You're going to have to talk to him eventually," Forrest supplies.

I shoot him a look as I pull open the pretzel bag with way too much gusto, sending pieces flying. "He wasn't very polite to you either."

Forrest shrugs. "He's allowed to be a jerk to me. Comes with the territory. I only got upset that night because he was rude to you."

I force a small laugh that sounds hollow and tickles my throat the wrong way. "It wasn't that bad. He's said worse things to me before. Dad isn't a bad guy, but he has his moments. When he's triggered, there's no filter. He's kind of like the Grinch during Christmas."

"So what's the game plan?" The phone rings again, and Forrest's eyes drop to the caller ID once more. "Ignore him until his heart grows a few sizes?"

"Ha. I'm optimistic, but not a fool. Dad's heart will be the size of a chicken liver until his dying day. I'm simply waiting until I feel...better." I don't want to face my dad and instantly break down into tears, replaying the disappointment and disapproval written in big, red block letters all over his face.

"Makes sense. Sometimes distance can help put things into perspective. I used to bump heads with my dad all the time until I moved to New York. After that, time was pressed whenever I'd go visit, and so we only focused on the good stuff."

After portioning out the pretzels in a small bowl, I move on to the toffee bits. "What's he like?"

Forrest's posture shifts slightly, a barely perceptible stiffening of his shoulders. "Boone? He's..." A small smile tugs on his mouth. "I don't know, he's Pops, you know? Old-school. Cowboy at heart. Eats red meat seven times a week. Drinks the same brand of beer he has since he was a teenager. Drives a ninety-five Chevy, that by some miracle still runs, when he makes a rare visit to town. He still has a flip phone if that tells you anything."

"A flip phone?" I parrot in surprise. "They still make those?"

Forrest fully laughs now. "Basically, he still thinks the world is flat and that the city is a disease. He wouldn't get on a plane if his life depended on it. It's why he's never met Dakota."

"Never?"

"I mean he's seen pictures, and talked to her a couple times, but no, he's never met her officially."

Fully captivated by this new revelation, I abandon my cookie fillings and place both hands on my hips. "Forrest, that's unbelievable. If Boone won't get on a plane, why don't you take Dakota out there to visit?"

"Hannah wouldn't let me. She claims for safety reasons, but I think it's because she would prefer Dakota not get attached to my side of the family. The only thing Hannah hates more than small towns is small-town people."

A shadow crosses Forrest's face, darkening his eyes to a stormy gray.

"So Boone doesn't get to spend time with his only granddaughter? That's awful," I say, automatically reaching for his hand. His fingers lace through mine with practiced ease. His thumb traces small circles on my wrist, a gesture he does often, and suddenly I don't think I can survive without it.

"You'd like him," he says, his eyes distant with memories. "He's rough around the edges, but genuine. He'd probably take one look at you and tell you that you're too pretty to be holed up in the city. He'd try to make a country girl out of you yet." He touches the tip of my nose, grinning ear to ear. "You'd look good as a cowgirl."

"Is that your not-so-subtle way of saying I should visit the ranch someday?" I ask playfully, but simultaneously searching for something deeper.

His eyes lock with mine, filled with something that looks a lot like sudden inspiration. "You might like it there. All the open space. Stars you can actually see at night. Air that doesn't smell like exhaust and piss and too many people. Dakota would love it too—plenty of room to run around, animals to play with. You know what? We should go visit."

The image of wide-open spaces under a vast sky is appealing in a way that surprises me. I've always been a city girl, more comfortable with concrete and taxis than horses and hay. "What about Hannah?"

Forrest releases a tiny exhale, his nostrils flaring. "Things are different now. I think it's about time I start deciding what I think is and isn't good for my daughter."

The determination in his voice sends a thrill through me, despite myself. This is a man who knows what he wants and is prepared to fight for it.

"I'm in, Forrest. You just say when."

He nods with a satisfied smile plastered all over his lips. But he doesn't say another word.

"Koda, let's add the chocolate chips now," I say, perhaps too brightly, turning back to the counter. The mixture in the bowl is creamy and perfect, waiting for our custom additions.

Dakota gleefully abandons her sorting project and grabs a handful of chocolate chips, scattering several across the counter in her enthusiasm.

"Whoa there, easy, tiger." Forrest laughs, moving to help her. He opens her hand toward him, unpicking the pieces off her sticky palm that hadn't fallen off despite her flourishing attempt. "You're supposed to put them in the bowl, not decorate the kitchen with them."

"I'm being an artist," she declares, her eyes narrowing in that way that makes her look so much like her father.

"You're baking," Forrest answers flatly.

"Out." I point toward the living room, dismissing him. "Cookies are artistry. Let the creatives work in peace."

Chuckling and licking his fingers, he retreats toward the stairs, leaving the kitchen so Dakota and I can further bond.

The rest of the baking process is a cheerful chaos of mixing, spilling, and tasting. The kitchen fills with warmth and the rich, comforting aroma of butter and sugar transforming into something greater than the sum of their parts. Dakota insists on adding rainbow sprinkles to her portion of the dough, along with the controversial gummy worms, her small hands diving enthusiastically into the mixing bowl despite my feeble attempts to maintain some semblance of hygiene.

"Not too much, sweetie. You're going to get salmonella," I warn when she steals a finger-scoop of raw dough.

"Sal-who?" Dakota asks, licking her fingers with obvious enjoyment.

"It's a bug that makes your tummy hurt," I explain, gently steering her toward the sink to wash her hands.

Dread fills her angelic little face. "There are bugs in the cookies?"

"Not that kind of bug."

"Phew," she says, "because I want to eat them all, Mommy."

Oh. Abandoning the cookie scooper, I squat down to meet Dakota at eye level. "Did you just call me Mommy, Koda?"

She hangs her head, puckering her bottom lip in shame. "I'm sorry. Don't be mad."

"Oh, sweetie, I'm not mad at all. I was just wondering if you're missing your mommy and maybe that's why you called me that. Have you talked to her recently?"

Dakota bites her bottom lip and nods sheepishly. "Today before lunch we talked on FaceTime, but Mommy couldn't talk too long because she had to go to sleep."

"I bet she misses you so much. Do you miss her too?"

She nods again with a look on her face that's mostly heartbreaking, but with a sprinkle of adorable.

"Know what? When I was your age, whenever I was sad and missing my dad, I'd make him a homemade card or draw him a picture. We could make something for your mommy and then mail it all the way to Tokyo. It's the best way to show somebody how much you love them, by making them something special."

"Like you're making Daddy cookies?" she cleverly asks.

"Well, I'm making them for you too, cutie." I wrinkle my nose at her.

"But, Sora…do you love Daddy?"

Dakota is incredibly blunt. I should've seen that question coming a mile away. "I um—"

"Dakota, that's enough chitchat. Let's do bath and PJs while the cookies are baking, okay?" Forrest says, suddenly reappearing in the kitchen. Dakota spins on her heel and races for the stairs, probably remembering she has brand-new bath toys to play with tonight.

"Sorry, she's getting so attached to you, she has no boundaries. If she asks you questions like that, you don't have to feel pressured to lie to her or anything."

I scrunch my bare toes against the polished wooden slats of the floor. "I'm surprised you didn't wait to hear my answer before interrupting."

"I don't want to know."

My face strains, contorted with surprise, confusion, and honestly, a little hurt. "Why not?"

He blows out a deep breath. "Because right now, I don't know if I could handle the answer, one way or the other."

"Oh."

He shows me a pitiful smile. "See you after bathtime?"

I nod, showing him a fake smile right back. "Yep, I'll be here. Just follow the smell of burning baked goods."

"Woman, please don't burn my cookies," he says a little too seriously.

Forrest's cookies look exactly like the Papa Beans version—M&M's, three types of chocolate, toffee pieces, and pretzel bits arranged in precise proportions. Mine got a heavy dose of cinnamon chips and dried cranberries, which earns me a raised eyebrow from Forrest.

"Cinnamon and fruit? In a kitchen sink cookie? Why are you trying to make junk food healthy?"

"Some of us have sophisticated palates," I reply with unnecessary decorum, which makes Dakota giggle.

"Yeah, Daddy," she chimes in, clearly delighted to have an ally. "We're so-fis-til-cated." I chuckle to myself, knowing Dakota refused to try my cranberry delights.

Forrest clutches his chest in mock betrayal. "My own daughter, turned against me by the cookie lady."

While the cookies cool, filling the brownstone with their sweet scent—butter and sugar caramelizing, chocolate melting into perfect puddles—Forrest disappears again upstairs. The floorboards creak above us, marking his path through the house to Dakota's room.

He returns a few minutes later with her large princess tent and an armful of pillows and blankets, the fabrics carrying the faint, clean scent of my lavender detergent.

"What's all this?" I ask, gesturing to the pile in his arms.

"Movie night," he announces with all the authority of a royal proclamation. "Not just any movie night—*fort* movie night."

Dakota squeals with delight, the high-pitched sound ricocheting off the kitchen tiles as she abandons her careful watch over the cooling trays to help her dad drag the coffee table aside. The legs scrape against the hardwood with a sound that would normally make me cringe, but tonight I find I don't mind.

Within minutes, Forrest transforms the living room into a cozy haven. The princess tent serves as the centerpiece, but he extends the fort using sheets draped over chairs and the sofa, creating a sprawling canopy. Inside, he arranges pillows and blankets in a nest-like configuration, complete with Dakota's favorite stuffed animals as sentinels.

The minute Dakota realizes Forrest forgot Mr. Flops, she's barreling up the stairs to retrieve him.

"Impressive architectural skills," I remark as he secures the last corner with a clothespin, the sheets billowing slightly in the warm cross-breeze from the electric fireplace.

"All those summers mending fences and building barns have prepared me for this moment," he replies with a wink. "Though I have to say, princess sheets are a lot more forgiving than barn timber."

My lids drop to half-mast, as I nibble my bottom lip playfully. "So, when you were barn-building in Wyoming...was your shirt usually on or off?"

He tries to hide his smile. "Depends on the season."

"Let's say summer..." I close my eyes. "I imagine you were extra tan, shirt off, cowboy hat on your head, maybe sweating a little here?" I skate my fingers across my chest, just beneath my collarbone. I end my sweat charades with a shiver of desire.

When I open my eyes fully, Forrest is staring at me, amused and bewildered. "I'm sorry, am I interrupting your wet dream over there?"

"No." I scowl. "Unrelated—do you still have any of your old cowboy hats, or..."

He bursts out in a rumbly laugh. "Subtle."

Dakota comes barreling back down the stairs, Mr. Flops in one hand, a Barbie doll in the other.

"How much longer do we have to wait?" she asks, eyeing the cookies with the intensity of a hawk tracking a field mouse.

I tap a cookie, the heat of it no longer biting. "I think we're ready."

I'm met by her squeals of delight. I half expect her to dive into the cookie sheet, inhaling them by the fistfull, but instead, like a little lady, she uses the step stool to retrieve three plates.

"Thank you for this," he says softly, his voice suddenly serious. "She's never been this self-sufficient. It's because she feels at home."

I turn to face him, our bodies close enough that I can feel the warmth radiating from him, smell the faint scent of his cologne mingled with the winter cold still clinging to his clothes. "You're more than welcome. And thank *you*."

"For what?"

"Making this place feel like home for me too," I answer.

His eyes search mine, looking for something I'm not sure I'm ready to give voice to. "Sora—"

Whatever he was about to say is cut off by Dakota's insistence on us eating cookies while they're warm. I've somewhat lost my appetite, probably somewhere in Forrest's hazel eyes. I tend to lose a lot of things in there: my thoughts, any semblance of resistance. It's all swept away in the vortex of the beautiful nuclear weapons he calls pupils.

I couldn't feel more full of love and warmth at the moment, especially with the aroma of warm cookies hovering in a sweet cloud, filling every corner of the brownstone. The three of us crawl into the fort with a plate of warm cookies—including Dakota's questionable gummy-worm creations—and a bowl of popcorn I've quickly microwaved, its buttery fragrance mingling with the cookies to create the perfect movie-night perfume.

"What movie should we watch?" Forrest asks, reaching for the remote, the plastic warm from sitting near the electric fireplace. Dakota's sitting crisscross-applesauce, sandwiched by me and her dad, backs resting against the couch.

She eyes me, overly pensive for someone her age, then declares, "Sora should pick. She's so nice and she made us cookies."

"That's very generous of you," I tell her, touched by her consideration. This child, with her uncomplicated kindness and easy affection, has wormed her way into my heart with alarming speed.

"What's your favorite?" she asks, her blue eyes wide and earnest in the fort's dim light, reflecting the glow from the TV screen.

I consider for a moment, the weight of this small decision feeling strangely significant. "How about *Lilo & Stitch*?"

"I don't think I've seen that one," Dakota admits, tilting her head curiously.

"Ma'am!" I declare with mock gravity. "You are missing out."

"The one about the blue alien-dog?" Forrest comments, eyebrows raised. Clearly I'm dealing with a tough crowd tonight.

"It's my favorite," I tell them. "It's about finding your family—not just the one you're born with, but the one you adopt along the way. About finding where you belong, even if the rest of the world sees you as a misfit."

Forrest gives me a look that's almost too knowing, like he understands exactly why I've chosen this particular film. His eyes hold mine for a beat too long, saying things we're not ready to put into words.

"Sounds perfect, right, Koda?" he asks her, but his gaze is still on mine. After she nods emphatically, he asks her to cover her eyes for just a moment. Her little hands fly obediently over her clamped eyes, and Forrest leans over his daughter to quickly find my lips.

The kiss shocks me. It feels new, and a little too risky. We can't explain to Dakota what we are, because we don't even know.

"What're you doing?" I whisper-mouth at him.

"How could I not after all that?" he murmurs back.

As the movie plays, we settle into a comfortable tangle of limbs. The fort cocoons us in a bubble of shared warmth and flickering blue light from the screen. Dakota nestles between us, munching contentedly on a gummy-worm cookie that Forrest was a good enough sport to try—then spit out once Dakota's head was turned. I find myself watching them more than the film—the way Forrest absentmindedly strokes his daughter's hair, the matching expressions of concentration on their faces.

"You have the same crease between your eyebrows when you're focusing," I whisper to Forrest over Dakota's head.

His grin lights up the whole damn room. "Do we?"

"Mhm. It's adorable."

"She's Hannah's mini-me," he says. "It's nice to think some of my traits fought their way through."

"She got your earlobes, your dimples, your toes"—I touch my forehead—"and that little concentration crease."

He laughs out loud, and is met by Dakota's serious scowl, her displeasure lit up by the television's light. "Shhh, *Daddy*."

"How come Sora didn't get shushed?" He acts playfully offended.

"Because she's a lady, *duh*," Dakota defends like her dad is the most clueless person on the block. "You don't shush ladies."

I hold my ribs, trying to push back against the giggly heaves.

"Only a couple months, and I'm already getting ganged up on," Forrest mumbles in displeasure, with glee splattered all over his face.

My eyes land on Dakota, investigating her bright-as-the-sun blond locks, a stark contrast from Forrest's rich brunette. "Does it bother you she looks so much like Hannah?" I ask in the lowest whisper I can so as not to interrupt what I'm convinced is Dakota's new favorite movie.

"No. Hannah's a beautiful woman."

I flash him a look. "That's strike three, mister."

He reaches for my cheek, but I pull away, pretending I'm mad. Okay, maybe I am a speckle...a smidgeon...a fairy whisper... *annoyed*.

"No, it's not what I meant. I—wait. What were strikes one and two?"

I hold up one finger. "Keeping my ten thousand dollars." Another finger joins the first. "Telling me I kiss like a fish."

He chuckles again, too loudly, earning another *shush* from Dakota. "*Got it*," he tells her, lowering his whisper another notch. "I meant Hannah is a beautiful woman the way a panther is a beautiful cat. And the way a butterfly is a beautiful insect."

I squint at him. "If you're trying to diffuse the bomb with confusion...you're succeeding."

He smiles, ducking his head low, then looking up at me with glorious puppy eyes. "Beauty is just a physical description. For me, it's really not enough to elicit an emotional connection. And for a man whose entire operation is based on lust, I can see how shallow it is."

I check Dakota's reaction to see if she knows by some disaster what *lust* means, but her eyes are glued to the movie.

"So are you saying I'm not beautiful enough to make you fall for me?" I ask teasingly.

"Sora," he says, dead serious. "You're magical. Whatever it is about you that makes men fall head over heels is in your bones… your soul. So the fact that you're gorgeous is just the cherry on top of something so much better."

I think it's the first time in my entire life I'm speechless. There's not an adequate response to a statement like that, except maybe…

"The end," I whisper.

His eyes widen in slight alarm. "What do you mean 'the end'?"

"It's just this thing I say when someone says the perfect line. Something worthy of ending a story on. *The end.*"

"I like that," Forrest says, staring at me like the entire room has melted away and he's trying to pour out his entire heart with one powerful look.

We're silent through the rest of the movie, eyes on the screen, but lost in our thoughts. Dakota begins to droop, her eyelids growing heavy despite her determined efforts to stay awake. By the time Stitch delivers his "ohana means family" speech, she's fast asleep, curled against her father's side like a contented kitten, her breathing deep and even.

Forrest isn't far behind. The warmth of the fort combined with the emotional comfort of the story lulls him into sleep. His head drops onto one of the pillows, his arm still protectively curled around Koda. I watch them sleep for several minutes, memorizing the peaceful lines of their faces, the way they mirror each other's expressions even in slumber.

I never noticed how different he looks when he's sleeping—vulnerable but unburdened, manly but still so delicately beautiful. That's Forrest, though. Full of contradictions and complications. And worth every mile of the journey.

And just like that, inspiration, for the first time in months, hits me like a runaway train.

Careful not to disturb them, I turn off the movie and tuck the blanket more securely around their sleeping forms. They look so comfortable, I decide to let them sleep in the fort for the night. Forrest will probably wake at some point and carry Dakota to her bed, but for now, they can rest together in their pillow nest.

I tiptoe into the office, retrieve my laptop, and settle into the armchair by the window. Outside, the city lights twinkle against the darkening sky, a few tentative snowflakes beginning to fall, dancing in the glow of the streetlamps.

It's a perfect backdrop for the words that suddenly flow right through me demanding to find life on the page. The inspiration that's been eluding me for months surges, filling my mind faster than I can type. I write without planning, without overthinking...I write from my heart, not my head.

Some of it's nonsensical, just lyrical descriptions of the metaphorical fullness I feel staring into Forrest's eyes like his irises are galaxies, and there are endless worlds to discover. Some of it is marking memories, describing the taste, feel, sound, and smell of the bliss of this evening. I jot down our conversations, like etching hieroglyphs in stone so that the magic between me and Forrest becomes the stuff of legends and myths.

Hours pass in a creative blur. It's intoxicating, liberating, and I feel so fucking alive. For the first time in my life writing just for...well...*me*.

A faint pinging sound from the kitchen pulls me reluctantly from my writing trance. It takes me a moment to identify the source—Forrest's phone on the kitchen countertop, a stone's throw from where he's sleeping.

Afraid the noise might wake them, I hurry to the kitchen, intending only to silence it. His screen lit up in an eerie blue glow in the darkened kitchen should've been my first clue that my peace was about to be disturbed. I shake off my intuition, and continue on my mission to silence the thing and flip it over.

The screen lights up once more as I reach for it, and I can't help but see the notifications.

> **Rina**
> **Job tomorrow night, 8pm. New client requested an overnight. Details to follow.**

My hand freezes midair, a cold weight settling in my stomach, as if I've swallowed ice water too quickly.

Of course. How could I forget this glaring alarm in the symphony of my budding romance? The ten-foot thorn in my rose garden. Forrest is an escort. He has clients. That's his job, his livelihood. The job that supports Dakota. The job he's never promised to give up.

So why does it feel like I've been sucker punched? Why does the thought of him having even apathetic sex with someone else make my chest ache as if all the air has been squeezed from my lungs?

The phone buzzes again, the *ping* now sharp with aggression.

> **Rina**
> **Last chance, Hawkins. Confirm ASAP, please.**

The warm glow of our domestic evening evaporates, replaced by a sick, chilly hollow feeling of dread. I set the phone back on the counter after setting it to vibrate.

I retreat back to the study and to my laptop, but the words that flowed so easily before now stick in my throat. The cursor blinks accusingly on the screen, a visual metronome marking the seconds of my naive foolishness.

What was I thinking? How much longer could we play house without reality ripping through like a tornado?

This life—cookies and forts and family movie nights—isn't

real. It's just...role-playing one small version of the story.

His phone buzzes, making me wish I'd completely silenced the dang thing. I don't need to look to know it's Rina again, wanting answers. I don't blame her; I do too. I want answers to questions I'm not allowed to ask. I made a deal. I said I could keep it together. My lie isn't Forrest's burden.

I close my laptop with a quiet snap, the sound unnaturally loud in the quiet night.

Some stories don't get happy endings. I should know better than anyone. Just because you love something, doesn't mean it's meant for you.

Love—I finally admit to myself.

CHAPTER TWENTY-SEVEN

Sora

Legendary... That's what I'll call it.

Daphne sits in stunned silence on my living room couch. My best friend being quiet is already unnerving enough, but the way her brows are pinched in perplexity has me vibrating with nerves. My whole arrangement with Forrest didn't seem that ridiculous...until I admitted it to someone out loud.

After Forrest saw the texts from Rina, like the emotionally mature man he is, he talked to me about it. He didn't want to go on the date that most definitely would end in something physical. But Dakota's school tuition is due, and apparently, still pissed about Forrest ruining their plans for boarding school, Hannah's boyfriend didn't pay their share this month. Not to mention, Rina gave Forrest a clear ultimatum. Start working, or find a new job.

Line cook or entry-level customer service are probably Forrest's only options until he manages to pay his dues to the law firm he's indebted to. And we both know those jobs aren't enough to make ends meet. Even if I had a million dollars to offer to him, he wouldn't accept. Providing for Dakota is something Forrest takes personally. It's not my place to tell him how to do that. Which is why I stupidly agreed to babysit Koda tonight while her dad whisks some other woman off her feet...into bed.

Untucking my legs, I poke Daphne's knee through her teal, terrycloth sweatpants. "Please say something," I beg.

"It's all still marinating," Daphne answers as she pours herself another glass of wine, the dark liquid sloshing dangerously close to the rim. "So run me through this again... Forrest is an escort."

"Correct."

"You met him at the wedding and then paid him to go home with you, except you didn't have sex. But wanting to make sure you got your money's worth, he pretended to be your boyfriend and went to the book signing."

I blink. "Right."

"Then even before bumping uglies, you decided to move him and his daughter into your dad's brownstone indefinitely in exchange for him acting out sexy romance fantasies with you?"

"They're not all sexy...just like—" I exhale. "Fine. Also, correct."

"And you've since been playing house, spending time with his daughter, banging like bunnies, and you're telling me you're *surprised* you fell for him?" She pauses, raising an eyebrow theatrically, her big eyes widening for effect.

Now I miss her silence a little. "A little..."

"And now the big hitch in your giddyup is that Forrest is currently out with another woman—excuse me, I mean client—while you're sitting at home, sulking and watching his daughter overnight."

"Yes, Daphne, based on the line-by-line reiteration you just provided, you have an impressive grip on the story," I snark before burying my face in my hands. I sink deeper into the couch cushions, hoping they might swallow me whole. The plush velvet of Dad's expensive sofa—my sofa now—feels like it's absorbing more than just my body weight. It's soaking up my shame, my confusion, my heartache. Dakota's small pink bunny slipper is wedged between the cushions. It must've fallen off when I carried her to bed an hour ago. I can't remember if she still has the other one on, tucked underneath her Disney princess comforter.

"I forgot to brush Dakota's teeth," I mumble, picking at a loose thread on the throw pillow clutched against my chest. "I suck at the bedtime routine. Forrest always does it. He never misses a step."

Daphne leans forward, her blond hair falling in a curtain around her face as she squeezes my shoulders. "Her teeth won't fall out from missing one night... Sora, babes, what the hell were you thinking letting him go tonight?"

"I wasn't," I admit, clutching the throw pillow tighter, like armor against her justified incredulity. "I was just trying to be supportive." It sounds ridiculous coming out of my mouth. *Let me support you right into the legs of another woman.* "I'll admit, I had some prejudices about what he does, but then I got to know him, and everybody has a story. The how, the why...it all makes sense. Forrest's story isn't about some playboy getting paid to take his clothes off, it's a dad enduring whatever he has to for his daughter. But his focus isn't on giving Dakota a glamorous life, it's about raising her to be a good person. He's had to make a lot of sacrifices for that."

The wine bottle sits half-empty between us on the coffee table, a silent witness to my unraveling. As usual, I've barely touched my glass. I thought the painful ache in my chest and gut-wrenching twists in my stomach might make liquid numbing more appealing, but I think I'm too sad to drink.

Outside, a taxi honks, the sound muffled by the brownstone's thick walls. The clock on the mantel ticks relentlessly, each second marking another moment Forrest is with someone else.

"Oh, honey." Daphne's expression softens as she scooches closer, the leather of the couch creaking beneath her. She wraps an arm around my shoulders, her familiar perfume—something with vanilla and spice—enveloping me. "I'm sorry. It's a lot to process. I think for once I don't have anything helpful to offer. On one hand, seeing you like this, I want to rip his head off. On the other, I can kind of understand where you guys are, and why. I'm just a little unsettled by it."

"Join the club." I laugh, but it comes out hollow, echoing in the quiet living room. "I should've told you sooner."

"Ya think?" Daphne rolls her eyes, the gesture so quintessentially her that it almost makes me smile. "Instead you let me believe he was some financial wizard you snagged at a wedding. I didn't realize he's a single dad selling his body to the highest bidder."

"Daphne," I hiss, though her bluntness is exactly why I love her. "It's not like that. He doesn't sleep with everyone." *I don't think?* "Look, it's all just complicated."

"Complicated?" Daphne snorts, tucking one leg beneath her as she settles back into the couch. "Girl, our senior calculus final was complicated. This is a whole new zip code of disaster."

"Thanks," I mutter. Leave it to Daphne to find the perfect imagery for my catastrophe.

"So what are you going to do?" she asks, her voice gentler now, tracing the rim of her wineglass with a manicured finger. "I mean, about tonight and…everything."

"What can I do? I signed up for this. I don't have the right to demand he change his entire life for me."

"Maybe not," Daphne says carefully, tucking a strand of hair behind my ear with maternal tenderness. "But you have the right to decide what you can live with."

My fingers trace the pattern on the throw pillow, following the loops and swirls like they might lead me somewhere better than here. The fireplace emits a gentle, electric glow, a poor substitute for real flames but warming nonetheless. The shadows it casts dance across the wall, a choreography of light and dark that mimics the war in my heart.

"I can't live with this," I admit, barely above a whisper. "The thought of him with someone else—" My voice breaks, and I swallow hard against the lump forming in my throat. "It's killing me, Daph. I keep imagining it—his hands on someone else, his lips, his body. I keep wondering if he likes it. If he's gentle with them the way he is with me. If he says the same things. If he means them."

"Did you tell him that?" she asks, her fingers now making

small, comforting circles on my knee.

"No." I shake my head, causing a tear to escape and slide down my cheek. I brush it away angrily. "How could I? 'Hey, I know we're not officially dating, but could you give up your livelihood because I'm jealous?' I'd sound like every possessive, controlling girlfriend cliché in the book."

"Or maybe you'd sound like someone who knows her own boundaries. Someone who values herself enough to ask for what she needs." Daphne takes my hands in hers, her skin warm against my cold fingers. "Look, I've watched you shrink yourself for years. Take up less space. Apologize for existing. Shrivel under every single trollish criticism. But, Sora, this isn't about controlling him. It's about being honest with yourself. This is *your* life. You need to live it in a way you won't regret. That means silencing some things, but roaring others into existence. You'll get more out of life the very minute you decide you *deserve* more."

The truth of her words hits me like a physical blow. I've spent so much of my life trying to be small enough not to inconvenience anyone, flexible enough to bend around other people's needs without breaking. I've made an art form out of accommodating.

"What if honesty costs me everything?" I whisper, voicing my deepest fear. The words hang heavy with implication. There's always the chance that everything I'm feeling between me and Forrest was fabricated. He promised me book-worthy moments. And I got them. *But were they just stories?* Are his feelings for me fiction or fact?

"What if dishonesty costs you yourself?" Daphne counters, her gaze unflinching. "Besides, this isn't just about Forrest anymore, is it? It's about Dakota too."

At the mention of Dakota's name, my chest tightens. Her sweet face appears in my mind—that tiny-toothed smile, those eyes that light up when I enter a room. The way she called me "Mommy" by accident, the memory still fresh enough to make my heart ache with a mixture of joy and terror.

"I think I love her too," I say simply, the words inadequate to express the depth of feeling that's developed in such a short time. "I wasn't prepared for that. For how fast it happened."

"Yeah, well, your ovaries are ripe. You would've fallen in love with his pet possum if he brought that along. This was really just a perfect storm, babes," Daphne says with a sad smile, squeezing my hands. "You're in love. The real, messy, terrifying kind. Not the sanitized version romance novels sell."

A montage of shitty reviews runs through my mind. Not *my* lackluster reviews, but the ones that would come out if Forrest and I were a love story on page. *He's a cheater*—one star. *Reformed playboy, I hate that trope*—one star. *Naive, pick-me heroine*—one star.

But then it hits me all at once...

I'd do for Forrest what I'm not allowed to do for my books. I'd stand up, clap back, and fervently defend him. I'd ask everyone who doesn't understand or can't relate to kindly sit down and shut up, because it doesn't matter how they feel about my love story. It matters how I feel. It matters what I want. I'd rather live a life in denial, full of hope, than allow the critics of the world to drench my books with their cynicism.

My story. My life.

"I have to stop him," I declare. I scramble for my phone on the coffee table.

"Thank *fuck*," Daphne exhales.

There's a momentary gleam of hope as I dial, preparing a monologue in my mind about how I'm in this with him. We'll figure it out together. I might be able to cover a portion of Dakota's tuition. I'll write more books. Hell, I'll take a job in finance if I have to, and write on the side. Whatever means necessary to keep our little odd ohana from being ripped apart.

Except his phone is off.

"Straight to voicemail," I mutter, shocked, as if the phone grew hands and slapped me across the face. "And I have no idea where he is."

"Glitch," Daphne says, her voice suddenly authoritative. "Try again."

And I do. Two more times for good measure. Each call goes straight to voicemail. Forrest shut his phone off...because he's busy.

Daphne knows what images are going through my mind without me needing to paint a word picture. I slump back into the couch, defeated. "Shit," I whisper. "What was I thinking?"

"You've survived one hundred percent of your bad days, babes. You're going to survive this too," Daph says, but the pained expression she's wearing vehemently disagrees. It almost looks like her heart is breaking as well.

Outside, a light rain begins to fall, pattering against the windows like hesitant fingertips. The brownstone creaks and sighs, a living thing holding its secrets.

"Speaking of secrets," I say, desperate to redirect the conversation away from the knot of pain in my chest, "when were you going to tell me about law school?"

Daphne's eyes widen, her hand freezing halfway to her wineglass. "How did you—"

"Forrest slipped. He begged me not to tell you. What happened to us never letting a man come between us?" I give her a gentle nudge, trying to inject some lightness into my voice.

"I didn't mean to tell him. I hadn't even decided—"

"You've decided," I interject. "And you made the right decision."

She hangs her head. "It's not Columbia Law. Can you imagine me in Lincoln, Nebraska? Cows, corn, and a whole lot of country boys."

I shrug. "I'm partial to country boys now. And look, if it's not the dream, then we change our dreams. Gut the vision board and rebuild it. I'm not a bestselling author. Doesn't mean we keel over and die. Our job is to make it make sense."

She looks down at her wineglass, tracing a finger around its rim. "Pep talks are my job."

"They should be my job too." Guilt washes over me, cold and harsh. "Is that why you didn't tell me? Have I been that selfish? So caught up in my writing and my problems that I made no room for yours?"

"No," she says firmly. "That's not why I kept it to myself."

"Then why?" I lift my gaze to meet hers.

"Because things are changing, Sora. For both of us. And that's really scary." She tucks her legs underneath her, downing the rest of her glass and setting it down with a decisive clink. "I can't wait tables and bartend forever. Law school was always the plan, you know that. Life just...got in the way for a while."

"Life, or me?" I ask quietly.

Daphne shakes her head, her blond hair catching the glow of the fireplace. "Not you. My own fears, maybe. It was easier to help you chase your dreams than to face my own. Safer. But now it's time to grow up and be brave."

"Time to grow up," I echo, letting the words sink in. "Is that what you think about my writing? That it's like waiting tables or bartending—just a placeholder until I decide to grow up too?"

"Not a chance." She squeezes my hand, her grip firm and reassuring. "Growing up doesn't mean giving up on your dreams. It means being brave enough to pursue them no matter what."

"Like becoming a lawyer, even if it isn't your first-choice school?"

"More like talking to Forrest about how you really feel, even though it terrifies you," she counters.

I close my eyes, letting the truth of her words settle into my bones, uncomfortable but necessary. "I'm afraid if I tell him how I feel, I'll lose him. And if I don't tell him, I'll lose myself."

Daphne laughs softly, the sound warm in the quiet room.

"What?" I ask, a little surprised at her reaction to my profound admission.

"The irony. You know that's a line right out of *Lovely*? You've written those exact words before, Sora. I know because I specifically remember highlighting and tabbing that paragraph. Now, you're living out the words you wrote. Sweet poetic justice. This was an experience you were always meant to have."

"When did you get so wise?" I ask, nudging her with my elbow.

"It's the wine," she replies with a wink. "The alcohol unlocks my powers." She shrugs. "I'm not the coolest superhero in the world, but I'm useful at times."

"Maybe if I had opted for wine instead of edibles that night, I would've made better decisions." *Stupid gummy bears.* Those bitter little fruit bites are what got my heart all tangled up into this mess to begin with.

We both laugh, the sound easing some of the tension in my chest. For a moment, it feels like old times—just Daphne and me against the world, figuring it out as we go along.

"So, law school in Lincoln," I say, genuinely proud. "When do you start?"

"Next semester. The accelerated program." She tucks a strand of hair behind her ear, a gesture that betrays her nervousness despite her casual tone. "The workload is going to be a bitch."

"Well, be a bitch right back," I say, the reality of it sinking in. "Go conquer Nebraska as fast as you can, and then come back to me, okay? We have big plans for matching rocking chairs and bifocals right on that stoop." I jut my thumb toward the front door. "Don't you dare bail on me."

"Never." She smirks. "We've come a long way since NYU freshman year, huh?"

"Remember our pact?" I ask, nostalgia washing over me. "That we'd both keep our ass out of trouble, graduate on time, not pregnant or in jail, and be disgustingly rich and successful by thirty? You'd be a hotshot lawyer; I'd be a bestselling author? We'd go to our college reunions dripping with condescension."

"I remember." Daphne smiles softly. "We've still got time, Sora. I still believe in us."

"Me too."

A sudden knock at the door interrupts us, three sharp raps that echo through the brownstone. Daphne and I exchange a confused look.

"Forrest?" she asks, half-rising from the couch.

I shake my head. "Can't be. He has a key."

Legs asleep from sitting too long, I wobble to the door. Through the peephole, I see the last person I expected—my father, shifting his weight from foot to foot, glancing nervously at his watch. His breath forms small clouds in the chilly night air, and there's something unusually vulnerable in his posture.

I open the door, my surprise evident. "Dad? What are you doing here?"

J.P. Cooper stands on my doorstep, looking oddly diminished in the soft glow of the porch light. His usual commanding presence is muted, his shoulders slightly hunched against the November chill. In one hand, he clutches a brown paper bag...perhaps an apology present? Which is unnecessary, because this is all I ever really wanted from him. *Show up.*

"You wouldn't answer my calls," he says simply, his voice lacking its usual resonance. "And I need to talk to you."

"It's almost eleven at night," I point out, crossing my arms against both the cold and my instinctive defensiveness.

"I know." He nods, his gaze dropping momentarily to his shoes—expensive Italian leather now spotted with rain. "But it couldn't wait."

"It's cold, come in." I nod over my shoulder, deciding who will be less thrilled to see the other, Daphne or Dad. When he hesitates, I add, "Forrest isn't here."

"It's not that. I'm not so great at this." His leg bounces in place, proving his point. "Would you take a walk with me? Around the block, maybe? I can get the words out better if we're moving."

I pause, glancing back at Daphne, who's now hovering in the hallway behind me, her expression curious.

"Go." She makes a shooing motion with her hands. "I'll stay with Dakota. She's fast asleep anyway."

"Let me check on her first," I say, more to buy myself time than anything else. I leave Daphne and Dad to awkward small talk in the foyer as I dart upstairs.

Pushing the door open carefully, like it's a sacred relic in an Indiana Jones film, I peek into Dakota's room. She's sound asleep, one small arm flung above her head, Mr. Flops clutched tightly in the other. Her breathing is deep and even, her face peaceful. The sight of her calms something in me, centering me in a way I desperately need at the moment.

Back downstairs, I grab my coat and pull on my fuzzy Muk Luks. "A quick walk," I tell my father, stepping out into the night.

The November air is crisp and sharp, filling my lungs with a bracing chill. The streets of the West Village are quieter than usual, most windows darkened, though a few still glow with warm light. Our footsteps echo on the damp pavement, a steady rhythm in the night silence.

"Where's Forrest tonight?" Dad asks after we've walked half a block.

I tighten my coat around me, the cold penetrating despite the wool. "Working."

"Does he often work late?" Suspicion lines his tone.

"Why?" I mutter, preparing myself for the worst.

"I've warmed up to the idea of you not living alone. I thought it was too quick to move in together, but, on the other hand, it's nice to know my little girl is being protected." Dad awkwardly crosses his arms and pats his shoulders. "He's a strong-looking guy. Could probably fight off an intruder."

I'm sure he's expecting a witty, Sora response. But I'm not in the mood for a multitude of reasons. "Probably," I mumble.

He sighs, the sound forming a small cloud in the frigid air. "I owe you an apology, Sora."

I nearly trip on an uneven piece of sidewalk. In twenty-seven years, I've heard my father apologize maybe three times, and never with much sincerity.

"For dinner the other night?" I ask, trying to keep my voice casual. "It's fine—"

"No, it's not fine." He stops walking, turning to face me under the glow of a streetlamp. Its light casts deep shadows across his face, highlighting the wrinkles I hadn't noticed before. "And it's not just about dinner. It's about everything."

A dog barks in the distance. Somewhere a car alarm goes off, then falls silent again. The city breathes around us, alive even in the late hours.

"I've been a terrible father in a lot of ways," he continues, his voice rougher than usual. "But the way I've treated your writing, your career...that's been inexcusable."

"Dad—"

"Let me finish." His eyes hold a type of shame I've never seen before. "I've been telling myself I was protecting you. That I was being tough because the world is tough, and you needed to be prepared." He shakes his head slowly. "But that was a lie. I was projecting my own fears onto you."

We resume walking, our pace slow, measured. A gust of wind sends dead leaves into a tango across the sidewalk, and I shove my hands into the pockets of my peacoat, which is starting to feel paper-thin against the glacial evening.

"What fears?" I ask, genuinely curious. "You're J.P. Cooper. You're successful, desired, respected, untouchable—"

"Depressed," he interrupts, the confession hanging low and heavy between us. "Every single day. I act like I'm immune to all the painful parts of being an author, but it's why I was so reclusive when you were growing up. I was emotionally tortured, constantly at the mercy of reader expectations, the pressure of providing for our family, the feeling that I was a failure every day."

I'm stunned into silence. This is the man whose confidence I've envied my entire life, whose certainty seemed unshakable.

"The truth is," he continues, "my apathy was a shield. In reality, every criticism felt like a knife. Every review, every sales report, every comparison to other authors—they all cut brutally deep. I built this persona, because I had to. You're either the king of the rock, or you'll get torn apart limb from limb by the hyenas. I was never brave enough to let the world see how vulnerable I really was... But you are."

"What?"

"I read your book—*Lovely*."

I halt. The fiery fear consumes me head to toe. My most daunting critic of all finally read my book and I can collapse from the anxiety. Because Dad's opinion...means *everything*.

I immediately get defensive. "Look, I'll be the first to say it—I was on a deadline. It was admittedly a little rushed. And there's a part two coming that'll fill in a lot of the gaps from *his* perspective. I'm not saying it's perfect, but—"

"It took me a few chapters to recognize the story," he cuts in. "It sounded so familiar, for a moment I was worried you ripped off some Lifetime movie I'd seen years ago—"

"*Hey!*" I bark out. "Rude."

"But then I realized why I knew it."

We lock gazes, and it's clear. Dad knows the secret about this book that no one else does. Every time I tell people what *Lovely* is about, I tell them it's a story about high school sweethearts who reconnect years later. A second-chance story. A promise of hope. Never once did I admit out loud that it's Mom and Dad's story.

Dad pulls my book out of the brown paper bag. It's worn and dog-eared. The pages are bent and the cover has a coffee ring stain on it. Basically Dad has committed every cardinal sin in the book girlies' manifesto. But it's proof. He read it. From the state of the book, it looks like he obsessed over it.

He puts the book into my hands, which teeters precariously because I'm still frozen in shock, my hands simply shelves attached to the wall of my body. Reaching back into the bag, he pulls out a black Sharpie. "I wanted to get the author's signature."

He spins around and hunches over, patting his shoulder, instructing me to use his back as my signing table. "Make it out to J.P. Cooper—not 'Dad.' Colleague to colleague."

I sniffle as I uncap the pen, my hand trembling so much I

know my signature is going to come out a squiggle. After opening the weathered book to the title page, I rest it against Dad's back, trying to savor what feels like the most monumental moment of my author life.

"One more thing," he says, right as the black ink dots the title page. I rip the pen away.

"What?"

"Sign it with your full name. Sora Cho-Cooper."

"Okay," I croak out. Just as I suspected, my signature comes out an ineligible scribble. Hands shaking from the cold and the magnitude of the moment, it's the best I can do. "Done," I tell him before he spins around. I hand the book back.

"Thank you," he says, studying my signature, pride glazing his cold, red cheeks.

"I can get you a better copy," I offer. "You massacred that."

He shakes his head. "No, thank you. I have notes in the margin I want to revisit."

I nod, pressing my frigid lipsicles together in a smile. The silence between us is hell-raisingly loud, bursting with all the broken promises, lost moments, and missed opportunities. We seem to relive them all at once in the chilly quiet. And then word by word, we rewrite our history. An unspoken understanding that from now on, things are going to be different.

"You said there's a book two?" Dad asks, lifting his bushy brows.

"Yeah. From the hero's perspective." I shrug. "I got it back from the editor, and she seemed unamused. I still have to go through her edits, format the book, and ask the cover designer to finalize the files. I'm supposed to publish it by December, but there's a part of me that doesn't want to. I can't bear to see it fail."

He gestures forward and we continue to walk as we talk, reaching a small park, deserted at this hour. A single swing moves slightly in the breeze, chains creaking. Dad leads me to a bench, and we sit side by side, breathing like dragons, our breath forming ephemeral white puffs of smoke in the midnight air.

"Can I give you some advice? Author to author?"

"Sure. I've only been begging for four years, but better excruciatingly late than never."

He rolls his eyes, and it comforts me. Like his grumbly annoyance is chicken soup straight to my soul. "A story can't fail. It exists, so it did its job. Don't fear the criticism. It's coming, Sora. It's as guaranteed as the sunrise and sunset each day. But it means nothing in the grand scheme of things. If you don't want to publish your story because you feel it isn't quite right, or you didn't get to say what you wanted to, delay it. Take your time. Experience every grisly part of being an author—the writing, the rewriting, overcoming doubt, fear, and shame. You have to let it all in, and give it room to breathe. Every single painful, harrowing part of this experience is *necessary*. The best stories are written from broken places."

I smirk at him. "Broken places? Is that why you kill off all your main characters?" I may not have read Dad's books. But I've read his glowing reviews.

He smiles. "You leave fantasy to the fantasy authors. Death is a necessary part of life. But what I meant is when you start a story from a broken place, it has a funny way of repairing your heart. The best stories come from pain, because they are intended to heal, Sora. That's the whole point of writing—*to heal something*."

I stare at him, this man I've spent my life idolizing and resenting in equal measure, suddenly seeing him through new eyes. Behind the impenetrable walls was a broken man, who wrote to mend all the wounds the world gave him.

My eyes water, washing my lashes with tears. "Thank you, Dad. That's all I ever wanted from you."

"I tried for so long to protect you from the hell I went through," he says, his voice softer now, more tender. "But I realize now the best way to protect you isn't to keep you from the fire. It's to stand in the fire with you."

He hands me the book I signed and taps the cover. "This is from your mom's perspective. And the second one is supposed to be from mine?"

A little embarrassed at his revelation, my answer is small. "Sort of."

"Do you have any idea how hard this was to read? All my mistakes documented on the page."

"I'm sorry. I wasn't trying to hurt you. It's just fiction, and I was convinced you'd never read it—"

"No, Sora, what I'm saying is that reading my mistakes helps me understand how to fix them. See, I need you to publish book two, because I really, *really* need to know they have a happily-ever-after. That's what all you romance writers do, right? Rainbows and sunshine at the end?" He gives me a teasing smile.

"Don't make fun of us," I say, glowering.

"I'm not. Rainbows and sunshine sound wonderful."

"I don't have the ending quite right," I whisper, my throat tight with unexpected emotion. I run my fingers over the cover, feeling the slight indentations of the spot-glossed title.

"How's it end?"

"They don't end up together. They go their separate ways, and find a different kind of happiness. She remarries. He ends up alone."

Dad shoots me a look. "Yeah, that's no good."

"Gee, thanks," I mutter. "It may not be rainbows and sunshine, but it's realistic."

"Maybe I can help you," he offers. "Let me read it. Let's write a new ending...together." He grabs my hand and clutches it tightly in his stiff fingers. "One where he's forgiven, and by some miracle, his family gives him another chance to make things right. Something that heals."

I squeeze his hand right back. "You'd do that? I thought you were going to be busy in Hollywood."

"I'm moving back to New York. I'm leaving the show as a producer."

"What? But what if they screw up your story? I thought you were there to police them a little."

He smiles slightly, the expression transforming his face, softening the hard lines. "So they screw it up. They'll have hell to pay with the die-hard fans, but that's the director's battle to fight. As for me? I'm going back to life before success warped everything. They don't need me hovering over everyone's shoulder."

"Wow." I'm genuinely shocked. Dad has been obsessed with controlling every aspect of the adaptation, treating it like his legacy, his immortality. "I can't believe you're choosing to walk away."

"I'm choosing what matters." The resolve on his face is determined. Full of confidence in his decision. "Your mother, for one."

"Mom?" I can't hide my surprise.

"That night opened my eyes," he admits. "Seeing Jennifer again, hearing her defend you...it reminded me of who she is. Who we were together. I've spent too many years chasing success, validation, acclaim. And for what? To come home to an empty house? To have my only daughter afraid to answer my calls?"

"I wasn't afraid," I protest automatically, but we both know it's not entirely true.

"You've been avoiding me, Sora. And I don't blame you." He takes his hand back, rubbing it furiously against the other, trying to produce some warmth. "I've been a harsh critic when I should have been your biggest fan. That ends now. So I'd love to help you with your story, if you let me."

"I'd love that, Dad." Truer words have never been spoken.

"But under one condition," he says sternly. "I want you to stop trying so hard to win my respect, my love, my approval." His voice roughens with emotion, cracking slightly on the last word. "You've had it all along, Sora. I'm sorry I failed to show you that. But it also doesn't matter. Be the person you want to be. Not the person anyone else thinks you should be."

Tears sting my eyes, hot against the cold night air. "All right," I promise with a sniffle. "From now on I won't give a rat's ass what you think of me." I flash him a shit-eating grin.

"Attagirl."

"So you and Mom are...?"

"Taking things slow," he says with a small shrug. "But she's agreed to give me another chance. Which is more than I deserve, honestly."

"And you're moving back to New York?" I parrot, trying to process this sudden shift in our family dynamic.

He nods.

"Do you want the brownstone back?" I ask quickly, thinking of the fort we set up in the living room, of Dakota's stuffed animals lined up on the window seat, of Forrest's coffee mug in the sink. My stomach fills with lead when I think about letting my newfound sense of happiness go.

"No. I gave it to you. *It's yours*," Dad says with a knowing look, a ghost of his old mischievous grin appearing. "It's probably ruined anyway, thanks to all the canoodling you've been doing with your boyfriend."

My face heats up despite the cold, the blush spreading from my cheeks down my neck. "Um...no...we don't."

"Spare me." He chuckles, the sound rich and warm. "And that Forrest fellow seems decent enough, despite our spat."

"He was defending me," I say, feeling the need to clarify even as I marvel at how easily my father is accepting Forrest's presence in my life.

"I know." Dad's expression turns serious again, the lines around his eyes deepening. "That's why I liked him, even while I wanted to punch him. Any man who will stand up to J.P. Cooper to protect my daughter is worth keeping around."

If only he knew the complications lurking beneath that simple assessment. The thought of Forrest, where he is tonight, what he's doing, sends fresh pulses of pain through me. But that's a conversation for another time. My heart is still feebly beating, fueled by this unexpected reconciliation.

A few snowflakes begin to fall, delicate and evanescent, melting almost as soon as they touch the ground. It's too early in the season for snow that sticks, but the brief white flurry adds a magical quality to the night.

"Should we head back?" Dad asks, standing and offering me his hand. "It's getting late, and I have a feeling you have a lot to think about."

I take his hand, the familiar calluses on his fingertips—writer's calluses, just like mine—a small testament to our shared DNA, our shared passion.

"Dad," I say, as we near the brownstone, our walk coming to a close. "The second book in the duet..."

"Yeah?"

"It's called *Lonely*. I know the cover designer will probably be pissed, and I'll have hoops to jump through with the publishing platform to update the metadata, but if we rewrite the ending, the title doesn't seem to fit after tonight."

I wrote *Lovely* because it's how I think of my mother. And now, I don't want to think of my dad as lonely anymore.

"What do you think fits better?" he asks, taking the concrete steps leading up to my front door slowly.

I stop behind him, before the first step, and look up at my dad's figure. With him three steps ahead, he looks so much taller. It reminds me of how I saw him when I was a little girl. The hero I always idolized...finally acting like a real hero. Coming full circle, fighting off his demons, and circling back to rescue his family from missing him. Righting wrongs, and fighting the beast of remorse.

"*Legendary*," I answer. "That's what I'll call it."

CHAPTER TWENTY-EIGHT

Forrest

It doesn't feel like a bomb going off in my intestines at all.

The November chill cuts through my jacket as I check my watch: 9:58 p.m. I've been wandering the streets of Manhattan for nearly two hours, no destination in mind, just putting one foot in front of the other. I had to shut my phone off, sick of it buzzing relentlessly in my pocket.

By now, Marianne Wescott must be furious. She booked me for the night—not for some charity gala or social function where she needed arm candy, but for what Rina diplomatically calls "the full package." Five thousand dollars for services I can't bring myself to provide.

I've never stood up a client before. Not once in four years. But tonight, as I stood outside Marianne's luxury high-rise on Park Avenue, something in me simply...refused. I can't do it. The thought of being with another woman, even professionally, feels like betrayal.

Because of Sora.

All I can see is her face when she found out about tonight's "appointment." The way she smiled too brightly and said she understood, that it was just business, that she was fine with it. But her eyes—those expressive eyes that can't hide a damn thing—told a different story. She tried to be brave, but the hurt in her eyes practically undid me. It kills me how Sora smiles right before she's about to cry, like she doesn't want to inconvenience anyone. And then she turned away, claiming she needed to work on her new manuscript, thinking I didn't see the tears.

The memory twists in my chest like a knife.

I'd rather scrub toilets or flip burgers than see that look on Sora's face again.

I can't lose her. I won't risk it. Not for anything. I just need a new plan. *Quickly.*

Somehow, my aimless wandering has led me to the Upper East Side, and now I find myself standing in front of Rina's elegant brownstone, staring up at the warm glow emanating from her windows. My finger presses the doorbell before I can talk myself out of it.

The door swings open almost immediately, as if Rina has been expecting me. She stands in the doorway wearing a burgundy silk pajama set, her tan skin glowing in the warm light of her foyer. Her dark hair, usually styled straight, falls in loose curls to her shoulders. Without her usual power suit and three-inch heels, she looks softer, but no less formidable.

She crosses her arms over her chest, one perfectly arched eyebrow rising. "Something told me you'd wind up here tonight."

No "hello." No "what are you doing here?" She's always been able to read me like one of her legal briefs.

"May I come in?" My voice sounds rougher than I intended.

She steps aside, gesturing me into the marble-floored entryway with a grace that reminds me why her wealthy clientele find her so intimidating and don't test her.

"I was about to pour myself a glass of Macallan. I think you might need one too." She turns without waiting for my response, leading me through to her study, where a fire crackles in the ornate fireplace. The room smells of sandalwood and old books, a comforting contrast to the chaos in my head.

"Marianne Wescott called me." Rina pours amber liquid into two crystal tumblers. "Four times."

"I'm sorry." I accept the glass she hands me, but don't drink.

"Don't be. That woman is insufferable." She settles into one of the leather armchairs by the fire, tucking her legs beneath her. "Though I do wonder what could possibly have made my most reliable escort stand up a high-paying client."

I remain standing, too wired to sit. "I quit, Rina."

There it is. All the words I'd been rehearsing during my hours of wandering, reduced to just those three. But they're out now. No going back.

She sips her whisky, studying me over the rim of her glass. "I can't say I didn't see this coming. But why?"

"I'm in love with someone."

A slow smile spreads across her face. "Ah, your private *client*, Sora." She shrugs. "Taio," she offers as an explanation to my unasked question.

I shouldn't be surprised. "Yes. She's not a typical client which is why I didn't tell you about her. I wasn't trying to do anything behind your back—"

She holds up her palm, stopping me. "I wasn't worried, Forrest. You know what happens when you build years upon years of trust with someone?"

"What's that?"

She blinks like I'm clueless. "You give them the benefit of the doubt. You're not on trial here, Hawkins."

It's not like Sora was a paying client. Well, technically, yes. But I never intended on keeping her money. The ten thousand dollars was just leverage so she'd have to see me again. Although now, I may need it.

"Thank you. But it doesn't change anything." I set my untouched drink on the mantelpiece. "I need to end this. All of it."

Rina leans forward, her expression suddenly serious. "And what exactly are you planning to do for money? Your debt to Sean's firm isn't going anywhere. Dakota's school tuition isn't going to pay itself. And let's not forget your father's ranch."

I run a hand through my hair, frustration bubbling up. "I don't know, okay? I haven't figured that part out yet. But I'll find something. Bartending, security work, hell, I'll deliver packages if I have to."

"All of which would pay a tiny fraction of what you've been making."

"I know that," I snap, then immediately regret it. "I'm sorry. I know how this sounds. Impulsive. Irresponsible. But I had to make a choice tonight, and I chose Sora. I'll have to figure out the rest."

Rina's dark eyes soften almost imperceptibly. "You're giving up financial security for a woman you barely know?"

"It's not just about Sora." I pace the length of the Persian rug. "It's about me. Who I am. Who I want to be. For years, I've justified this job because it was the only way to keep my life from falling apart. But now..." I trail off, struggling to articulate the shift I feel inside.

"Now it's keeping you from building the life you actually want," Rina finishes for me.

I nod, grateful for her understanding.

"Sit down, Hawkins. You're making me dizzy."

I comply, sinking into the chair opposite hers. The fire pops and hisses between us, casting dancing shadows across the bookshelves lining the walls. There's an entire row of old academic books, from Rina's teaching days. The days I knew her as Professor Colt.

"I'm sorry to let you down," I say quietly. "After everything you've done for me. You saved me when I had no other options. I'll never forget that."

"I know what you're thinking, and you are not in my debt. You did a job, you were compensated. I've never pitied you, Forrest, and I respect your choices."

A small, reluctant smile tries to tug on my lips. It barely succeeds. "You sure? I'm not close with my mother, but if I were, I imagine the look on your face right now would be similar to what I'd see if I'd deeply disappointed her."

Rina places her glass on the side table, leaning forward to

meet my gaze directly. "On the contrary, I'm incredibly proud of you."

That catches me off guard. "Proud? I'm bailing on you, on my responsibilities—"

"You're choosing integrity over convenience. Don't misunderstand me—I'm not saying there's anything inherently wrong with what we do. But it's clearly no longer right for you. And recognizing that takes courage."

I feel something tight in my chest begin to loosen. "So...you're not mad?"

"Oh, I'm furious about Marianne Wescott. I'll have to send Saylor or Marcus to salvage that disaster, and I just know she's going to be insufferable about it." She waves a dismissive hand. "But *at* you? No, I'm not mad."

She rises gracefully, crossing to a sleek desk in the corner of the room. From a drawer, she withdraws a manila folder, which she hands to me before returning to her seat.

"What's this?" I ask, opening it to find what looks like legal documents.

"A way out," she says simply. "I've been thinking about this for weeks."

I scan the first page, confusion mounting. "These are loan papers."

"From my personal accounts, not the business." She meets my startled gaze calmly. "Enough to pay off Sean's firm and keep Dakota in her school through the end of the year. That should give you time to find your feet."

Shock renders me momentarily speechless. It's nearly a million dollars. "Rina...I can't accept this."

"You can, and you will." Her tone brooks no argument. "Instead of being indebted to Sean, you'll be indebted to me. The difference is, I'm not going to blackball you out of the legal industry. Go take the bar. Find a good job. I'll do as much damage control as I can. Not every single law firm in the city is under Sean's reach. We'll find you something."

"But it's *a lot*, Rina. I don't know when I can pay this back. This is more of a gift than a loan."

"It's not a handout. You're a big boy, Hawkins, and this is the real world. The interest rate is favorable but not charitable. Let's both assume you'll be paying me back for quite some time." A hint of mischief flashes in her eyes. "I may be proud of you, but I'm still a businesswoman."

I stare at the papers, struggling to process what she's offering. "Why would you do this for me?"

Rina is quiet for a long moment, staring into the fire. When she speaks again, her voice holds a note I've never heard before—something raw and honest.

"Do you know why I started this business after my divorce from Sean?"

I shake my head. "Revenge?"

"Partly." She gives a short laugh. "I love the idea of scandalizing his arrogant, blue-blooded family. But it actually started with something else—my own encounter with an escort four years ago. I would've never done something that daring and risky, but..." She trails off, getting lost in some memory.

I blink, terrified she's about to give me details about a risqué night she had with a hired date. In a weird way, Rina can pimp me out no problem, but hearing about her sex life is quite frankly like hearing about my own mother having sex. I can't think of anything more uncomfortable.

"Um..."

"Now, I don't kiss and tell—"

"*Thank god*," I mutter a little too loudly, and am met by her icy stare.

"But," she continues, still glaring at me, "one night changed my entire perspective on life. I was inspired to change people's understanding of what being an escort means. It's not all about sex. It's about connecting and companionship. Sometimes you need the right person, at the right time, to pull you out of a rut you didn't even know you were in. I like the idea of giving people an opportunity, even if it's just for a night, to be valued, cared for, loved, protected, fought for... It's sad there are so many women out there who need that fabricated because the men in their real lives are so severely lacking. But nonetheless, while it's fleeting, it doesn't mean it's not real. Even a momentary feeling can inspire big change."

"So, you mean you didn't sleep with that escort? You just talked?"

She levels her gaze, face completely straight. "No, Hawkins. I rode the hell out of him. All night. Then, the morning after."

"*Dammit*, Rina." I cup my hands over my ears like a child, so I can watch her fall into a giggling fit.

"Sorry," she says through breathy laughter. "My point is, one person changed my entire life for the better, even if he did end up breaking my heart. So, if this young lady is somebody worth changing your life for—do it."

"But you said he broke your heart...your guy." I watch the last flicker of humor disappear from her eyes as she's taken over by something a bit darker.

She nods. "Because I couldn't keep him. That's all."

"What was his name?"

"Dalton," she answers simply, back to tight-lipped Rina when it comes to her personal life. "You lose yourself helping everybody else. Dakota, Hannah, your dad, and now Sora. You're selfless to your detriment. But I see the man you could be if you weren't constantly scrambling to keep your head above water." She gestures to the folder. "Consider this an investment in that man."

My throat tightens with emotion I can't quite name. "I don't know what to say."

"Say you'll be smart about this. That you'll use this to set yourself up for something great." Her expression grows stern. "And then say you'll definitely pay me back."

A laugh escapes me, half relief, half disbelief. "You're something else, you know that?"

"So I've been told." She picks up her whisky again. "Now,

about this Sora. Tell me everything."

I finally reach for my own glass, taking a grateful sip. "She's nothing like anyone I've ever met. Brilliant, funny, completely neurotic in the best possible way. She writes these romance novels that she thinks aren't good enough, but they're actually amazing—full of heart and humor and these characters that feel so real you forget they're made up."

"And she's completely upended your life in what, two weeks?" Rina's tone is teasing, but her eyes are kind.

"Two months." Although truthfully? Two minutes. I knew from the moment she narrowed her eyes at me in Papa Beans that this woman was going to star in my dreams for the foreseeable future. "It sounds crazy, I know."

"Not crazy." Rina swirls the amber liquid in her glass. "Inconvenient, certainly. Potentially foolhardy. But not crazy."

"That's reassuring," I say dryly.

"She must be quite special for you to risk everything."

"She is." The certainty in my voice surprises even me.

Rina studies me for a long moment, then nods as if confirming something to herself. "Well then. I suppose there's only one question left."

"What's that?"

"Does she feel the same way about you?"

The question drenches me like a bucket of ice water. In my rush to make this grand gesture, to reshape my entire life around the possibility of a future with Sora, I haven't actually confirmed that she wants that future too.

"I...I think so," I stammer. "We haven't exactly had that conversation yet."

Rina's eyebrows shoot up. "You're quitting your job before telling this woman how you feel about her?"

Put that way, it does sound monumentally stupid. "I was going to tell her tonight. After I talked to you."

"Good lord." She rubs her temples. "You really are a romantic at heart, aren't you? No wonder you're so good at your job." She catches herself. "*Former job.*"

I groan, burying my face in my hands. "This is too much, too fast, isn't it? She's going to think I've lost my damn mind."

"Probably." Rina shrugs. "But sometimes the grand gesture pays off. Just..." She hesitates, an unusual occurrence for her. "Be prepared for the possibility that she might need time to process all this. It's a lot."

I nod, suddenly nervous in a way I haven't been since my first day at Columbia Law. "Any advice?"

"Be honest. All cards on the table." She sets her empty glass aside. "And maybe lead with 'I'm falling in love with you' before 'I just quit my job and took out a massive loan so we could be together.'"

Despite everything, I laugh. "Noted."

Rina stands, signaling the end of our conversation. "Keep me updated. And if it doesn't work out..." She gives me a pointed look. "You always have a place here. No shame in that."

I rise too, clutching the folder of loan papers. "Thank you. For everything."

Impulsively, I step forward and hug her. She stiffens initially—Rina isn't exactly the hugging type—but after a moment, her arms come around me briefly before she steps back.

"Enough sentimentality for one night." She straightens her silk pajama top. "Go get your girl, Hawkins."

As I step back into the cool night air minutes later, the weight that has been pressing on my chest for weeks—maybe years—feels lighter. The path ahead is uncertain, fraught with financial challenges and the terrifying possibility of rejection. But for the first time since Columbia Law, since Dakota was born, since Hannah dumped me, I feel like I'm making a choice rather than reacting to circumstances beyond my control.

I pull out my phone, turn it back on, and call an Uber. It's time to tell Sora the truth—all of it. Time to find out if the future I suddenly want more than anything is one she wants too.

The brownstone is eerily quiet as I slip through the front door. It's well past midnight, and exhaustion weighs on my bones after the emotional conversation with Rina. But there's one more thing I need to do tonight—one conversation I can't wait until morning to have.

I creep up the stairs, avoiding the third step that creaks like it's auditioning for a horror movie soundtrack. The house is dark except for a sliver of light coming from the fourth floor—Sora's bedroom. She's still awake.

My heart rises and falls in my chest like it's riding a roller coaster as I approach her door. I've spent years perfecting the art of charming women, knowing exactly what to say and how to say it, but right now, I feel like an awkward teenager about to ask someone to prom.

I knock softly, then turn the knob.

"*Aaaahh!*" Sora yelps, brandishing a stainless-steel water bottle like a baseball bat. She's cross-legged on her bed, laptop balanced precariously on her knees, hair piled in a messy bun that's tilting precariously to one side. She's wearing an oversized T-shirt with the words "I like big books and I cannot lie" stretched across her chest. "Christ, Forrest! You scared the crap out of me!"

I can't help but smile at the sight of her—future bestselling author Sora Cho, armed with hydration to defend herself against home invaders.

"Planning to drown the burglars?" I nod at her weapon of choice.

She lowers the water bottle, her cheeks flushing adorably. "It was the closest thing at hand, you lurker. And what are you doing here? I didn't expect you until...you know, morning."

There's a shadow behind her words, a careful distance in the way she's looking at me. She thinks I've just come from another woman's bed.

"Were you really going to fight off an intruder with that?" I ask, deflecting for a moment as I close the door behind me.

"This thing is solid steel and holds forty ounces of ice water. I could do some damage." She lifts her chin defiantly. "I've seen enough crime shows. Go for the kneecaps, then the groin, then run."

"Solid strategy. But maybe invest in a baseball bat. Or pepper spray. Or literally anything designed to be a weapon."

"Noted. I'll add 'instruments of self-defense' to my shopping list, right below 'milk' and 'sanity.'" She sets the water bottle on her nightstand with exaggerated care. "So...why are you home so early?"

"Early?" I ask, knowing it's almost one in the morning.

"I assumed I wouldn't see you until morning. Dakota and I made pancake plans. We were going to save some for you."

"That's sweet." I perch on the edge of her bed, suddenly very interested in the pattern of her comforter. "What are you working on so late?" I ask, nodding at her laptop.

She eyes me suspiciously but allows the subject change. "Edits for *Legendary*."

"*Legendary*? New book?"

"The new title for the reworked version of *Lonely*." A small, genuine smile lights up her face. "My dad stopped by unannounced tonight."

"Your dad?" I straighten up, surprised. "J.P. Cooper himself descended from his literary throne to visit the peasants?"

She swats at my arm. "Be nice. It was good. *Incredible*, actually. We talked—like, really talked—for the first time in... maybe ever. He read my book."

My heart shudders. But she's smiling, so it can't have been that bad. "And?"

"And he liked it." Her voice is soft with wonder. "So much so, he's going to help me with book two, just so I get it exactly right."

"You trust his opinion when it comes to a romance story like this?"

She smiles at me, secrets safeguarded behind her closed lips. "More than you know."

"Then that's wonderful. I'm very happy for you. I know how much your parents mean to you." There's too much distance between us, an entire queen-sized bed's worth, so I blow her a kiss. I bet she doesn't want me to touch her right now.

"It feels like a new beginning for me and Dad." Her eyes are bright with unshed tears. "We finally broke through a wall I thought would keep us separated forever. So liberating. I never thought we'd get here."

The perfect opening. I take a deep breath.

"Speaking of new beginnings," I say, shifting to face her fully. "I was wondering if we could have one too."

Her eyebrows draw together in confusion. "What do you mean?"

"First, I need to address the elephant in the room," I say. "About tonight."

Her expression shutters slightly. "Right. How was your evening?"

"Nonexistent." I hold her gaze, wanting her to see the truth in my eyes. "I didn't go through with it, Sora. I didn't meet with the client. I couldn't."

Her lips part in surprise. "You...what?"

"I stood outside her building for twenty minutes, then I just walked away. Spent two hours wandering around the city before I ended up at Rina's." I comb a hand through my hair. "I stood her up."

"Was Rina angry? She said she wasn't going to give you any more work if you bailed again." Her voice rises an octave. "Forrest, what are you going to do about—"

"That's tomorrow's problem," I cut her off gently. "Tonight, I just need you to know something."

She waits, her dark eyes wide and uncertain.

"Do you know what makes me so attracted to you?" I ask.

A mischievous glint replaces the uncertainty. She cups her

breasts through her oversized T-shirt and pushes them up slightly. "Obviously these double-Ds," she jokes. Though to me her breasts are the definition of perfect; we both know she can barely fill a C-cup.

I laugh, the tension breaking. "Yes, obviously your massive rack. But know what else?" I crawl across the bed and plant myself right next to her. I take her hands in mine, growing serious again. "It's how vulnerable you make yourself. How you show the world your bleeding heart with every book you write. Even when it hurts, even when you struggle, you wear your heart on your sleeve. It's so brave."

She looks down at our joined hands. "That's not bravery. That's just me not knowing how to be any other way."

"That's exactly what makes it brave." I squeeze her fingers. "You're genuine. Kind. Tender. Sweet. Despite the garbage the world throws at you, you're still powerless but to be yourself. It inspires me. It makes me want to be honest too."

"Honest about what?"

"About how I feel. About what I want." I take a deep breath. "I want to start over, Sora. From the very beginning of our story."

She tilts her head, curious but still wary. "What do you mean?"

"That day at Papa Beans, the only reason I didn't ask for your number was because of the baggage of my job. I want to go back to the very moment I laid eyes on you and try again."

"Like a do-over?" she asks, amusement lingering in her tone.

I let go of her hands and stand up. Then, with exaggerated formality, I extend my hand toward her.

"Hi," I say, putting on my most charming smile. "I'm Forrest Hawkins. I noticed you from across the room, and I just had to introduce myself."

Understanding dawns in her eyes. She straightens her posture and delicately places her hand in mine.

"Sora Cho-Cooper," she replies, playing along. "It's a pleasure to meet you, Mr. Hawkins."

"Cho-Cooper?" I furrow my brow in mock concentration. "Do I know you from somewhere? Aren't you a mega-famous bestselling author?"

She laughs, the sound warming me from the inside out. "I'm trying to manifest it."

"I'm sure it's not too far away. And you are stunning, by the way. Are you Asian by chance?" I ask, still holding her hand longer than strictly necessary for a handshake.

"My mother is Korean. And I should warn you right now, Forrest, I only date men who love spicy food."

I smirk. "I *love* spicy food. It doesn't feel like a bomb going off in my intestines at all."

She chuckles. "Good to know."

"So what are you working on these days?"

"A fantasy romance about a mermaid warrior princess and the dragon she falls in love with. It's hot. Enemies to lovers. Rage sex and all that good stuff," she says sarcastically.

"Sounds hot. Literally."

She groans at my terrible pun, but her smile remains. "What about you, Forrest Hawkins? What do you do for work?"

I hesitate, suddenly aware that this game we're playing has veered into real territory. "This is kind of embarrassing, but I used to be an escort. I actually quit tonight."

The air falls silent between us. Our playful facade slips, reality reasserting itself.

Sora's expression grows serious. "How are you going to make ends meet? What's next? Why would you give up everything for—"

"Whoa, whoa, lady," I interrupt, trying to steer us back to lighter ground. "That's a lot of invasive questions for a first meeting." I wink at her. "But I like your moxie. How about we talk about something else? What do you do for fun when you're not writing steamy dragon romance?"

She recognizes what I'm doing and plays along, though I can tell from the look in her eyes that we'll be revisiting those questions later.

"I stress-bake," she says.

"So you're comfortable in the kitchen?" I ask skeptically.

"Oh, yes. A bona fide professional."

I peer at her, trying to call out her obvious lies with one gaze. "Okay, Sora. What can you cook that's not in the microwave?"

She narrows her eyes. "Just yesterday I made salmon croquettes with Creole aïoli."

"First of all, that sounds delicious. Second of all, you really want to start our new relationship with just *utter* bullshit? I've seen you cook, woman. You 'boiled' spaghetti noodles in barely lukewarm water and were shocked they came out crunchy."

"Oh my god," she shrieks in frustration. "For the last time, they were rice noodles and they're delicate! The water isn't supposed to get too hot." She groans in frustration as I chuckle at her huffiness.

"Tell the truth, Ms. Cho-Cooper."

"Fine. My culinary skills are capped at microwaveable popcorn. I struggle with grilled cheese sandwiches. Happy?"

"It's not a problem. I can cook. I could teach you if you'd like?"

"Can you?" she asks seriously. "I didn't know that."

"Well, my current roommate is pretty territorial in the kitchen, so I try to make myself scarce. I think she's trying to prove her domestic skills."

She laughs. "She probably learned that the way to a man's heart is through his stomach. I bet she's trying to improve her cooking skills to keep you interested."

"It's not necessary," I say. "She could screw up a peanut butter and jelly sandwich, and I'd still think that woman walks on water."

"Well, Forrest, that's...problematic." She purses her lips and shakes her head.

"What?"

"Two minutes into our conversation, and now I know you have the hots for your roommate. *Red flag*," she mouths.

Laughing, I stretch out on the bed beside her, careful to

maintain a respectable distance. "Let's forget about my roommate for a minute."

"Fine," Sora says with a cute smirk. "We'll circle back to that later. So, are you from around here?"

"*Your bedroom*?" I ask. "I wasn't born here, but I know my way around. Are you looking for some tourist attractions? Because the important parts are the vibrator hidden underneath the caboodle in the nightstand cupboard, and the secret stash of candy bars in the locked cashbox underneath the bed." I point to the door leading to the bathroom. "The key is hidden on top of the doorframe."

"I hate you," she deadpans.

I burst out in a deep belly laugh again. "In all seriousness, I grew up in Wyoming, but came to the big city to be a hotshot lawyer."

"How'd that work out for you?"

"Had a moral crisis, tanked my career before it started, became an escort instead. You know, the usual career trajectory."

"Naturally," she says with a solemn nod.

"And you?"

"I'm a born-and-raised city girl. I walk or take cabs. My driver's license is purposeless outside of getting me into R-rated movies and buying occasional wine coolers. But you know what I've always regretted? Not learning how to drive a stick shift."

I sit up, suddenly excited. "Yeah? I'll teach you."

"You will?"

"Absolutely. My old truck is still parked at my dad's ranch. It only runs if you sweet-talk it and sacrifice a quart of oil to the automotive gods. Perfect learning vehicle. If you can drive that thing, you could drive a semi."

She giggles. "Sounds great. The only problem is last time I checked the map, the cab fare from Manhattan to Wyoming is a little out of my budget."

"How about we fly? Next weekend?" Rina loaned me more than enough to fly my girls home.

Her eyes pop wide open. "What?"

"I know it's a big step for a first date," I say, watching her carefully, "but I want to take you home to meet Boone. Wyoming is beautiful in the winter. Cold as hell, but beautiful."

Her smile grows to the point her cheek muscles look strained. "I'd love to go. It sounds like a perfect first official date."

"Good." I reach for her hand again, my thumb tracing familiar circles on her palm. She leans in closer, her lips relaxing as she flutters her lashes. I disappoint her with a brief peck on the lips.

"What the hell, Forrest?"

"I've been thinking about something else... Some rules we should implement."

"Rules?"

I sigh, dreading the words about to spill out of my mouth. "I think we should wait to have sex. At least three official dates. Like a future couple, not like—"

"An escort and a client?" she finishes for me, understanding the sentiment.

"Exactly."

She rolls her eyes so hard, her pupils poke her brain before returning to stare at me, unimpressed. "Forrest, what is waiting going to accomplish? You've already had me in every position imaginable."

"Come on. For me?" I pucker my bottom lip, trying to look irresistibly adorable. "This is for real. I want to do this right."

She studies me for a moment, then nods. "Okay. Not until three dates, then?"

"Agreed." I glance at the clock: 1:23 a.m. "Starting now."

"Starting now," she echoes, her eyes dropping briefly to my semi-bulge before meeting my gaze again. We look at each other for a long, charged moment.

"This is a terrible idea," she whispers.

"The worst," I agree, not moving.

"I mean, we've already seen each other naked."

"Multiple times," I add.

"And we're adults."

"Very adult."

"And we're both clearly consenting," she emphasizes.

"So consenting."

Another beat of silence.

"But this is our second chance, and we're doing this right," I say firmly, as if reminding myself.

This time I'm met with a baby eye roll. Not nearly as theatrical as the first. "Fine," she mutters. "Starting tomorrow."

"Technically today, but yes."

She closes her laptop and sets it aside, then scoots down under her comforter. "You're welcome to stay," she says, patting the space beside her. "Just for sleep."

"Just for sleep," I agree, kicking off my shoes and sliding in next to her.

She turns off the bedside lamp, plunging the room into darkness. I can feel the warmth of her body inches from mine, the subtle shift of the mattress as she gets comfortable.

"Forrest?" Her voice is soft in the darkness.

"Yeah?"

"I feel selfish saying it, but I'm glad you quit your job. You can keep my ten thousand dollars. I think you're going to need it."

I reach for her hand beneath the covers, threading our fingers together. "Would you still be with me if I was broke, living under a bridge?"

She squeezes my hand. "Definitely."

"Good." I pull her closer until her head is resting on my chest, her hair tickling my chin. "I promise it'll be a really nice bridge. Lots of colorful graffiti. Tire-burning bonfires every night for the added romance."

She laughs softly against my shirt. "Lovely."

I press a kiss to the top of her head, marveling at how right this feels—just holding her, talking, laughing. No expectations, no performance, just us.

"Forrest?" she murmurs again, her voice growing sleepy.

"Hmm?"

"I'm glad we're starting over."

I smile into the darkness, overwhelmed by the simple joy of this moment. "Me too, my little conch shell. Me too."

Within minutes, her breathing evens out, her body growing heavy and relaxed against mine. I lie awake a while longer, savoring the feeling of having her in my arms, of knowing that tomorrow brings not just another day, but the first day of our real story together.

I'm getting a second chance at a first impression.

And this time, I'm determined to do it right.

CHAPTER TWENTY-NINE

Forrest

I make it wimpy-style for him.

"That's him," I say, nodding toward the unmistakable figure leaning against a dusty, red pickup truck in the Jackson Hole Airport parking lot.

Even from a distance, my father cuts an impressive silhouette—tall and lean, with a well-worn Stetson pulled low over his eyes. At sixty, Boone Hawkins could still star in *Yellowstone*, fully equipped with his silver handlebar mustache and the don't-mess-with-me squint that terrified my teenage friends.

"Papaw!" Dakota shouts, tugging her hand free from mine to race across the parking lot.

I watch, throat tight with emotion, as my daughter runs toward the grandfather she's only ever seen in photos. This moment—their first real meeting—has been a long time coming.

My dad's weathered face breaks into a wide smile that shaves a decade off his age. He crouches down, arms open but hesitant, as if unsure how to greet a granddaughter he's never held. Dakota shows no such uncertainty, barreling into him with the force of a tiny missile.

"There's my girl," he says, his usually gruff voice gentle as he carefully wraps his arms around her. "Even better looking than your pictures, that's for sure."

Dakota beams up at him, completely at ease. "You look just

like your pictures, Papaw! Daddy showed me so many!" Without an ounce of trepidation, she tugs at the tip of his mustache, as if familiarizing herself. Dad makes a funny face and then chuckles, uncharacteristically, giving Koda far more grace than he'd ever give me. If I tugged on his mustache as a kid, he'd dropkick me across the room.

My dad's eyes find mine over her head, saying everything his old country soul can't articulate with sappy words: *She's precious, good to see you, son, thank you for bringing her home.* I answer his unspoken words with a simple nod of my head as we approach.

Beside me, Sora fidgets with the sleeve of her jacket, and I give her hand a reassuring squeeze.

"Dad, this is Sora." I nudge her forward, her feet glued to the concrete like a child nervous on their first day of school. I'm not used to her this bashful, which warms my heart because it means this is important to her. "Sora, I'd like you to meet the one and only Boone Hawkins."

My father straightens up, one hand still on Dakota's shoulder as if afraid she might disappear. His sharp eyes immediately focus on Sora, a look of genuine interest and warmth replacing his usual stoic expression.

"So you're the city girl," he says, extending a callused hand.

Sora looks like a fish out of water as she takes Dad's hand. "Yes, sir. Born and raised in Manhattan."

There's a beat of tension-ridden silence, and then Dad throws in the biggest plot twist I could've imagined. "It's good to know some good things can come out of the city," he says amidst a barking laugh. He yanks Sora awkwardly into his chest and gives her a bear hug. "Been looking forward to meeting the woman who got my son to finally come home."

Sora freezes for a millisecond, then melts into the hug. All the acceptance and validation she needed flooding out of one embrace. "Mr. Hawkins, thank you for having us. I've heard so much about you and the ranch," Sora says when Dad finally releases her.

"Boone, please," he insists, his smile revealing the crow's-feet around his eyes. "And I hope some of what you heard was good."

"All of it," she assures him.

My dad looks pleased, if a bit flustered. He's a man of few words by nature, and that hug probably satisfied his social quota for an entire month.

"You don't look a damn thing like Pumpkin's mama," Dad says, surveying Sora head to toe before he flashes her a sly grin, then turns his attention back to Dakota, leading her to the truck.

"Is that a bad thing?" Sora asks, lowering her voice so only I can hear.

"Oh, that was a Boone Hawkins compliment. Pay attention, they are few and far between, and oftentimes nonsensical," I offer.

"You said Hannah was beautiful...and I look nothing like her."

I grasp her shoulders, positioning her so she's facing me. "He's saying I'm making better choices. But he can't come right out and say that because—"

"Ah, yes. Country boys don't trash-talk their baby mamas."

"And country men don't talk smack about their granddaughter's mom." I tap the tip of her nose. "Just so you know, I can count the number of people Dad's ever hugged on one hand. High honor. He likes you."

"Good," she coos. "I like him too."

I wink at her. "It's still early and he's on his best behavior. The grump is coming. Prepare yourself."

She chuckles as Dad calls out to us.

"Daylight's burning. Let's get on with it, you two," he says while helping Dakota climb into a car seat in the back of the truck.

I load our luggage into the truck bed, then point Sora to the back seat. She climbs in beside Dakota. I hoist myself into the front passenger seat, and Dad scowls at me from the driver's side.

"Hold up now," he says, his frown deepening. "You're putting the lady in the back? Didn't I raise you better than that?"

"The buckle's still loose up front, Dad," I explain, barely tapping my seat belt clasp, which releases without protest. This seat belt is mostly for show. Wouldn't protect me against an ill-mannered kitten, let alone a head-on collision. "I'd rather have Sora and Dakota where it's safest."

He considers this, then nods, apparently satisfied with my reasoning. "Attaboy." Then, to Sora: "Sorry about that. Truck's seen better days, lil lady."

"It has character," she replies with a genuine smile. "And I'm happy to be back here with Dakota. We're going to count cows on the drive."

The engine roars to life with a rumbling growl that vibrates through the floorboards. Dad peels away from his parking spot, the truck's suspension groaning in protest.

"Sounds like a dinosaur!" Dakota exclaims delightedly from the back seat.

"Sounds like you've been neglecting repairs," I murmur to Dad.

"She's fine. Bessie's got some miles on her," my dad agrees, patting the dashboard affectionately. "But she's reliable. And plus it's the cold season, every spare penny I have is going to feed. Prices keep climbing. If Deacon keeps robbing me blind, I'm going to start making the trek to Cheyenne for better prices," he grumbles bitterly.

"Then you'll need a better truck," I note, mentally calculating what I can afford to help him with. Obviously the money I send home every month is barely putting a dent toward his needs.

As we pull away from the airport, I notice my father glancing in the rearview mirror more often than necessary, his eyes finding Sora each time. Not checking up on her—more like reassuring himself that she's really there. That we're all really here.

"So," he says, breaking the comfortable silence that had settled over us, "how was the flight? Always did hate those tin cans myself. Haven't been on a plane since—"

"Since Grandma's funeral," I finish quietly. "My mom's mom," I quickly explain to Sora through the rearview mirror.

"Once and never again," Dad adds.

"If you'd hop in a tin can every now and then, you'd get more time with Dakota," I reason.

He nods, a shadow crossing his features before he deliberately brightens again. "Pumpkin, how'd you like flying? Scary?"

"It was the *best*!" she announces. "My ears went pop. And I got pretzels and apple juice and the clouds looked like vanilla cotton candy and I could see tiny cars from the window!"

My dad chuckles, a rusty sound that suggests it doesn't happen often. "Is that right? Sounds like quite an adventure."

"It was! And Daddy let me have the window seat, and Sora told me stories about sky dragons that live in the clouds, and—"

She's off, chattering away about every detail of the flight as if it were an epic journey rather than a four-hour trip in economy class. My dad listens attentively, asking questions at just the right moments, drawing out more excited descriptions from her.

For a man who typically communicates in grunts and nods, it's an impressive display. I catch Sora watching him with a mix of surprise and appreciation, also recognizing the effort he's making.

"Thought we'd make cowboy chili for dinner," he says during a rare pause in Dakota's narrative. "Forrest's favorite."

"Chili is your favorite, but you don't like spicy food?" Sora asks.

"I make it wimpy-style for him," Dad says, earning a giggle from Sora.

"Ah, that's the secret. We have to make Forrest's food *wimpy*-style," she emphasizes.

"I hope by 'we' you aren't referring to yourself, because we both know even *edible* is a stretch for your cooking."

She smacks my shoulder. "How dare you," she sasses to me, then sweetens her tone as she addresses Dad. "Would you teach me how to make your chili, Mr. Hawkins? I'd love to learn."

"I appreciate your manners, but Boone is fine, hon. And I'd be happy to show you the family recipe. You'll cook with me today and I'll show you all the steps."

Sora clasps her hands together in glee. "Wonderful."

"You've still got good insurance on the house, right?" I ask loudly. "Protection against fire and such?"

I'm met with another smack from the back seat, this one with a little more oomph behind it.

The rest of the drive over, the scenery I know so well is filled with easy conversation—it's familiar but new at the same time. My dad has always been a quiet man who values his solitude, but there's a lightness to him today I haven't seen in years. Having Dakota and Sora here is drawing out a side of him I didn't know existed.

We turn off the main highway onto a dirt road that winds through a barren stretch of land. The truck bounces over the uneven terrain, and Dakota squeals with each jolt, finding it hilarious.

"Son, you're set up in your old room, and I put a cot in there for Dakota. Got the spare room all ready for you, Sora," Dad says. "Put in a space heater too. That side of the house gets cold in the mornings."

"You didn't have to go to all that trouble," she says.

"No trouble." He pauses, then adds with uncharacteristic openness, "Been a long time since I've had guests worth fussing over." My father isn't a demonstrative man—never has been—but in his own way, he's screaming from the rooftops how much this visit means to him.

The road curves sharply, and through a break in the field, the ranch appears before us—a sprawling, single-story house with a wide front porch that's seen better days. The paint on the main barn, just a stone's throw away from the house, is peeling, and one of the fence sections near the road needs repair.

"There she is," my father says with quiet pride. "Hawkins Ranch. Been in our family for four generations." He glances back at Sora. "Not as fancy as New York, but—"

"It's beautiful, Boone. Very impressive. How many acres?" she asks, and the genuine awe in her voice makes him sit a little straighter.

"A little over a hundred."

"Wow. That's a lot of upkeep. Do you use ranch hands with horses or sheepdogs to herd?"

I turn my neck to glance curiously at Sora. She widens her eyes at me in the universal symbol of: *Be cool.*

"Sheepdogs?" Dad asks with a chuckle. "Honey, Hawkinses haven't used sheepdogs even in my lifetime. They take too much to train. I've still got Redd, but he's old and fat. The only thing he can wrangle these days is a nap. We use ATVs mostly. I heard Riggins Ranch is using drones now. Offered to loan me one. Supposedly effective, but I'm not messing around with that technology mumbo jumbo."

"You're talking to Riggins?" I ask, acknowledging Dad's old nemesis, the nicer ranch just up the road.

Dad shrugs, trying to hide his embarrassment. "Rivals become more friendly in tough times. At the end of the day, we all take care of each other. He lent me some hands for the last calving season."

Translation: Dad's broke and has resorted to taking handouts. I know his pride is hurt. My stomach sinks a foot lower. *Fuck, I feel terrible.* It's another reminder of why I don't visit often. It's been two years since my last trip home. The guilt is physically painful. I should be here, helping him. Dad has been letting ranch hands go left and right, unable to afford them. He's carrying this burden all on his own, his only son abandoning him for city dreams.

"And, Boone, when is your calving season? Do you breed your heifers to give birth in the winter season or spring?"

I turn around to face Sora again. "Heifers? Did you spend a lot of time on Google before this trip?"

She shushes me aggressively, trying adorably to impress Dad with her ranch knowledge.

"I don't have any heifers, lil lady. All my current cows are seasoned."

"Right...right," Sora says, squinting one eye, clearly confused by Dad's reply.

"A heifer is a young female who hasn't given birth yet. Dad's current cows all had at least one calf." Or more accurately, Dad had to let his heifers go early to try to make money at market. It's expensive to maintain and breed.

"Our calving season is winter," Dad adds. "We start them early so they have time to get a little bigger before market. More weight, more money."

Dakota decides to insert herself back into the conversation at the most inconvenient time. "Why do the cows go to market?"

Turning once again, Sora and I meet each other's eyes with wide stares. "Papaw goes to market to sell the cows to other families who need them."

"Like pets?" Koda asks.

"Yup," Sora annexes my lie seamlessly. "Exactly."

Dad shoots me a look. "I thought you told me she was advanced? The lil one doesn't know what a burger is?"

"Hush," I hiss. "She's four. And unless you want her in tears for the rest of the day, as far as we're concerned, you sell cows like puppies, okay?"

We pull up to the house, and my dad cuts the engine. The sudden silence feels thick after the constant rumble of the truck.

"Home sweet home," he announces, a hint of nervousness creeping into his voice as if he's suddenly worried it won't measure up to expectations. "Let's get inside and warm up. November air's got a bite to it, even in the morning."

As he helps Dakota out of her car seat, there's a tenderness to his movements that belies his rugged exterior. He may have only just met her in person, but it's clear my daughter has already wrapped him around her little finger.

"I brought my coat, Papaw. Can I go outside and see the ranch later?" she asks, looking around with eager curiosity.

"Course you can," he confirms. "I'll give you the grand tour. Show you the barn, the old chicken coop, even the creek that runs along the back of the property."

"And then we can make chili?" She bounces on her toes.

"That's right," he promises. "You can be my special helper."

"And Sora too! She makes really good cookies. Maybe we can have cookies for dessert?"

My dad looks at Sora with amusement. "Thought Forrest implied you were a little...inexperienced in the kitchen."

"Cookies are my one exception," she admits with a laugh. "Everything else is a disaster, but somehow cookies always work out."

"Well then," he says, "sounds like we've got ourselves a plan. Chili for dinner, cookies for dessert."

The image of my stoic father cooking alongside Sora and Dakota makes my heart constrict with a mixture of love and regret. All the years we've missed, all the moments he should have had just like this...

But we're here now, at least.

I help Sora out of the truck while my dad leads a hopping Dakota toward the house, pointing out features of the ranch with an animation I never knew he possessed. I start unloading our bags from the truck bed, pausing to take in the sight of them together—my father, my daughter, and Sora, framed against the backdrop of home, *my real home.*

As I close the truck door, something catches my eye—a small plastic tag still affixed to the side of the car seat through the truck window. Curious, I move closer to read it: $249.99.

Nearly half a month's worth of groceries for my dad.

My stomach twists with even more guilt. I know exactly how tight money is for him these days. The ranch hasn't been profitable in years, and the support I send is barely enough to keep the place running. Yet he spent over two hundred dollars on a car seat that will be used for what—three days?

And the space heater for Sora's room. And who knows what else he's done to prepare for our visit in the past week, stretching his limited resources to make us comfortable, to make this homecoming special. *He wants them to love being here, so I'll bring them back.* And he won't feel so alone.

"Need help with those bags?" my dad calls from the porch, Dakota now excitedly pointing at something in the distance as he patiently explains what it is.

"Got it," I holler, swallowing past the lump in my throat.

Sora appears at my side, taking one of the bags. "Your dad is wonderful," she says softly. "I can see where you get your heart."

I look at her, surprised and touched by the observation. "He's really making an effort. He's usually much more..."

"Reserved?" she supplies.

"That's a polite way of putting it." I grin. "But Dakota brings out the best in people. And he seems to really like you."

"The feeling is mutual." She looks toward the house, where he's now showing Dakota how to stomp the mud off her shoes before entering. "I'm glad we came, Forrest. This feels so important."

"Yeah," I agree, the weight of the moment settling around us. "It is."

Together, we carry the bags toward the house, the clean, crisp November air filling our lungs with each step. Whatever else happens this weekend—however many uncomfortable questions I have to answer, however many truths I have to face—this moment, right now, feels like coming home in the truest sense of the word.

For once in my life, I'm not pretending. I'm showing Sora my true colors, my humble life almost a world away from New York City, and she's still looking at me like I'm the prize.

All the times I was bitter that Hannah wouldn't visit Wyoming with me. All her resistance and rejection pissed me off at the time, but now I'm grateful. I had to wait, because it was never just about coming home...

It was about coming home with the right girl.

CHAPTER THIRTY

Sora

The story of this land.

"Now, you'd normally make this with cayenne pepper, but I leave it out for Forrest," Boone says, demonstrating each measurement of various spices with weathered hands that move with surprising grace for a man who spends his days with farm equipment and cattle. His fingers, though callused and marked with the tiny scars of manual labor, handle the delicate spices with unexpected precision. "The secret's in the balance. Too much spice overpowers the meat. The meat is the star, we're just dressing it up."

I nod solemnly, treating his chili recipe with the reverence of ancient scripture. Here in this warm kitchen with the scent of spices hanging in the air, I feel a connection to something primal and essential.

"Now do we add the brown sugar?" I ask, my wooden spoon poised over the pot.

"Not yet," he cautions, his bushy eyebrows drawing together in a way that reminds me so much of Forrest when he's concentrating. "Sugar goes in last. Let the spices marry first." He taps the side of the pot with a gnarled knuckle. "Gotta give 'em time to get acquainted."

Through the kitchen window, I can see Dakota darting across the front yard in gleeful pursuit of actual, honest-to-god wild rabbits. Her delighted squeals float through the glass as she zigzags between patches of grass, hands outstretched but never quite fast enough to catch her prey. Her jacket—a bright pink spot against the muted browns and hidden greens of the Wyoming landscape—has come partially unzipped, and her hair streams behind her like a flag.

"She's having the time of her life," I observe, smiling at the sight.

Boone's expression softens as he watches his granddaughter, the lines around his eyes crinkling deeply. "City kids don't get much chance to chase real critters, I reckon."

"The only thing close to wildlife in Brooklyn—outside of the two-legged variety—are feral squirrels. They're basically tiny mobsters who've figured out how to mug tourists for pretzels."

Boone chuckles, the sound warm and so unexpectedly youthful, it's like Forrest flashes before my eyes for a brief moment. He stirs the chili with practiced motions, his plaid shirtsleeves rolled up to reveal forearms mapped with blue veins and old scars. Each mark tells a story of this life he's built.

"Dakota was supposed to be our sous-chef, wasn't she?" he asks, glancing out the window again where his granddaughter has now stopped to examine something in the dead grass with intense four-year-old concentration.

"The call of the wild was too strong to resist," I say with a dramatic sigh. "She abandoned us for bunny hunting after about forty-seven seconds."

"Kids her age have the attention span of a hummingbird," Boone says wisely, a fond smile playing at the corners of his mouth. "It's good for her. She needs country air." He tastes the chili, considers for a moment, then adds a touch more salt with a flick of his wrist that speaks of decades of cooking this same recipe.

I stir the simmering pot, inhaling the rich aroma of spices and slow-cooked beef. The kitchen is cozy, lived-in, with well-worn countertops and cabinets that have witnessed decades of family meals. Photos line the refrigerator—mostly of Forrest at various ages, from gap-toothed kindergartner to serious high school graduate. In one corner, I spot a newer addition: a school portrait of Dakota that I recognize from Forrest's wallet.

Looking at these snapshots of Forrest's life before I knew him creates a strange ache in my chest—a wistfulness for the moments I missed, for the boy who became the man I'm falling for. Here he is at seven or eight, proudly holding up a fish nearly as big as himself. There, astride a pony with a look of determined concentration. Gangly teenage Forrest in a football uniform, his smile uncertain but hopeful.

"You know," I say, nodding toward the window where we can see Dakota back in hot pursuit, "I didn't play much outside as a kid. Don't get me wrong, I didn't have a bad childhood or anything, but my memories as a kid are of going to *Wicked* on Broadway, or dinners out on the town. Nothing like this."

"That so?" Boone measures out a careful portion of corn starch, his hands steady despite their slight tremor—a detail I hadn't noticed before. He glances at me with genuine interest, his eyes attentive beneath the brim of his indoor hat, which I've learned is different from his outdoor hat, though they look identical to my untrained eyes.

"Oh yeah. White dresses, patent-leather shoes, the works. I was like a miniature adult at social functions." I laugh, though it comes out a bit hollow. "This might be better," I say, jutting my chin to the window where Dakota is darting in and out of view. "Messier, but...better."

"Nothing wrong with a little dirt," Boone says, holding out the canister of brown sugar. His hand brushes mine in the exchange, rough and warm. "Builds character." He nods toward the pot, indicating it's time for the sugar to go in.

Through the window, I watch Forrest emerge from behind the barn, toolbelt slung low on his hips. Even from this distance, I can see the determined set of his shoulders as he surveys the property, mentally cataloging every repair needed. He's been at it since breakfast, disappearing almost immediately after our arrival to tackle one project after another.

Boone follows my gaze and makes a tsking sound, shaking his head slowly. "Boy's trying to cram about three months' worth of work into one weekend because he feels guilty." His voice holds equal measures of pride and concern, the complex emotion of a father watching his son push himself too hard.

"Guilty?" I prompt, as I sprinkle the sugar in, more and more, until Boone nods in approval that it's enough.

"For not being here." Boone stirs the chili, his movements methodical, almost meditative. A lock of silver hair falls across his forehead, and he brushes it back with the back of his wrist, leaving a smudge of chili powder that I don't have the heart to point out. "Always was too hard on himself."

I watch the chili change colors before my eyes. Bright red from the tomato sauce, turning into a rich amber as the spices marinate. "He mentioned the ranch has been struggling."

"Has its challenges," Boone admits, a shadow crossing his face. He looks down at the pot, avoiding my eyes for a moment. I suspect he's not accustomed to discussing the ranch's financial realities with strangers, but after a moment, he continues. "But it's not his cross to bear. I always wanted more for Forrest."

"Columbia Law?"

Boone nods, a flicker of pride lighting his eyes and straightening his posture. "Supported him going to that fancy-pants law school." His mouth quirks up in an almost-smile. "Couldn't have been prouder when he got in. I couldn't do much in the way of paying for it, but my boy figured it out." He pauses, watching his son through the window as Forrest kneels to examine a section of fence, his shoulders squared against the November chill. "Still am proud of him. Not because he's some hotshot city guy, but because of what a good dad he is. Better than me."

The sincerity in his voice touches something deep in my chest, and I find myself blinking back unexpected tears. This man, with his coarse hands and sparse words, loves his son with a quiet fierceness.

"He is amazing with Dakota," I say softly.

"Puts her first, always." Boone tastes the chili with a small spoon, considers, then adds another whisper of cinnamon. "That's what matters." He taps the spoon against the pot's rim twice, a gesture I've noticed he repeats often, like a small ritual. "Nothing more important in this world than being there for your kids."

I think about Forrest's devotion to his daughter, the way he restructured his entire life to accommodate her needs. The way he lights up when she enters a room. The way he quit his job the moment he realized it might jeopardize his chance at building something real with me—*with us*.

Dakota appears at the window, face pressed against the glass, her breath creating a small foggy circle. She waves enthusiastically, then disappears again in a blur of pink jacket and bouncing blond curls. Boone watches her go, his expression soft with a joy that transforms his usually stern features.

"I'm a little nervous, to be honest," I admit, surprising myself with the confession. The words tumble out, encouraged perhaps by the calm presence of this man who listens more than he speaks.

"About what?" Boone asks, reaching for the salt and adding a pinch more to the pot.

"About my role in Dakota's life," I say, focusing on stirring the chili to avoid his gaze. "Being with Forrest means being with Dakota, and while I'm completely on board with that, I sometimes feel...ill-equipped."

"How so?" Boone pivots to face me fully, leaning against the counter with his arms crossed. His stance is relaxed, but his eyes are attentive, missing nothing.

"I don't have much experience with kids." I set the spoon down, fidgeting with a dish towel instead. "I'm an only child. My best friend is childless. I'm doing my best, but what Forrest has with Dakota is instinctual. Maybe something that only happens if it's your own kid, you know? What if I'm not the mom to her he expects me to be?"

The last part comes out in a rush, giving voice to fears I hadn't fully acknowledged even to myself. In my novels, I can revise any scene, delete any misspoken word. Real life offers no such safety net. If there's one thing that would make Forrest walk away, it's me screwing up with Dakota.

Boone considers this for a moment, then gestures for me to sit at the kitchen table. His face is thoughtful, the lines around his mouth deepening as he presses his lips together, formulating his response. After lowering the heat under the chili, he joins me, the wooden chair creaking slightly beneath his weight.

"Let me tell you about Forrest's mom," he begins, folding his hands on the aged wooden surface. His knuckles are enlarged from years of hard work, and a faded scar runs across the back of his left hand. His wedding ring is still there, a plain gold band worn thin by time.

I lean forward, hungry for these pieces of Forrest's history that he rarely shares. It feels like a treasure, Boone entrusting me with his past, with the story that shaped his son.

"Marnie was a firecracker. Beautiful, wild, full of big dreams." His eyes take on a faraway look, and for a moment, I can see the young man he once was, captivated by a woman who burned too bright to stay. "I fell for her hard and fast."

The kitchen seems to recede as he speaks, his deep voice painting pictures of a younger Boone and the woman who captured his heart—dark-haired Marnie with her restless spirit and city dreams that couldn't be contained by the vast Wyoming horizon.

"Problem was, she got cabin fever something fierce." He runs a thumb over the scuffed edge of the table, tracing a pattern only he can see. "Life on a ranch wasn't enough for her. She wanted to travel, explore, live more...extravagantly than I could provide." His eyes meet mine briefly, then drift back to the window, where the landscape stretches endlessly beyond. "So she left. When Forrest was just nine."

"That's awful," I say softly, imagining a small Forrest

watching his mother walk away.

"Would've been easier if she'd stayed gone," Boone continues, a muscle working in his jaw. He takes off his hat, setting it on the table, and runs a hand through his silver hair—another gesture so reminiscent of Forrest that my heart twists. "But she'd keep popping back in when things fell apart for her elsewhere. She'd play house for a few months, get Forrest's hopes up, then disappear again when something more exciting came along."

My chest aches thinking of a young Forrest, repeatedly abandoned by the person who should have been his constant. I want to reach across time and hold that boy, tell him it wasn't his fault, that he deserved better.

"This went on until he was about sixteen," Boone says, his voice roughening with the memory. He clears his throat, blinking rapidly, and I pretend not to notice the sheen in his eyes. "As a boy, I told him that was his mama, like it or not, and he'd respect her while he was under my roof. But when he was sixteen, that's when he finally told her he didn't care to see her anymore. He made that choice as a man, and I respected it."

He picks up his hat, turning it in his hands, examining the frayed edge of the brim as if it holds the answers to questions he's spent decades asking himself. The gold of his ring catches the glint of the sunlight through the window.

"You're divorced but you still wear your ring?" I ask, then immediately choke on my words. "I'm so sorry, Boone. That's overstepping, and not my business. Please excuse me."

He smiles at me. "You're full of manners, aren't you, city girl?"

"Careful there. 'City girl' is starting to sound like a compliment." I wink at him.

"It is," he assures me. "And you didn't overstep. Marnie and I are still married on paper. That's why I wear my ring. But in every other sense..."

He doesn't need to explain. I can fill in the blanks. Marnie probably had a dozen other relationships, while for Boone, it seems he found solace in work.

The weight of this revelation settles upon me. Now Forrest makes so much more sense than ever before. It always seemed odd how despite everything, he was still so supportive of Hannah having custody. He wanted Dakota to have what he didn't—a relationship with her mom.

"The best way to be there for Dakota," Boone says, meeting my eyes directly, his gaze steady and clear, "is to just be there. The way Marnie wasn't." He echoes my internal sentiments as if he can read me like a book.

I nod, understanding blooming like a sudden light. This is why Forrest finally made his big change. Hannah committed the ultimate sin in his eyes by moving to Tokyo with her boyfriend without Dakota. Her arrogant, entitled personality was tolerable, but when she chose to abandon her family, she became another Marnie—the one thing he couldn't forgive.

"I can do that," I say firmly, determined suddenly and completely. "Be there, I mean."

Boone studies me for a long moment, his eyes searching mine as if gauging the weight of my promise. What he sees must satisfy him, because he nods, a small smile softening the hard planes of his face. "I know you can."

He rises, setting his hat back on his head with a practiced motion, and returns to the stove. "Now come on. Let's get the cornbread started. We've got a hungry bunny hunter to feed."

"Yes, sir," I say, pushing my chair back and rising to my feet.

"Tell me about your books," he says, surprising me. "Forrest mentioned you write romance books."

I blink, trying to picture Forrest discussing my writing with his taciturn father. "I do."

"Never read much romance myself," Boone admits, his cheeks coloring slightly. "But I reckon yours are good." He gathers the cornbread ingredients, which in the country is apparently not just a box of Jiffy. "What's your latest one about?"

It seems too overwhelming to explain, really. So I answer as simply as I can in true Boone fashion. "My parents. They had a strained relationship as I was growing up. They got divorced when I was a teenager. But ten years later, they're dating again."

Boone lets out a low hum. "Well, how about that. You think they're going to last this time?"

I smile to myself, warmth filling my cheeks and my heart. "Yeah, I think so."

Dakota bursts through the door at that moment, face flushed with cold and excitement, clutching something in her small hands. "Look, look, look! A special rock! It's got sparkles!"

Boone immediately crouches to her level, hat tipped back, face alight with genuine interest. "Well now, let's have a look, Pumpkin."

As Dakota displays her find, chattering about where she discovered it and all its magical properties, I stir the chili and watch this unlikely pair—the reticent cowboy and the tiny, chatty city girl—heads bent together over an ordinary quartz pebble as if examining the Crown Jewels.

All I can think as I watch them together is that this place is full of all the things I put in my stories, but have never experienced for myself. Love, family, warmth, and security.

And maybe it's time for me to start living.

The barn door grinds as I push it open, balancing a large picnic basket against my hip. The interior is dimly lit, with dust motes dancing in the slanted beams of late-afternoon sunlight that filter through high windows. The smell of hay and old wood wraps around me like a blanket, earthy and comforting in its unfamiliarity.

"Forrest?" I call, stepping carefully over the uneven floorboards. "You in here?"

"Back here," his voice echoes from the far end.

I follow the sound, navigating past stacked hay bales and abandoned farm equipment. A rusty tractor part. Coils of wire. A saddle stand missing one leg, propped against the wall like a wounded soldier. Each piece a chapter in the story of this land.

I find him in what must have once been a stall, surrounded by feed bags and various tools. He's changed into what I can only describe as full-on cowboy mode—faded jeans, scuffed work boots, and a buffalo-plaid shirt hanging open over a white tee that's smudged with the dirt of a day's honest labor.

My heart does a ridiculous flutter. City Forrest is undeniably sexy in his tailored shirts and designer jeans, but Country Forrest? With his tousled hair and that casual confidence that comes from being in his element?

I might need to sit down... And cross my legs.

"You missed dinner," I say while shamelessly gawking.

He glances at his watch, genuine surprise crossing his features. "Shit, really? I lost track of time."

"You've been at it since breakfast," I point out. It's not that late, actually. It's just past five o'clock. I've quickly learned that out here, dinner happens when the sun's still high. Very different from New York, where "dinner" typically coincides with sane people's bedtime.

"Sorry I disappeared on you all day," he says with an exhausted sigh.

"Your dad explained you were trying to compress three months' worth of ranch work into one weekend." I lift the picnic basket. "I brought leftovers. Here's your 'wimpy chili,' not a hint of spice in sight."

Forrest laughs, the sound echoing in the cavernous space. "Keep teasing me, Sora. See what happens."

I pump my eyebrows at him. "I'm feeling daring, wimpy boy. Do your worst."

He smirks. "Three dates. Remember?"

Damn his resolve.

"Your dad took Dakota into town to buy her cowgirl boots," I say, setting the basket down on a relatively clean hay bale.

"I thought I heard the truck." Forrest's smile falters. "He doesn't need to spend money on that. They're unnecessary."

"He wanted to," I say gently. "And he agreed to watch her and put her to bed tonight so you could show me around town. Maybe go out?"

His expression softens, and he wipes his hands on a rag tucked into his back pocket. "That was thoughtful of him."

I kneel to unpack our makeshift picnic. "We had a nice talk while making chili. He told me some things about your mom."

Forrest stills, his posture tensing slightly. "Did he now?"

"Mmm," I affirm, pulling out containers one by one. "I brought cowboy chili, cowboy butter, cowboy cornbread, and cowboy coffee."

Forrest fetches a blanket, discarded in the corner. He shakes it out aggressively, hay, dust, and dirt making a dust cloud. He lays it on the barn floor, gesturing for me to sit. "You know we don't actually put 'cowboy' in front of all our food, right? It's cowboy chili and butter. The cornbread is just cornbread."

"Shhh, don't ruin my Wild West fantasy," I tease. "I've been picturing you lassoing stray cattle all day."

"Hate to disappoint, but I've been mending fences and checking supplies." He gestures to the feed bags. "Glamorous stuff."

We settle on the blanket, and he graciously accepts the container of chili I packed him. For a few minutes, we eat in comfortable silence, the only sounds the occasional distant groans of cattle and the soft rustle of hay beneath the blanket as we shift our weight.

The barn is surprisingly cozy, the ancient wood holding decades of warmth within its frame. Old lanterns hang from hooks, their glass cloudy with age. Forrest follows my gaze, examining the barn. "This place is going to shit."

"It's not. It's just a little worn."

"I feel bad. Dad's getting older. He needs help around here, and I'm not here to give it."

"He understands," I assure him. "He told me he's proud of you—not for being a 'hotshot city guy,' but for being a good father."

Forrest's eyes soften. "He doesn't even know what I actually do. Did," he corrects himself. "What I *did* for a living."

"I don't think that would change his opinion," I say honestly. "He sees how you are with Dakota. That's what matters to him."

Forrest nods, then sets aside his empty container. "You know, I've been thinking. Why am I in New York now? With the escort job over, what's keeping me there? Dakota's school, I guess, but there are other options, you know? She seems to really like it here. I think Dad thought I was bringing home a prissy princess, but that's not the case."

"Is prissy princess in regards to Dakota, or me?" I ask, scowling.

"Hey, is that the coffee?" Forrest points to the tin canister by my thigh.

"You jerk," I playfully mutter, handing over the canister.

"You're both doing great," he says with a teasing grin. "Makes me want to stay here."

My heart does a strange leap in my chest, part exhilaration, part panic. "Are you saying you want to move back to Wyoming?"

"I'm wondering if I should," he says carefully, his eyes studying my face for any sign of my reaction. In the dimming light of the barn, his features are partially shadowed, giving him a rugged mysteriousness. "If Dakota and I did move...would you come with us?"

For a full two minutes, the question takes up residence with us, big and fat and overwhelming. The barn seems to hold its breath, waiting for my answer as much as Forrest is. I set down my fork.

What would it mean to leave New York? My apartment, my few friends, my familiar routines? My mother would be horrified—her dreams of me marrying a nice Korean doctor or lawyer already dashed by my writing ambitions, potentially compounded by a move to rural Wyoming.

But then I think of Dakota's face this morning, bright with the simple joy of chasing rabbits. I think of Boone in the kitchen, patiently teaching me his chili recipe. I think of Forrest now, in this barn that holds the echoes of his childhood, looking at me with hope and uncertainty mingled in his beautiful eyes.

"That's a big ask for a first date," I finally say, my tone deliberately light.

His face falls slightly, and he nods, accepting what he thinks is rejection. "You're right. It's way too soon—"

"Ask me on the third date," I interrupt, meeting his eyes. "You might get the answer you're hoping for."

Understanding dawns, followed by a slow smirk that makes my stomach flip. "Is that so?"

"Can't say for sure. I'm a very unpredictable woman."

He laughs, the tension dissipating. "That you are." He reaches out, tucking a strand of hair behind my ear, his fingers lingering on my cheek. His touch is gentle despite the day's hard labor, and I lean into it instinctively. "Thanks for bringing dinner. And for spending time with my dad today."

"I like him," I say honestly. "He reminds me of you—or you of him, I guess."

"Poor you," Forrest jokes.

"Actually"—I lean in closer, the hay crinkling beneath me—"I was thinking how similar you look in this light. Especially now that you're in full cowboy form." I let my gaze travel appreciatively over him. "It's working for you, Hawkins."

His eyebrow arches. "Is it, now?"

"Mmm," I confirm. "Turns out cowboy is my new favorite trope."

"You ain't seen anything yet, ma'am," he announces with a deep, sexy cowboy drawl. "I've got something I want to show you tonight," he says. "I made plans for our first official date. Let's finish eating, and then I'll get cleaned up and show you how country boys do romance."

I reach out, running my hand down the front of his open shirt. The cotton is soft from years of washing, warm from his body, and beneath it, his chest is solid and real. "Don't fuss on my account. I like you just like this."

His eyes darken at my touch. "Covered in hay and smelling like the barn?"

"Authentic cowboy experience," I quip. "The burly, manly outdoorsman with his toolbelt and flannel. Very romance novel cover-worthy."

"So we're back to role-playing?" he asks.

I shake my head. "I don't think so. I kind of think...this is the real you. Right? If it isn't, lie to me."

Forrest laughs, catching my hand and bringing it to his lips. The gesture is old-fashioned and sweet, sending a shiver down my spine despite its innocence. "You're something else, cookie girl."

"So I've been told." I lean forward and press a light kiss to his lips. "What's this mysterious something you want to show me?"

He smiles against my mouth. "The stars. You've never seen them like this before—without city lights drowning them out. You'll see, sweetheart. I'm going to romance the heck out of you. By the end of tonight, *you'll* be the one dropping down on one knee."

I burst out in a raucous laugh, but the funny part is...the way he's looking tonight...

I wouldn't rule it out.

CHAPTER THRITY-ONE

Sora

Have you ever fucked a jealous cowboy?

"Sora, your hands are slipping," Forrest shouts over the rumble of the ATV's engine.

"I know," I murmur, but surely he can't hear me. Seated behind him, my arms wrapped around his body, I let my hands wander to the familiar bulge I've been missing during our sex drought.

"Hold on to my *waist*, woman," he shouts. "I'm going to crash if you keep touching me like that."

Giggling, I tighten my grip around his waist obediently, pressing my cheek against his broad back as we bounce along the uneven terrain. The setting sun paints the Wyoming landscape in breathtaking hues of gold and amber, the vastness of it still overwhelming to my senses. I've never seen a sky so enormous, land so wide open it seems to stretch into infinity.

"Where are we going?" I call, my voice nearly lost in the wind.

"Patience!" he answers, although the excitement in his voice is palpable even over the engine's roar.

We've been driving for about fifteen minutes, leaving the main ranch property behind and winding our way through rolling hills dotted with scrubby pine trees. I'm starting to regret my outfit choice—blue-jean shorts and a white tank top might have seemed like appropriate "cowgirl" attire when I packed in

New York. I severely underestimated November in Wyoming. Especially riding the ATV, the cold wind bites to the bone.

We crest a small hill, and Forrest slows to a stop. Ahead of us stands a structure I hadn't noticed on our drive in—the wooden skeleton of what looks like a half-built barn, silhouetted against the darkening sky.

"We're here," Forrest announces, cutting the engine.

The sudden silence is profound, broken only by the soft whisper of wind through the tall grass and the distant call of a bird I can't identify. Forrest climbs off the ATV first, then offers me his hand.

"What is this place?" I ask, accepting his help.

"My house. Or what was supposed to be my house, anyway. It's a barndominium."

I follow him toward the structure, curiosity piqued. As we step in, I can see it's much more than a barn—it's the framework of a home, with clearly defined rooms and large windows facing the breathtaking view of the mountains.

"My senior year of high school, Dad and I started this project," Forrest explains, his hand warm against the small of my back as he ushers me in farther. "Said I could build my own place here if I wanted. We started that summer—laid the foundation, framed it out. We were going to work on it each summer until I graduated. Then, I'd move in."

"But you never finished it?" I guess, understanding dawning.

"I met Hannah. I got into law school. We got pregnant with Dakota. And a million and one other excuses as to why this didn't make sense anymore."

"This would've been amazing," I say in awe, spinning around in place, soaking up every inch of potential.

He runs his hand along one of the support beams. "Now it's unfinished business."

"What was this part going to be?" I lightly stomp my foot against the floor.

"This would have been the living room," Forrest says, guiding me through the space. "Big windows to catch the sunrise. Kitchen over there—Dad insisted it be big enough for a proper table. 'No eating on the couch,' he said."

I smile, imagining a younger Boone and Forrest working side by side, planning it all out together. "It's beautiful, Forrest. Even unfinished."

"Down here would've been two bedrooms," he continues, leading me through what would have been a hallway. "And this..." He stops in a large space at the back of the structure. "This would have been the master bedroom. Windows facing west for the sunset. Planned to build a deck off it right there."

I stand in the center of the would-be bedroom, closing my eyes and picturing it finished. Through the open framework, I can see the mountains in the distance, painted in deepening purples as the sun continues its descent. Despite its incomplete state, there's something magical about this place—a dream deferred but not forgotten.

"Promise me something," I say, turning to face him.

"What's that?" He tilts his head, eyes curious in the fading light.

"Promise me you'll finish it someday. This house. If for nothing else, it deserves to be completed."

Something shifts in his expression—surprise, then warmth that reaches his eyes. "I promise," he says softly, and I believe him.

A gust of wind sweeps through the open structure, and I can't suppress a shiver. My bare arms pebble with goose bumps, and I wrap my arms around myself in a futile attempt to ward off the chill.

Forrest shakes his head, mouth quirking in amusement. "Why in the world would you wear shorts and a tank top in the middle of November in Wyoming?"

Heat that has nothing to do with the temperature rushes into my cheeks. "I, um, may have underestimated the seasonal differences between New York and Wyoming. I brought what I thought was cowgirl attire..." I gesture at my outfit with a self-deprecating shrug. "Summer cowgirl, apparently."

His laugh is warm and rich as it echoes through the home. "So you were willing to freeze your ass off to play dress-up."

"You said I'd look good as a cowgirl. I was trying," I protest, but I'm laughing too.

"I asked you a million times on the way over here if you were cold. You lied through your teeth every single time, hm?"

"Indubitably."

Without hesitation, Forrest shrugs out of his plaid flannel shirt, leaving him in just a snug white tee that does nothing to hide the contours of his chest and shoulders. He wraps the flannel around me, his body heat still clinging to the fabric.

"Better?" he asks, his voice dropping to a lower register that sends a different kind of shiver through me.

"Much," I manage, tying the shirt's hem at my waist to keep it in place. The sleeves hang well past my fingertips, and I have to roll them up to free my hands.

Forrest removes his cowboy hat and places it carefully on my head, adjusting it with a tenderness that makes my heart flutter. "There. Now you're a proper cowgirl."

"How do I look?" I strike a pose, one hip cocked.

His eyes darken as they roam over me—his oversized shirt, my bare legs, the too-big hat perched on my head. "Like every fantasy I never knew I had."

The intensity in his gaze makes my breath catch. "Forrest Hawkins, are you flirting with me?"

"Darlin', I'm way past flirting." He steps closer, his fingers tracing the open collar of the shirt where it meets my collarbone. "Come on. I've got something else to show you."

He takes my hand, leading me back outside. The sun has nearly set now, the first stars beginning to appear in the darkening sky. It's then that I notice what I missed upon our arrival—Forrest's old truck parked about fifty yards from the house frame, its bed facing the open view.

As we approach, I realize the truck has been transformed. A

mattress fills the bed, covered with blankets and pillows. String lights have been hung around the edges, casting a warm, golden glow. Most surprisingly, a white projection screen has been attached to poles at the end of the truck bed, and a small projector sits on the roof of the cab.

"What is all this?" I ask, amazed.

Forrest's smile is touched with shyness—an unexpected and endearing look on him. "Our official first date. Movie night under the stars."

"When did you have time to set this up?"

"Squeezed it in between fence repairs and feed inventory," he says with a casual shrug that doesn't quite hide the effort this must have taken. "I do have one serious question, though."

"What's that?"

"Have you ever seen *The Princess Bride*?"

I laugh, delighted. "Only about a thousand times. I'm pretty sure Westley was the original book boyfriend."

His smile widens. "I've never seen it, but Taio told me it was the epitome of date-night movies."

"Taio said that?" I arch one brow.

"I paraphrased. He might've said it was panty-dropping material. Anyway, is this corny?" he asks, suddenly looking uncertain.

I reach up, taking his face in my hands. "This is perfect. *Absolutely perfect.* I'm already a big fan of country-boy romance."

Relief floods his expression. He helps me climb into the truck bed, then retrieves a small cooler from the cab. "Drinks and popcorn," he explains, opening it to reveal bottles of soda and a container of what looks like homemade caramel corn.

"You think of everything."

"I try." He settles beside me on the mattress, arranging blankets around us against the growing chill. With a click of a remote, the projector hums to life, and the familiar opening scene appears on the screen.

For a while, we simply watch the movie, cuddled together

under the blankets. The unique combination of comfort—the soft mattress, warm blankets, Forrest's solid presence beside me—and the wild openness of our surroundings creates a bubble of intimacy that feels both safe and thrilling.

Above us, more stars emerge as true darkness falls. I've never seen so many in my life—a glittering tapestry spanning the entire sky, unimpeded by city lights or tall buildings. The movie plays on, but I find my attention increasingly drawn to the man beside me, to the way the string lights catch the angles of his face, to the steady rise and fall of his chest beneath my cheek.

"You're not watching the movie," Forrest murmurs, his voice a pleasant rumble against my ear.

"I'm distracted," I admit.

"By what?" His hand traces lazy patterns on my shoulder through the flannel shirt.

I prop myself up on one elbow to look at him properly. "By you. By this. By how surreal it feels to be here. Best ten thousand dollars I've ever spent."

"Excuse me, ma'am. I'm no longer available for hire," he teases, before his expression turns serious, his eyes searching mine. "I'm happy, Sora. For the first time in a long time, I'm really happy."

On screen, Westley and Buttercup reunite in the fire swamp, but neither of us is paying attention anymore.

"I think," I say slowly, my fingers playing with the collar of his T-shirt, "that we might need to revisit our third-date rule."

His eyebrow arches. "Is that so?"

"Mmm." I lean closer, my lips brushing his jawline. "I mean, technically, we had stale snacks together on the plane—date one."

His expression pinches. "Please dump me if I'm ever dim enough to call that a date."

"And we had chili in the barn—date two."

"Better," he agrees, "but not by much."

"We never stipulated that they had to be *good* dates. Our focus was quantity over quality, correct?"

"No, you horndog. Quality was always part of the plan." He playfully bats my hand away when it goes searching again.

"Forrest Hawkins, pony up. It's date three and I'm getting what I came for."

His mouth forms a small O at my demand. "Bossy, bossy little thing." Hand sliding up to cup the back of my neck, thumb tracing my cheekbone, he whispers against my ear, "What'll it be, Ms. Cho-Cooper? Am I taking the lead or are you?"

In answer, I close the distance between us, pressing my lips to his. The kiss starts soft, tentative, but quickly deepens into something more urgent. Forrest responds immediately, his arm snaking around my waist to pull me flush against him.

"What would a cowboy do?"

His eyes darken. "Toss you around like a bale of hay. Take you however I want to, right here, right now."

"Out here?" My gaze darts along the rolling hills, but there's nothing and no one in sight besides the shadowy fences and half-built home behind us.

"Out here," he echoes in a slow, seductive drawl, eyes fixed on my chest.

I gesture at the movie, the lights, the carefully arranged bed. "You've got me right where you want me, cowboy. Now do something about it."

His answering smile is equal parts boyish and wolfish. "That mouth of yours. I'm going to put it to good use."

I slide my hand beneath his T-shirt, feeling the warm skin and firm muscle. "You are so sexy, have I ever told you that? I can't believe you're all mine now."

A growl rumbles in his chest as he flips our positions, pressing me into the mattress with delicious weight. "Nothing new. I've been yours since the minute I laid eyes on you, Sora."

"Good to know," I say, desperately trying to get my voice steady, as desire pools low in my belly. "Me, on the other hand, I'd like to keep my options open. All this talk of ranch hands, maybe I need to head up to Riggins Ranch and see what's available."

The cowboy hat falls from my head as Forrest attacks my mouth in a bruising kiss. "Have you ever fucked a jealous cowboy, Sora?"

"I'm trying to." The fiery glare in his eyes tells me I might be poking the bear too hard.

"Well, fuck around and find out, then." Then, his hands are everywhere—tangling in my hair, tracing the curve of my waist, skimming beneath the hem of my tank top with deliberate slowness that makes me arch against him, seeking more.

"You're mine, *only mine*," he murmurs against my lips, barely letting me catch my breath from his aggressive kiss. "All night. All of your nights."

His eyes lock with mine briefly before he trails kisses down my neck softly, his intention changing. His stubble creates a delicious friction against my sensitive skin as he coos sweet nothings in my ear. "I'm going to keep you safe...keep you warm...adjust your attitude by adjusting your hips, whenever you get sassy."

I chuckle against him, as if a thorough Forrest-fucking could be considered punishment.

"When you doubt yourself, I'll believe for both of us. When your heart breaks, I'll fix it. When you talk, I'll listen. When you write, I'll read."

Just like that, it's not funny anymore. The mood shifts. Desire surges, but it's not just the ache beneath my navel. My heart is swelling, desperately wanting to be cradled in his hands.

He unties the flannel shirt, then slips it off, one sleeve at a time. When he notices me shiver, he covers as much of my body in warm kisses as he can. His touch is electric against my bare skin, and a small gasp escapes me when his hand slips under my tank top, thumbs brushing the undersides of my breasts.

"You're so beautiful," he says, his voice rough with desire. "Do you have any idea what you do to me?"

Before I can respond, he tugs my tank top up and over my head, leaving me in only my bra and denim shorts. If I ever was cold, I've forgotten. He's creating all the warmth I need with his tender touches. Forrest's mouth finds my collarbone, then dips lower.

"You all right?" he asks, his breath hot against my skin.

"In heaven," I manage, threading my fingers through his hair to guide him back to my lips.

Our kisses grow more heated, more desperate. I tug at his shirt, needing to feel more of him, and he breaks away to pull it off. My eyes devour the sight of him shirtless in the golden glow of the string lights—all defined muscle and taut, tan skin. Wordlessly, I trace the planes of his chest with my fingertips, exploring the dips and curves of his body with unhurried appreciation. When I reach the waistband of his jeans, I feel his muscles tense in anticipation.

"Sora," he groans, the sound of my name on his lips like a prayer and a curse wrapped into one.

I've never felt more powerful, more desired, than in this moment. Under the vast Wyoming sky, with stars as our only witnesses, I feel free in a way I never have before—free to want, to take, to give without hesitation.

Forrest's hands find the button of my shorts, a question in his eyes. I nod, lifting my hips to help as he slides them down my legs, leaving me in nothing but my underwear and anticipation. I hold my breath, almost not wanting it to start, because eventually we'll have to stop. Is there a way to stay suspended here forever? How do I keep this moment from turning into a memory?

"God, look at you," he says, his voice filled with awe. "Like you belong here."

"I do belong here. Under the stars. Under you." I reach for him, pulling him back down to me, reveling in the feel of his weight, settling me still. His hand slides between us, fingers finding the edge of my panties, then slipping beneath with careful deliberation.

"Always so wet," he groans against my neck, his touch finding my most sensitive spot with unerring accuracy. "Say it's for me, baby. Only for me."

"Yes," I gasp, arching into his touch. "Only for you."

He works me with skilled fingers, alternating pressure and pace until I'm writhing beneath him, teetering on the edge of release. Just when I think I can't take anymore, he withdraws his hand, earning a whimper of protest from me.

"Not yet," he says, his voice a low command that thrills every sensitive part of me. "I want to taste you dripping wet first."

Before I can process his words, he's moving down my body, pressing open-mouthed kisses along his path. He pauses at my breasts, lavishing attention on each nipple through the lace of my bra until I'm squirming with need. Then he descends, across my stomach, lower, *lower*.

He hooks his fingers into my panties, looking up at me with those striking eyes that have so quickly claimed my soul. "Okay?"

"*Please.*"

He slides my underwear down with torturous slowness, his callused hands leaving trails of fire on my skin. Finally he settles between my thighs, his breath hot against my center.

The first touch of his tongue is electric, pulling a sharp gasp from my lips that echoes in the open air. Strong hands grip my thighs, holding me open for him as he deftly explores, focusing on rhythms that make me moan, then tremble.

"Show-off," I simper.

"Mmm. You taste so damn good," he murmurs, his words vibrating exquisitely against me. "Sweet and sexy, and fuck's sake, baby, I want your taste to live on my tongue."

I tangle my fingers in his hair, beyond words, beyond thought, reduced to pure sensation as he works me higher. When he slides a finger inside me, curling it to hit exactly the right spot while his tongue continues its relentless attention, the tension building within me snaps.

My release is an overwhelming, rapid-fire assault of sensation. The pulses of pleasure annihilate me, becoming almost painful as I whimper through his playful post-orgasm teasing. He continues with persistence until I have to push his head away with my shaky hand, too sensitive to withstand any more contact until the rapturous pings still firing through me eventually subside.

He moves back up my body, wearing a self-satisfied grin that would be so arousing if I weren't completely boneless with pleasure. "Beautiful," he whispers, pressing a kiss to my lips that allows me to taste myself on his tongue.

Selfishly, I'm so sated, I could pull up the covers to my chin and fall asleep under the stars. Forrest would let me. That's how good he is to me. If he knew I was tired, he'd cuddle me until I was passed out and dreaming of this night all over again. But I inhale a few deep, brisk breaths, reenergizing myself because I want to give him what he gives me: *everything*.

His breath catches as I work his jeans open, then slide my hand inside to wrap around him tightly. I twist my wrist, coaxing his thick cock to a full erection. "Shit, Sora," he hisses, his nostrils flaring on the out breath.

"Problem?" I ask innocently, stroking him through his boxers.

"Only that you're going to end this party before it really starts if you keep that up." He captures my wrist, bringing my hand to his lips to kiss my palm. "And I'm not nearly done with you yet."

In one smooth motion, he stands to remove his jeans and boxers, then rejoins me on the mattress. The sight of him fully naked in the string lights' glow is breathtaking—all lean muscle and perfect proportions, his arousal evident and more than impressive. Truthfully? Maybe too much. *Almost* too much.

His eyes darken as he watches me take him into my mouth. The weight of him on my tongue is substantial, the taste a heady mixture of salt and skin that sends renewed desire spiraling *right* where I was just excessively replete. I work my way down his length, taking him as deep as I can, reveling in the way his thighs tense beneath my palms.

"Christ, Sora," he groans, one hand clasping a fistful of my hair, not guiding but anchoring himself. "Your mouth...*fuck*."

The raw need in his voice spurs me on. I establish a rhythm, alternating between long, slow strokes and focused attention to his sensitive head, my hand working what my mouth can't reach. His breathing grows more ragged with each pass, the muscles in his abdomen tightening in the golden glow of the string lights.

The scent of him is criminally erotic—clean sweat but with a hint of earth and something uniquely Forrest that I crave beyond measure. *How would a heroine describe that scent...? No—stop that. Stop working.* When I glance up, the sight brings me right out of my head and nearly undoes me completely—his head thrown back, throat exposed, lips parted as broken sounds escape him. I could do it: write a bestseller, hang the flippin' moon, all the things. What could be as profoundly satisfying as reducing this strong, controlled man to wordless pleasure?

"Baby, stop," he finally manages, his voice strained. "I need to be inside you."

I release him with reluctance, pressing one final kiss to the tip, letting his salty precum vanish on the tip of my tongue, while allowing him to hoist me up into his arms. He crushes his mouth to mine, the kiss desperate and claiming, his hands roaming over my body with renewed urgency.

"Turn around," he murmurs against my lips. "I want you from behind, cowgirl."

The command sends a fresh surge of electricity between my thighs. I comply, positioning myself on hands and knees, feeling intensely vulnerable and powerful all at once. The cool night air whispers across my heated skin, raising goose bumps along my spine that Forrest soothes away with warm palms.

"Look at you," he breathes, reverence clear in his voice as his hands trace the curve of my hips, the dip of my waist. I wiggle my hips, egging him on. "Good girl. Make me want it. So fucking perfect."

I feel him positioning himself, the blunt pressure of him seeking entrance. When he pushes in, it's with exquisite slowness that has us both gasping. The stretch is intense, borderline uncomfortable, but then he's fully seated, sheath to hilt, and the discomfort transforms into bone-deep satisfaction.

We can't abstain from sex this long. What stretches snaps back, making the girth of him like losing my virginity all over again. A momentary break and it feels like the first time. But maybe that's not so bad. What I wouldn't do for a thousand more first times with Forrest.

"You okay? You're shaking," he says, his voice tender despite the evident strain of holding himself still.

"Yes," I manage, the word more breath than sound. "You can move."

He complies, drawing back and then pressing forward in a measured thrust that sends sparks of pleasure cascading through me. His pace is controlled at first, each movement deliberate, but soon builds in intensity. His hands grip my hips with bruising pressure, guiding my body to meet his thrusts.

The truck rocks gently beneath us, the blankets bunching under my knees. Above, the vast Wyoming sky stretches endlessly, stars bearing silent witness to our union. The distant soundtrack of the forgotten movie mingles with our sounds—his grunts of effort, my breathless moans, the rhythmic creak of the truck's suspension.

"Touch yourself. Rub your perfect little clit," Forrest commands, his voice rough with exertion. "I need to feel you come on my cock."

I balance on one arm, slipping my free hand between my thighs to find the bundle of nerves already swollen and sensitive. The dual stimulation is overwhelming, pushing me rapidly toward another peak. Forrest's thrusts grow more erratic, his breathing harsh in the night air.

I'm nearly at the cusp when he slows. Before I can ask why, he spreads my ass cheeks apart, surely surveying *all* of me. I'm glad I'm turned around, so my self-consciousness is somewhat kept at bay.

He silently spits, only evident because a glob of lubrication hits my asshole before dripping down to my sex. "Curious?" he asks dangerously.

"A little," I admit, but I can barely handle him where I'm meant to take him. A tighter hole seems unreasonable. "I'm scared though."

"Just my finger," he coos, circling his new target. "Tell me if you don't like it."

His finger circles gently, applying just enough pressure to tease but not enter. "Relax for me," he whispers, his voice a velvet caress against my heightened senses. "Trust me."

I take a deep breath, trying to will my body to soften. His other hand strokes my lower back in soothing circles, his cock still buried deep inside me but motionless now, allowing me to adjust to this new sensation.

"That's it," he encourages as I gradually relax. The tip of his finger slips just past the tight ring of muscle, and a strange new pleasure ripples through me. "Good girl. You're doing great, baby. I wish you could see yourself. So fucking hot."

The dual sensation—his thick length filling me completely while his finger explores this forbidden territory—is staggering. A moan escapes me, primal and unrestrained, carried away by the Wyoming wind.

"You like that?" he asks, though the answer must be obvious from the way my body shudders around him.

"Yes," I gasp. "Don't stop."

He begins to move again, short, rhythmic thrusts that build in intensity as his finger works in tandem with his cock. The pressure is divine, hitting places inside me I didn't know could feel pleasure. Each movement sends sparks dancing behind my closed eyelids, building a tension so sweet it's almost excessive.

The night air cools the sweat beading along my spine, creating a delicious contrast to the heat of Forrest's body against mine. The sounds of our coupling—slick flesh meeting flesh, ragged breathing, half-formed words of encouragement and need—seem amplified in the endlessness surrounding us.

"Fuck, Sora," Forrest growls out, his free hand tightening on my hip. "You're squeezing me so tight. So perfect."

His words push me closer to the edge. The pressure of his finger increases slightly, pumping deeper, harder. The truck rocks beneath us, the springs creaking in protest, but neither of us cares. In this moment, we're reduced to our most primal selves—seeking, claiming, giving, taking.

My arms begin to tremble with the effort of supporting myself, but before they can give out, Forrest withdraws his finger and wraps his arm around my waist, pulling me upright so my back presses against his chest. This new angle drives him impossibly deeper, tearing a cry from my throat that echoes across the landscape.

"I've got you. Come hard for me. Fucking lose it, baby. I'll hold you."

His free hand slides down my belly to where we're joined, fingers finding my swollen clit with unerring accuracy. It's too much—I shatter around him, surges of ecstasy crashing through me with such force that tears spring to my eyes. My inner muscles clench around his length, drawing a guttural groan from deep in his chest.

"That's it," he praises, working me through the aftershocks. "I can feel it, baby. That's what drives me over the edge."

My climax triggers his own building release. His movements become less calculated, more desperate. His teeth graze my shoulder, not quite biting down but threatening to mark me. Possessing me.

"Where?" His voice is strained with the effort of holding back. "Not inside tonight."

He's right. We're a ways away from a bathroom to get properly cleaned up.

"Wherever you want," I permit without hesitation.

He pushes me back down on all fours, and after a few more demanding thrusts, he places the tip of his sex against my tender ass, coating me with his warmth. The sensation triggers a reaction in me. Maybe it's because something that once felt forbidden is now so unapologetically explored. The idea of Forrest knowing every single part of my body... I come again, with every shred of energy I have left. I crash from my knees to my stomach, flattening myself against the mattress as my final orgasm fades into the night.

Forrest collapses to my side, rolling me over so he can hold me in his arms, shielding me from the cold.

For a time, we remain locked together, our breaths gradually slowing. Then, with infinite tenderness, he brushes damp hair from my forehead, his touch patient, reverent.

"How was that?" he asks, his voice rough around the edges. "I didn't hurt you, did I?"

"I'm perfect," I assure him, pressing a kiss to his palm. "That was..."

"Yeah," he agrees, understanding my inability to find adequate words. "It was."

A comfortable silence moves in as our bodies cool down. He peels away from me with a groan. "Stay here."

Still butt naked, he hops down from the truck bed, retrieving a clean cloth from the cab. I smile into the mattress as he wipes me clean. When he's finished, Forrest reclaims me in his arms and repositions us to the top of the mattress. Reaching down, he pulls a blanket over us, effectively making a cocoon for our body heat to nestle. On the forgotten screen, the movie continues, casting flickering blue light that dances with the golden glow of the string lights.

I trace idle patterns on his chest, memorizing the texture of his skin, the rhythm of his heartbeat beneath my palm. His fingers comb through my tangled hair, gently working out the knots.

"We have to start the movie over," he murmurs after a while, his voice barely audible. "I missed everything."

I prop myself up on an elbow to see his face better. "Good idea." I peck his chest. "Let's start over. All the way from the beginning. We won't miss a minute this time."

"Not a damn minute," he muses, eyes on me, not the screen. "We'll rewrite everything exactly the way we want."

Look how far I've come. The writer who creates love stories

but never stopped to write her own. I can't remember the last time I checked a sales dashboard, or stressed about a crummy review. The last couple months have been too full of meaning to worry about meaningless things.

Forrest agreed to help inspire me to write a bestseller. Instead, he inspired me to live a life.

I nuzzle into him as the opening credits of *The Princess Bride* play once more. He scoots me closer, tucking my head under his chin, his heartbeat steady against my ear. He rubs my shoulders furiously. "Cold? Should we get dressed?"

"Don't move a muscle, cowboy. Stay in this moment with me."

We lie in comfortable silence, limbs tangled, skin cooling in the night air but warmed by our shared body heat beneath the blanket. Above us, millions of stars continue their silent dance across the royal, dark purple sky.

"Thank you," Forrest says suddenly.

"For what?"

"For another chance to be the real me. For turning a blind eye to what I used to do, and loving me anyway—" He stops short, nearly choking on his words. "Shit, I didn't mean *love*, I meant—"

"I do, Forrest. Isn't it obvious? *I love you* beyond reason. I love you so much, I don't know what it even means anymore."

"What?" he asks, confusion covering his face.

"It's too easy to write '*I love you*' in the final chapters of a story. That's how it's supposed to go. There's a blueprint for romances—act one, then two, then three. 'I love you' belongs in the final chapters, but you know what? Now I see that's just stories. In real life, we started with love, not ended with it. It brought us together from the very beginning. It was the lack of love we were feeling at first, maybe. Then, the desperate search for love once we got a taste. Finally, now, the acknowledgment of how we've felt all along. But it was always there, lurking. From our very first dance outside that pretzel cart, love planted a seed. Right now is where it blooms."

Forrest pauses the movie and stares at me in silence for what seems like eternity. "I'll build that house," he finally says, "if you promise to write another book." He strokes my cheeks. "Put your words on page, Sora. Until your dying day, share your heart with the world, not because they deserve it, but because you deserve to be heard. And by the way..." He stamps another tender kiss against my lips. "I love you, too. More than you can imagine."

I smile. "If I write that book, and you build that house, what then? What if I write another book after that?"

"Then I'll build you another house," he says. "I'll fill up this entire damn ranch as long as it keeps you writing."

I press a kiss to his chest, right over his heart. "You're going to be a busy man."

He plays the movie, restarting it yet again, then recommits to our cuddle.

"Can I tell you something?" I ask, my voice small in the vastness of the night.

"Anything."

"I think I could be happy here. In Wyoming, I mean." The admission surprises even me, but as the words leave my lips, I know they're true. "Someday."

I feel him go still, his breathing caught in a lasso before it resumes. "Yeah?"

"Yeah," I confirm, feeling suddenly shy. "With you and Dakota. If that's something you might want too."

His hand comes up to cup my face, tilting it so he can look into my eyes. The kiss that follows is different from the heated ones we shared earlier—softer, sweeter, but somehow fuller. Full of promise, a beginning, a silent agreement to explore this possibility together.

When we part, I settle back against his chest, listening to the steady pace of his heart. This time we watch the movie through. Actually, I mostly watch Forrest, appreciating the subtle scrunch of his face, or lift of his brows at various scenes. The movie earns quite a few chuckles, a few eye rolls, and even a cringe when Westley gets slashed open by a sword or giant rat—I'm not quite sure. But it's the *"aw"* at the end, during the final kiss, that makes me smile. I might make a romance girlie out of Forrest, yet.

"We should probably head back soon," he says reluctantly when the credits roll. "Dad will worry if we're out too late."

"Five more minutes," I negotiate, snuggling closer.

His chuckle rolls through his chest. "Five more minutes," he agrees, pressing another kiss to my hair.

But time creeps by, and neither of us makes any move to leave our starlit sanctuary. The world beyond doesn't exist. For now, there is only this moment, this connection, this feeling of having found something precious and unexpected.

As I drift toward sleep, wrapped up in Forrest's warmth, I find myself believing in the kinds of happily-ever-afters I've always written about but never quite trusted could be true.

Until now.

CHAPTER THIRTY-TWO

Forrest

I did this. I caused this.

Steam rises from the pan as the batter hits the hot surface, filling the kitchen with the sweet scent of vanilla and chocolate. Morning sunlight streams through the windows, casting everything in a soft golden glow. There's only one way to describe it—perfect.

"Daddy, they need more chocolate chips!"

I glance over at Dakota, who's perched on a stool at the kitchen island, her small face serious as she supervises my pancake-making technique. Her hair is still rumpled from sleep, and she's wearing the unicorn pajamas Sora bought her last week. Mr. Flops is tucked securely under one arm, his droopy ears spilling onto the countertop.

"More chocolate chips, huh?" I ask, feigning skepticism. "I don't know, Koda. The pancake-to-chocolate ratio is already pushing these away from hearty breakfast, and into the realm of dessert."

"But they're so much better with extra chips," she argues, eyes wide with conviction. "Isn't that right, Sora?"

Sora looks up from where she's cutting fruit at the counter, a smile playing at her lips. "I'm going to have to side with Koda on this one. Chocolate-chip pancakes should be at least fifty percent chocolate."

"Two against one," I sigh, reaching for the bag of chocolate chips. "I'm outnumbered in my own kitchen."

"It's my kitchen, actually," Sora reminds me, bumping her hip against mine as she passes with a bowl of freshly sliced strawberries. "And in this kitchen, we believe in chocolate supremacy."

A smile spreads across my face as I watch her arrange the fruit on the table—the easy grace of her movements. How every time she passes Koda, she sweetly touches her—smoothing her hair, tapping the tip of her nose, running her thumb over her cheek. I can't believe she was ever nervous about her maternal energy. She's a natural.

This past week has been surreal in the best possible way. After returning from Wyoming, we've settled into a routine that feels both novel and utterly natural. Sora working at her desk in the study while I pore over legal textbooks, preparing for the bar exam. Dakota drawing pictures that now cover the refrigerator. The three of us making dinner together, watching movies, reading bedtime stories.

I'm living the dream I gave up on years ago.

I drop another handful of chocolate chips into the batter, earning an approving nod from Dakota. "Now stir it clockwise," she instructs, "or the pancakes get sad."

"We can't have sad pancakes," I agree seriously, following her directions.

"Daddy, can we go to the park after breakfast?" Dakota asks, swinging her legs beneath the counter. "I want to show Sora how high I can swing now."

"Higher than any four-year-old should legally be allowed to go," I confirm, flipping a perfectly golden pancake. "And yes, we can go to the park if you bundle up, and the weather holds." It's bizarre to have bright sunshine this late in November. I'm all for Koda taking advantage of the slides and swings today.

Sora returns to the counter, reaching around Dakota to grab a napkin. She drops a kiss on top of Dakota's head as she does.

"I was thinking after the park we could stop by the bookstore," Sora suggests, arranging napkins beside the plates she's set out.

"Our bedtime stories are falling apart at the seams. Time for some new ones perhaps?"

Dakota's face lights up. "Can we? Please, Daddy?"

"Absolutely," I agree, sliding the first batch of pancakes onto a waiting plate.

"Can we go see your books in the store too, Sora?" Dakota asks innocently.

"They're not there, sweetie," Sora says without flinching. She's not so sensitive these days.

"Yet," I add, firmly catching Sora's gaze. "They're not there, *yet*."

The knock comes as I'm pouring the second batch into the skillet—three sharp raps against the front door, authoritative and impatient.

"I'll get it," Sora offers, wiping her hands on a dish towel.

"Babe, I've got it." I hand her the spatula. The aggressive knock gives me pause, and I don't want either of my girls in harm's way. "Just don't let these burn."

As I make my way through the brownstone, I can't help marveling again at the fact I live here now. Not as a guest or a temporary resident, but as someone who belongs. My jacket has point of pride in the hallway closet. Dakota's toys are neatly stacked in a basket by the couch, her tiny sneakers lined up beside mine and Sora's by the door—tangible signs of our shared life that fill me with quiet contentment.

I smile to myself, thinking about how different things look from just a month ago. I've signed up for a bar exam prep course that starts next week. I've been reviewing my old law school notes, surprised by how much I've retained despite my detour into a very different profession. The prospect of finally becoming a lawyer, of building a career I can be proud of, feels well overdue.

When I open the door, the world tilts on its axis.

Hannah stands on the doorstep, perfectly put-together as always in a cream cashmere coat and designer boots. Her blond hair is swept into an immaculate updo, not a strand out of place.

But her eyes—cold, hard blue—are rimmed with red, her lips look thin and brittle like she's pressing them together so hard they might burst.

For a moment, I simply stare, unable to reconcile her presence with the reality of my morning. *Hannah. Here. Now.* The careful compartmentalization I've built—Hannah and the complications she represents in one box, my new life with Sora in another—shatters instantly.

"Hannah?" I manage, shock rendering my voice barely audible. "Are you okay?"

Her laugh is short and humorless. "No, Forrest. I am extremely not okay." She steps past me into the entryway without waiting for an invitation. "Henry and I broke up. I just got back from Tokyo last night."

I close the door, mind spiraling. Hannah is here. In New York. In Sora's house. This encounter wasn't supposed to happen for months, if at all.

"I'm sorry to hear that," I say carefully, maintaining a neutral tone despite the fire alarm screaming in my head. "But why didn't you call first?"

She shrugs one elegant shoulder. "Would you have answered?"

The truth is, I don't know. Hannah and I have developed a guarded dance over the years—civil but distant, focused entirely on Dakota. The less actual interaction, the better.

Before I can respond, there's the rapid patter of small feet on the hardwood.

"Mommy?" Dakota freezes at the entrance to the hallway, her eyes wide with disbelief.

"Koda." Hannah's voice softens as she bends toward our daughter, her arms opening. "There you are, sweetheart."

Dakota hesitates for a heartbeat, then races forward, throwing her arms around Hannah's legs. "You came back! I missed you so much!"

Hannah kneels down to hug Dakota properly, pressing a kiss to her forehead. "I missed you too, baby. Look how tall you're getting." She smooths Dakota's hair back from her face, though her eyes keep darting elsewhere, her affection feeling forced. She's going through the motions of a loving reunion, but something feels off. "Mommy just had to take care of some things, but I'm here now."

Sora appears behind Dakota, wiping her hands on a kitchen towel. Her eyes meet mine, questioning. I give a small, helpless shrug.

Hannah's gaze shifts to Sora, her expression cooling as she takes in the oversized T-shirt—which is obviously mine—sleep shorts, the messy bun, and bare feet. I recognize the look—Hannah sizing up potential competition, assessing weaknesses, plotting strategy.

"You must be the girlfriend," Hannah says, her tone perfectly pleasant but her eyes sharp as cut glass.

"Sora Cho-Cooper," Sora confirms, stepping forward with an outstretched hand. "It's nice to meet you, Hannah."

Hannah accepts the handshake with the briefest possible contact. "You too." She turns back to me, dismissing Sora completely. "Forrest, I need to speak with you. Privately."

Dakota tugs at her mother's sleeve. "But, Mommy, we're making chocolate-chip pancakes! You can have some too!"

"Later, sweetie." Hannah extracts herself from Dakota's grip with exercised ease. "Mommy needs to talk to Daddy about grown-up things."

I look to Sora, torn. She gives me a small nod. "I'll finish making pancakes with Dakota," she says. "You two can use the study to talk."

Thank you, I mouth silently as Hannah follows me down the hall.

The study has become Sora's workspace—her laptop open on the desk, reference books stacked on shelves, notepads filled with her elegant handwriting. My bar exam materials are piled neatly on one corner of the desk, sticky notes marking important pages. It feels like an invasion to bring Hannah into this room.

I close the door behind us, gesturing for her to take the leather armchair while I perch on the edge of the desk.

"What's going on, Hannah?" I keep my voice low, conscious of how sound carries in the old brownstone. "Why are you really here?"

She sinks into the chair with the fluid grace that once captivated me, crossing her legs and adjusting her coat. "Like I said...I'm back." When she's met with silence, she elaborates. "Henry left me, okay? For his twenty-two-year-old assistant." Her laugh is brittle. "Such a cliché, right? After everything I did for him—moving to Tokyo, giving up..." She trails off, but we both know what she was about to say. *Giving up her daughter.*

"I'm sorry," I say, and I am. Despite everything, I never wanted Hannah to get hurt. "That's rough."

"It's more than rough, Forrest." Her composure cracks slightly, revealing the devastation beneath. "It's humiliating. I went all-in on Henry. I thought he was the upgrade I'd been waiting for. Wealthy, connected, ambitious." She swallows hard. "Turns out I was just a placeholder until something younger and shinier came along."

I shift uncomfortably, unsure how to respond. Hannah and I don't talk like this anymore. Our interactions have been limited to terse text messages about Dakota's schedule and needs.

"What can I do?" I ask finally. "Do you need help finding a place to stay, or—"

"I want another chance," she interrupts, leaning forward. "With you. With us."

The words hang in the air between us, impossible and absurd.

"Hannah—"

"I know what you're going to say," she rushes on. "That I walked away. That I broke up with you. But I've changed, Forrest. I've learned that money isn't everything. I could settle for this." She gestures vaguely at our surroundings. "A brownstone in need of upgrades. A simpler life. I'm willing to live more humbly now."

The irony of her calling Sora's multimillion-dollar

brownstone "humble" would be laughable if the situation weren't so painfully awkward.

"Hannah," I say gently, "that's not going to happen."

"Why not?" A flash of the old Hannah—entitled, imperious—surfaces briefly before she smooths it away. "We have history, Forrest. A child together. We could be a real family again."

I run a hand through my hair, searching for the right words. "Look, I understand you're going through a hard time. And I'm genuinely sorry about that. I know what it's like when life turns out differently than you planned."

Her eyes sharpen with interest. "What do you mean?"

I hesitate, then decide that honesty might be the only way to make her understand how much things have changed. "I haven't been a financial consultant, Hannah. That was a cover. I've been working as an escort for the past four years."

Her jaw drops. "An escort? As in—"

"As in women paid me to be their date, yes." I meet her gaze steadily. "Sometimes more than that. It was the only way I could make enough money to keep Dakota in that fancy school you insisted on and still handle my other financial obligations."

"I don't believe you." But her expression says otherwise—shock giving way to calculation as she reassesses me.

"It's true. I quit recently. I'm starting over from the ground up, trying to figure out what's next." I gesture toward the bar exam materials on the desk. "I'm finally taking the bar. Building a legitimate career."

"You're going to be a lawyer?" She sounds genuinely surprised. "After all this time?"

"Yes. It's what I studied, after all." I lean forward slightly. "My point is, if I can rebuild my life after that mess, so can you. You don't need to chase after men like Henry. You're smart, capable. You always talked about interior design. Maybe now's the time to pursue that. You'd be great at it."

"That's not what I want." Something shifts in her expression—a softening, a vulnerability I haven't seen since our early days together. She stands, moving toward me with purpose.

"Maybe fashion design?" I ask awkwardly.

"What I want," she says softly, "is you."

Before I can react, she's leaning in, her hands coming up to frame my face as she tries to press her lips to mine. I jerk backward, nearly toppling over the desk in my haste to create distance.

"Whoa! No, Hannah, stop." I raise my hands defensively.

"But you're being so nice, Forrest—"

"You've misunderstood. I was trying to be kind, to give you hope about your future, not—*not this*."

Her face flushes with humiliation. "You're seriously rejecting me? For her?" The way she says *her* drips with disdain. "How can you choose a fling over our history?"

"Not a fling. I'm in love with Sora," I say firmly. "I live here with her. We're building a life together."

Hannah scoffs. "Please. You barely know her. What's it been, a month? Two?"

"It doesn't matter how long it's been. What I feel for her..." I pause, searching for words that won't wound Hannah further but also won't diminish what Sora means to me. "I've never loved anyone the way I love her. Not even you, Hannah. I'm sorry, but it's the truth."

The color drains from her face, then returns in two angry spots high on her cheekbones. "You're saying you love this—this nobody more than you ever loved me?"

"She's not a nobody. And yes, that's what I'm saying."

Hannah's eyes narrow to slits. "Well. Thank you for your honesty." She straightens, adjusting her coat with jerky movements. "I think this conversation is over."

She strides to the door and yanks it open. Panic builds in my chest as she stalks down the hallway toward the kitchen.

"Hannah, wait—"

She ignores me, entering the kitchen where Sora and Dakota are stacking pancakes on plates. Dakota looks up, face brightening at the sight of her mother.

"Mommy! We made extra for you! They have chocolate chips and Sora cut strawberries in heart shapes!"

"Get your things, Dakota," Hannah says, clipped. "We're leaving."

Dakota's smile falters. "But...our pancakes..."

"Now, Dakota." Hannah's tone is bone-breakingly harsh. "We're going to Grandma and Grandpa's house."

I step forward. "Hannah, you can't just take her." I try to keep my voice level despite the heat lashing my throat. "Our agreement—"

"Was based on lies. You were a sex worker while caring for our child. I wonder what a judge would make of that."

Dakota looks between us, confusion and distress clouding her features. "I don't want to go," she says in a small voice. "I live with Daddy and Sora now."

Hannah crouches down to Dakota's level, her expression softening into something almost sincere. "If you don't come with Mommy right now," she says, her voice gentle but her words venomous, "you will never, ever see me again. Is that what you want? To lose your mommy forever?"

"That's enough," I growl, stepping between them. "You don't get to manipulate her like that."

But the damage is done. Dakota's face crumples, tears welling in her large eyes. "I don't want to lose Mommy," she sobs. "But I don't want to leave Daddy!"

The sound of her crying guts me, a physical pain like someone's reached into my chest and squeezed. The crying turns to wailing, and I can feel her sobs pulsing through my body like a wretched heartbeat. I can't bear to see her torn apart like this, forced to choose between parents who should be putting her needs first.

I kneel down beside her, gently wiping her tears. "Hey, baby, it's okay. *It's okay.*" With Koda safely in my arms, I throw daggers at Hannah with my eyes. "You really want to do this?"

Hannah delivers back an ice-cold look. "I said what I said.

Me or you. She can decide."

Koda's small body heaves with sobs that seem too big. "I don't w-want to ch-choose."

"You don't have to," I assure her, though each word costs me. "You can go with Mommy now, and I'll come get you as soon as I can. I promise."

Her tear-filled eyes search mine. "But what if Mommy doesn't let me see you again?"

"That won't happen," I say firmly, glaring up at Hannah over Dakota's head. "Daddy will always be here for you, whenever you need me. Nothing will ever change that."

Sora bends down beside us, her face pale but composed. "Dakota, why don't I help you pack Mr. Flops and some of your favorite things?"

Dakota nods miserably, and Sora takes her hand, leading her toward the bedroom.

"This is cruel, and you know it," I say once they're out of earshot, keeping my voice low but unable to hide my anger. "You abandoned her for Henry, and now you're using her as a weapon because I rejected you?"

"I'm protecting my daughter from living with a man who sells his body for money," she bites back. "Did you really think I'd let her just stay here?"

"She's been happy here, Hannah. Safe and loved. You know that."

"What I know is that you've been living a lie." She glances around the kitchen with contempt. "Playing house with your little girlfriend while hiding your sick secrets."

"At least I was here," I counter, the words sharp with years of pent-up resentment. "I didn't ship her off to boarding school so I could follow some cheater halfway around the world."

Hannah's eyes sharpen dangerously. "Don't you dare judge me. You have no idea what it's like to be a woman trying to secure a future in this world."

"A future that didn't include your own child?"

"A future I was building for both of us! Henry would have provided everything she could ever need."

"Except what she needed most! A mother who put her first. A mother who was there for her."

The barb lands, and for a moment, I see genuine hurt flash across her face before it hardens into resolve. "I'm taking her home with me today. If you want to see her again, you'll need to go through proper legal channels."

Before I can respond, Sora returns with Dakota, carrying a small backpack stuffed with Dakota's essential comfort items—Mr. Flops, her favorite blanket, several picture books, and the dinosaur pajamas she insists on wearing at least three nights a week these days.

Sora kneels to give Dakota a hug. "I'll miss you, sweetheart."

Hannah makes a small, dismissive sound. "Not a threat," she mutters under her breath, loudly enough for me to hear. "She's not even pretty."

Then, to me, "Don't bother trying to see her. I'll be contacting a lawyer first thing Monday. You'll be lucky to get supervised visits once the court learns about your work history. This little arrangement we've had is over, Forrest."

She takes Dakota's hand, dragging her toward the door with barely disguised impatience. Dakota peers back over her shoulder, her face streaked with tears, her free hand clutching Mr. Flops.

"Bye, Daddy," she squeaks. "I love you."

"I love you too, baby," I manage, my throat so tight it hurts. "So, so much."

The door closes behind them with a soft click that sounds like a gunshot to my ears. For a moment, I stand frozen, disbelief warring with despair. Then the smell of burning pancakes registers, and something inside me splinters.

My knees give way, and I sink to the floor, a raw, animal sound escaping my throat. Sora is beside me instantly, her arms encircling me as I break apart completely.

"She took her," I gasp, my voice unrecognizable. "She took

Dakota."

"I know," Sora murmurs, rocking me gently. "I know."

"I should have fought harder. I should have—"

"You did the right thing," she interrupts my self-deprecation. "You put Dakota first. You didn't force her to choose. That would've traumatized her."

"What am I going to do? Why the hell did I tell Hannah the truth?" The reality of it hits me anew, another wave of agony. "She'll use it against me in court. I could lose Dakota forever."

"That won't happen." Sora cradles my face between her hands, her gaze fierce and determined. "We'll fight this, Forrest. Together. Hannah doesn't get to swoop in and destroy what you've built."

I want to believe her. I want to find strength in her certainty. But all I can see is Dakota's tearstained face, all I can hear is her broken goodbye. My daughter, my heart walking outside my body, taken from me by a woman who sees her as a possession to be claimed rather than a child to be cherished.

"I can't lose her," I whisper, a confession and a prayer.

"You won't," Sora promises, holding me tighter as I collapse against her, sobs racking my body. "We'll call a lawyer today. We'll get ahead of this. Surely you know someone?"

Of course I do. And when I call her, Rina will unleash hell.

But for now, all I can do is grieve. The weight of Dakota's absence already feels unbearable. The brownstone—so warm and full of life just minutes ago—now seems like a graveyard of shame. *I did this. I caused this.*

In the kitchen, the pancakes burn, filling the house with acrid smoke. But neither of us moves to save them. Some things, once broken, can't be salvaged.

And right now, I'm afraid my heart might be one of them.

CHAPTER THIRTY-THREE

Forrest

From here on out...meddle away.

The town car's leather seat creaks beneath me as I shift positions for the tenth time in two minutes. Through the tinted windows, the mediator's office building looms—six stories of gray concrete that will determine the course of my daughter's life. My life.

"Stop fidgeting," Rina says, not unkindly. "You're making me nervous."

"Sorry." I force my hands to be still in my lap. "It's been twenty days." The words catch in my throat. "What if Hannah's poisoned her against me already?"

Rina's expression softens, the hard lines of her usually formidable demeanor gentling. "Dakota adores you, Forrest. Children are resilient, but they're not easily swayed when it comes to genuine love. And that little girl knows you love her."

I nod, though the knot in my stomach only tightens. These weeks without Dakota have been the longest of my life filled with sickening nerves—worse than any finals period in law school, worse than the terrifying early days of fatherhood when I was alone with a newborn and no idea what I was doing. It's not just how the brownstone feels hollow without her laughter, her endless questions, her small shoes by the door; it's that I can't believe some stranger gets to decide the relationship I have with my kid. It's maddening.

I haven't been myself the last few weeks—broody, distracted. I pretend to study at all hours of the night, just to stave off conversation. Sora knows I'm going through hell. She's officially seen me at my worst, and yet, she's stuck by me. Lately, where I've lacked, she excels. She even made me cowboy chili one night—better than my dad's, but we promised we'd never tell him that.

"Remember what we discussed," Rina says, drawing me back to the present. "Today's goal is to keep this out of court. Mediation will be far more pleasant for everyone if we can resolve this now."

"And if Hannah's unreasonable?" The question haunts me. "If we have to go to court?"

A cold smile spreads across Rina's face. "Then we go to court and aim for the jugular." She straightens the lapels of her impeccable suit. "But let's hope it doesn't come to that."

The town car pulls to a stop at the curb. Through the window, I can see the revolving doors of the building, each turn bringing us closer to the moment of truth.

"Forrest." Rina waits until I meet her eyes. "I'm with you, every step of the way. Hold your head high. You have nothing to be ashamed of if Hannah brings up your past employment."

"Easier said than done." Three weeks of Hannah's threats have worn deep grooves of shame into my psyche.

"You connected with people, Forrest. You made lonely women feel treasured, wanted, even if just briefly." She holds my gaze, unflinching. "At least you were adding something to these women's lives. All Hannah does is take from people."

Her words settle over me, a small balm to my raw nerves. "Thank you. For everything."

"Of course." She glances at her watch. "We should head in. Punctuality makes a good impression."

"Sora wanted to come for support," I say as we exit the car. "I told her not to. I didn't want to put this stress on her shoulders. And after how cruel Hannah was to her..."

Rina gives me a knowing look but says nothing as we approach the revolving doors. Her silence speaks volumes.

The lobby of the building is all polished marble and echoing spaces. Our footsteps ring out as we cross to the elevator banks, the sound oddly ominous. I'm so focused on the brass elevator doors ahead that I nearly miss the small gathering of people to our right.

"Forrest!"

I turn, and my heart catches. The lobby isn't empty as I'd expected. It's filled with familiar faces—Taio and Saylor, dutifully standing with military precision in suits that would make James Bond envious. Beside them is Celeste, dressed to the nines, looking graceful as ever. Her dark hair fancily coiffed. Daphne, wearing her waitressing uniform, but no matter, she's here, fist bunched in the universal *get 'em, tiger* gesture.

And then, stepping forward from the group—Sora. Not alone, but flanked by her parents.

"Surprise," Sora says, her smile wavering slightly as if uncertain of my reaction.

I stand frozen, floored by the show of support. Rina gives me a gentle nudge forward.

"Did you know about this?" I ask.

"I might have made a few calls," she admits. "Your girl did the rest."

Sora reaches me first, her hands finding mine. "Don't be mad. I know you said not to come, but I couldn't let you face this alone. We won't be in your way," she continues quickly. "We'll stay down here in the lobby, but I wanted you to walk into that room knowing how much love and support you have behind you."

I look past her to the others—Taio giving me an encouraging thumbs-up, Saylor with his nod of solidarity, Celeste holding her hand over her heart, beaming at me. Even Sora's parents, hand in hand, stand firmly behind me.

"Boone wanted to be here too," Sora adds. "He's planning to call right after. He's here in spirit."

The lump in my throat threatens to choke me. I've spent so much of my life standing alone—against my mother's abandonment, against the crushing debt, against Hannah's rejection. The sight of these people gathered for me is almost too much.

"Thank you," I manage, my voice a mere croak. "All of you."

Sora rises on her tiptoes to press her forehead against mine. "You've got this," she whispers. "No matter what happens in there, we'll figure it out together."

I kiss her forehead, breathing in the familiar scent of her shampoo—vanilla and something floral—that has become synonymous with home. "I love you," I tell her. "Thank you for being here, for everything."

Her answering smile is like sunrise after the longest night. "I love you too. Now go get your daughter back."

With one last look at the unlikely assembly—escorts and clients, colleagues and friends, all united for me—I turn and follow Rina to the elevators.

As the doors close, separating me from Sora and the others, I straighten my shoulders. For the first time in three weeks, I feel something other than despair.

I feel hope.

Sora

The lobby of the mediator's office feels both too large and too small—vast in its hollow marble expanse, but confining in the way all waiting rooms are. There's nothing to do except exist, trapped in the shallow tank of my anxiety and nerves.

I pace in front of the seating area where my parents wait, taking five steps in one direction before pivoting and retracing my path. Mom watches with the patient-ish resignation of someone who's witnessed this particular habit for twenty-seven years. My father's attention is divided between the legal pad on his lap, where he's been scribbling notes about God knows what. Maybe story ideas before they leave his head and dissipate into the abyss of reality.

"Sora, you're going to wear a track in the floor," Mom finally says, patting the empty seat beside her. "Come sit. Your pacing won't make time move faster."

"I can't help it," I reply, but I do stop, turning instead to stare at the elevator bank as if I could will the doors to open and reveal Forrest with good news. "It's been over an hour."

"These things take time," Dad says without looking up from his notepad. "Legal proceedings are notoriously slow."

"It's not a legal proceeding per se," I explain. "It's a mediation." It's more of a hope-and-pray-Hannah's-pulled-her-head-out-of-her-ass type deal. But that's obviously a mouthful, so "mediation" it is.

I resume pacing, ignoring my mother's grievous sigh. Taio and Saylor left to find lunch, promising they'd return before everything was over. Celeste departed shortly after Forrest's arrival to a meeting she couldn't miss, but not before pressing a business card into my hand with instructions to call her if we needed anything—"anything at all, darling"—delivered with a wink that suggested her resources were both substantial and discretionary. Daphne had to get back to work.

Now, it's just my parents and me, waiting.

"I still don't understand why Hannah would use Forrest's past against him like this," my dad says, finally setting his notepad aside. "What exactly did he do that's so terrible?"

I gnaw the inside of my cheek, searching for words that will explain without revealing too much. "It's complicated. Forrest had to take a job that some people might consider...morally gray. But it was legal," I add quickly. *Well, mostly.* "Just not the kind of thing that looks good in custody proceedings."

His eyebrows rise. "He wasn't running drugs or something, was he?"

"No. Of course not." I cross my arms defensively. "He was helping people. In his own way."

"Hmm." Dad taps his pen against his knee. "And now he's looking for more conventional employment? That's the issue?"

"That, and his financial situation." I sigh, pulling at the ends of my hair. "He has a lot of debt from school, and without a steady income right now..."

"It makes him look unstable," my father finishes for me. "At least in the eyes of a family court."

"Exactly." I sink into the chair beside my mom, suddenly exhausted. "It's been nearly three weeks since he's seen Dakota, Dad. It's killing him. She's everything to him."

Mom squeezes my hand. "He sounds like a good father."

"The best," I confirm. "He's always put her first, even when it meant making sacrifices. Even when it meant..." *He'd resented it, but stayed in the profession to provide for his daughter.* But my mouth clamps over the words. How can I say *anything* that won't beg more questions?

A thoughtful expression crosses my dad's face. He stands abruptly, gathering his notepad and pen.

"Where are you going?" I ask.

"Upstairs," he says, as if it's the most obvious thing in the world. "To the mediation."

"What? No, Dad, you can't." I scramble to my feet. "It's a closed proceeding. They won't let you in."

He's already striding toward the elevators. "They'll let me in."

"Dad, seriously, you'll just complicate things and make Forrest look bad." But I'm already following him, knowing from experience that once J.P. Cooper sets his mind to something, there's no dissuading him.

"What floor?" he asks as we reach the elevators.

"I—that's not the point! You can't just burst in there and—"

"What floor, Sora?" he repeats, this time in Dad Voice.

I groan, recognizing defeat. "Third. Conference room three-twelve."

The elevator ride is brief but tense. I try one more time to talk him out of whatever he's conspiring, but he just smiles that infuriating smile—the one that's graced author photos for decades, the one that says he knows exactly what he's doing.

"Trust me," he says as the doors open. "I have a plan."

"That's what I'm afraid of," I mutter, following him down the hallway.

Outside conference room 312, I make one last desperate plea. "Dad, please. This is important. This is Forrest's daughter we're talking about."

"I know." He places a hand on my shoulder, his expression suddenly serious. "Let me help, Sora. For once in our complicated relationship, let me be the one to save the day."

The sincerity in his tone stops me short. This is new territory for us—my father and I, trying to find our way back to each other after years of distance. I think of the work we've done on *Legendary*, the bridge we've started to rebuild.

"Okay," I concede. "But please, be..." What's the right word here? I want to say "not an ass," but that seems too direct. "*Civil*."

He nods, then opens the door without knocking.

The mediator looks up in alarm as we enter. "Excuse me, this is a private—"

"I know, I know." Dad waves his hand dismissively. "Never been great at following rules. But there's something everyone here needs to know."

I see Forrest's shocked expression first, then Hannah's irritation, then Rina's raised eyebrows that quickly transform into understanding as my father continues.

"Forrest Hawkins is my agent," he announces to the room.

Forrest looks completely bewildered. "I'm your what?"

"*My agent*," Dad repeats firmly. "He's helping me broker a deal for my next series." He glances around the room, his gaze settling on Hannah's lawyer. "Seven figures at least, if you're curious. Probably eight, depending on the audiobook situation."

Understanding dawns on Forrest's face. He glances at me,

and I give a small, encouraging nod.

"That's right," Forrest says, picking up the thread seamlessly. "J.P. and I have been discussing terms for a while now."

"Indeed." Dad clasps his hands behind his back, looking like a professor delivering a lecture. "Forrest's commission alone will cover his outstanding debts and provide quite comfortably for his daughter." He smiles thinly. "So, excuse me for being crass"—he shoots me a sly smile—"but isn't that what had your panties bunched up in a wad?" He looks at Hannah. "Problem solved, yes?"

Rina, quick on the uptake, leans forward. "You see? As I told you earlier, you don't have a case. Forrest's prior employment was perfectly legal." She pauses significantly. "He's never missed a custody day. And if we're looking at facts, he's been the more stable parent for the entirety of Dakota's life."

Hannah's lawyer looks shaken. She leans over to whisper something to Hannah, who nods reluctantly.

"If this is true," the lawyer says slowly to Hannah, "and if Mr. Hawkins is indeed working as Mr. Cooper's agent... Then his past employment isn't a concern, if his current employment is solidified. He doesn't have a criminal record, Hannah." She sighs. "In court, this would likely come down to your decision to leave for Tokyo. And given the evidence—including the boarding-school enrollment forms with Mr. Hawkins's signature—I'm not confident in our position to request full custody."

"You're saying?" Hannah asks flatly.

"Your very intelligent lawyer is saying if we go to court, you'll lose," Rina delivers.

Hannah's lawyer idly taps her pen. "It's not about winning or losing, but—"

"Don't patronize me, Judith." Hannah turns to face Forrest directly, her expression unreadable. "You win. Congratulations."

I watch Forrest's face, expecting to see triumph or at least relief. Instead, I see something more complex—a man looking at the mother of his child and seeing beyond his own hurt to what really matters.

"Hannah," he says quietly. "Does this feel like winning for anyone? I didn't ask for this. This isn't what I wanted."

Hannah looks confused. "Then what do you want?"

Forrest stands, addressing her directly. "I want us to split custody fairly. Whatever makes most sense for our daughter." He takes a step toward her. "I never wanted to hurt you. And I certainly never wanted to keep Dakota from you. She needs her mother."

Hannah's composure wavers, a touch of vulnerability in her eyes. "You're saying you'll share custody? After everything?"

"I'm saying I want to do what's best for our daughter." Forrest spreads his hands. "I'm not trying to rip our family apart. I'm trying to build a stronger one, to let new love in." He glances at me, standing quietly by the door, and my heart swells with pride and love. "Dakota deserves to have both her parents in her life, plus as many people who love her as possible. But from here on out, we do what's fair and what's right. No more threatening me. No more keeping my kid from me out of spite. You either work with me, or against me...in court, where a judge will tell you what my rights are, if you won't respect them coming from my mouth."

Something shifts in Hannah's demeanor—a softening, a surrender. "I assume you want to see her?" she asks. "Today?"

Hope alights Forrest's face. "Yes. Today. *Right now.*"

"She's with my parents. I'll call them. How about we bring her to you this evening? You guys can get reacclimated... She misses you."

"*Good.* I miss her too. And we should talk about Christmas," Forrest adds. "Work out a schedule that gives her time with both of us. Your parents have that big Christmas dinner every year, right? So I'll take the morning, and send her to you in whatever fancy dress you want her in. I'm more than willing to compromise, okay?"

Hannah nods slowly. "That seems...fair."

"More than fair," Rina snarks.

Hannah looks down at her hands, then back up at Forrest. "I'm sorry. I shouldn't have..." Her gaze darts to me, then back to him. "I shouldn't have used Dakota against you."

"No," he agrees. "You shouldn't have. But we can do better going forward. For her sake."

The mediator, who's been watching this exchange with evident relief, clears his throat. "It sounds like we're making progress. Are we ready to draw up a custody agreement?"

"Yes," Hannah and Forrest say in unison.

As the mediator and lawyers dive into logistics, Dad and I step back toward the door. He looks highly content, like a chess master who just executed a particularly clever move.

"Dad," I whisper. "That was amazing. I know I told you not to meddle, but from here on out...meddle away."

"Noted," he replies with a wink.

The meeting concludes with remarkable speed after that, everyone eager to capitalize on this unexpected breakthrough. Hannah's lawyer looks relieved to have found an amicable solution, Rina seems smugly satisfied, and Hannah herself appears thoughtful, as if reassessing her priorities

They file out of the conference room—Hannah and her lawyer heading one direction, Forrest and Rina joining us down the hallway toward the elevators.

"J.P.," Forrest says once they're caught up to us. "I don't know how to thank you. That lie saved us."

My father looks truly puzzled. "Lie? What lie?"

"About me being your agent."

"Oh, that wasn't a lie, son." He claps Forrest on the shoulder. "I sincerely hope you know your way around a contract, because we have work to do. Sora speaks highly of your legal background. You're going to need it. The publishing industry is like bathing in chum, then swimming naked in Australia. Buckle up."

Forrest blinks at him, dumbfounded. "You're serious?"

"Deadly." My dad holds out his hand. "We can discuss terms later. You'll need to draw up a contract of representation. And do a good job, buddy, because I read every word. But right now, I believe you have a little girl to see."

Forrest takes his hand, a slow smile breaking his face wide. "Thank you, sir. I won't let you down."

"See that you don't." With that cryptic parting shot, my father joins Rina in the elevator to head down to the lobby, leaving Forrest and me alone in the hallway.

"Did that just happen?" Forrest asks, looking shell-shocked. "Did J.P. Cooper really just make me his agent?"

"Apparently." I slip my hand into his. "Are you okay with that? It's not exactly practicing law."

"Are you kidding? It's perfect." He squeezes my hand. "It's a legitimate legal job that lets me use my degree without having to join some soul-crushing firm. And the commission on an eight-figure deal..." He whistles low. "That would solve a lot of problems. Hey, maybe I can be your agent too and get you into bookstores."

I turn up my nose and pretend to be put off. "Eh, I don't know. You're pretty inexperienced. Are you even any good?"

"Listen, lady, I'm your best shot. No one would work harder for you."

"Well, I know that for fact," I say.

He pulls me closer, his arms encircling my waist. Around us, the business of the mediation office continues—phones ringing, people passing, lives being rearranged in conference rooms all around us. But in this moment, it's just us.

"I love you," he says softly. "Whether we're in Wyoming or New York or anywhere else in the world. Home is wherever you are."

"I love you too," I answer proudly, still delighted at the way the words dance off my tongue. I don't think I'll ever get sick of saying it.

"Things will be less messy from here on out, I promise you," Forrest says with as much sincerity as he can muster.

"Doubtful," I sass. "Our whole journey has been messy and chaotic and definitely not the stuff of fairy tales."

"No?" A smile plays at his mouth.

"No," I confirm. "It's been better. It's been real." I reach up to cradle his clean-shaven cheek. I admire the face of this beautiful, complicated man who's changed my life in ways I'm still discovering. "A story well worth telling."

His lips meet mine in a kiss that feels like a promise, like a beginning. Pulling away, he looks into my eyes as he borrows my line...

"The end," he whispers.

EPILOGUE

Sora

It's the beginning.

Kitchen sink cookies. Papa Beans. The same table where my life fell apart and somehow began to rebuild itself all at once.

Five months after the mediation, and almost a year since that fateful meeting with Dane Spellman, I find myself back in the cozy coffeehouse, two kitchen sink cookies balanced precariously on a small plate as I weave through the crowded tables.

"I can't believe our luck," I announce, setting the plate down in front of Forrest. "Last two cookies in the case. And not a crying kiddo in sight."

Forrest's smile—the one that still makes my heart skip a beat despite seeing it every day—spreads across his face. "Does this mean we're having a lucky day?"

"I think so." I slide into the chair across from him, the same one where Dane Spellman delivered his brutal rejection. "Last time I snagged the final kitchen sink cookie here, I met you."

"Best day of my life," Forrest says with such sincerity, I can't help but blush.

"Really? Because I think I called you an asshole," I muse.

"It might've been deserved," he says, laughing, breaking a piece off our dessert and popping it in his mouth. "Mm, yours are better."

So much feels familiar. The same barista, April, still works behind the counter, still chews gum too loudly, still pretended not to see me at the counter, and I had to remind her twice I was waiting on my cookies. It's the same murmur of conversation filling the space, punctuated by the hiss of the espresso machine.

But I am not the same Sora who walked in here late last summer, desperate for validation, clinging to a meeting with an agent who couldn't be bothered to show up on time. That Sora feels like a distant relative—someone I know well but haven't seen in years.

"You're thinking deep thoughts," Forrest observes, reaching across the table to brush a stray hair from my face. "Care to share?"

"Just reflecting on everything that's happened since I first walked in here." I capture his hand, pressing a kiss to his palm. "It's kind of funny to be back here, once again meeting with an agent."

"An agent?" Forrest asks, mock-offended. "I prefer *boyfriend*, or *love of your life*, or I'll even settle for *Sora's sexy cowboy*. 'Agent' feels like a demotion."

I flutter my eyelashes at him, before taking a giant bite of cookie. *He's right.* Mine are better. Maybe my days of chasing kitchen sink cookies for luck is over, especially when I have all the luck I need right in front of me. "Okay, my sexy cowboy."

"Thank you. That's all I ask." He pushes our plate aside. "Are you all packed for Wyoming?" he asks, the teasing glint in his eye softening to something more tender.

"Almost. I just have a few more things to go through." I take a sip of my latte—caramel with extra whipped cream, exactly how I like it. No more trying to impress anyone with sophisticated coffee orders.

Forrest lifts his brows. "Translation? You haven't even started yet, have you?"

"Nope," I admit, flashing him a toothy grin. "Don't worry, I'll be all set by tomorrow, promise."

The decision to spend summer in Wyoming was simple. Even Hannah's blessing, which we thought we'd have to wrestle out of her like an unruly alligator, came easily. She's traveling this summer, with a new boyfriend, even richer than Henry apparently, because some things don't change. But at least the new guy loves kids. He and Forrest get along well enough.

"Dad's excited. He bought Dakota a pink fishing pole. Let's see how that goes," Forrest says with a scoff.

"What do you mean?"

"Picture Dakota's face with a slimy, wet fish flopping around in her hands. She's been to the ranch *once*. My baby girl is still a little prissy."

"Well, we have a summer to fix that, don't we?"

"Should we get you a pole? Are you going to fish?" Forrest asks.

"Ew, gross. Picture *my* face with a wet, slimy fish flopping around in my hands. *No, thanks.*"

Forrest barks out a laugh. "Okay, city girl. One summer to fix you, too."

"Spare me the trout, but I'll be your dutiful helper with the barn house. I bought some thick work gloves so I will be splinter-free all summer."

"That's sweet. You can help paint when it comes to that, but the country boy in me is not putting his girl to work during the hot summer. And plus, you've got a book to finish this summer, yeah? Your agent's waiting on you. How's progress going?" He winks.

I duck my head, blushing slightly. "I'm taking my time with this one. Enjoying the ride. Don't rush me."

"Not rushing...*inspiring* you to get your tush to work."

"Save it, cowboy. These next few months are going to be all about building and bonding. I'll write when I can, but I'm soaking up every second of the Wyoming summer. I've got a stick shift to learn to drive, a horse to learn to ride, and your dad told me someone dropped a red heeler puppy on his doorstep and it won't leave. We have a cattle dog to train."

"Oh, you and Boone making big plans, hm?"

"That's right."

"Will I get to see you at all this summer?" Forrest asks teasingly.

"Perhaps if you play your cards right." I beam at him, picturing the endless movie nights in his truck, stars overhead, Forrest owning my body in the cloak of twilight.

Forrest's phone chimes with a reminder—Dakota's school pickup in forty-five minutes. I shove another big bite of cookie in my mouth, and chew rapidly. "We still have time," he says, as if reading my thoughts. "Plenty of time."

His expression is carefully neutral, but I've learned to read the tiny tells—the slight tension in his jaw, the way his fingers tap a soft rhythm against the table.

"What's going on?" I ask. "You're acting weird."

"Am I?" His smile is innocent, but his eyes give him away. "Just enjoying my cookie."

I narrow my eyes suspiciously but let it drop. Whatever he's planning, I'll find out soon enough. Forrest has never been able to keep secrets from me for long.

"So, tell me more about your plans for the barn house," I prompt, breaking off another piece of my cookie. "Are you still planning on building a deck off the master bedroom?"

He shakes his head. "I'm reconfiguring the floor plan a little. The master is going to the other side, and I'm going to make that room into your office. I'll still build the deck, but it'll be outside of your space. West-facing, so you can watch the sunsets while you write."

The thought of writing in Wyoming, surrounded by vast, open spaces and clear air, stirs something in me. I wonder what I'll think of there, under the big sky, inspired by the beautiful Wild West.

"That sounds perfect," I tell him. "I might actually get some writing done with a view like that."

"Speaking of your writing..." Forrest reaches into his messenger bag and pulls out two thin stacks of paper, each folded neatly in thirds. My heart skips a beat as he places them on the table between us.

"What are those?" I ask, though I have a suspicion.

"Contracts," he says simply, his eyes watching my reaction carefully. "Offers for the duet. I'm struggling with them, to be honest."

My jaw gapes at the way he drops this bomb with such nonchalance. I'm over here choking on my cookie. "What offers? What are you talking about?"

"Oh, did I not tell you?" He smirks, and I resist the urge to snatch them off the table.

When Forrest agreed to become my agent—in addition to being my boyfriend and now my live-in partner—I was skeptical. Not because I doubted his abilities or his connections, but because I worried that mixing our personal and professional lives might strain our relationship. But he's proven me wrong. As my agent, Forrest is shrewd, professional, and relentless. He read every draft of my manuscript, offered thoughtful critique, and then championed it to publishers with the same passion he brings to everything he does.

"I've been in negotiations with both publishers for a couple of weeks," Forrest explains, his agent voice mixing with his boyfriend tone. "One is offering a bigger advance. It's a Big Five publisher." He points to the contract on his right. "The other is from a smaller press. They're offering a much smaller advance—all they can afford, really—but a higher royalty rate."

I stare at him like he's grown a second head. "And you're struggling with this why? The Big Five is obviously the way to go."

My mind is racing with possibilities. A Big Five publisher. The kind of legitimacy I've been chasing for years. The kind of validation that might finally make Mom understand why I've chosen this difficult path. The kind that might silence the voice in my head that sometimes, late at night, whispers that I'm not good enough.

"That's what I thought at first," Forrest says. "But after talking to both editorial teams, I'm not so sure."

"What do you mean?"

He leans forward, his expression serious. "The smaller publisher is passionate about your work, Sora. The editor read your manuscript twice in one long weekend because she couldn't get enough. She has marketing plans, creative ideas for reaching readers. She's in love with your story."

"And the Big Five?"

"They'll put it out there, of course. But from everything I've learned, your books will be just two of hundreds they publish this year. They'll hit the shelves, maybe get a brief promotional push, and then....." He makes a falling gesture with his hand.

I frown, the excitement dimming slightly. "But the advance—"

"Is bigger, sure. But my job as your agent is to think long term." His eyes hold mine, intensity radiating from them. "And my instinct as the man who loves you is to build a team for you that believes in you as much as I do. I think there needs to be more decisions made with heart versus statistics in this industry."

I consider his words, turning them over in my mind. The old Sora—the one desperate for a seat at the table—would have grabbed the Big Five contract instantly. But the woman I am now, the one who's learned the hard way that external validation doesn't equal happiness, isn't so sure.

He pushes both contracts toward me. "But ultimately, it's your choice. I will support whatever you choose."

I look at the contracts, then back at Forrest. His expression is carefully neutral, but I can see the hope in his eyes. This man, my roommate, my friend, my lover, and now my agent and partner, has never steered me wrong.

"Which one is the Big Five again?"

He points to the contract on his right.

I reach for the one on the left. "I trust my agent's advice," I say, "but I trust my boyfriend's heart even more."

The smile that breaks across his face is worth more than any advance. I unfold the contract, eager to see the details of the offer, when something tries to blind me. Something that definitely isn't part of a standard publishing contract.

A ring.

Not just any ring, but a delicate pavé band with a small, star-shaped diamond that catches the light from every angle. Identical to the one I'd admired during our billionaire trope date all those months ago.

My hand flies to my mouth. "Forrest..."

"It's a replica," he immediately says. "That's not actually Celeste's ring."

"I don't care," I muse in a whisper-sob. "It's stunning...what... but...how'd you know I was going to pick this contract?"

"Because I know your heart, cookie girl." His smile has turned wobbly now, a rare vulnerability showing through his usually confident demeanor. "I know you have a lot of questions, and I'll address them all," he says softly, "but I'd really like mine answered first."

Before I can process what's happening, he gathers the ring, moves from his chair, and drops to one knee beside our table. The ambient noise of the coffee shop dims as heads turn in our direction.

"Sora Cho-Cooper," Forrest murmurs, taking the ring from where it had been nestled in the contract and holding it up. "When I walked into this coffee shop a year ago, I was a different man. I had walls built so high around my heart that I couldn't see past them. But you—with your determination, your talent, your tenacious belief in love despite all evidence to the contrary—you saw through those walls like they were made of glass."

Tears are already streaming down my face, but I make no move to wipe them away.

"You wrote your way into my life," he continues, his voice steady despite the emotion in his eyes. "And now I can't imagine a single chapter of my future without you in it. Will you do me the honor of being my happily-ever-after?"

The question bobs in the air between us, but only for a split second. Because there has never been a question with an easier answer.

"Yes," I croak through my tears.

He slides the ring onto my finger, and it fits perfectly—of course it does. This man has planned everything down to the last detail. As he rises, the coffee shop erupts in applause, strangers sharing in our moment of joy.

Forrest pulls me to my feet and into his arms, his lips finding mine in a kiss that tastes of chocolate chips, caramel, and promises. I melt into him, into the safety and excitement of our future together.

When we finally break apart, both breathless, he lays his forehead on mine. "I love you, Sora."

"I love you too."

As we settle back into our seats, both of us unable to stop smiling, I find myself staring at the ring on my finger. The small star catches the light, sending prisms dancing across the table.

"How long have you been planning this?" I ask.

"A while." His smile is soft, reminiscent.

I shake my head, amazed at how life works out sometimes. "And you thought to hide the ring in a publishing contract?"

"I figured it was fitting. Your writing brought us together, after all." He gestures to the contract, still open on the table.

"So this publisher...they really love my books?"

"They do. And they'll do right by them." He reaches across the table to take my hand, his thumb brushing over the new ring. "Just like I'll do right by you."

A year ago, I would have given anything for a Big Five contract. It was all I could think about—the prestige, the confirmation that I'd finally "made it." But sitting here now, with the perfect man, a ring on my finger, and a contract from a publisher who truly believes in my work, I realize how much my definition of success has changed.

Success isn't a big advance or seeing my name on a bestseller list, though those things would be nice. Success is having people who believe in you, who support you through the hard times, who celebrate your victories no matter how small. Success is finding joy in the process, not just the outcome.

Success is *this*—a man who loves me despite my neuroses and obsessions, who sees my value even when I can't, who wants to build a life with me in two different states because home isn't a place, it's wherever we're together.

"We should get going," I say, reluctantly. "Can't be late for Dakota's last day of school."

Forrest nods, gathering our things. As we stand to leave, I take one last look around the coffeehouse—the scene of so many pivotal moments in my story. The place where a cocky, hot dad and his adorable daughter stole my cookie and inadvertently changed the course of my life.

The woman I was a year ago would have ended this moment with a whispered, "The End"—my signature way of punctuating a perfect, storybook conclusion. But now, with Forrest's hand in mine and the weight of a star on my finger, that phrase no longer fits.

Because this isn't an ending at all.

It's the beginning.

Playlist

Ruin My Life - Zara Larsson
Sailor Song - Gigi Perez
Slow It Down - Benson Boone
Hold Me While You Wait - Lewis Capaldi
Breakaway - Kelly Clarkson
What About Us - P!nk
White Flag - Dido
run for the hills - Tate McRae
Close - Nick Jonas, Tove Lo
Wildest Dreams - Taylor Swift
Fallin' For You - Colbie Caillat
Yours - Russel Dickerson
Write a Book - SoMo
Dirt - Florida Georgia Line
Unwritten - Natasha Bedingfield

Acknowledgements

To Mr. Cove, my partner in crime and biggest supporter of all my harebrained ideas. Your endless patience for my shenanigans makes me laugh and smile, even when I don't feel like it. Most of all, you remind me daily that this life is worth living to the fullest. Also, thank you for loving spicy food. I think I'll keep you.

To Michelle, my incredible editor, who guided this story all the way to the finish line. You've done more than elevate this book in every way—you made me believe in myself again. This story, and many more of mine, will exist because of you, my friend. You made writing a joyous adventure, even when we felt like we were wrangling an octopus into a mason jar (IYKYK). "Thank you" isn't a big enough phrase, but I'm still here shouting it from the rooftops. Thank you.

To Kristin, my extremely talented cover designer and emotional support human. Thank you for burning the midnight oil with me and bringing this special project to life. It wouldn't have been possible without you answering every call and steering me back whenever I fell off track. Among everything I have to thank you for (and the list is long), I especially appreciate you allowing "orange" into your heart forever. Cheers to many more adventures together.

To Trisha, who has been here since the very beginning of this idea. In the midst of a hurricane, I called you with the unhinged thought of writing a series about male escorts...but romcom style. You told me to put my foot on the gas pedal and GO! When I was at my lowest, you convinced me to keep dreaming big. Now, here we are, one colossal book later. Masked man Forrest is for you, my friend. Enjoy.

To Team Kay, Tatyana, Brooke, and Trisha, thank you for your unwavering support when I had to disappear like a ghost to finish this book on schedule. You work tirelessly every day to keep my sky from falling. Because of you all, I'm able to focus on my passion, and I'm immensely grateful for that gift.

To Aga, and all your beautiful work. Every time I fatigue or lose momentum, your incredible artwork inspires me to craft my stories with full gusto. Thank you for joining Team Kay. I appreciate you more than words can express.

To Meredith and the entire Page & Vine family, for believing in me and my stories. Thank you for being the easy, clear choice in my publishing journey. I am grateful for each one of you.

To Judy, for fearlessly tackling the mammoth manuscript I dropped on your lap last minute. Thank you for helping me polish my book baby with all the magical final touches.

To Shaima, for being the beautiful soul who always keeps me motivated. You believe in me fiercely, and your contagious energy is making me believe in myself, too. Thank you, bestie.

To Sarah and the Literally Yours team, for your enthusiasm and innovative idea of choosing your own adventure book boxes. Thank you for your time and advice, and Sarah, an extra big thank you for grabbing the spray bottle whenever I get too far in my head.

To Shaye, Lindsey, and all the Good Girls, for welcoming me and my book babies into your bookish family. Your support means the world to me.

To all my readers—those who have been with me from the beginning and new-to-me book friends just getting acquainted—THANK YOU. Truly. If you took nothing else away from this story, it's that while the author path is full of obstacles, you amazing readers are the prize, the ultimate goal, the giant pot of gold at the end of the rainbow. I am forever grateful for every moment you spend with my stories.

About the Author

Kay Cove, a Korean American, Amazon best-selling author, known for Camera Shy, is a wife, boy mom, and accidental entrepreneur. After (surviving) a career in HR she ultimately decided to pursue her dream of becoming a published author. She writes contemporary romances filled with angsty characters, green flag MMCs, and witty banter.

She currently resides in Georgia with her husband and two sweet—albeit rambunctious—little boys. When she's not writing she can be found drinking copious amounts of coffee and watching true crime documentaries—all while keeping her tiny humans alive.

Some of her works include the Lessons in Love, PALADIN, Real Life, Real Love, and Off the Books series.

Also by Kay Cove

Lessons in Love
Camera Shy
Snapshot
Selfie

Real Life, Real Love
Paint Me Perfect
Rewrite the Rules
Owe Me One
Sing Your Secrets
First Comes Forever

Paladin
Whistleblower
Tattletale
Snitch - Coming 2026
Canary - TBD